THE COMPLETE OBSESSED SERIES

PART ONE, PART TWO, PART THREE &
PART FOUR

DEBORAH BLADON

PART ONE

OBSESSED

Part One of
The Obsessed Series

Deborah Bladon

CHAPTER ONE

THIS IS WHAT I'M SACRIFICING MY FRIDAY NIGHT FOR? I TILT MY HEAD to the left hoping to gain some much-needed perspective. I find nothing. I tilt it back to the right so swiftly that the chandelier earring in my left ear bounces against my neck. It's not helping. I'm still at a loss. The large canvas hanging on the gallery wall directly in front of me still looks like something my three-year-old nephew might have created if given an abundance of finger paints and five minutes of unsupervised time to use them. I sigh heavily. How did I end up at another of these pretentious, stuffy, art events? It's all Liz's fault. My best friend had whined for days about not wanting to attend the opening of Brighton Beck's collection alone.

I turn, my eyes quickly scanning the few familiar, and the many unfamiliar faces in the gallery. No Liz. I try to discreetly adjust the neckline of the extra low cut black dress I'd hastily chosen for the occasion. I feel like the definition of cleavage all wrapped into one ill-fitted, overpriced creation of an up and coming designer who doesn't understand the concept of women's breasts. I regret not giving myself a once-over in the mirror before rushing from my apartment. I also regret not trying this on last month when I found it on the discount rack at a boutique in Chelsea. I'm uncomfortable. I'm hungry, and I'm quickly resenting Liz for abandoning me as soon as we walked through the gallery doors an hour ago.

As I circle back towards the enormous and all-encompassing piece of questionable artwork before me, I fumble in my clutch for my phone. If I can't find Liz by sight, surely she'll answer a quick text suggesting we make a hasty exit to grab some dinner.

"This is called Seduction." I feel the rush of a man's breath on my neck. He smells of cologne, soap and there's the subtle hint of a woman's perfume.

I stand silent for a moment, imagining the man attached to the voice. It's a game I first played when I was a freshman in high school. He'll be mid-height I decide, perhaps five or six inches taller than my five-foot-two inch figure. His hair will be black and cut short, in direct contrast to mine, which is shoulder length and blond. And his eyes, his eyes will be a deep blue that will draw me in the moment my green eyes lock with his.

I turn slowly.

My gaze is met with the chest of a man, dressed sharply in a crisp white shirt, open at the collar and a dark blue, flawlessly tailored suit. Even though I'm wearing heels, he towers over me. He's at least six-foot-two.

"You consider breathing on a stranger's neck seduction?" I smile coyly.

"It can be." He tucks his hands into the pockets of his slacks as he lazily runs his eyes over my body.

"Does that work for you?" My face flushes at the thought of being seduced by a man like this. My heart pounds as I try to level my breaths. I'm reacting as if I've never been this close to a man before. If I'm being honest with myself, I've never actually been in the presence of a man who exuded so much raw magnetism.

A hint of a smirk brushes across his lips. "More often than you'd imagine."

What am I supposed to say in response? "*I imagine you've bedded many women just by glancing in their direction and if you stand any closer, you can take me right here on the gallery floor.*"

"For the record, I was referring to the painting." He points to the wall behind me with a sudden flick of his wrist. "That piece is titled Seduction."

"Confusion might have been more appropriate," I say quietly, disappointed that I'd assumed he was trying to seduce me when all he was doing was appreciating the art.

He smiles. When his grin opens, his brown eyes widen just a touch. He runs his hand through his thick brown hair, pushing it back from his forehead.

I study his face while he looks over my head at the painting. His jaw is uncompromising. There's a quiet sophistication woven into his features. He's strikingly handsome and the way he carries himself suggests he's very aware of it and its usefulness in getting what he wants.

"Do you like it?" His voice is deep and rich.

Again, I'm not certain what to offer as a reply. Do I like it? I like it so much I want to run my hands along its face, down its chest and torso before wrapping my fingers and lips around its...

"Are you a fan of the piece?" He gestures over my head towards the wall behind me. The raised eyebrow that accompanies the question rattles me. Does he realize where my mind keeps wandering to?

I hesitate briefly before blurting out, "not especially." I shake my head faintly back and forth, wrinkling my nose.

He laughs. Not a voracious laugh, but more of a chuckle. "Honesty. Nice." There was that smile again.

My hand jumps to my mouth. I'm mortified by the sudden realization that in my dazed state I may have accidentally insulted one of Liz's most promising allies. She's been chasing after the illustrious Brighton Beck for the better part of the past three months and I could have destroyed all of her hard work within a minute of meeting him. Why the hell didn't I Google him so I'd recognize him tonight? I briefly contemplate making a mad rush for the gallery doors but there's the little matter of the hundreds of people standing in my way.

"Are you alright?" His voice takes on a softer tone.

"Please tell me you're not Brighton Beck." I wince as I say the words knowing that if this is indeed the star of tonight's gallery showing that I'll be dealing with a very pissed-off best friend.

"Not." He leans down so his breath grazes my forehead. "I'm Jax." He offers his hand and I reach for it. It's much larger than mine. He cradles my hand in his right as he covers it with the left. "It's nice to meet you."

"Ivy..."

"Marlow," he interrupts. "You're the jewelry designer. I read the piece The Dialogue did on you. What did they call you? You're one of the hot twenty-five entrepreneurs under twenty-five."

I'm stunned. I instinctively retreat, pulling my hand back with a quick jerk. I've never been recognized by a man. Ever. It made sense given that my jewelry line was an eclectic mix designed just for women. Yet here was a man who knew exactly who I was.

"I'm flattered." I blush slightly realizing that he recalls an article written about me more than a year ago in the alumni newsletter of the small community college I went to in Rhode Island.

"You're very talented, Ivy." He shifts closer until his lips are mere inches from my cheek.

I close my eyes, inhaling the subtle scent of his breath. It's a heady mixture of bourbon and peppermint. I take a deep, heavy mouthful of air, placing my hand on my abdomen to steady myself. I can feel him step even closer, the warmth of his body radiating.

"Is this one of your designs?" I feel his fingers lightly graze my neck before there's tension pulling softly on my earring.

I nod, reaching for his shoulder to steady myself.

"What about this?" His hand glides back to my neck. His index finger traces a pointed line down the gold chain until it reaches the black onyx pendant hovering between my breasts. My eyes are glued to his finger as it brushes against the top of my red lace bra that is peeking boldly past the neckline of my dress.

My breathing stops as my body tightens. "It's all mine," I whisper.

"Yes." His lips sweep against my ear. "But for a price it can all be mine."

"Ivy! Ivy!" Liz's voice breaks the moment.

I glance at Jax, the grin on his face a clear sign that he has enjoyed our brief rendezvous in the middle of the crowded gallery. He steps back allowing Liz to march right up to me.

"I thought I lost you, sugar." Liz Sander's southern drawl, although misplaced at an event like this in the heart of New York City, is always a pleasant surprise. She still looks as perfectly put together as she did when we left her apartment two hours ago. Her makeup impeccable, her brunette hair tied tightly into a chignon and her blue Chanel dress clinging to her slender frame like a glove.

I sigh, disappointed that Liz has decided to pick this second to come looking for me. Where had she been ten minutes ago when I was ready to bolt for the door in search of a glass of Chardonnay and something decadent to ease my ever growing hunger?

I open my mouth to speak, but Liz isn't done yet. "I need you to come with me, Ivy. There's someone you absolutely must meet." She gingerly grabs my elbow to direct me to walk with her.

"It was nice meeting you, Jax." I reach for his hand, forcing Liz to halt in her tracks.

"Your pleasure was all mine." He lightly runs his fingertips over my palm. "Wait...I mean..." His dark eyes look directly into me as he continues, "no, that's exactly what I mean."

I stare at him unable to pull myself free from his gaze. Liz pulls harder on my arm, forcing me to turn and follow her.

We aren't more than five feet from Jax when the expected inquisition begins. "What on earth was that?" Liz is pulling me towards a group of people gathered across the gallery.

"Apparently it's a painting but I'd beg to differ." I try to keep a straight face as she stops mid-step to frown at me.

The heavy groan she exudes is more dramatic than necessary, which is a character trait of Liz's that I both love and loathe. "Ivy. Be serious. You know exactly what I'm talking about."

"Where's Brighton?" I feign searching the room for the artist I have little interest in. "I'd love to meet him."

She takes the bait. "He's there. Come." She jerks my arm and pulls me unexpectedly to the left.

I turn for one last lingering glimpse of Jax, but he's not where I left him. "Damn," I grumble under my breath. He certainly had potential.

Liz steers me towards a group of men and I instantly pick Brighton Beck out of the bunch. He's average height, slight, with expressive hands, vibrant blue eyes and light brown hair. He's excitedly telling a story to the spellbound crowd. His hands are rushing to keep up with the words as they effortlessly flow from his lips. He has artist written all over him.

He stops mid-sentence. "Liz, there you are." Brighton reaches to kiss her, first on the left cheek, then the right.

Liz giggles which in turn makes me smile. Her preoccupation with male artists, those of the straight variety, has become fodder for much good natured teasing by me.

Brighton turns his attention to me. "You must be Ivy." I offer him my hand, which he graciously accepts, bringing it to his mouth in one fluid movement. I feel his moist lips press against my skin, lingering there for a moment too long.

"Are you enjoying yourself?" His smile is infectious.

"Yes, thank you. I am." Or I was, I think to myself when I was talking to that delightfully tall creature named Jax.

"Do you have a favorite piece, Ivy?" Brighton asks confidently.

I shift my focus to Liz who has a look on her face that screams, "Get this right Ivy or I'll never let you hear the end of it."

"Seduction..." I pause for effect, "is breathtaking." For good measure I raise my left hand to my chest and let out a deep sigh. I instantly realize that it's over-the-top but Brighton strikes me as the type of man who has women praising his work, among other things, on a daily basis.

He beams and looks at Liz. "I like her."

"Brighton, we must talk." Richard Feist has appeared out of nowhere. I've never been happier to see New York's premier art critic before.

"Liz. Ivy." Richard doesn't look our way as he brusquely acknowledges our presence.

"Brighton, I..." Liz's voices trails in disappointment as Richard places his hand on Brighton's shoulder briskly guiding him away from us.

"Hell," she says under her breath causing me to laugh out loud. It's always amusing to hear Liz curse. She is the personification of a southern belle right down to her aversion to four-letter-words.

"Let's get some dinner." I look at Liz who is on her tip toes, trying unsuccessfully to see over the growing crowd. I assume her radar is still locked on Brighton.

"Maybe we should stay a spell more," she calls over her shoulder to me.

"You'll see him tomorrow." I plead my case. "He's busy. You're not going to get time with him tonight."

She twists around and grabs my shoulders pulling me into an embrace. "I can't leave without saying goodbye to him. Go on without me. I'll text you later."

With that, she disappears into the crowd and I'm left alone to weave my way to the exit.

Thirty minutes, and two conversations with acquaintances later, I'm still working on breaking free of the gallery and the now almost-to-capacity gathering.

"Ivy, wait!" A vaguely familiar voice rises above the buzz of the room just as I have the door within my sight.

I turn to my left to see Brighton rushing towards me. Unfortunately, Liz is nowhere in sight.

"Liz is looking for you." I smile at him. I realize this is my opportunity to sell all of Liz's artistic attributes to her current idol.

He frowns slightly, the disappointment flowing into his voice, "She's not with you?" He skims the room behind me and his expression speaks of his frustration.

"No. She set out on a search for you. Do you want me to text her and let her know where we are?" I reach inside my clutch fishing for my phone.

He touches my forearm softly. "That's not necessary. Can we talk for a moment?" He motions to the glass doors that lead to Ninth Avenue.

Brighton holds the door open for me as the welcome rush of cool spring air greets us.

"You're Brighton Beck!" a woman entering the gallery shrieks. The man accompanying her looks horrified by her outburst.

Brighton stops to talk with the woman and her companion. I can hear him expressing his delight in their desire to preview his latest creations.

I stand a few feet away, waiting for Brighton to finish, rehearsing in my head what I'll say about Liz and her watercolors. She's gifted. She's eager and she's in need of a moment to shine.

While I run through my mini-speech I turn to the street. There hailing a taxi is Jax. Next to him a beautiful, tall brunette is attached to his other hand. The subtle suggestion of women's perfume that he carried with him now has a face, a fabulous figure and a pair of gold Louboutin pumps my feet are instantaneously infatuated with.

A taxi rushes to the curb as Brighton joins me. "My apologies, Ivy but an adoring fan is impossible to ignore."

I nod, my eyes still fixed on Jax as he opens the door of the taxi and helps the leggy brunette in.

I turn my attention back to Brighton and my quest to help Liz. "It's wonderful that so many people appreciate your unique talents, Brighton." I'm optimistic that he hears sincerity in my words. I can already tell that coddling his ego will get me everywhere.

Brighton reaches for my hand, once again bringing it gently to his lips. As he does, I look over his shoulder to see Jax, standing next to the open door of the taxi, his eyes fixed on us. A female hand reaches out of the back seat encouraging him to get in. He's frozen. I can't hold back a grin.

"What's so fascinating over there?" Brighton turns to look at what I'm obviously fixated on. "Jax." He calls with a wave.

Jax raises his hand in a weak wave, shakes his head and lowers himself into the taxi.

"You know Jax?" I ask meekly not wanting to seem overly curious.

"Of course." Brighton offers nothing more. I inwardly curse.

I decide to shift the conversation back to the reason I'm shivering in the chilly May air, starving and sleepy. "You see the potential in Liz, yes?"

"She lacks confidence," he says with little emotion.

I'm slightly offended. "I don't understand." I'm being genuine. If he knew Liz the way I did, he'd never question her level of self-assurance.

"She's brilliant, Ivy. Liz is very talented. Her belief in herself is lacking." His voice takes on a softer tone and I feel myself relaxing. "She's not like you."

I ignore his remark, and keep my thoughts focused on Liz and her aspirations to one day have a showing of her work as extravagant as this evening has been for Brighton. "Please consider her for the mentorship program you offer. It would mean the world to her."

"And what would it mean to you?" he counters.

"It would mean my closest friend would be within grasp of her dream." Those are the words I manage to say to Brighton. Internally, they translate within my own mind to, "*Not a moment in a bed with you.*"

I can't read his reaction so I quickly turn on my heel and walk towards the street in search of a taxi. As much as I want to help Liz attain her goal, I have to draw the line somewhere. She might find Brighton captivating but he's definitely not my type.

He calls after me, "I bought one of your rings last week at Veray, Ivy."

I stop. I'm in shock. Not by Brighton's restrained proposition but by the fact that in the space of an hour two, attractive, refined men have recognized me as a jewelry designer. One even bought a piece at the store that commissions my work. Maybe the evening wasn't such a waste of time after all.

CHAPTER TWO

A CAN OF TUNA AND A GLASS OF MERLOT DO NOT MAKE A DINNER. They do, however, qualify as a late night snack when your best friend bails on you. They also managed to keep me up most of the night tossing and turning with an uneasy stomach. Food shopping is definitely on my to-do list this Saturday morning.

Before I do that, I need to check on Liz. I reach for my phone perched on the pillow next to me, and dial her number. No answer. I leave a short voicemail telling her to call me when she pulls herself out of bed.

I decide it's time to rally my body as well. Just as I place my left foot on the floor, there's a faint knock on the door. The clock on the stand next to my bed reads eight fifteen. I mutter under my breath about who could be at my door this early on a Saturday and how did they get past the doorman.

I pull a short robe around my body, covering up the red lace bra and matching panties I'm still wearing from last night. Hunger overtook practicality.

The person knocking is bolder now. The rat-a-tat-tat is loud enough to wake the neighbors who share the third floor with me.

I look cautiously through the peephole. It's Mrs. Adams, the self-proclaimed, one woman, building security patrol. She's just shy of ninety-years-old, meddlesome, overly curious but vaguely endearing.

I swing open the door. "Good morning, Mrs. Adams."

She gives me the once over, a disapproving look taking over her face. "Dear, have you combed your hair today?"

My hand jumps to my hair in reflex. I work to flatten it. "I just woke up." I continue, "Come in please, Mrs. Adams." I step back from the threshold of the door to make way for her.

She strides into the room her cane tapping out a rhythmic beat on the hardwood floor. "Oh, this just won't do." She walks directly to the vase of flowers sitting atop the antique table in my foyer. She picks it up and starts in the direction of the kitchen. "These are dead, Ivy. You should have thrown them out days ago."

"I've been busy," I say, re-adjusting the sash on my robe.

She tosses the flowers in the trash, placing the now empty vase on the counter. "Yes, I've noticed. You've been out every night this week."

The words ready to leave my lips are, "*I'm twenty-three-years-old, single and aching to do things with a man that would make you blush.*" But I keep my attitude out of the conversation with my conservative, widowed neighbor.

It's obviously time to change the subject. "I'm going shopping this morning. If you put a list together, I'll stop by before I leave and pick up what you need."

Her demeanor softens. "You're such an angel, Ivy. I'm not sure what I'd do without you."

I start walking towards the door, hopeful that she'll take the not-so-subtle hint and follow me. She doesn't.

"Your mail was delivered to me by mistake again." She hesitates briefly before continuing, "There's another letter for Mark, dear. I'm sorry. "

I feel an instant heaviness in my chest. "I'll get it from you when I pick up your shopping list." I avoid making eye contact with her. The pity that's always present in her gaze isn't welcome.

She moves towards the door, stopping to touch my cheek. "Time will help, dear."

I smile meekly, knowing she means well. "I know it will. I'll be by within the hour."

————

"I'M TIRED OF THIS." I toss the white envelope addressed to Mark on the table as I take my seat across from Liz in a busy mid-town bistro.

"It's about time you got here." She glances at the gold watch on her left wrist. "You're late again."

"Not today." I wave my index finger at her as the waitress approaches. "Just don't, Liz."

She picks up the envelope as the friendly woman asks for my drink order. "Iced tea," I say as I iron my hands across my lap, smoothing the blue cotton fabric of the dress I'm wearing.

"He's doing this on purpose." She pushes the envelope back to me. "Mark wants you to get his mail so he has an excuse to see you again."

"Why? We have been over this so many times I've lost track." I slip the letter into my purse. "I just want this to be over. It's been six months."

Liz takes a long sip of the water in front of her. "He feels bad for what happened. I think he just wants you to forgive him."

"You're kidding, right?" My voice is slightly raised. "Don't side with him, Liz. He was the one who cheated on me."

"I'm not, sugar." She reaches across the table to cradle my hand in hers. "I'm really not. I just hate seeing you like this."

"I'll handle it." I motion to her that the waitress is once again approaching. "What are you having?"

We eat lunch in silence. The uncomfortable subject of Mark, my ex fiancé, clouds the air. It isn't surprising given the fact that Mark and Liz had been friends well before I'd fallen head over heels for him. Even if she didn't want to admit it, I knew that she always felt torn when we talked about him. As the waitress clears our plates I decide to touch on Liz's focus of the moment. "Did you see Brighton after I left last night?"

Her face brightens instantly. "We went for a drink."

"Do tell." I lean in anxious to hear if her encounter with the famous artist was anything like my awkward curb side exchange with him.

"It was rushed. He had to get home. I'm seeing him again tonight or rather we are." She motions toward me and then herself.

"We?" I ask cautiously, unsure of where this is heading.

"Brighton's having a small dinner party tonight." There's some trepidation in her voice. "He insisted I bring you, Ivy. We both know this could mean that he's going to give me one of the placements in the program."

"Or it may mean he's going to give you something else." I raise my eyebrows playfully.

"Ivy!" She giggles. "I don't think he likes me that way."

"Likes you that way?" I tease. "Gosh, Liz, maybe you could pass him a note in second period and tell him you have a crush on him."

She pulls her hand to her mouth in mock surprise.

"You're twenty-seven- years-old. If you want him, tell him." I press on, "you haven't been on a date in months. Come to think of it, I can't remember the last time you were really interested in a man."

She sighs. "I'm not sure I want him and besides he doesn't see me that way."

"You won't know until you try." With that I pull some cash out of my wallet. "What time is this dinner party I don't want to go to?"

A smile returns to her face. "A car will pick you up at eight o'clock. Be ready, Ivy. Don't be late."

"I'll be ready." I turn to leave.

"It's black tie so wear something appropriate." Her voice calls after me.

CHAPTER THREE

THE CAR ARRIVES PRECISELY AT EIGHT. I PEER DOWN FROM MY bedroom window and see Liz emerge dressed to the nines in a tight black cocktail dress, her hair tumbling in waves down her back. I take one last look at myself in the mirror. Presentable enough I decide and I grab my clutch and race for my apartment door. I want to be in the elevator before Liz buzzes.

I make it. I step into the elevator breathless and anxious. Brighton Beck may be a world renowned artist but I'm much more curious about Jax. The man who had literally breathed down my neck at the exhibition opening last night has been dancing through my thoughts all day. Hopefully I can probe Brighton this evening into sharing more information about the mysterious Jax and how serious things are with him and the woman he left the gallery with.

The elevator reaches the lobby with a jerk and I brace myself for Liz's reaction to my non-traditional, black tie ensemble.

I step out to the grinning face of Oliver, one of the building's doormen. "Ms. Marlow, you look lovely."

"Thank you, Oliver." I reach to kiss him on his cheek. "How is your wife feeling today?" I can see Liz standing a few feet behind Oliver, her face twisted in panic.

"She's fine, Ms. Marlow. I'll tell her you asked about her."

As Oliver moves to open the front door of the building, Liz steps up beside me. "I said black tie. Why are you wearing that?"

I look down at the red, knee length, halter dress I'm wearing, my left leg peeking out beneath the curiously high slit. Strappy black heels complete my outfit. "I think I look fabulous."

I can hear her grumble something under her breath as the driver opens the car door for us. "After you." I smile at my disgruntled friend.

"Fine," she says with a huff as she slides in.

The driver winds his way through traffic as Liz briefs me on what she's hoping to accomplish this evening. "I want to impress him." She absentmindedly plays with the silver bangle on her left wrist. "This placement could make all the difference in my career."

I grab Liz's hand to steady it. "You'll do fine. Your work speaks for itself." I try to reassure her although I know it's doing little good. When Liz feels apprehensive about anything, her body language always gives it away.

She pulls away from my touch to continue twisting her bracelet. "If it was all about my work, he would have given me the spot already. He's offered placements to two others, there's only one left."

I nod. "I understand."

"Your hair." Liz reaches to tame the loose tendrils from the quick upsweep I've pinned my hair into. "It's everywhere."

I follow her lead, tucking a few stray strands of hair behind my ears. "Is that better?"

She looks at me momentarily, then her gaze shifts to the buildings we're passing as the driver maneuvers the car up Fifth Avenue.

I pull a small mirror from my clutch along with my lipstick. My reflection speaks of someone who wasn't all that interested in putting on her dinner party best for a man she's not sure she ever wants to lay eyes on again. I apply the dark red color to my lips, take one last fleeting glance and ready myself as the car comes to a halt in front of a high rise on Park Avenue.

———

WE STEP INTO A LAVISH, open concept space, filled with classical music, the fragrance of fresh flowers and an eclectic mix of artwork and furnishings.

Brighton rushes over. "Liz, Ivy, I'm so delighted you're here."

"I'm so excited." Liz's voice has taken on a higher pitch.

I give her a glare, trying to silently warn her to calm down. She ignores me, her eyes fixated on Brighton who is dressed in a black suit, white shirt and a red tie that is the same hue as my dress.

"Great minds think alike, Ivy," he says as he lifts the tie and play-fully nods towards my dress.

"I agree, Brighton." I smile. "Your apartment is wonderful."

Liz interjects, "this is a penthouse."

"Whatever," I say as I watch Brighton's reaction.

He grins, obviously entertained by our mindless banter about his living quarters.

"Please, ladies, come in." He motions towards a small group of people gathered across the room. I don't recognize any of them which isn't surprising. The world of New York art is not where I spend my time. This is Liz's element.

Liz leads the way with Brighton right behind her. I study the surroundings, not particularly enthralled with the idea of meeting a bunch of people I have nothing in common with, who I'll likely never see again.

"Ivy." Jax's voice is in my ear the moment his hand touches my back.

I close my eyes, relishing in the sound. It's soft, the tone strong and vibrant.

"You look beautiful." His index finger is slowing circling a small spot on my back.

"Thank you." I turn around and look up. His face is even more arresting in this light. He has a small mole above the left corner of his lip that I didn't notice last night. I find myself staring at it.

His hand trailed my body when I turned, never losing contact with the silk of my dress. It's now resting very gently on my waist.

"You look..." I glide my eyes over the black suit, soft blue shirt and bold patterned tie he's wearing. "You look formal."

"Formal?" The mole shifts slightly as a small grin takes over his mouth.

"Formal," I repeat with a smirk.

"I'll take formal." His hand starts a path from my waist to my arm, moving sensuously and slowly up its entire length until it's resting on my exposed shoulder. "I didn't expect to see you here."

"I could say the same for you." I take a deep breath. I desperately try to change the mood, certain that the thin fabric of my dress is doing little to veil my arousal. My nipples are hardening just from the gentle touch of his fingers on my skin. "Or are you a Brighton Beck fanboy?"

"A fanboy?" He cracks a wide smile. "I'm not familiar. What's a fanboy?"

"If you have to ask, you're not one," I tease, grateful for the reprieve from his seriousness.

"I take it that's a good thing?" His hand jumps from my shoulder to my chin, tilting it slightly upward so I'm looking directly into his face. The curtain of intensity that was in his eyes when I first turned is now replaced by playfulness.

I perch myself on my tiptoes, resting my hand lightly against the center of his chest. "It is a good thing," I whisper quietly. "Did you see the price of some of his paintings? Someone should tell him he's no Leonardo da Vinci."

I'm greeted with a hearty laugh. "Indeed, they should."

"Jax. Ivy." Brighton appears out of the corner of my eye, rushing towards us. "I didn't realize you knew each other." He casts a disapproving glare at my hand on Jax's chest.

"We met last night." Jax pulls back, straightening his tie.

"Isn't that nice?" Subtle sarcasm is obviously not a part of Brighton's repertoire. "Dinner is served."

CHAPTER FOUR

DINNER IS DELICIOUS AND THE CONSTANT LULL OF MINGLED VOICES keeps me occupied. Jax is seated on the same side of the table as I am. The problem of the three people dividing us has been enough to quash any chance I have of engaging him in idle dinner chatter. Assigned seating is not working in my favor this evening. The only promise I can see right now is that the brunette with the Louboutins from last night is nowhere in sight.

"I said, y'all haven't seen nothing yet." Liz's voice carries above the noise. I look across the table to where she's seated next to Brighton. Her cheeks are flushed. It's no wonder given the fact that she's on her third glass of wine. Everyone around her bursts out in laughter. I smile knowing this is her realm and she's taking full advantage of the spot-light she's honed in on herself.

"What about you, Ivy?" Brighton directs his attention to me. "Any fun stories of your childhood you'd care to share?"

Liz cuts me a look. I know her well enough to realize she doesn't want any of this man's attention diverted.

"Not any like Liz's." I continue, "Liz, tell Brighton about the time you chased the man who stole your purse."

Liz launches into an embellished description of a night four years ago when she was mugged in Alphabet City. My recollection was that of a man demanding her purse which she readily handed over along with mine before she took three or four steps in his direction as he raced off on foot. Liz's memory involves some serious ninja moves on her part, half the NYPD and a very battered and bruised mugger.

"Excuse me," I say quietly as I rise from the table.

Brighton throws me a quizzed look.

"The powder room," I mouth under my breath, not wanting to interrupt Liz's tale which now includes a heat seeking helicopter and tear gas.

Brighton motions for a man standing near the hallway entrance. He comes over to guide me towards a much needed, temporary break from the evening.

I close the heavy door of the restroom behind me. I look at myself in the mirror. My hair is a bit less controlled than it was when I left my apartment. I wet my fingertips lightly and comb them through the stray ends. After applying a fresh coat of mascara I gingerly re-apply my lipstick. I look down at my phone to gauge how much time I can spend in here hiding just as there's a gentle knock on the door.

"Dammit," I whisper under my breath, certain that another woman has taken my lead and removed herself from that awful dinner chatter.

I take one last look at myself in the mirror. I adjust the front of my dress, smooth my hands over the skirt and open the door.

Jax is blocking the doorway. He takes a step in. I take a step back. He closes the door behind him, locking it.

"I decided to come looking for you, Ivy." His breath is peppered with the aroma of wine.

"I was trying to escape."

"From me?"

"No." I shake my head slowly. "Not from you."

"Good." He moves closer to me, forcing me to retreat until my back is against the wall.

I can feel his entire body pressed against mine. I struggle to catch my breath.

"Where's Mark?" His question rattles me.

"Mark?" I can barely form the word.

"Your fiancé? You said he was your inspiration in The Dialogue piece."

I'm speechless. This is the last person in the world I want to discuss Mark with. The room feels claustrophobic. I've been wary of discussing Mark with anyone. It's too raw and too painful.

"You're not wearing his ring." Jax has obviously indulged in just as much wine as Liz, if not more. "Is it over?"

"I'd rather not talk about him." I try to sound determined.

"Why not?" He leans down until his forehead is touching mine.

"It's personal." I try in vain to push him away from me. He swiftly grabs my wrists, holding them tightly against the wall. I don't struggle, my body betraying my mind's desire to break free.

"Answer the question, Ivy."

"It's none of your business," I spit back.

'You're wrong. It's more my business than you know." I feel his lips barely graze mine as I struggle to absorb his words.

"How the hell is my relationship with Mark your business?" I fight the desire to push myself into him. The nearness of his lips is tempting me even though his words are incensing me.

"I don't like complications." His breath caresses my cheek. "Mark is a complication."

"A complication? What does that mean?"

"You belong in my bed," he says it with purpose as if it's already fact.

I take a deep breath. My mind is telling me that he's a stranger yet my body is agreeing with his bold declaration. "I don't even know you," I whisper.

"I want to drown in the taste of you, Ivy, in the feeling of you."

I feel lightheaded. The scent of him permeates every one of my pores, overwhelming my senses. As much as I know I should push him away and run out the door, I don't move. All my body wants in this moment is his. I close my eyes, hoping to find some balance. I'm greeted with the mental image of him ripping my dress off and taking me on the spot.

"You're...you're...drunk," I manage to stammer out.

An enthusiastic laugh escapes his lips. "I'm not drunk."

"So you're always this direct with women you barely know?" I feel the strength returning to my legs now. I'm certain I can stand my own ground as long as he doesn't push his body closer to mine.

"I'm always this direct with women I want to fuck."

"I...." my voice trails as he runs his tongue over my lower lip.

The doorknob rattles violently. "Ivy, are you in there?"

It startles Jax who pulls back, his hands freeing my wrists.

I stumble forward feeling dizzy and disoriented.

"Ivy? Open the door!"

"I'm here, Liz. Give me a minute." I reach to hold the edge of the sink to steady myself.

Jax stands motionless, his eyes fixed on the doorknob.

"I need to go," I mumble under my breath. I skim my hands over my dress before I open the door slightly, slip out and close it. I don't want Liz to realize I'm not alone.

"You look flush, sugar." Liz brushes her hand across my forehead. "Are you fevered?"

"I'm fine." I start walking down the hallway, determined to move Liz away from the door before Jax emerges. I'm stopped when I almost run right into Brighton.

"Liz? Ivy?" A look of genuine concern washes over his face. "You both disappeared. Is everything alright?"

"I'm fine. We're fine," I say breathlessly.

"She's not fine. She doesn't feel well," Liz mumbles with a noticeable slur in her speech. "I should take her home."

"No, Liz, that's not necessary," I say, trying to regain my composure. "I can get there myself."

"Nonsense," Brighton interjects. "I'll have a driver take you."

I nod in agreement as I turn around to look at the restroom door. It's still closed.

CHAPTER FIVE

"THANK YOU. I CAN MAKE IT UP ON MY OWN," I SAY TO THE BURLY driver Brighton assigned to drive me back to my apartment.

"Are you sure, Ma'am?" His face shows concern as he closes the car door behind me. "Mr. Beck said you weren't well and I should see you to the door."

I place my hand on his shoulder, pointing to the front door of my building with the other. "There's the door, we both see it."

He smiles. "Yes, Ma'am."

I watch him get back in the car and drive away. I breathe a sigh of relief. My mind keeps playing the encounter with Jax over and over again. I'm still feeling a lingering breathlessness from his boldness. His brazen words made me feel as though he'd take me against the wall in the locked restroom if Liz hadn't interrupted us. Those thoughts are sprinkled with images of the woman he'd left with the night before. That was a line I didn't want to cross. I absentmindedly press the elevator button for the third floor after exchanging niceties with Oliver.

I'm met with a rush of cool air as I enter my apartment. "The open window," I say out loud. I put my keys on the foyer table as I rush down the hallway to my bedroom to shut the window. I shiver and decide a hot shower will not only warm my body but help clear my mind. The door buzzer interrupts my thoughts of the soothing water washing away the guilt that's pressing on the corners of my conscience.

"Hello?" I ask hesitantly into the intercom.

"Sweetheart, it's me. Let me up." The sound of Mark's voice immediately causes my body to tense.

"I'm busy, Mark. What is it?" I know the frustration is evident in my tone and I'm glad.

"I heard you had a letter of mine." He continues, "I want it."

"I'll bring it down." I don't want Mark back in my apartment, even for a moment.

"Oliver will let me up." With that the line goes dead.

"Dammit." My heart races, knowing that within two minutes, the man I was devoted to for more than four years is going to be standing back in the home we shared together.

I brace myself as I hear the elevator stop on my floor.

I feel unsteady as I open the door. "Here's the letter."

He grabs the envelope from my hand, folds it and pushes it into the pocket of the jeans he's wearing.

"Bye Mark." I start to close the door, only to feel the resistance from his hand on it.

"Sweetheart, let me in." His voice is just as I remember it. The word sweetheart pulling at my heart, while at the same time bubbling up a feeling of rage within me.

I stand my ground in the doorway. "There's nothing for us to talk about. Nothing."

"It's about my mother." His voice is tinged with sadness.

I instantly form an image of Mark's mother in my mind. She had become the mother I had longed for after the death of my own when I was an infant. Mark's mother, June, and I had struck a close bond instantly. I move to the side so he can enter.

"How's June?" I ask expectantly, knowing that her health has been fragile in recent years.

Mark sighs heavily before speaking. "She's at Lenox Hill Hospital. She was asking for you."

"How serious?" I ask not certain I want to hear the answer.

Mark's blue eyes well up with tears. "I'm scared, Ivy."

I study his face. His usual beard is unkempt, his blonde hair in desperate need of a cut. The deep bags under his blue eyes that have always been a sign of his insomnia are even more pronounced now. His face is gaunt. I can tell he's lost weight off his small frame.

"I'll go up to see her tomorrow." I open the door, wanting Mark to leave before my heart takes over and wants to comfort him.

He ignores me and walks farther into the apartment, settling himself down on a taupe chair in the living room. I grudgingly follow him.

"I miss you so much." He looks up at me. "I'm sorry for everything, sweetheart."

"Stop calling me that, Mark." My tone is stern and serious. "I hate when you call me that."

"I can't help it." He shrugs. "That's who you'll always be to me."

My temper is rapidly racing to the surface. I want to shout at him, "*You have no right to call me anything after what you did. You slept with three other women while I was planning our wedding.*"

I hold my self-control, not wanting to waste any more emotional energy on him. "You need to go, Mark. There's nothing for us to talk about."

He rises slowly. "I'm hosting a broker's open house at Carleton Towers next Thursday night. I want you to come."

I smirk at the mention of his last name. I'm not surprised he named his latest luxury condo complex after himself. After all, only one person matters to Mark.

"I won't be there, Mark." I hold the apartment door open. "Go now."

"You're a shareholder, Ivy. The building is as much yours as it's mine."

I turn to him and chuckle. "We both know I didn't want those shares. You gave them to me because you felt guilty. Just go." I hold back the urge to bring up his multiple affairs again but I'm in no mood to rehash the past.

He stops briefly before stepping out of the apartment. His blue eyes lock on my face. "I did it because I was scared, Ivy. I loved you so much it scared me."

I hold back the instinct to laugh. "It doesn't matter anymore."

After closing the door, I feel the tears instantly fill my eyes. Damn Mark. Damn him.

———

"YOU'RE NOT GOING to believe who came to see me last night." I hand Liz one of the cold lemonades I picked up for us on my way to her studio.

She takes a long drink from the straw. "Is there any sugar in this at all?" Her brow furrows as she purses her lip.

"Half-sweet." I take a drink from my own. "We're already sweet enough."

She ignores my attempt at humor. "It's too sour." She pushes it aside and turns back to the canvas she's working on.

"Aren't you going to ask who?"

"Who what?" she asks with her back to me.

I sigh, dismayed that this is becoming very anti-climactic. "Who came to my apartment after I left Brighton's."

"Just tell me." She turns, the paint brush, brightly adorned with blue, waving in her right hand.

"Mark."

I watch the brush fall and hit her stark white shoe. I leap forward in an effort to help.

"Rats!" Liz yells at she bends down to pick up the brush.

I laugh in reflex to her reaction. "Rats?" I grab the brush from her hand, playfully waving it in the air. "This is more like a fuck moment. You've ruined your shoe."

We both look down. We're standing toe-to-toe now and it's blatantly obvious that Liz's white flats cost much more than the worn out sneakers I've matched with my jeans and t-shirt.

"They're just shoes, sugar." She reaches to cradle my face in her hands. "How was it? It must have been hard."

I cover her right hand with my left briefly before stepping away. "It was fine. He wanted to talk about June and pick up the letter."

"How's June?" Her voice rings with genuine concern.

"I saw her this morning. She's fine. Just as feisty as ever." I smile remembering my brief visit hours earlier with Mark's mother. "She's getting over pneumonia. She said she'll be home in a few days."

Relief washes over Liz's face. "That's great news. How's Mark?"

"Mark is Mark." I take the brush to the sink. I'm hopeful that Liz won't press for more.

"Did he talk about anything else?" There's a suggestion of real anxiety in her voice.

"No." I turn around, shaking my head. "He didn't."

"Did he talk about his feelings?" Liz's gaze falls to the floor.

"He tried." I sigh heavily. "He also mentioned that he's throwing a party at his new building next Thursday night. It sounds like another one of those ridiculous lavish parties with all his rich friends."

She raises a brow. "Are you going?"

"Of course not," I snap back. "Have you forgotten what he did? He... " I stop myself before blurting out that it wasn't just one woman Mark slept with, there were three. My pride, to this point, has stopped me from sharing that juicy bit of Mark gossip with anyone, even Liz.

She rushes over to hug me. "I could never forget."

"Can we please talk about something else?" I turn back around to wash the paint brush, hoping Liz will let the subject of Mark rest in peace.

"Brighton?" Her voice takes on a lighter tone.

I glance back over my shoulder at her. "Did you spend the night?"

"Ivy Marlow!" She pulls her hands to her chest. "I barely know him."

I laugh heartily. "This is Manhattan. If you've spoken to him once, you know him well enough."

"Never mind me." Liz's face flushes crimson. "What about you and Brighton's brother?"

I completely turn to look at her. "Brighton's brother?"

"Jax." A small smile pulls at the corner of her lips. "Technically they're half-brothers. They have the same mother, different dads. His last name is Walker, or Walters…something with a W."

I stand in silence trying to process this news. I flash back to the moment in the gallery when I referred to Brighton's so-called-masterpiece as Confusion and my flippant remark last night about Leonard da Vinci.

"He asked about you after you left." There's excitement in my best friend's voice.

"What did you tell him?"

"I said you were the most remarkable woman I knew." Liz's eyes start to well with tears.

I'm surprised by her emotional reaction. "You're so sweet to me."

She looks down at the cement floor of her studio, slowly shaking her head from side-to-side. "I'm not. You've always been the better friend."

"That's not true," I say gently. I'm hoping that my words will comfort Liz enough that she'll bounce back to the topic of Jax.

She smiles weakly at me. "He seems taken with you. He talked non-stop for ten minutes about you and your jewelry."

"Really?" I know I sound overly excited but I'm completely enthralled with the man. "What do you know about him?"

"Let's see," Liz pauses as she settles down on a stool next to the canvas. "He's twenty-six, single, and no kids. He moved back here from Los Angeles a few months ago. He just bought into a business here, I think."

"Wow," I say, taken back by the biography of Jax I've just been handed. "Single is good, although I did see him leaving the opening with a gorgeous woman the other night."

"Celeste Gladu," Liz reveals. "She's a model."

I feel my heart sink at that announcement. "That's not surprising," I say under my breath.

"No." Liz holds back a chuckle. "They weren't together. Jax is friends with her beau, Jeremy. Jax was seeing her home that night as a favor."

"How do you know all this?" I ask in bona fide amazement.

"I saw Celeste at the opening. I was coming to fetch you to meet her when we got sidetracked by Brighton." Liz rambles on, "I met Celeste years ago when we lived in the same walk up in So-Ho."

"And you saw her with Jax at the opening?"

"Yes." She continues, "after you left Brighton's last night I mentioned Celeste to Jax and we started talking and before you know it, I had a fistful of information to give my best friend."

"Very helpful information." I grin widely. "I like him."

"I could tell at the opening." She winks at me before turning back to her painting. "I should get back to this. Brighton is coming by later to see more of my work."

I walk up next to her and give her a hug from behind. "I love you, Liz."

"Love you too." She squeezes my arm.

I pick up the small straw purse I brought with me. "Did you tell Mark about the letter?"

She sits silently before slowly turning on the stool to face me. "Did you mention it to anyone else?"

"Mrs. Adams knew."

"It must have been her," Liz responds before turning back to her work.

"Yes, it must be her," I say as I walk out the door.

————

"MS. MARLOW." Oliver greets me as I arrive back at my apartment. I'm not certain walking the eight blocks from Liz's studio was such a good idea in the heat of this very humid, Sunday afternoon.

"Oliver." I smile at the elderly doorman as I use my hand to fan my face.

"There's a delivery for you."

I'm wary. Surprises have never been something I embrace. "What is it?"

"It's there." Oliver gestures to a grand package leaning against the wall near the elevators. It's square and at least four feet across wrapped completely in brown paper.

"I'm going to guess it's not flowers."

Oliver laughs. "No Ma'am. I'll get Phil to help me bring it up in the freight elevator."

I give Oliver a quick peck on the cheek. "You're a doll."

I stare at the mystery package as I wait for the elevator to arrive in the lobby. It's hard to focus on it given all the Jax details that Liz so willingly offered up this afternoon.

The elevator doors open and Mrs. Adams steps out.

"Mrs. Adams." I give her a quick hug. "How are you today?"

I watch the doors close behind her as the elevator races up to retrieve someone else.

"Dear, were you jogging?" She reaches to wipe some errant hairs that have clung to the perspiration on my forehead.

"No." I instinctively smooth my hair back into place. "I was walking. It's hot out today."

"That's why I brought this." She pulls a small black umbrella out of her bag. "Rule number one is a lady must always be prepared."

"Do you want me to walk with you?" I ask, concerned by the idea of her wandering on her own.

"Absolutely not." Her mouth transforms into a sly grin. "I have a date."

"Who's the lucky fellow?" I raise my eyebrow playfully.

"Rule number two." She holds up two fingers. "A lady never kisses and tells."

"That's a very wise rule."

"I'm not one to mind anyone else's business, but I noticed Mark paid you a visit last night." Her voice has become a whisper now.

"He did," I whisper back knowing she's trying to keep our conversation out of the range of Oliver's ears. "He came to get that letter."

"How's Mark?" She places her fragile hand on my arm.

"He's fine," I say a bit puzzled. "Didn't you ask him how he was when you called him about the letter?"

"Dear?" Her voice stops at that. Her expression is one of bewilderment.

"Didn't you call Mark to tell him about the letter?" The confusion is mutual now.

"I would never," she declares strongly. "After what that boy did to you, I want nothing to do with him." She waves her hand in Oliver's direction.

"Thank you. Enjoy your date and play safe." I give her a small wink.

"Ivy!" She grins as Oliver comes over to help her out to the car that just arrived for her.

I take the elevator up to my apartment, the entire time wondering how Mark found out about the letter. It makes no sense. One of those two women had to have told him.

Within twenty minutes there's a knock at my door. Oliver has enlisted Phil Johnson to help him bring the enormous mystery package to my apartment door. It easily slides in as I make small talk with Phil about his parents, who manage the building. The conversation shifts to his sophomore year of college and all his challenges. I listen attentively while wishing I could politely slam the door in his face so I could deal with the package.

He finally says he needs to run and follows Oliver to the elevator.

I turn to look at the package. The only writing on the brown paper wrapper is my name and address. There's nothing indicating who sent it. My stomach begins to turn because of my always present dislike of surprises.

I take a deep breath and pull the paper from the corner. It falls revealing a canvas covered with bright colors. I start to laugh as I rip off the remaining paper. It's Brighton's painting from the opening. I stop for a moment to survey it in its entirety in the natural light of my apartment. I still don't see the appeal. I turn it around and find a small white envelope with my first name written in blue ink. I excitedly rip it open.

.   .   .

IVY,

PLEASE ACCEPT this offering as an apology for my behavior last night. Let me cook you dinner tonight. I'll send a car for you at 8:30. You bring the wine.

YOUR FANBOY

I RUN into my bedroom to find the perfect outfit for tonight. My heart is pounding as I consider all the possibilities this night can offer me and the obviously interested Jax.

CHAPTER SIX

WE DRIVE THROUGH CENTRAL PARK IN SILENCE. THE DRIVER FOCUSED
on the road, while I'm focused on what's waiting for me at Jax's apartment. I'm clutching the bottle of Shiraz so tightly my knuckles are turning white. I giggle to myself, realizing that I haven't felt this anxious about seeing a man since I first met Mark.

The driver makes a few quick turns and now we're on Amsterdam heading uptown. He manipulates the dark sedan around a couple in the crosswalk and brings the car to a stop on Eighty Ninth Street. Without a word, he comes around to open my door.

"Thank you." I smile at him.

He only nods in return and points to the charming townhouse we're parked in front of.

I turn to see Jax standing near the open front door. He's dressed in tailored gray slacks, and a dark blue shirt. His strong features are so much more vibrant in the soft evening light.

I walk up the steps while carefully holding closed the skirt of my navy wrap dress. I've paired that with the nude four inch heels I found at the back of my closet. Once I reach the top step I realize that even with the added height my shoes afford me, Jax still towers over me.

"You're look beautiful, Ivy," he whispers into my ear as he gently embraces me. "Thank you for coming."

"Thank you for the invitation." I kiss him softly on his cheek.

He pulls back and takes my hand, leading me into the building. "I'm on the second floor."

I nod, even though his back is still turned to me. I follow him up the stairs, the entire time breathing in the subtle scent of his cologne.

"This is me." He motions to an open apartment door and I step through into a space filled with the aroma of spice and vanilla. The lights are low and there are several small candles burning. The sound of jazz music wafts through the air. The decor is clearly all male. A dark leather couch sits next to an oak coffee table, magazines strewn everywhere.

"I told you I admire your work." He nods towards the table where several Veray jewelry boxes sit.

I smile faintly. "Yes, I can see that you do."

"Are you hungry?" He walks towards the kitchen.

I walk into the living room, still clutching the bottle of wine I've brought with me. I immediately notice several photographs displayed on a shelf. One is of two small boys. "Is this you and Brighton?" I call in the direction of the kitchen.

Jax appears around the corner. He moves next to me. "That's us."

"How old were you here?" I stare at the photo noticing the younger boy is missing a few teeth.

"I'm six I think. Brighton would have been ten then." His voice becomes more expressive, "I always looked up to him. He picked on me constantly until I was taller than him."

I chuckle. "When did that happen? When you were eight?"

"Witty, are we?" His index finger lightly brushes against my nose.

"I am," I counter. "I haven't figured out if you are yet."

That brings up a laugh. "I'll take that," he says as he reaches for the wine. He disappears into the kitchen again as I sit on the couch.

"You bought a lot of my pieces," I say under my breath as I pick up one of the crimson plush Veray jewelry boxes. I open it and see a necklace I designed more than a year ago. I silently close it and grab another from the pile. This one contains a bracelet I remember working on with Mark. With shaking hands I reach to place the box back on the table.

"That's one of my favorites." Jax hands me a glass of wine as he settles in next to me on the couch.

"Mine too." I smile faintly taking a small sip of the fragrant, red liquid.

"I was out of line when I asked about Mark."

I look up and into his eyes. "You were curious."

"I was." He nods slightly. "I still am. You two were engaged, weren't you? I read it online."

I take a second, heartier drink from my glass. "We were for a time, yes."

"He was a fool to end it." Jax raises the glass to his lips, taking a healthy swallow.

I do the same, realizing the wine is helping calm my reservations about talking about Mark. "I ended it, actually."

"Would it be out of line to ask why?"

"It would. But seeing how you were so generous to give me that...um...shall we say, interesting piece of artwork, I think I can oblige with an answer."

He laughs. "I heard from my brother that you found it breathtaking." He emphasizes the last word, while holding his chest, mirroring my response to Brighton at the gallery.

"You are..." I let my voice trail as I lean closer to Jax. "Almost as witty as me."

"Almost?"

"We can work on that." I run my finger along his strong chin. "I'll teach you things and you can teach me." I'm shocked by my shameless desire for this man.

He moves back slightly, raising the glass to his mouth. He empties it in one gulp. "You have no idea how much I want that."

"You can show me how much," I whisper, my lips almost touching his. "After you feed me."

He smiles and stands, offering me his hand.

I reach for it and allow him to help me off the couch. Holding my hand he leads the way to a small, simply decorated dining table.

"Ivy." He stops and turns to me. "Tell me why. Why you ended things with Mark."

Sensing that he'll press the subject until I share, I sigh. "He travels a lot for his work and he was easily distracted."

"I understand." I feel his lips gently brush my forehead.

———

"DINNER WAS DELICIOUS. THANK YOU." I take the linen napkin from my lap and place it next to the plate. The remnants of the seafood pasta Jax prepared still tempting me.

"It was my pleasure." He reaches the short distance across the table to cover my hand with his. "Can I get you anything else? A coffee? Maybe some tea? Scotch?"

I smile at his willingness to please me. "Another glass of wine would be perfect."

"Of course." He reaches for the bottle and half-fills both our glasses. "Let's go back to the living room. It's much more comfortable."

I pick up my glass and follow Jax. I stop along the way to admire a small painting on the wall.

"That's one of Brighton's earliest works." He's standing next to me now, his voice soft.

"I'm surprised. It's so different than what he's doing now."

"He's so different now than he was then." There's an unmistakable edge of displeasure to his voice.

I sigh. "Success can change people."

He studies my face for a moment. "It does. I know you understand."

I turn to walk back towards the living room. I sit in the same spot I was earlier. He settles in closer to me than he was before. He reaches for my wine glass, placing it next to his on the coffee table before picking up a jewelry box and opening it.

"Your work is really brilliant." He pulls one of the soft pink crystal earrings from the box. "When did you decide to start designing jewelry?"

I take it from him and place it back in the box. "Before I do that, can you tell me why you find my jewelry so interesting?" I raise my eyebrow mischievously as I continue, "I'm used to women buying my stuff. I don't think men buy it. I mean, I just get checks from Veray but I think it's mostly women...or maybe I've just always guessed it is." I stop as I realize I'm rambling.

He hesitates before answering. "I was dating a woman a few months ago and she was wearing one of your bracelets. It was stunning. I asked her about it, and she mentioned Veray so I went to check it out."

"I see." I feel a pit in my stomach at the mention of him dating another woman. What's wrong with me? We just met and judging by his behavior in the powder room last night, he's likely dated a lot of women, or at the very least slept with them. "So you rushed out and bought all of these to give to that woman?" I cringe at my own words before picking up my glass and bringing it my lips.

"No, I never saw her again after that night," he admits.

I try to hold in a smile while swallowing the wine. "That's too bad." I place the glass back down on the table, moving my hand to rest on his thigh.

"I just think they're beautiful." He inches his entire body closer to mine on the couch. "Much like the woman who created them."

"That's very flattering."

"You do all the work yourself?" He cradles the earring I'm wearing between his fingers. "It's all so intricate. Where's your studio? I'd love to stop by sometime and see you in action."

I pull in a deep breath, savoring the intermittent brush of his fingers against my ear. "I work alone at home. I don't have a studio."

"No studio?" His voice is a low whisper as I feel his breath rush against my neck. "That's a shame."

"I'd love to have a dedicated space to work in. One with more natural light. Ideally, I'd find a different apartment that was more suited for me to work and live in. Not that my place now isn't great. It is. I mean, it's not great but it's okay. It's enough for now."

I'm digressing partly because the smell of his cologne is intense and alluring and partly because I'm so nervous. My experience with men is restricted to Mark. That's it. Having any other man this close to me is unchartered territory for my hormones and I'm worried that my incessant talking is making that ever apparent. I pull in a deep breath willing myself to calm down and embrace the experience. When would I ever get to be this close to a man like this again?

"I think your talent is less about the space you're in and more about you," he whispers, his index finger gently moving my hair away from my neck.

I can feel him sigh deeply as I move even closer to him, raising my hand up his thigh. I look down to see his obvious growing erection straining against his slacks. I take in the scent of his skin which combined with the wine is making me feel lightheaded.

"Do you have a favorite piece?" My lips are close to his cheek now.

"I loved the necklace you were wearing the other night at the gallery," he says under his breath.

"Tell me what you like about it."

"The shape of it was exquisite."

"What else did you like about it?"

"That it was touching you." He shifts to the side, his hand grasping my waist to pull my body close to his.

"You couldn't take your eyes off of it."

"No. I couldn't take my eyes off of you." His mouth finds my neck. He leaves a line of small kisses, his tongue playfully tempting my sensitive skin.

He pushes his lips into mine and I soak in the taste of them. I sense the subtle pressure of his tongue on my lips forcing me to open my mouth more. His kiss becomes more aggressive as my lips follow his lead. His teeth pull at my bottom lip sending a tender feeling of pain through my mouth.

As a moan escapes his body, I pull back from the kiss. I trace my open lips down his cheek to his jaw line, running my teeth along it. I move towards his neck, biting softly along the path.

"I kept thinking about you...about the scent of your skin, the curve of your neck." His words are rushed as his lips find mine again. His breath is labored and wanton.

"I thought about you too," I whisper. "I can't stop."

He cradles my face in his hands, pulling me into him. "I won't stop."

A small moan runs through my body.

Deftly he pulls me onto his lap so I'm facing him. My lips rest against his cheek. I slowly run my tongue over the bristle of evening stubble, tasting the salt in his skin.

His hands find my thighs. I'm certain he can feel my arousal as I subtly push my now damp panties into his lap. His hands inch upwards. My breath catches.

"When I saw you at the gallery..." He reaches for the sash holding my dress closed. "I wanted to take you home with me right there."

I nod. My voice stuck in my throat. I watch him pull on the sash, my dress falling open revealing the white lace bra and matching panties I'd chosen for the evening.

"You're so much more beautiful than I ever imagined." His hands push the dress from my shoulders, leaving me exposed and open. "I've thought about this moment for so long."

I catch his gaze and smile gently. "You've thought about me?"

"You have no idea." He runs his finger down my neck.

I jump slightly at the intimacy of his touch. "Tell me what you've thought."

"Your skin is so soft." He grabs my hand with his, gliding my fingers over the flesh at the top of my right breast. "Feel it?"

"Yes." I slide myself across his erection, pressing my body into his.

He smiles. "That's what you do to me."

He guides my hand down my breast, tracing my finger over my swollen nipple as it pushes against the fabric of the lace.

He presses his lips to mine. "You want me too, don't you?"

I moan as I feel his tongue once again claim mine.

He continues our joint exploration with my fingers, running them over the soft curves of my stomach until they're shyly grazing the top of my panties.

"Let's see how badly you want me." He pushes my fingers below the lace.

I'm instantly greeted with the warm wetness of my arousal.

"Touch yourself for me, Ivy," he whispers into my ear.

I feel for my clit. I gasp the moment my finger brushes against it. I'm so aroused already.

"Think about all the things I'm going to do to you." His warm breath runs over my neck. I quickly find my rhythm. I rock my hips slightly on his lap while my index finger circles my swollen clitoris.

I lock eyes with him, my lips parted, my breathing quickening as I rush to find release.

"I'm going to own your pleasure. Nothing will feel as exquisite to you as coming under my direction, under my touch, under my tongue."

"Please."

"Please what?" His hands inch up my thighs pulling my desire to the surface. "Please make you feel things that no man has made you feel before?"

"Yes," I barely whisper the word. "Yes. I want that."

"You want to come."

"Yes, now," I whimper, knowing that I'm close to the edge.

"Not now. Not yet." His voice is low and melodic as he gently pulls my hand from my panties.

I stare, mesmerized as he runs my moist fingers along his lips. A low growl escapes his body.

"I need to be inside you." His hands both move to his shirt, making quick work of the buttons.

I reach for his belt. My fingers struggle to unfasten it as I tremble from within.

"Sweetheart," he says hoarsely.

Time stops. I freeze. Images of Mark pour into my mind.

"Sweetheart?" His large hands cover mine now. "Don't stop."

I look into his eyes, willing him to understand, knowing that I can't form the words to tell him to stop calling me that without my emotions spilling over.

I see a flash of frustration covered by disappointment in his face. He pushes me to my feet and stands. Breathing heavily he runs his hand through his hair. He reaches for his wine glass, swallowing the contents in a single gulp. "Fuck," he whispers under his breath.

He barely glances at me, before pushing past me to walk towards the kitchen. "You're not ready. You should have told me it was too soon."

"No. You're wrong. It's not that way. It's not too soon. It was just that..." I'm a step behind him, my emotions quickly rising to the surface.

"You're too fragile." He takes a long drink directly from the wine bottle before turning to face me. "I knew by the way you reacted yesterday when I mentioned Mark's name. I saw it again today. I shouldn't have pushed. I don't know what I was thinking."

"You're wrong." I feel the sting of tears. "I'm ready. Please let me explain."

He walks back to the coffee table and picks up my dress and my clutch. "You have no idea how badly I want this. How badly I want you. How long I've waited for you, but not yet. Not like this. Get dressed."

I tear my things from his grasp my eyes settling on his undone belt. I've never felt more embarrassed.

"I'm taking you home. I'll call for the car. Wait right here." His voice is stern and commanding.

I watch him leave the room before I bolt for the door, my hand over my mouth silencing the sobs.

CHAPTER SEVEN

"I was so humiliated." I sigh as I continue, "I froze when he called me sweetheart."

Liz drops the fork holding the crisp piece of romaine lettuce destined for her mouth. "He did what?"

"I started to undo his belt. He said it and I stopped."

She motions for me to continue.

"He got up off the couch, pushed me aside and walked away." I swallow hard, hating the sound of the words.

"What did he say when you told him Mark used to call you that?"

"I didn't. He wouldn't let me get a word in. He just assumed I wasn't ready yet."

"So you just left?" Liz quizzes.

"As fast as I could. I put my dress back on in the hallway and ran to find a taxi."

"Maybe you overreacted a bit, sugar. I mean, it's been months since Mark called you that."

I shake my head from side-to-side. "Days, not months."

"Days?" Her voice is quickly becoming the loudest in the near capacity diner. "What do you mean days?"

"When he came to get the letter, he was all sweetheart this and sweetheart that." I roll my eyes.

"How dare he still call you that? He can't call you that. It's just...it's so wrong."

I nod silently.

"So it's been three days and you've heard nothing from Jax?"

"Not a word."

"I'm sorry."

"What about Brighton?" I ask wanting to shift focus. "What's going on with you two?"

She shrugs her shoulders. "Nothing. He said he'll make a decision on the final spot in the next week."

"You'll get it, Liz." I pull a French fry through the ketchup on my plate before popping it into my mouth. "You've got to be the most talented candidate he's seen."

Liz pushes the remaining salad on her plate around with the fork. "I hope you're right."

I glance at my phone. "I need to go."

"Where to?"

"I've been summoned to Julia's office for a meeting. I'm sure it's about the deadline for my new bridal pieces." I groan.

"She's back from maternity leave?"

"I think so." I reach for my wallet.

Liz motions with her hand for me to stop. "It's my treat today. What do you mean you think she's back?"

"I haven't talked to her since the baby was born. Her assistant sent me an email yesterday, asking me to be at Julia's office at two o'clock today which means I need to leave now. Thanks for the lunch."

"Good luck," Liz calls as I race out of the restaurant.

———

AS THE TAXI slowly snakes its way up Lexington, I think about Jax and how he reacted so strongly when I hesitated. I fully expected to hear from him Monday, it's Wednesday now and not a word. I'm beginning to wonder if my pause stalled his interest for good. Maybe a potential one night stand was all I was.

I shake off the thought as the taxi pulls up to the corner of Lexington and Fifty Fourth Street. I run as fast as my red heels will take me to the building's entrance and then to the elevator. It's almost two fifteen now and Julia, the head of consignments for Veray Jewelers, is not a patient person. I'd had enough gentle lectures over the past few years to know better.

"Ms. Marlow, there you are." Graham's cheerful voice greets me as I step off the elevator onto the seventh floor. He pulls me into a warm embrace.

"It's great to see you." I step back and wait for his once-over. Graham, Julia's assistant, has always been the last eyes on me before I enter Julia's office. He gently pushes my straightened hair back off my shoulders and fastens the top button of the white shirt dress I'm wearing.

"Perfect." He grabs my shoulders with both hands. "We need to talk."

"About your latest conquest?" I tease.

"No." He shakes his head overly dramatically and then holds up his left hand. "I'm engaged!"

I reach to embrace him again. "What? When did this happen? Who's the lucky guy?"

"We'll talk about it later. You need the scoop on what's going on around here." He grabs my hand pulling me in the direction of his office.

"Ivy, stop." A woman's voice calls from behind me.

I turn to see Madeline, the owner of the company standing in the hallway. Her hands are resting firmly on her hips. She looks striking dressed in a dark suit and patterned blouse. Her black hair is pulled harshly back into a tight knot completing her always intimidating look.

"Madeline," I gulp. "It's wonderful to see you. How are you?"

Her face softens. "I'm well. Come." She motions me towards her office.

"I'm sorry," Graham whispers in my ear as he straightens the buckle on the thin red belt around my waist.

"For?" I mouth under my breath.

"You'll see." He puts his hands on my shoulders and pushes me in Madeline's direction.

I follow her into her office waiting silently as she closes the door behind us.

"Please have a seat." She points to two chairs in front of her desk. I settle into one crossing my legs.

"Will Julia be joining us?" I glance at the door again, willing it to open.

"No." Madeline stops as if to gather her thoughts. She sits in the impressive leather chair behind her desk. "Julia isn't with us anymore, Ivy."

"I don't understand what you mean." I feel my chest tightening.

"Motherhood was too tempting I suppose." Madeline smiles as she glances at two framed pictures of her own teenage children hanging on the wall. "We've had to restructure and Julia decided to take advantage of that and devote herself to her family."

My head is spinning with this news. Julia was the chief advocate for my jewelry line. She was my cheerleader. "Restructure?"

"I've had to let a few people go." Her voice hints of subtle disappointment. "I've also reorganized some of the other departments."

I sit in silence wondering what this means for the collection I've just finished.

"You're one of our stars, Ivy. You're a very important part of the Veray family and we're not going to let you down."

I smile weakly, nodding my head up and down in acknowledgment.

"I've partnered with someone to help ease the financial burdens the company's been facing. He's got some brilliant ideas, including being hands-on with many of the departments." Her voice is enthusiastic, or at least that's the intention she's trying to convey. "He's going to handle all the marketing and publicity for your collection himself."

A knot forms in my stomach. "He?" I ask knowing that a man can't understand my designs the same way a woman can. The same way Julia did.

"He's up to speed on your work," Madeline explains. "He's studied all the current pieces we have on hand and loves them. He's anxious to see everything new you have to offer."

"That's helpful," I say quietly, wishing I could talk to Julia.

"I know this must be surprising." Her voice shows little emotion. "But we're focused on moving forward and we're all going to work together to make the bridal collection the biggest success you've had yet."

"Yes," I say, unsure of anything other than my disbelief that I have to work with a stranger, a man, to market my new pieces. This collection is cherished, personal and I can't hand it over to just anyone. I feel panic rushing through me but I take a deep breath realizing that without Veray my jewelry would likely be sitting in the small studio in my apartment gathering dust.

She reaches for the phone on her desk and punches in three numbers. "We're ready for you now."

Almost instantaneously there's a soft knock at her office door. As she moves to open it, I rest my head in my hands, trying to process all of this.

"She's right here." Madeline's voice feels very far away although I know she's only a few feet from the chair I'm still glued to.

"It's lovely to meet you, Ms. Marlow." His voice is intimately familiar.

I turn slowly. My eyes following a line that begins at his blue trousers. I start to raise myself from the chair when I catch sight of the fingers of his right hand resting on his belt. Before I can make eye contact with his face, I'm falling back into the chair, my legs too weak to hold me up.

He kneels next to the chair. "Ivy, are you alright?"

"I'll get her some water." Madeline moves into my line of sight, reaching for a bottle of water on a table next to her desk.

I take the bottle and open it, still staring straight ahead, my body preventing me from turning to look at him.

"Are you still feeling faint?" Madeline is sitting in the chair next to me now. She rests her hand gently on my arm.

I turn to look at her. "I'm fine. I'm sorry."

"You're probably just dehydrated." Her voice has a motherly tone to it now. "Take a sip."

I do as I'm told and swallow a mouthful of the cool water. I take a deep breath, knowing that this is the moment I have to face him.

"Ivy, this is Jax Walker." Madeline's excited voice cuts through the silence in the room.

"Jax, this is her." Madeline stands and spreads her arms above my head. "This is our Ivy Marlow."

I stand before turning to look at him. "Mr. Walker, it's a pleasure."

He takes my hand in his, his gaze locked on my eyes. "Ms. Marlow. I've been looking forward to this moment. May I call you Ivy?"

I nod, searching his eyes for some sort of glimmer of understanding. There's nothing.

"And you should call him Jax." Madeline pats me on the back. "We're all family."

"Family," I repeat after her, casting my eyes down to the floor.

"I can't wait for you two to start working together." Madeline is holding both my shoulders now. "It's a match made in heaven."

I glance up to Jax's face again. "It's been lovely meeting you, Jax, but I need to leave."

I push past him and swiftly move in the direction of the door. "Madeline, I'll be in touch next week with the final pieces."

She pulls her hands together, clasping them in front of her chest. "I can't wait, Ivy."

"When did you join the Veray family, Jax?" I try my best to convey a sweet and endearing tone.

"We became partners six weeks ago," Madeline interjects, wrapping her arm through Jax's.

"I see." I swallow hard. "It's been an interesting afternoon. Thank you, both."

I bolt for the bank of elevators as soon as I'm through the door of

Madeline's office. I lean against the wall, trying to catch my breath as I repeatedly punch the call button.

Once the heavy metal doors open, I'm inside the small space, pushing the round button for the lobby. Just when the door starts closing, Jax steps in.

"No," I snap. "I don't want to talk to you right now."

He allows the doors to close behind him before he speaks. "I want to explain."

The elevator jolts to a heavy stop on the fifth floor. The doors open and four people flood in. They're all talking about the same seemingly evil boss they work for. I stand in silence with Jax next to me.

He leans down, his breath reaching my neck. "It's not what you think."

Again, the elevator jars us as it stops. This time it's the third floor and as a small group of people enter, I quickly push through the crowd and slip off. I breathe a heavy sigh of relief as the elevator continues its downward flight to the lobby with Jax still onboard.

CHAPTER EIGHT

I GLANCE AT MY RINGING PHONE AGAIN. IT'S THE SAME NUMBER FOR the sixth time since I left Veray this afternoon. It has to be Jax. I slide back down into the bathtub, letting the water and remaining bubbles rush over my body. Since I left the elevator I've replayed every interaction with the man over and over again in my mind. He knew when he met me at the gallery that he practically owned my business. My pulse quickens just thinking about how foolish he's made me feel.

I pull myself from the now tepid water and walk to my bedroom with a towel wrapped around me. I need fresh air so I decide a walk in Central Park will help. I throw on a pair of loose fitting jeans, a white t-shirt and a light pink cardigan. I rummage through my cluttered closet to find a comfortable pair of blue flats.

"Ivy." I hear the recognizable sound of Mrs. Adams' voice as I lock my apartment door behind me.

I turn to look at her. "Mrs. Adams. How are you today?"

"I'm fine." She gives me the once over. "Are you wearing a brassiere, dear?"

"I glance down at my full breasts pushing against the thin fabric of the t-shirt. "Oops. I guess I'm not."

"You should close this then." She reaches to fasten several of the buttons of the soft cardigan.

I smile. "How was your hot date?"

She giggles in response. "I'm eighty-nine-years-old. My suitor is eighty-six. Hot dates are for the younger crowd."

I laugh with her. "I'm going for a walk. Would you like to join me?"

"Not tonight. I'm rather tired. I just stopped by to give you this."

She hands me another letter addressed to Mark. "Thank you," I say in a hushed tone.

"I don't have to keep giving them to you." She reaches to take it back. "I know it must be hard."

"No." I hold the letter tightly. "It's fine. I'm going to take care of this with Mark."

"Good," she says. "You need to get that boy out of your life for good."

I nod in silent agreement as she turns to walk away.

———

SIXTY MINUTES later I march into the lobby of my apartment with Mark's letter still clutched in my fist. The instant Oliver approaches me I see Jax sitting on the bench near the elevator.

"He's been waiting for almost an hour, Ms. Marlow." Oliver's voice is apologetic.

"It's fine." I smile weakly. "We work together."

Jax stands as I approach him. "Ivy, we really need to talk."

"Let's talk." I stand in front of him, perspiration gathering on my forehead from the brisk walk I've just finished.

"Not here." He glances in Oliver's direction.

"He's paid not to hear." I know my voice sounds harsh. I suddenly feel overheated so I quickly remove the cardigan.

"Your apartment would be better." Jax reaches to push the call button for the elevator, his eyes lingering on my breasts.

I hold the cardigan to my chest as we share the elevator ride with one of the students subletting the apartment next to mine.

I close my apartment door behind him and throw my cardigan, keys and the letter on the foyer table.

"You can sit down in there, Jax." I motion towards the living room. "I'm going to get some water. Would you like anything?"

"Water sounds good." He stands motionless in the foyer, his hands tucked into the pockets of his jeans. The grey polo shirt he's wearing is wrinkled just a bit.

"Please, have a seat," I say as I walk out of the room.

I steady myself against the kitchen counter as I take a long drink of water to quench my thirst. This is the conversation I've been dreading all day and now I realize it's unavoidable. I pick up both bottles of water in my hands and walk back to the living room.

Jax is still in the foyer, his back turned to me. I silently walk up behind him and instantly realize he's holding the envelope addressed to Mark.

"What are you doing?"

He jumps slightly, the letter falling from his hands to the floor. He quickly reaches to pick it up and place it back on the table. "I'm sorry."

"That's personal."

"Do you still see him?"

I motion towards the living room. "That's none of your business."

"He's bad for you." He doesn't budge. "You shouldn't be anywhere near him."

I push the bottle of water at him. "I can do whatever I want."

"Stop acting like a child." Jax wraps his large hand around my wrist. "He hurt you. Why put yourself through more of that pain?"

"I refuse to discuss Mark with you." I stamp my foot for effect, pulling my arm free from his grasp.

"You can't trust him." Jax moves to sit on the edge of the couch.

"I can't trust you either, can I?" I seethe. "You conveniently forgot to mention that you were going to be my boss when you had me sitting half naked on your lap."

He runs his long, slim fingers through his tousled hair. "No. It's not like that. I'm not your boss."

"What's it like then?" I sit on a chair opposite the couch with my arms firmly crossed.

"I've never met anyone like you, Ivy." His eyes lock on mine. "When I saw you at the gallery, I couldn't believe it was you."

"Because you already knew that you owned the company that consigned my work." I stand, my voice loud but shaky.

"I did know then, yes." I watch him squirm in his seat. "But seeing you there, standing there, so beautiful, so close. I just wanted you so much."

I walk closer to the couch, my anger brimming near the surface." You had my jewelry at your apartment because it was your job. You let me want you when you knew we'd have to work together and then you rejected me."

"No." He stands now. "I recognized your talent long before I talked to Maddie about buying in."

"Maddie?" I step back. I've never heard anyone refer to the head of Veray as Maddie before.

"Oh, shit." He runs his hand through his hair again. "Madeline, I meant Madeline."

"No, Jax. Why did you call her that? How well do you know her?"

"It doesn't matter, Ivy." His voice is strained. "Just drop it."

I step towards him grabbing the arm of the chair to steady myself. "Tell me now."

"We dated briefly when I came back to New York."

I close my eyes to absorb the information. "Are you dating now? Is that why she took on a business partner?"

"It's more complicated than that." He takes a drink from the bottle of water. "This isn't coming out the way I wanted it to."

"What way?" I can feel my chest burning. "That you flirted with me at the gallery knowing you were my boss? That you and your lover practically own my jewelry line? Or that you tossed me aside like an old shoe when I needed to catch my breath the other night?"

"Ivy, please." His voice is pleading now. "You have to let me explain."

"Why?" I can feel my eyes flooding with tears. "You're playing games with me. I don't want to play anymore."

"I'm not. I'm not playing any games." He takes two large steps towards me. "I want you."

I push him away, my hands resting on his chest. "No. Leave."

"I don't want to go."

"You blindsided me today." I look directly into his eyes. "You let me walk in there knowing you'd be there. You rejected me the other night and then knew I'd have to face you today. It's so cruel."

"I should have told you," he says quietly. "I'm sorry I didn't."

"It doesn't matter anymore." I walk swiftly to the door, holding it wide open. "As I told Maddie, I'll have the rest of the collection to the two of you next week."

He turns as he reaches the threshold. "I care about you. You have no idea how much."

I silently close the door behind him.

———

"HEAVENS." Liz's voice startles me as she exits the elevator. "What on earth is that?"

"An unwelcomed gift," I say smugly turning back to the delivery men standing at my door. "Mr. Walker at Veray Jewellers. I wrote the address here." I point to my messy handwriting on the front of the brown packaging I clumsily pulled together with tape.

"Will do," the older of the two says as he directs the other to pick up the edge of the painting before they carry it out of my apartment and life for good.

"Mr. Walker at Veray?" Liz walks back into the foyer after helping herself to a glass of wine in the kitchen.

"It's not even noon." I motion to the half-full glass.

"It's been a bad week." She takes a small sip. "Which Mr. Walker at Veray?"

I had hoped to explain all of this to Liz next week, or maybe next month, or perhaps never. "Jax. He's the new co-owner."

"What?" Liz's southern drawl is all too apparent when she raises her voice.

I shrug my shoulders. "I had no idea."

She moves to sit in the living room. "Was that what the meeting with Julia was about yesterday?"

"Yep." I sit on the arm of the chair. "Julia is out and Jax is in."

"But you and he...you almost...you know." She finishes the glass of wine in one gulp.

"I know." I lean closer to where Liz is sitting on the couch. "And he...you...you know with Madeline."

"Madeline Veray!" Liz shrieks.

"Maddie to him," I say sarcastically as I settle into the chair.

"I'm sorry, sugar."

"It is what it is." I feel a need to change the subject. "What are you doing here? For that matter, what are you doing out of bed at this hour?"

"I can't sleep much anymore." Liz walks towards the windows. "I'm worried about the placement. If I don't get it, maybe I need to rethink my dream."

"Ridiculous." I try to sound encouraging, "Never give up that dream."

She lets out a slow breath. "It's all I have left."

"What do you mean?"

"Nothing." She half-smiles. "I'm just tired of living off Daddy's trust fund."

"You're the next big thing in art. I can feel it."

"What would I do without you?" She turns on her stilettos and struts to the door. "Let's go shop."

"I can't. I need to work on the rest of the pieces for Jax and Maddie."

Liz picks up the envelope addressed to Mark. "Another one?"

"I'll take care of it."

She places it back down and nods as she swings open the door and tosses her hair back. "See you later."

CHAPTER NINE

"Is Ms. Veray in?" I quiz the unfamiliar middle-aged woman seated behind the reception desk.

"She's otherwise engaged." A weak smile crosses her thin lips. "May I ask whose inquiring?"

Otherwise engaged? What does that even mean? "I'm Ivy Marlow. I'm here to drop off the final pieces of my bridal collection."

"You're Ivy Marlow?" Miss Meek and Unassuming has shot to life.

"That's me." I extend my hand over the desk to her.

She jumps to her feet. "I'm Teresa. I love your jewelry. I …well…I mean my husband and I love it. He gave me one of your necklaces this past Valentine's Day. He gave it to me right after we made love and now I wear it every time we do it."

"I'm flattered." I'm assaulted by a mental picture of her naked with one of my necklaces bouncing off her chest as she's on all fours with a faceless man behind her. I shake my head subtly, trying to chase the image away.

"Can I see what you brought?" She's giddy and not afraid to show it.

I lean closer and in a whispered tone say, "I can do one better. I'll have a set of earrings that didn't make the collection delivered right to your desk."

I'm met with a high pitched squeal of delight.

"But there's one condition." I smile.

"What is it?"

"You have to promise to wear them when you go out with your husband," I say half-teasingly, looking for reassurance that she's not just going to wear my pieces only when she's being fucked.

She throws me back a wicked grin before sitting back down behind the desk. "I know Ms. Veray would want to see them right away, Ms. Marlow. Why don't you take them in to her? I'm sure she won't mind."

I'm puzzled. "Maybe you should call her and tell her I'm here?" I point towards the phone sitting on her desk.

"She's not really busy." She continues, her voice barely more than a whisper, "I'm supposed to tell people she's busy when she's waiting for her lunch to be delivered."

"Gotcha." I wink at her.

I knock softly on Madeline's slightly ajar office door.

"That must be lunch." I hear her say. "Come in."

I push open the door and I'm instantly greeted with the image of Madeline sitting uncomfortably close to Jax at the table next to her desk.

"Ivy! It's you!" Madeline leaps from her seat.

"Hello." The word somehow forms on my tongue and leaves my mouth.

"I thought you were lunch." She giggles and throws Jax a knowing glance.

"I've been told I'm delicious," I say without thinking.

Jax coughs and Madeline laughs a bit too hard. "You've always been such a card, Ivy. That's why we love you so."

I know it's all in my imagination, but I feel as though the walls are rapidly closing in on me. I place the box containing my jewelry on her desk. "Here's the rest of the bridal collection." I push it towards her.

"This calls for a celebration!" She turns to Jax. "Let's take Ivy to lunch."

"No," I say louder than necessary. "I can't."

"Nonsense," she says as she rounds her desk to place the box in a drawer. "It's not open for discussion. This is an important day for all of us."

"I agree," Jax chimes in.

I look directly at him, my breath stopping briefly when his eyes catch mine. He stands and puts on the blue suit jacket that had been carefully placed on the chair behind him.

"I'm not dressed for lunch." I'm hopeful that my hastily thrown together ensemble of jeans, red knit top and black flats will be enough to grant me a raincheck.

"You look stunning as always, Ivy. I'll tell Teresa to cancel our lunch." Madeline marches out of her office in the direction of the reception desk.

"I don't want to go," I whisper to Jax as he approaches me.

"I promise it will be fine." He reaches to touch my shoulder.

I instinctively pull back.

"We're all set." Madeline pops up by the open office door. "Lunch awaits."

———

TWO HOURS and a few bites of braised cod later, I'm ready to make my timely exit.

Madeline, on the other hand, has settled nicely into our lunch and into a lengthy conversation about how her divorce and how amazing it's been to reconnect with Jax.

"Can I get you anything else?" The waiter's voice is a welcome reprieve from Madeline's incessant ramblings about herself.

"I'll have another vodka soda." Madeline holds up her empty glass. "What about you, Jax?"

"I'm fine." He turns to me. "Ivy?"

"No, thank you." I sigh, knowing that Madeline's desire to have a third drink means at least another thirty minutes of chit-chat with her and Jax.

"Ivy." Madeline turns her attention and gaze on me. "I've always wanted to ask you something."

I silently curse hoping she's not about to ask me a question about Mark. She never hid her obvious infatuation with him when we were together. It wasn't surprising given the fact that he is one of Manhattan's preeminent real estate investors and he's much closer to her age than mine, which she eagerly reminded me of constantly. Madeline has a reputation for chasing after men with money and Mark unequivocally fit into that category.

She leans in, her warm breath tickling the hair on my arm. "What's Mark like in bed?"

"Excuse me?" I ask, my face flushing instantly.

"We're all friends here." She presses on, "there's something about him. He's got that certain je ne sais quoi as they say. I've always wondered what it would be like to fuck him."

I swallow hard wanting my legs to pick me up and run me right out of the restaurant. I look at Jax who has a small grin on his face. He raises his brow expectantly when my eyes lock with his.

"He's so hot. I...." She falls silent as the waiter delivers her drink to the table. She snatches it up before downing half in one single gulp.

"I need to get going." My voice is shaky. Talking about Mark and what we used to do in bed isn't something I want to do with Madeline, especially in front of Jax.

"I always wanted to do him." Madeline ignores how uncomfortable I obviously am as she continues, her words now slurring from one into the next. "He's single now, right? Would you mind if I called him?"

I shake my head, unable to string any words together into a coherent sentence.

"I couldn't even get this one into bed." She points her index finger in Jax's direction.

I feel a way of nausea wash over me. "I'm not really comfortable..."

"Madeline," Jax interjects, his voice tinged with anger. "That's enough."

"I've waited three years to ask her this." She raises the heavy glass to her mouth, swallowing a good dose of the clear liquid. "So tell me, Ivy, what's he like?"

I take a moment and look first at her and then at Jax. I know that if I give her what she wants I'll be able to walk out of the restaurant sooner rather than later.

"As good as you imagine him to be, multiply that by a thousand." I giggle internally knowing that it's exactly what she wants to hear and also hoping that it will sting Jax to hear the words.

Madeline leans in closer, the glass still firmly fixed in her hand.

"Giving your body to a man like that is liberating." I sigh heavily to get my point across. "He takes intimacy to a completely new level."

Madeline stares at me wide-eyed as she quickly finishes her drink. "Christ. I knew it. Do you miss it?"

"Miss it?"

"You know..." Her voice shifts to a whispered tone. "Do you miss the sex?"

"What woman wouldn't miss it?" I smile at Jax now. It's clear from his expression that he's lost in our conversation.

"Do you still want him?" Madeline's voice is filled with confusion.

"Let me explain it this way." I take a deep breath before continuing, "When a man takes control in that way, he's completely focused on you. He owns your pleasure. He wants you to feel amazing bliss that lasts and lasts. Long after it's over your body still longs for it."

"Oh. My. God. I need another drink," she says before bringing her glass to her lips and emptying it in one last gulp.

"I do need to go." I move to pick up my purse, pushing my chair back.

"But, Ivy, do you think I have a chance with him? Do you think he'd want me?" She barely whispers the last two words.

"Yes," I say even though I want to blurt out that I'm shocked he wasn't fucking her when we were engaged and as long as she's got a pulse and she's willing he'll be all over her. I start to stand and Madeline grabs my arm to pull me back into my seat.

"How do you know? Do you know how long I've wanted him?"

She's almost gasping for air now, her words running shamelessly into each other. Madeline has reached her limit in more ways than one.

I look at Jax who sits motionless in his chair, absorbing every word we're both saying.

"I think you should go for it and call him. Mark loves beautiful women. I do have somewhere I need to be," I say convincingly, even though the only place I have to be is outside the restaurant and away from these two.

"I'm having a meet and greet for Jax at my place on Thursday night." Madeline sits up straighter in her chair. "I'd like you to come and bring a date."

"She can come alone." Jax finally speaks.

"Nonsense." Madeline winks at me. "I bet she's got men lined up to be with her."

I smile. I'm beginning to enjoy this relaxed version of Ms. Veray save for her fascination with my ex.

"No." Jax's tone is more adamant now. "She's obviously still getting over Mark."

"It's time for her to move on," she states. "The past is the past. Who will you bring, Ivy?"

"Brighton," I blurt out.

Jax's jaw drops. Madeline's face radiates.

"Brighton, as in Brighton Beck?" Madeline asks, obviously flustered.

"Yes." I stand to leave. "Jax's brother."

"How would you rate him compared to Mark?" Madeline giggles.

"I don't know yet, but soon I'll have more to report." I grin as I lean down to give her a quick hug. "Thank you for lunch, Madeline and for everything. You have no idea how much I've enjoyed this."

"I'll have Teresa call you with the details for Thursday."

"Perfect." I turn to Jax. "See you then."

He nods in response, his expression doing little to veil his anger.

CHAPTER TEN

"This afternoon I may have told Madeline that Brighton was going to be my date for her meet and greet thing for Jax."

Liz bursts out laughing.

"Obviously it wouldn't be a real date." I continue, "You know I'd never run after someone you're interested in."

"Sugar, I'm not interested in Brighton, other than getting the placement."

"Really?" I'm a bit stunned by that admission. "I thought you were all hot and heavy about him."

"It was mostly about his talent. He's not my type." Liz reaches to clear both our plates from the small dinner table on her terrace.

"Do you think he'll go with me?"

"I know he will." Liz motions for me to follow her back inside her apartment. "He's talked about you more than once."

"I'm not interested in him like that though." I sigh as I settle into Liz's overstuffed sofa. "I don't want to lead him on."

Liz hands me a bowl of lemon ice cream for dessert. "He's more interested in himself than anyone else. Just ask him to go with you for Jax's sake."

"Good idea." I smile as I swallow my first taste of the cold treat.

"Did you ever get that letter to Mark?"

"Not yet." I shake my head. "I haven't wanted to call him."

"I don't think you should."

"I don't like talking to him. I know you understand what I mean."

"I do." Liz puts her dish down on the small table next to the chair she's sitting in. "It's been over a week now. It might be important. I can take it and have someone get it to him."

"That's sweet." I smile at her. "But I'll take care of it."

"Do you want some coffee?"

"Coffee would be good." I stand to follow her into the kitchen. "Do you want me to sing your artistic attributes to Brighton if he agrees to go with me to Madeline's?"

"Pretty please, yes." A huge grin takes over her face. "I can't believe he's still undecided."

"He's an artist," I tease. "You know how they can be."

"Funny." She pushes a hot cup of coffee towards me. "Now tell me what you're going to wear to make Jax seethe with jealousy."

I laugh. "His brother on my arm?"

"The perfect accessory." She winks at me before pouring cream into her mug.

———

"I WAS SO delighted when you called." Brighton smiles as I step out of the elevator into his apartment.

"Thank you for seeing me," I reply as he reaches for my hand to bring to his lips which I've now realized is his signature move.

"You said you had a favor to ask?" He leads me into the main room, motioning for me to sit on a leather couch.

"I do, yes." I sit down, carefully adjusting my red pencil skirt to ensure its covering everything I want it to cover.

"Can I get you anything? Coffee, tea, or something stronger?"

"I'm fine, but thank you."

He settles in close to me.

I shift slightly hoping to gain some space. "Your brother has become a partner in Veray Jewellers. As you already know, they commission my work. "

"Oh, yes. He said something about that a few weeks ago."

I study his face and it dawns on me that he looks much more like Jax than I first realized. "Yes, well, there's an event on Thursday evening to welcome him into the business. I was wondering if you'd like to go...go...with me?"

He sighs and I panic just a bit. "I was wondering when you would get around to asking me?"

I stare at him, certain that my mouth is open. "What do you mean?"

"Jax called me after you two had lunch and gave me a lecture on the reasons why I shouldn't go with you."

I'm shocked given the fact that our lunch was yesterday. "I'm sorry. I should have called and asked sooner."

"You didn't think Jax would get in touch with me that quickly?"

I shake my head from side-to-side.

"My brother is obsessed with you, Ivy." His gaze darkens as he continues, "you have no idea the lengths he has gone to."

"The lengths?"

"You don't know, do you?" He stands, walking to the bar to pour a drink of something deep amber.

"I'm lost." I shrug my shoulders, unable to process what Brighton is telling me.

"He..." The words stop as his eyes travel to a painting on the wall of a woman. She looks to be in her thirties, tanned, brunette, her smile wide, and her eyes a deep brown. She's resting in a lounge chair near a pool wearing a black one piece swimsuit. The artist obviously captured her bright spirit.

"He what?" I stand and move closer to where Brighton is.

"That's our mother, Ivy." Brighton points to the grand painting. "My father painted that before they divorced. I hung it there the day she died."

"It's beautiful. She was beautiful."

"She was extraordinary. Strong, independent, loving, fearless."

"I'm sorry for your loss. When did she pass?"

"She died a year ago. It still feels like yesterday."

"I know how hard that is." I verbally console him although emotionally I'm still stuck on his almost confession about Jax.

"She lived with Jax in Los Angeles before she died. He was so devoted to her. He nursed her the last few years of her life."

The Jax surprises keep coming. "I didn't know that," I manage. Of course I didn't know I scold myself. I know nothing about the man beyond the fact that he bought into Veray.

"What's your mother like?" Brighton turns to face me directly, his eyes still filled with so much sadness.

"I never knew her." I sigh. "She died when I was a baby."

He stares at me before a single tear slides down his cheek.

———

"YOU'RE AN ANGEL, IVY." Brighton smiles up at me from his seat on the couch as I bring him a cup of tea.

"That's kind of you to say." I hand it to him and sit next to him.

"I'm sorry I was so emotional."

"No, please," I say warmly. "I'm glad you showed me the painting. It's incredibly special and I can see where your talent comes from."

"My father is a remarkable artist. He's been my greatest inspiration."

I smile listening to him telling me a story of the first time his father showed him how to paint. My mind skips briefly to an image of Jax at his mother's funeral. His body must have been rife with grief. I feel a pang in my heart thinking about how much I wished I had been there to comfort him. I shake the thought from my head remembering his omission about being Madeline's new partner.

"Ivy?" Brighton's voice breaks through my thoughts.

"Yes?"

"I'll definitely go to Madeline's event with you on one condition." His sly grin has reappeared.

"I can't sleep with you."

"Whoa." He bursts into a loud laugh. "Ivy, you're great, but you're not my type."

I can feel my face turn a bright shade of red and I instantly start laughing too. "But at the gallery, I thought you..."

"No!" His laughing slows. "I was trying in my roundabout, awkward way to see if you'd hook me up with Liz."

"Oh!" My hand jumps to cover my mouth as my laughing begins again.

"She's not interested in me, I'm afraid."

"We haven't discussed it that much."

"I thought she was." He continues," we had a few drinks one night and then when I visited her at her studio, she almost kissed me."

"Almost?" My curiosity is racing.

I don't know what happened." He shrugs his shoulders. "We were close, she seemed really into it, and then pulled back and said that she was in love with someone else."

"What? Who?" This is the first I've heard of Liz being in love with anyone.

"She didn't say."

"I'm baffled." I run every man Liz has dated the last few years through my mind. I can't imagine who Brighton is referring to.

"Back to the favor, Ivy."

"Yes." I look directly at him. "What is it?"

"Put in a good word for me with her," he says with a mischievous smirk. "You know, extol all my wonderful virtues."

I nod even though I'm caught at the point in the conversation when he told me Liz was in love. We've always shared everything and now a virtual stranger is telling me she's crazy about some invisible man.

"Of course." I smile back. "I'm supposed to be doing the same with you except in an artistic way."

"What do you mean?"

"The placement. Liz is very hopeful she'll get it."

"She will," he assures me. "I'd like to tell her myself in the next few days. Can you keep it a secret?"

"Absolutely," I say excitedly.

———

"WHO IS HE?" I say the moment Liz opens the door of her apartment.

"What are you doing here so late?"

Judging by Liz's lack of makeup and her sweat pants it seems a call ahead might have been in order.

"You don't sleep anyways, remember?"

"It's midnight." Liz moves aside so I can step in. "What is it?"

"Who is he?" I repeat.

"Who?" Liz shrugs her shoulders before turning to walk into the kitchen to turn on the espresso machine.

"The man you're in love with."

Liz's face turns ashen. "Who told you?"

"Brighton," I say, reaching to grab a cookie off a plate sitting on the counter.

"What did he say?" Her voice is trembling.

"He said you're head over heels for some mystery guy."

She stares at me, her eyes beginning to fill with tears. "No."

"No?"

"I'm sorry, Ivy." She turns and runs down the hallway, slamming the bathroom door behind her.

I knock softly. "Liz, please come out. I didn't mean to ambush you. I was just confused." I hear water running and the sound of Liz blowing her nose.

"I'll be right out."

I sit back in the kitchen nursing my cup of espresso and second almond cookie.

"I'm sorry." Liz appears around the corner, no trace of tears left.

"No. I'm sorry I upset you."

"You didn't, sugar." Liz sits across from me. "I told Brighton that so he'd stop pursuing me. I'm not fond of mixing business with pleasure."

"Ah. That makes perfect sense."

She nods her head.

"Why did you get so upset when I mentioned it?"

She sighs heavily before answering. "I just wish a man really loved me, I guess."

"Me too," I say, my mind jumping instantly to Jax.

"It's been a long day."

"You don't have to tell me to get lost twice." I wink at her before giving her a quick hug and heading to the door.

CHAPTER ELEVEN

"Ivy, you look good enough to eat." Brighton's voice greets me as I step out the front door of my building.

"I'm not your type, remember?" I tease.

"Ouch." Brighton feigns grabbing his heart.

"You look wonderful too." I take in the sight of him wearing a tailored gray suit, black shirt and silver tie.

"Red really is your color, Ivy." His gaze follows the neckline of my dress which precariously hovers in a deep v just above my navel. "You brought out the big guns tonight, I see."

I giggle. "I brought out the double-sided tape." I adjust the hem of the dress, which falls just below my knee.

"The car awaits." He motions his hand towards the street.

As we walk in that direction, I decide that now is as good a time as any to revisit the conversation we almost had about Jax and the great lengths he's gone to. I'm still not sure what Brighton meant but some clarification is definitely in order before I see his brother again.

"The other day you mentioned Jax going to great lengths...um...something about him and I?" I fumble for the right words as Brighton and I reach the car.

"You first." He gestures for me to get in the backseat as the driver holds the door open.

"Thank you," I mumble hoping that the conversation isn't going to get sidetracked again.

"Give us a minute," Brighton says to the driver before closing the door. "After I tell you this you may decide you don't want to see me or my brother again."

My heart instantly starts pounding. "I'm really confused."

Ivy." Brighton reaches for both my hands cradling them in his. "My brother...he's...well...to put it mildly...he's obsessed with you."

"Obsessed?"

"He's been in a string of empty relationships. He's dated so many women over the past few years I've lost count."

"I didn't know."

Brighton looks down at my hands. "Are you sure you want to know all of this?"

I nod.

"It started when he was in high school. He was the typical high school heart throb." He pauses to take a long, slow breath before he continues, "it was one girl after another. He'd date one, bed her and dump her."

I shrug feeling somewhat let down by his admission. I don't speak, hoping he'll elaborate.

"Jax has always been about the conquest. That's not just with women but everything." He scowls and I can see that he's not completely comfortable sharing so many details about his brother.

"I thought as much. He does have that air about him," I offer.

"After his father died, it just intensified." Brighton's eyes dart to the people quickly passing by the car. "He would set a goal for himself and then do whatever it took to achieve it."

"And I'm a goal?" I whisper the words, not wanting to hear them myself.

"You are." He reaches for my hand. "But you're different than the others."

"How so?" I bite my lip feeling the unexpected rush of tears approaching.

He squeezes my hand. "Are you sure you want to know all of this?"

"I have a right to know."

He nods and shifts his body so he's looking directly at me. "There was something different about you. He started talking about you right after he moved back to New York." There's a pause and I realize he's waiting for me to respond.

"He told me that a woman he was dating was wearing one of my bracelets and that he sought out the designer," I offer. I share it with him because it's really all I know about Jax's interest in me.

"That makes sense. He saw a write up in one of the papers about your broken engagement and mentioned you and your jewelry."

"He had a lot of my pieces at his apartment."

"He was fascinated by the beauty of your work. He talked about it constantly. He talked about you constantly."

I feel my pulse quickening. I'm not sure whether to feel flattered or upset by this news.

"He left L.A. to come here to find you."

"The jewelry company..."

Brighton nods. "He told me he was going to do that, but until you came to see me the other day I didn't put two and two together. He convinced Madeline to sell half to him so he could be closer to you."

"But at the gallery...at your showing, that was fate." I'm desperately trying to make sense of everything Brighton is sharing with me.

He hangs his head. "No."

"No?"

"Jax asked me to put Liz on my short list of potential placement candidates so you'd be at the opening. We discussed it months ago. It was before he bought into Veray."

"None of this makes sense." I feel my face becoming flush. I just can't absorb everything he's telling me.

"He was so distraught after our mother died. His dad died just a few months before that. When he asked me to help him get close to you I couldn't say no. I told Liz she was a placement candidate before I even saw her work."

"But the other night you said she would be in the program." I think about Liz and how manipulated she's been by all of this.

"She will be, Ivy." He rests his hand on my forearm. "She's so talented. I'm so grateful Jax insisted on her."

"I don't understand any of this." I feel the muscles in my neck tightening.

"Jax is very controlling." Brighton continues, "Our mother was like that too. When he wants something, he'll take it. Right now he wants you."

I sit quietly, listening to Brighton's voice and the distant sounds of the streets of Manhattan outside the cocoon of the car.

"I've told him it worries me." His voice becomes softer. "You're all he thinks about."

I lower the window. "We're ready, sir."

The driver nods.

"You're sure?" Brighton asks with apprehension in his voice.

"Positive, " I say. "I can't wait to see Jax."

―――――

"THE GUEST of honor has yet to arrive," Madeline says to me even though she's staring straight at Brighton.

"Oh, Madeline, this is Brighton Beck." I step back allowing Madeline space to greet Brighton.

She doesn't waste a moment before she pulls him into a tight embrace. Brighton throws me a quizzed look and I giggle.

"I'm such a huge fan, Brighton. I have one of your paintings in my den. Come." With that Madeline pulls a hesitant Brighton down the hall.

I survey the room quickly, waving to a couple of acquaintances. My mind is still reeling from the information Brighton threw at me before we arrived. Part of me feels flattered by Jax's almost compulsive like interest. The other part is deeply concerned that his fascination is dangerous.

I feel my clutch vibrating and realize I didn't set my phone to silent before Brighton picked me up. I scoop it out of my bag and with one quick glance spot that it's Mark calling. I push the ignore button. The last person I want to deal with tonight is him.

"Ivy Marlow, is that you?" An unrecognizable woman's voice breaks through my thoughts.

I turn to see Jennifer, one of the first buyers I worked with at Veray. "Jen, it's been how long?" I reach to hug her.

"Too long." She smiles warmly. "Where's Mark?"

"We're not together anymore," I say wishing I didn't have to keep explaining Mark's absence to people.

"Really?" She seems genuinely shocked. "I thought you two would do the whole white picket fence, two kids, happily-ever-after thing."

"It wasn't meant to be." Jax's voice interrupts before I can form any sort of reply.

I don't turn to look at him but I realize from Jen's expression that she finds him just as attractive as I do.

"You're Jax Walker, aren't you?" Jen holds out her hand as Jax comes into my peripheral vision.

"And you are?" Jax reaches for her hand, while his other hand finds its way to my back.

"Jennifer Flanagan. I'm a buyer. Well, I used to be a buyer. Although sometimes Ms. Veray will have a special project for me. "She's rambling and apparently isn't aware of it. "I..."

"It's a pleasure to meet you, Jennifer." Jax's voice calmly saves us both from Jennifer's overenthusiastic greeting. "If you'll excuse us, Ms. Marlow and I have some business to discuss."

Before I can protest, Jax has me by the arm and is guiding me through the same hallway, Madeline and Brighton disappeared into moments before. As we step through the doorway of a bedroom I get my first frontal glimpse of Jax since I've learned he's semi-stalking me.

As much as I try not to stare it's impossible. He's just shaven, his facial skin glowing gently in the soft light of the room. He's wearing a dark suit, and a light pink shirt opened enough that several small chest hairs are finding their way into my line of sight. I shake my head trying to gain some perspective.

"Where's Brighton?" Jax demands.

"With Madeline," I offer.

"Are you interested in him?" Jax hasn't let go of my arm yet.

"He's interesting."

"That's not what I asked, Ivy." I can tell from his tone that he's losing patience.

"We're friends," I say softly.

"Friends?" His expression turns to uncertainty.

"Yes."

"Are you going to sleep with him?"

"I haven't decided," I lie.

I see the pain in his eyes the moment I say it. "No. You can't."

"Why?" I can feel my heart racing as I stare into Jax's eyes. "Why can't I?"

"He's completely wrong for you." He grabs my other arm now, pulling me closer to him. "I want you."

"You don't want me." I try to pull back but his grasp on me is too strong. "You want to fuck me. As soon as that's done, you'll be done with me."

"I what?" His voice has a hint of anger. "Why would you say that?"

"Brighton. He said...he..." I grope for words, my mind darting back to what Brighton shared with me less than an hour earlier. "Brighton told me all about your past. I know you just use women and then throw them away. "

Jax's hands drop. "He doesn't understand."

"What doesn't he understand?" I press on, "it makes perfect sense to me. When I was at your place, you almost fucked me and that was what? Two days after we met? That's impressive."

"It's not like that with you. I feel things," he states boldly.

I stop. I can't breathe. I stare at him. "It's the same thing you feel each time you chase a woman and catch her." I look past him to the wall, not wanting to meet his gaze. "I'm just a conquest to you."

"You're wrong." He pulls his hand through his hair, pushing it back from his forehead.

"I'm not wrong." I poke my index finger into his chest. "You even used my best friend to get me into bed. Why the hell would you insist on Brighton adding her to his list of candidates? Why go to so much trouble? Why?"

"Brighton's mistaken. The two aren't related. Your friend has real talent."

I scan his face trying to pull out the truth. "Mistaken? Is that your story?"

"It's not a story."

"She means so much to me. You don't understand that. You don't know me," I manage to say.

"I do know you." He reaches for my hand gently cradling it in his. "I know that you were devastated when the person you loved cheated on you. I know that you're a kind, talented and exceptional woman. I know that you deserve to be with a man who cherishes you for the gift that you are. I don't want to hurt you."

I close my eyes hoping that will stop the tears. It doesn't. "Please don't say those things. Please." I feel my clutch vibrating again.

"Ivy, your phone." Jax has obviously noticed the irritating rumble as well. "Do you need to get that?"

"No," I whisper. "We should get back."

"I want to explain more." Jax inches closer to me, his right hand pushes my hair back behind my ear. "Brighton doesn't know what I feel. The other night when we were together, you pulled back because I called you sweetheart. When I saw the pain in your eyes I knew Mark must have called you that too. I hated myself for doing that. For making you think of that bastard and for making you feel pain because of him again. I panicked."

I feel overwhelmed by everything he's saying. "Madeline will be looking for us by now."

"I want to protect you, Ivy." His breath runs across my cheek." I want to help you heal. I want to help you love again."

I look into his eyes, seeing something I hadn't before. There's a vulnerability that wasn't there before tonight. I need time to think. "We need to get back now. You're the guest of honor."

He stares silently at me for a moment before releasing my hand. "You're right."

As he walks out of the bedroom door, my phone once again starts vibrating.

"Go to hell, Mark," I say under my breath before I follow Jax.

CHAPTER TWELVE

NINETY MINUTES, AND SEVERAL DOZEN STOLEN GLANCES AT JAX LATER, I'm ready to leave. I search the room for Brighton and spot him delicately kissing the hand of a woman who works in the sales department at Veray. I smile realizing that Liz was right in her decision not to pursue a relationship with such an obvious playboy.

"I'm going to call it a night, Madeline." I reach to give her a quick embrace. "Thank you for including me."

"You know you're part of our family." Madeline looks past me to where Brighton is. "Are you taking him with you?"

I giggle. "No, he's all yours." I give her a quick wink before turning to leave.

As I ride the elevator to the lobby I fish in my clutch for my phone. Five missed Mark calls in total. I sigh thinking that a good night's rest will give me the emotional energy I need to deal with him.

I quickly dial Liz, hoping that I can secure some best friend time tonight. I could really use her perspective to help me sort through what I've learned about Jax and his unexpected confession about his feelings.

"Hello?" Liz screams as she answers. There's a surge of loud background noise wafting through the phone.

"Liz? It's me." I raise my voice hoping she can make out what I'm saying.

"Ivy? Hold on. I'll find a quieter spot."

I exit Madeline's building into an unpredicted rain shower. "Damn," I say as I take cover under the awning hanging over the door.

"Are you still there?" I bring my phone back to my ear.

"I'm here, sugar."

"Where are you?" I ask. "Sounds like way more fun than my night."

Liz laughs. "I'm just out grabbing a drink with a few friends. What's up?"

"I could use some best friend time."

"What happened?"

"Mark. Jax." I sigh heavily. "You know how it is."

"What about Mark?" Liz's voice is clearer now.

"He's called a bunch of times tonight." I step back into the rain, trying to hail a taxi. "Where are you? I'll grab a taxi and come meet you."

"No." She's resolute. "I'll come to your place. Give me an hour."

––––––––

"DEAR, I believe you put your dress on backwards." Mrs. Adams greets me as I step off the elevator.

I laugh. "No, it's supposed to look like this."

"Really?" She frowns. "It leaves very little to the imagination."

"That's the idea," I whisper.

"In my day, women kept their assets hidden until their wedding night." She adjusts the soft, pink, terry cloth robe she's wearing.

"It's very late." I glance at my phone realizing it's already past eleven. "Are you all right? Shouldn't you be asleep?"

"It's been a troubling night, Ivy. Walk with me to my apartment."

I gently grab her arm helping her down the hallway. "What happened?"

"Mark was here." She reaches into her pocket for her keys. As she fumbles with all three of the locks on the door I smile knowing she locked her door up tight even though she was only going a few feet to my apartment.

"When?" I help her inside, turning on the light for her.

"It was hours ago." She sits in an oversized, blue chair that has seen much better days.

"Can I warm you some milk?"

"Yes, thank you." She nods. "He was looking for a letter he said you had and demanding to know where you were."

"I'm sorry you had to deal with that."

"He buzzed me when you didn't answer and I let him up." Her hands are shaking. "He was so angry."

"He tried calling me several times tonight." I sigh. "I should have talked to him."

I set the mug of warm milk and a linen napkin on a small tray that I place on the table in front of her. I kneel down so I'm at her eye level. "I'm going to take care of this. I won't let him bother you again."

"Be careful, Ivy." She rests her weathered hand on mine. "His temper is so bad."

"I'll handle it." I lean down to kiss her forehead. "Lock the door before you go to bed."

"Thank you." She manages a small smile. "I will."

———

I CHANGE into a pair of jeans, and a pink t-shirt while I wait for Liz. As tempted as I am to call Mark right now, I want to gather my thoughts and my best friend's input before I confront my ex fiancé.

I stare silently at the envelope addressed to Mark on my foyer table before being hit with a realization. I scurry down the hall to my bedroom, heading straight for the bedside table. I pull the drawer out before dumping it on the bed. I rummage through the papers in search of an old love letter Mark sent me a year ago when he was in Tokyo on business. I grab for it before running back down the hallway in my bare feet. I take a deep breath as I pick up the envelope I've been holding for Mark.

The buzzer startles me. "Liz?" I say into it.

"Let me up."

I buzz her in, my heart racing.

I open the door to my apartment, the two letters still clutched in my palm.

"He sent this envelope to me." My words assault her before she's even stepped foot off the elevator.

"Who sent you what?" Liz pushes past me. "I need a drink."

"Mark." I motion towards the kitchen. "He sent me this envelope."

"I haven't a clue what you're talking about." She calls from the kitchen amidst the sound of the cupboard opening and something liquid being poured.

"Mark has been sending me these envelopes." I push both letters towards her as she re-enters the foyer a full glass of white wine in her hand.

"Why pray tell would he do that?" There's obvious sarcasm in her voice.

"I don't know." I try to hand her the envelopes again. "Look."

"You know something." The slurring in her voice is now distinctively obvious as she slaps the letters from my hand. "Not every man wants you, Ivy."

"What?" I'm appalled by her comment, but quickly decide that it's all the alcohol she's obviously consumed this evening talking and not her.

"He cheated on you remember? Why would he want you again?" She empties half the glass in one swallow.

"What's wrong with you?" I reach to take the wine glass from her hand realizing she's way past the point of being tipsy.

"Don't!" she screams, pulling the glass back from me.

"Liz, you've had enough."

"I need to use the bathroom." She stumbles down the hall, the glass teetering in her hand.

I call down to the lobby and Oliver quickly answers. "Ms. Marlow? What can I do for you?"

"I need a taxi for my friend, Oliver." I try to calm my quivering voice. "I'll bring her down shortly."

"Of course," he replies. "I'll take care of it."

I reach down to pick up the envelopes from where they landed on the floor. Once again I hold them side-by-side, noting that the writing is identical.

There's a knock at the door. I jump. "Oliver," I say quietly thinking that he must have come up to help me with Liz.

I swing the door wide open. It's Mark. He pushes past me.

"No," I say. "No. Out." I point at the open door.

He pushes it closed with his foot. "I'm not going anywhere, sweetheart. Where the hell were you tonight?"

"That's none of your business," I shout at him. "Why did you come here and terrorize Mrs. Adams?"

"That crazy old bat?" He shakes his head. "I can't believe she's not dead yet."

"I have nothing to say to you." I try to push past him to get to the door. He grabs my shoulders.

"I'm not leaving." The anger in his voice is palpable. "We have some things to settle."

"Like the fact that you keep sending letters addressed to yourself here?" I point at the envelopes on the table.

"I did that so I could see you."

"I hate you." I can feel the tears coming. "Don't you get that? You cheated with three women Mark. Three."

The sudden sound of breaking glass causes us both to turn abruptly.

"Three?" Liz is standing at the entrance to the hallway, the wine glass in broken shreds by her feet. "Three?"

"That's right," I snap. "He slept with three other women right before our wedding."

Mark's face turns white. "Lizzie, what are you doing here?"

"Three?" she repeats, her body beginning to shake from sobs. "You said it was only me, Mark."

"I didn't love them." Mark rushes across the room.

I stare at them both, bitter realization washing over and through me.

"You bastard," she screams at him, her fists pounding into his chest. "Who were they?"

"You...you both..."I stumble to steady myself against the table. "You and Mark?"

"You weren't supposed to find out like this." Liz's voice is barely more than a whimper.

"How long?" I shake with anger. "When...when did it start?"

They both stand in silence staring at me.

I rush towards them. "When did you start sleeping with him?"

"It's been on and off for years." Mark moves to block me from reaching her. "It started about a year after we met. It was when you went to Baltimore for your aunt's funeral."

I mentally push myself back to that day. It had to have been more than two years ago, maybe three.

"Liz came over to keep me company," he pauses drawing a heavy breath, "before you know it we were in the bedroom."

"My bedroom? My bed?" I feel nauseous.

"Oh God," Liz gasps.

"When did it stop?" My gaze is still locked on Liz, who is glaring at Mark.

"It hasn't," she whispers. "I was with him when you called earlier. I went to the broker's open house."

I feel my body go numb. I can hear the words but they don't make sense.

"Why?" I barely can hear my own voice.

"I love him," she wails.

"All this time you've been lying," I scream at her. "Was it you? Were you the one he meant to send that email to?" My head is spinning. I'm assaulted with memories of all the times I talked to her about Mark. She was there when I donated my wedding dress and watched as I shredded all the invitations and reception place cards. She had been my rock and sole support when all my dreams had come crashing down.

"What email?" She's livid again.

"That's how I found out he was a cheating bastard." I glare at Mark. "He mistakenly sent me an email saying he was ready in his hotel room one night when he was in Chicago."

She shakes her head violently, letting out a blood curdling scream. "No! I was here when he was there."

"It didn't mean anything." Mark reaches to touch her arm.

She slaps it away before turning her attention to me. "Why didn't you tell me there were others? Why?"

"You've got to be kidding," I seethe.

"How did you find out about the others?" She's sobbing heavily again.

"He told me." I point my index finger directly at Mark. "Call it a guilty conscience."

"I hate you." Liz grabs my shoulders and pushes me.

The instant I fall I feel a deep pain in my head. It takes me a moment to realize I hit the corner of the foyer table on my way to the floor.

I start to pull myself up. "Get out. Both of you," I scream.

Liz lunges for me again. I raise my hands to stop her, but she pushes me. I fall hard against the door.

"Stop it, Liz." Mark grabs her from behind. "You're going to hurt her."

"Let go of me you bastard." Her arms flail wildly behind her head as she desperately tries to make contact with Mark's face.

I stand, staring at them. I can feel the doorknob in my fist. I twist it, quickly opening the door and running out into the hallway. I hurriedly press the elevator button before hearing the sound of more breaking glass coming from my apartment. I panic, slipping through the door for the stairs.

CHAPTER THIRTEEN

"Look, Lady, I'm not leaving until I get paid, kapeesh?"

I nod as I press the buzzer for Jax's apartment for the sixth time.

"It's raining cats and dogs. I need my money now." The taxi driver barks at me through the open window of his car.

I press the buzzer again, hoping Jax is asleep and this last time will wake him. "Please answer," I whisper as I shiver on the front step of his building, my bare feet numb, my clothing completely drenched.

I curse as there's no response. My eye catches the sight of headlights coming around the corner. A dark sedan stops and the driver gets out and opens a large black umbrella. Before he can walk around the car, Jax swings open the back passenger door, darting up the steps.

"Ivy! Jesus!" He quickly removes his suit jacket, wrapping it around my quivering body. "What the hell happened to you?"

"Hey! You! I need to get paid." The taxi driver honks his horn ensuring Jax, and the entire block hears him.

"Leonard, take care of that," Jax calls to his driver who is still standing under the umbrella near the car.

"You're bleeding." He runs his hand over the back of my head. "Where are your shoes? Were you mugged?"

I shake my head back and forth, unable to form any words.

"We need to go to the hospital." He scoops me off the ground and into his arms.

"No. Please, no," I murmur against his chest. My hand clutching the front of his now drenched shirt.

"Leonard, the door. Help us."

The driver jumps into action, unlocking the door and leading the way up to Jax's apartment.

Jax places me gently on the couch before walking back to talk with Leonard. Jax's voice is hushed but I hear him say Mark's name, my apartment address and something about shoes. I hear the muted click of the apartment door closing as Leonard takes his leave.

"Did Mark do this to you?" Jax is kneeling next to the couch now, his right hand stroking my forehead.

I feel my lips tremble as my eyes, once again, fill with tears. "Liz," I manage to say.

"Liz? Your friend, Liz?"

"Yes...her... she... and then Mark came to my place." My body starts to shake, the coldness overtaking me now.

"You're shivering. You need a shower." Jax picks me up again, taking me down the hallway to a bathroom.

He places me on my feet before reaching into a large, black marble shower stall to turn on the water. "Can you raise your arms?"

I nod. I cringe from a sharp pain in my left shoulder as I lift my arms above my head. I feel him pull the saturated t-shirt over my head, my breasts instantly visible. His eyes don't leave my face.

"Lean on my shoulder." His voice is gentle. He kneels to unfasten my jeans, sliding them and the pink panties I'm wearing off.

"I can't believe anyone would hurt you." He embraces me, his arms locked around my mid-section, his head resting against my breasts. "You're so beautiful."

He stands and looks directly at me as he unbuttons his shirt. "I'll kill whoever did this to you."

"Please don't say that," I whisper, raising my hand to cradle his cheek.

He places his hand over mine. He closes his eyes, pulling my hand to his lips before placing a kiss on my palm. "I wish I had been there to protect you."

I nod silently, feeling my body trembling from the coldness in the air. I'm so overwrought. I feel as though the last few hours have been nothing but a nightmare. I don't know how I went from sitting in that limousine with Brighton to standing naked and shaking in his brother's apartment.

"What am I doing?" Jax swiftly finishes undressing. "We need to warm you up."

He walks past me to open the door of the shower. I scan his body, noticing how firm the muscles in his back are, how defined his legs are. My eyes linger on his round buttocks, wanting him to turn. He does as he reaches his hand out to me.

"Come."

I place my hand in his allowing him to lead me into the warmth of the shower.

"Thank you," I whisper through sobs as the water rushes over my body.

"Shhh." He takes my hands in his, placing them on his hips. "Hold onto me. I'll wash your hair. But first, let me look at that nasty cut."

I nod, leaning my head forward, my eyes now in a straight line with his groin. I breathe deeply seeing him naked and exposed for the first time. Even in a semi-hard state his cock is magnificent.

"I don't think you'll need stitches." His hand finds my chin, tilting my face up so our eyes meet.

"I'll take care of you, beautiful."

I stand silently as he takes his time gently washing and conditioning my hair. He turns my body slowly before soaping my back with a lavender fragranced wash. His hands lightly skim my buttocks then trail down as he washes my legs and feet.

"You cut your foot." There's disappointment in his voice. "Did you come all the way here in bare feet?"

"Yes."

He stands before turning me back around to face him. "I'll bandage that for you."

I catch my breath when I realize he's lathering his hands to continue his cleansing mission. He smiles gently before placing his warm hand on my chest above my breasts. We lock eyes as his hand moves lower, sliding over each of my breasts, stopping to circle my now hard nipples.

"I've wanted to take care of you for so long." His hand runs down my body, stopping to caress the subtle curve of my stomach.

I take a deep breath knowing that his journey isn't complete yet. I look down watching his hand disappear between my legs. He moves it slowly, separating the smooth folds, his finger just barely grazing my clitoris before his hand continues its path down my right leg.

"Step back so I can rinse you." He gently pushes me back so I'm under the flow of the warm water. I close my eyes, feeling him carefully rinsing the area that was cut again. His touch is light and gentle.

"It's time to dry you off." I open my eyes to see him reaching behind me to shut the water off. He grabs a thick white towel from a shelf above the showerhead. I feel the softness swathe me as he wraps it around my body. He quickly wraps another around his waist. His hair dripping onto his face, he pulls his hand over it, pushing it back. "I'll take care of that nasty cut on your head and the one on your foot."

———

"YOU'RE TICKLISH, AREN'T YOU?" Jax, now clad in sweatpants is trying desperately to apply antiseptic cream to the cut on my right heel. My giggling isn't helping matters.

"A little, yes." I smile at him from my spot on his bed where he laid me after dressing me in one of his t-shirts and a pair of navy boxers.

"Hold still or I'll tie you down." He throws me a wicked grin.

"Promise?"

He shoots me a glance and a wide smile before going back to work on my foot. "All done," he announces as he places the box of bandages down on the bedside table. "Now I'll find a brush for your hair."

As he leaves the room I reach up to feel my hair and my fingers lightly skim the cut and now good-sized bump near the back of my head. My mind instantly forms an image of the anger in Liz's eyes before she pushed me. I tear up, my heart beating faster thinking about the depth of her betrayal and my naivety.

"What's happened?" Jax's hand cradles my face as his thumb reaches to push away a tear that has fallen down my cheek. "You were thinking about earlier?"

"Yes." I sob now, thinking about how terrified I was of Liz and how overwhelmed I was learning that she was one of the women Mark had been unfaithful with.

Jax motions for me to move forward. He settles in behind me on the bed, his back resting against the black headboard, and his legs around me. He pulls my back to his chest, his arms circling me.

"I didn't know where else to go." I feel a need to explain how I ended up on his doorstep. I'm not sure of it myself. It was an inner drive to be near him after hearing him tell me earlier that he'd protect me.

"You're exactly where you need to be." I feel him gently pull a brush through my now damp hair.

I nod silently enjoying the feeling of him taking care of me.

"I think you should talk to the police tomorrow," he says very matter-of-factly. "I'll take you there to file a report."

"No." I turn my head to look at him. "I don't want that."

"Ivy." He stops brushing my hair. "You were badly hurt."

"I fell." I turn back around, pulling my knees to my chest, wrapping my arms around them. "I stumbled when Liz came running at me."

"She pushed you." His tone is more serious. "I know that she pushed you."

"She was so angry. I've never seen her that angry."

"Was it because you went to the party with Brighton tonight?"

"No." I feel the tears rising to the surface again. I take a deep breath trying to steady my emotions. "Mark came and she heard him and she lost it."

"Did Mark threaten you?" I feel Jax's body tighten.

"No. It wasn't like that." I hold my head in my hands wanting to forget that tonight ever happened.

"We don't need to talk about it." He stands now. I look up to see him towering over me. "It's time for you to sleep."

He hops off the bed. I move slightly as he pulls back the covers, revealing tan sheets. "Get in, beautiful."

I shift my body so I'm now under the covers. I look at him expectantly, not certain of what his next move will be.

He leans down, brushes his moist lips against my forehead before he whispers, "Sleep well. I'm in the next room if you need me."

I stare silently as he closes the door behind him, my eyelids suddenly feeling very heavy.

———

"DO YOU WANT COFFEE?" Jax's voice greets me as a walk into the kitchen.

"I think I overslept and yes, please." I sit in one of the chairs next to the small dining set.

"Cream, sugar?" He smiles as he hands me a ceramic mug filled to the brim with rich smelling coffee.

"No, thank you."

"Does your hair always look this way when you wake up?"

"What way?" I reach to touch it, quickly realizing that the natural curl I so desperately dislike took control when I went to sleep with damp hair. "Not always, no."

"I love it."

I see that he's already dressed in navy trousers and a light blue dress shirt. "You're dressed," I say under my breath, feeling very out of place.

"I've been out. I needed to take care of some things."

"Things?"

"Ivy things." He winks at me before walking out of the room.

"Ivy things?" I repeat quietly.

He returns carrying two shopping bags. "I went to your apartment."

"You what?" I'm startled and instantly unsure of how he could have gotten past the doorman.

"Fred Johnson and I have done business together." He continues, "I mentioned that you'd had a problem in your apartment last night and he was more than happy to let me in."

"You know the man who manages my building?"

"I do." He grins.

"Please tell me you haven't bought the building." I try to cover the anxiety in my voice.

"Not yet." His voice is teasing.

I raise my eyebrow before taking a small sip of the coffee.

"If I did own it, I'd lower your rent." The smile on his face is widening.

"You couldn't. I own," I counter.

"You own? Or you and Mark own?" There's surprise in his voice.

I hesitate before I reply, "Actually, Mark owns the apartment I live in." I take a deep breath and look directly at him. "I want to be able to move out on my own but I'm still working on how to make that happen."

"I understand." He holds his hand out to me. "Come with me."

I follow him down the hall to the bedroom. He motions for me to sit on the edge of the bed as he places the shopping bags on the floor.

"Ivy." He kneels in front of me. "There were some broken things at your place."

"Yes." I sigh. "Liz broke a wine glass and then I heard more glass when I ran out."

"I cleaned it up." He stops as if to gather his thoughts. "But it was more than just a wine glass."

I raise my eyebrow giving him a quizzed look.

He leans to the left, reaching inside one of the shopping bags. I gasp the moment I see the edge of the weathered picture frame. It's bent, splintered and the glass shattered.

I can't stop tears from filling my eyes. "Oh no. No." I stare at it unable to move.

"This is you and your mother, isn't it?"

I nod. "It's the only photograph I have of the two of us." I stare at it resting in his hands. "She ... my mother..." I sob, trying to say the words. "She made the frame herself."

I reach out to run my finger along my mother's beautiful face in the image. She's cradling me as she sits beaming in the hospital bed the day I was born.

"I'll have it fixed." His voice is so calm.

"It's destroyed," I whimper.

"It's bruised. Trust me with it, please."

I look from the frame to his face. I study his eyes, seeing the deep and genuine concern in them. "Yes. I trust you. "

CHAPTER FOURTEEN

"Thank you for picking up some of my things," I say to Jax as I walk back into the kitchen after having a warm shower and getting dressed.

"I knew you'd look lovely in that dress." He smiles at me. "Purple is really striking on you, Ivy."

I look down at the simple sundress and white strappy heels he brought for me from my place.

"I haven't seen you with your hair pulled back like that." He stands next to me, running his hand down my cheek, past my chin and unto my neck.

I sigh, enjoying his touch. "I'd like to go to my apartment now."

"I'd like to stop somewhere before we do that, if you don't mind." There's a playful tone to his voice.

"Please say it's not the police station." I frown as I look up at him.

He gently moves his hand from my neck back to my face, cradling my right cheek with his palm. "Ivy, last night you said no police. I wouldn't push you to do anything you don't want."

"Thank you." I place my hand over his relishing in the feeling of his touch.

"No. I should be the one thanking you." His other hand finds my left cheek and our eyes meet.

"For?" I search his eyes for an answer.

"You came here last night. I was the one you wanted when you needed help." His voice is soft, gentle and soothing. "That means more than you know."

I smile. "I'm not sure why but you make me feel so safe."

His tone becomes more serious. "You're safe with me, Ivy. I loved taking care of you. That was a gift for me and so today..."

"Today?" I ask, wondering what he has in store for me.

"Today I repay the gift."

I 'm puzzled and I'm certain he can read that within my expression. "I should be the one repaying you for everything you did for me."

"You will." He reaches for my hand. "All of the pleasure I'm going to take from you today, tomorrow and every day after that will be my compensation."

I stand silent while my mind jumps to an image of him in the shower, nude, semi-erect and wanting.

"You want that don't you, Ivy?" he asks with confidence. "You want me to help you feel pleasure, don't you?"

I nod, unable to form any coherent response. I'm certain if I open my mouth at this point, nothing but high pitched gibberish will spill out.

He smiles. I watch intently as he pulls my hand to his lips and kisses each of my fingers slowly and methodically.

"Time to go." He steps towards the apartment door. I follow, unsure of what I've gotten myself into.

———

LESS THAN THIRTY MINUTES LATER, Leonard parks the car in front of my apartment building. We had stopped on our way in midtown in front of a non-descript storefront. Jax had run in and emerged within moments with a bright, mischievous grin on his face.

I had questioned him as the car weaved through traffic towards my building, but the only response I received was a smirk and a wink.

"Are you sure you're ready to go up?" His voice pulls me from my thoughts.

"I am."

Leonard opens the door as I make my exit from the car, followed quickly by Jax. I instantly feel his hand on my waist as we begin walking side-by-side towards the building.

"Ivy!" Mrs. Adams almost runs directly into me as I step into the lobby. She's holding tight to Oliver's arm. "Dear, there you are. I was worried sick."

"I'm sorry. I should have called."

Her gaze swiftly jumps from me to Jax. "I'm so glad that you've hired a bodyguard. Now Mark and that Elizabeth woman can't get anywhere near you."

"Actually, he's not..."

"I'll be certain to take the best care of Ivy," Jax interjects. "I'm not a bodyguard though. I'm a friend."

"A boyfriend?" Mrs. Adams rattles on, "Ivy has needed a boyfriend since the Mark fiasco. Now, young man, you better take care of her heart. It's fragile, you know."

"Yes. I know. Ivy is a treasure. You have my word I'll take very good care of her." He glances down at me before continuing, "I'm Jax Walker and you are?" He extends his hand waiting for Mrs. Adams to place her diminutive, weathered hand in his.

"It's a pleasure, Mr. Walker." She reaches to shake his hand. "I'm Rose Adams. I live next door to Ivy."

"She's a wonderful neighbor," I offer. I'm eager to get upstairs to my apartment to see whether there's any permanent damage from last night's argument.

"I need to be on my way now." Mrs. Adams looks towards Oliver who stepped back inside. "Oliver is going to help me find a taxi."

"Absolutely not." Jax extends his arm to her. "My driver, Leonard, will take you anywhere you need to go and I'll have him wait and bring you home."

"Nonsense." Mrs. Adam gestures in the air with her hand as if trying to hit a wayward fly. "A taxi suits me just fine."

"You can trust Leonard." Jax winks at her. "He'd enjoy keeping himself occupied."

She throws him a skeptical glance before nodding once in agreement.

I watch as he speaks to Leonard after helping Mrs. Adams into the backseat of the sedan. I can't help but notice how tender he is as he takes her arm to guide her in.

"Onwards and upwards, Ivy," Jax says as he walks towards me. "Your apartment and my surprise awaits."

––––––––

"EVERYTHING LOOKS JUST as I left it." I place my purse down on the foyer table. "The letters. They're gone."

"I didn't see any letters when I came by earlier." Jax walks from his place near the door to stand next to me. "Do you mean the letters addressed to Mark?"

I nod, knowing I should explain to Jax more about what happened last night but not feeling the inner strength to relive those moments yet so I don't elaborate.

It's as if he reads my mind. "I can take you somewhere else if this is too much for you."

"No, it's not." I try to sound convincing. "I'm fine."

"You're certain?"

"I just want to put last night behind me. I have to." I try to find strength in my words all the while knowing that it will take me a long time to get over the realization that Liz betrayed me.

"Try not to think about last night right now. I have a surprise for you, remember?"

"How could I forget?" I sigh, feeling slightly unnerved by what the surprise entails.

"I take it you don't like surprises?" He moves closer to me, his hand reaching into the inner pocket of his suit jacket.

"I don't." My eyes are glued to his hand waiting to see what he's about to reveal.

"This you'll like." He pulls a plain white envelope from his pocket. "It's something very special." He holds it in his hand dangling it in the air between us. "It's yours right after we take care of a small, but very significant detail."

"What detail?" I ask suspiciously.

He leans in closer until his lips are lighting touching my ear. "The detail of your pleasure." He drops the envelope on the foyer table next to us.

"My pleasure?" I stand frozen in place, not wanting to lose the sensation of his breath on my neck.

"You wanted me in the shower last night."

I don't respond. What can I possibly say? I can't deny that I wanted him then and that I've wanted him ever since I turned around at the gallery and was consumed by his very presence.

His lips move from my ear to my neck. Light kisses combined with the sensation of his teeth nipping at my sensitive skin. A moan builds deep within me and softly escapes.

"That's right, beautiful. You know you belong to me."

I reach for his hair, needing and wanting to feel his lips on mine. I pull his head up and push my lips into his. He thrusts his tongue into my mouth, gently coaxing mine to join his in a slow, circular dance. He bites my bottom lip, causing me to pull back slightly.

"You're going to learn never to refuse what I want," he growls.

He steps back. His hands grip my shoulders as he turns me abruptly around.

I whimper. "Please."

"Please what?" His breath is on my neck again as I feel his hands deftly undoing the zipper at the back of my dress.

"Please let me touch you."

"Not now. Not yet." He pushes the dress to the floor. His hand tracing a path down my bare back to the edge of the white lace panties I'd found in the bag he brought me earlier. "Put your hands on the wall. Lean forward."

I feel exposed and aroused, certain that soon he'll discover how wet I've become just from the anticipation of his touch.

There's brief movement behind me and I realize he's on his knees.

"Your body is amazing," he says quietly.

I jump slightly at the touch of his lips on my lower back. His tongue makes contact with my skin, forming small circles.

"Last night, after I put you to bed..." He stops as he runs his tongue over the white lace of the panties, "I couldn't stop thinking about how you would taste."

I moan again as his tongue runs back up the panties to the bottom of my back.

"It's such a shame."

I feel him pull back slightly, disappointment immediately washing over me. "A shame?" I manage to say as I glance down and over my shoulder.

"They're so pretty," he says as he looks up into my eyes. At that moment I feel his hands grab the thin material at the sides as he rips the panties off my body.

I stumble. His hands steady me as he gently nudges my feet farther apart making me feel even more exposed.

"You're so perfect. So smooth." His hands pull my buttocks apart as his tongue traces a long, pointed line up my cleft.

I almost come from the sensation.

"Ivy. Listen to me." His breath is caressing my wetness as I try and focus on his words. "Do not come until I tell you to."

My body reacts. I push myself towards him, longing to find his tongue once again.

"No coming until I say." He thrusts his tongue between my folds. "Understood?"

"Yes. Please," I say without thinking.

He stabs his tongue sharply into me, before pulling it back and tracing a circle around my engorged clitoris. I stumble again from the sensation. He uses the opportunity to turn my body around before his mouth swiftly claims me again.

I look down to see him still fully clothed, his face between my legs. I wrap my hand through his hair, pushing him further into my wetness.

I feel his finger near my entrance as I work to control my arousal. I'm so wet, so open, so wanting. I've never felt so utterly exposed before, yet nothing could have made me stop.

He runs his finger once over my clit before gently sliding it into me. I gasp as he immediately hones in on my most intimate spot. His tongue skillfully works my clit, tenderly running circles over it, the pressure changing from soft to more direct before he pulls it into his mouth sucking on it.

My hips start to move involuntarily, keeping pace with his finger. He slides another in and I'm immediately assaulted with an image of his cock. I want to come, but more than that I want to feel him inside of me, stretching me, pulling at my arousal.

"Jax..." My voice turns into a low moan as he pushes harder on my clit. "Fuck me, please."

His groan vibrates through my folds entering me just as his fingers have.

"I'm so close." I push his face harder into me, wanting him to let me come.

He slows the pace. His movements suggesting it's not time yet.

I pull on his hair, willing him to suck on my clit harder. "Let me come." I know my voice sounds impatient. It's a clear reflection of what my body is feeling.

He stands swiftly. I work to catch my breath before feeling his moist lips crush mine. I taste him and my arousal and I immediately feel myself moving towards the brink of orgasm again.

"I want you," I moan into his mouth.

"You want me to fuck you," he says as he pulls on my bottom lip with his teeth again.

"Please." I press my body into his.

In one fluid movement he reaches down, pulling my thighs around him before his hands slide to cup my ass. The index finger of his left hand finds my clit as I wrap my legs around his waist. I move my body slightly back and forth enjoying the pressure of his finger.

He kisses me hard before turning and walking down the hallway.

He lowers me onto the bed, his eyes running over my exposed skin. He pushes his suit jacket from his shoulders before undoing the buckle of his belt. I stare as he reaches into his slacks pocket to reveal a small foil packet.

"Touch yourself for me." I stare at his lips as I watch him reach for my hand guiding it to my still aching clit.

I follow his instructions, gently running my fingers in slow circles. I feel myself inching close to the edge yet again. "It feels so nice." I'm breathless and wanting.

"That's the way, Ivy." He catches my glance as he unzips his slacks. I watch him pull the edge of the packet open with his teeth before releasing the condom. My eyes are glued to his knowing that I'll soon feel him completely inside of me.

He kneels on the bed, still almost fully dressed, sweat forming on his upper lip. I gasp when I feel the tip of his cock touch my clit. I move my hands to his shoulders trying to pull him closer toward me.

"Not now. Not yet," he says again.

I whine with disappointment.

"Take the pleasure I give you," he whispers as he reaches forward to brush his lips against mine. With that I feel the tip of his cock skim my clit.

He shifts his body so he's kneeling between my legs. I look down. His full, erect cock, resting heavily in his hand as he expertly glides it back and forth across my clit. My body is aching. I try to maneuver my hips so he'll slide himself into me.

"I want you close to the edge." He kisses me again, this time with more force. I groan from the desire building within me.

"Please," I beg. "Please fuck me now."

"If you come you belong to me."

"Yes. I want..." I stifle a scream as I feel the entire length of his cock enter me.

"Look at me," he demands as he rapidly finds his rhythm.

I look into his eyes seeing the same pleasure I'm feeling in his face.

"You're mine now," he growls as he pushes deeper.

"Yours."

He thrusts harder, his eyes never leaving mine.

"I'm so close," I say breathlessly feeling my body tense.

He slows and I search his face for an explanation. I grind myself into him, wanting him to fuck me even harder. I watch him bring his thumb to his lips. It disappears between them briefly, wetness glistening just on the tip.

"Jax..." I manage before I feel pressure on my clit.

His thumb traces circles around my clit as he moves his body slowly. He pushes as deep as he can. His cock is stretching me. The pain of his size within me mixed with sheer pleasure.

"Please," I beg wanting him to tell me I can come.

"I don't want this to end," he hisses before moving to kiss me. I hungrily open my mouth to his, allowing him to pull my tongue between his teeth.

I breathe heavily in his mouth, his thumb now pressing harder, moving faster against my swollen clit. His thrusts become stronger again.

He pulls back from our kiss, his face mere inches from mine. I stare into his eyes willing him to let me find my release.

"Now," he rasps through clenched teeth, his eyes boring a hole into me.

I feel an orgasm wash over me as I watch his face. His lips open slightly, his breathing stalls and I know in that instant he's come at exactly the same moment I have.

"Ivy," escapes his lips before he leans down, gently placing his head on my chest. His right hand reaches to cup my breast before he places a gentle kiss on the sensitive skin between my breasts. "You're so beautiful."

I nod even though I know he can't see the movement. I softly run my hand through his hair as I take a deep breath.

"You're okay?" He looks up at me.

I smile before I nod again. I want to tell him that was the most intense orgasm I've ever experienced but I've yet to fully catch my breath.

He sighs heavily before pulling his body away from mine. I feel an instant void as I watch him remove the condom and tie it before wrapping it in a tissue from the box on the nightstand. He throws it in the wastebasket and refastens his slacks and belt before he turns back to me.

"There's a silk robe in your bathroom." He walks towards the doorway. "I saw it earlier when I was here."

I pull myself up to sit on the edge of the bed finally removing my shoes.

He returns with the white robe, helping me put it on before tying it tightly around my waist.

"Don't move." He kisses me lightly on the forehead before disappearing out of the room again.

I listen intently, hoping to get a clue as to where he's gone. Part of me is fearful that he's heading for the door, his conquest completed. I hear water running before I hear his heavy footsteps coming back in my direction.

He pushes a glass of water towards me. "Drink this."

I take the glass. The sudden realization that he looked through my cupboards to find it brings a small smile to my lips.

"Ivy. Drink." He motions towards my mouth with his hand. "You've barely had anything to drink today. I don't want you getting dehydrated."

I raise the glass to my lips. The cold water a welcome reprieve from the thirst I'd been ignoring. I finish the entire glass before handing it back to him.

"Thank you," I say as he moves to kneel in front of me.

He smiles before running the fingertips of his right hand across my forehead, pushing back the hair that has fallen into my eyes.

I relish in his touch, still wanting to express how wonderful it had felt to come under his direction. I clear my throat, readying myself to speak.

"I have to go." Jax cups my left cheek with his palm. "I have a meeting I can't miss."

"At Veray?"

"No." He leans in to kiss me tenderly before standing and reaching for his suit jacket. "Another business interest." I watch as he pulls his phone from the jacket's inner pocket.

I nod, realizing that I know so little about him, yet we just shared one of the most amazing experiences of my life.

"I left the envelope on the table. Don't open it without my permission."

I raise my left eyebrow. "Or?" I teasingly ask.

"Or I'll be thoroughly disappointed in you." He doesn't look up from his phone. His eyes scanning the screen, his thumb scrolling through messages I assume.

"I won't then." I stand and adjust the robe, readying myself to walk him to the door.

He takes my hint and motions for me to lead the way. I do in silence, feeling slightly abandoned after what just happened.

"Leonard will pick you up for dinner at eight o'clock." He rests his hand on the doorknob. "Wear the red dress hanging in the middle of your closet and bring the envelope."

I glance over to the table at the envelope still sitting exactly where he dropped it.

"And, beautiful..." he reaches forward to brush my lips with his. "Don't under any circumstances speak to Mark or Liz."

"I don't want to talk to either of them today."

"Good." With that he opens the door, slips through and quietly closes it behind him.

I lean against the door listening to the elevator's bell signaling Jax's brisk departure.

CHAPTER FIFTEEN

"I KNEW YOU'D LOOK GORGEOUS IN THAT DRESS," JAX GREETS ME AS HE opens the door of the sedan.

"You have impeccable taste in clothing, Mr. Walker," I tease as I reach for his hand before stepping out of the car.

"And women," he quips before giving me a quick kiss.

The remark bites. I'm not foolish enough to believe that I'm the first woman Jax has swept off her feet, and that has me wondering how many have come before me.

"Let's go up." His fingers interweave with mine as we silently walk up the stairs to his apartment.

I place my purse and the plain white envelope down on the coffee table before I turn to him. "How did your meeting go?"

"Fine," he says brusquely. "I'll get us some wine."

I settle onto the couch my eyes scanning the room, noticing all of the jewelry boxes have been removed from their spot on the table. I don't see them anywhere.

He reappears carrying two half-filled wine glasses. "For you." He hands one to me before sitting beside me. He crosses his long legs as he skims his hand across the black material removing a stray piece of lint. His black trousers, coupled with the black dress shirt he's chosen offers a muted look I haven't seen him in before.

I take a long sip. "It's delicious."

He smiles before speaking. "How was your day?"

"It was fine." I enjoy another swallow.

"What did you do?"

"Nothing exciting. I rested, sketched some new designs ideas, and tidied." I place the wine glass down before turning to face him. "What did you do?"

He ignores the question as he leisurely takes a sip. "Did you talk with Mark or Liz today?"

I sigh out of sheer frustration. "No. I didn't."

"Are you going to?"

"I should at some point, no?" I retort.

"No, you shouldn't, Ivy." He once again brings the wine glass to his lips, his gaze falling from my face to the glass.

"I should. I need to."

"Why?" He places the glass down next to mine before turning his body to face me.

"I need to put this to rest and I can't do that until I talk to Liz, at least."

"What exactly happened?" He rests his arm on the back of the sofa, his index finger leisurely running a small circle along my bare shoulder.

I shiver from the touch knowing that my erect nipples are pressing against the material of the sheer sleeveless dress Jax chose for me to wear. I search his face looking for some of the understanding I saw not more than a few hours ago.

"It will help if you talk about it, beautiful." His hand reaches for mine. "Please tell me."

I take a deep breath. "They've been sleeping together for years."

"Who?"

"Mark and Liz," I say the words quickly, hoping that it will help to ward off the tears I can feel approaching.

"Mark was sleeping with your best friend?" His hand drops mine as he reaches for his wine. He empties the glass in one gulp before I have a chance to answer.

"Yes. I found out last night."

"He told you?" He leans back just a bit as if to gain more perspective. His eyes scan my face searching for answers.

"No." I shake my head slowly from side-to-side. "Liz was already at my apartment when he got there and she overheard us talking and she put two and two together, and..."

"Jesus." He stands quickly picking up his wine glass. "Nothing is off limits to that asshole."

"What does that mean?" I call after him as he disappears into the kitchen.

He strides back into the room, the wine glass, now completely full, gripped firmly in his hand. "You didn't know until last night that she was one of the women he was sleeping with?"

"How do you know there was more than one?" I try to recall when Jax first asked about Mark and if I offered that he had more than one lover.

He sits and turns so his body is completely facing me. He stares at me before answering. "I guessed, Ivy. Usually when a man cheats he'll do it more than once."

"I suppose he will." I look down at my hands before taking a deep breath. I can feel my emotions swiftly coming to the surface. I don't want to cry over Mark again.

"How many in total?"

"How many what?" I try to divert the question not wanting to continue the discussion.

"How many women did Mark cheat with?" He takes another healthy drink.

"Why does any of this matter?" I bite my lip to hold back the tears.

"How many?"

"Three." I jump to my feet. "Three. Are you happy? Mark fucked three other women when he was supposed to love only me. One of which is...or...was my best friend. And he did her in my...in my bed."

He stands and reaches to embrace me, guiding my head so it rests on his chest. "I'm sorry. Upsetting you wasn't what I wanted."

I pull back so I can look up into his face. "Why are you so curious about Mark?"

"I'm not." He motions for me to sit again. "I'm curious about you and what you're feeling."

I take a drink before settling in next to him on the couch again. "I'm devastated." I draw in a deep breath before continuing, "It was much easier when I didn't know who any of the women were."

"So Mark never told you about the other two?"

"No." I sigh. "I don't want to talk about Mark anymore."

Jax stares at my face before he reaches for my hand again. "No more Mark talk. Let's eat."

———

"YOU'VE BARELY EATEN ANYTHING," he says before taking another mouthful of the perfectly prepared mushroom risotto he's served alongside the grilled swordfish.

"I'm just not hungry," I confess. "It's delicious though."

He smiles before finishing the last bite on his plate. "You should eat, Ivy. You're going to need nourishment for later."

"For later?" I raise my eyebrow teasingly. My heart jumps a beat thinking back to earlier when Jax took me so brazenly, so wantonly that he didn't even undress himself.

"You'll see," he offers before standing to remove both plates from the table.

The distant ringing of my phone from the other room startles us both. I don't move from my spot knowing that it's very likely to be Liz calling yet again. Before I left my apartment there were eight missed calls all from her number.

"You're not going to get that?"

"No. I know who it is."

"Mark?"

I frown at the mention of his name yet again. "No, it's Liz. She's been trying to reach me all day."

"From now on it would be best if you turned off your phone when we're together."

I flash back to earlier in my apartment, right after we made love when he was eagerly checking the messages on his phone.

"You should turn it off now." His voice pulls me from my thoughts.

"And you'll turn off yours?" I counter.

He smirks as he answers, "Of course not. I run several businesses, Ivy. I can't be unreachable under any circumstances."

"But...but that hardly seems fair," I stumble with my words. "You..."

As if on cue, his phone rings. He reaches into his pocket and glances at it before raising his index finger signaling my silence. "I need to take this. Wait right here."

I nod as I watch him rush down the hallway towards his bedroom, quietly closing the door behind him. I know I'm not imagining that there's been a drastic shift in the way Jax is acting. He went from sympathetic and loving to dismissive and preoccupied. I sit in silence, listening for any murmur that may escape his bedroom. There's nothing but stillness. The sound of my phone ringing yet again brings me to my feet. I rush into the other room, pulling it swiftly from my purse, before pressing the Ignore button. Just as I expected it's Liz calling yet again. I scroll through the flood of text messages she's left for me. All either saying she's sorry or expressing her need to talk to me. I turn off my phone, throwing it back into my bag.

"Ivy."

I turn to see Jax standing behind me.

"I was turning it off, just as you ordered, sir." I try to smile.

"That's not important now."

"It's not?" My eyes follow him as he walks towards the envelope I brought with me. He picks it up before turning to face me again.

"I have to leave."

"Leave?" I stare at his face as he motions for me to sit next to him on the couch.

"Tonight. Now." He adjusts the envelope in his hands, moving it back and forth, his gaze never leaving it.

"I don't understand."

"That call, Ivy." He finally looks directly at me. "There's a situation in Los Angeles I need to tend to now. It can't wait."

"But it's Friday night," I whisper.

"I'll be back Sunday evening." He reaches to place the envelope in my lap, his hand lingering on it. "I wouldn't go unless it was an emergency."

I stare at my lap, trying to stifle my disappointment.

"Open it." His voice is curt.

"Now? I question.

"Now."

I pick it up hesitantly and run my nail along the flap, pulling it open easily. I peer into it and struggle to make out its contents in the low light of the room. I look at Jax whose face has suddenly turned very serious.

"Take it out."

I do and my breath catches as I realize it's a check with my name on it signed by Jax. A blank check.

"What's this?" I'm lightheaded. After our intimate encounter this afternoon he's now trying to write me a check? My guard rises as I question what's really going on.

"It's a check, Ivy." He takes the envelope from my lap and places it on the table before he rests his hand on my knee. "A gift so you can start that life away from Mark that you want."

"I don't understand." I place the check on the arm of the couch suddenly feeling dirty. I don't want his money. Who does he think I am? "Why are you giving me a blank check?"

"I'm sorry." He moves his hand to clutch mine, squeezing it gently. "I just wanted to help."

"By giving me a blank check?" I pull my hand from his. "What is it? A loan? Payment for services rendered? Please, Jax, explain."

He says nothing but I can see the pained look in his eyes.

"I don't really know you." I reach to put the check on the table, wanting it farther away from me. "I know we slept together today but we just met and now you're giving me carte blanche with your checking account. That makes no sense. You get that it makes no sense, right?"

"I've clearly offended you."

"I can find a way to get out from under Mark's thumb myself." I stand to leave. "I don't need your pity money."

"How?" he barks.

"How what?"

"Christ, Ivy, don't play dumb." He stands next to me. "You're horrible at it. How the hell are you going to get away from Mark when you live in his apartment and he pays all of your expenses?"

The words slice through me. I don't need this man reminding me of how the last man I slept with is financially providing for me months after he humiliated me. "He doesn't pay all of my expenses," I spit the words at him.

"Ivy, I own Veray now." He reaches to touch my arm but I pull back harshly before he can make contact. "I've seen your commission checks. You can't survive on that."

"I'm thinking of selling some pieces online," I say simply.

"You can't," he counters.

"I can't?" I place my hands on my hips determined to show this man that I can stand on my own two feet even if they feel incredibly shaky and unreliable at this moment. "You can't tell me what to do."

"Actually I can." He leisurely reaches for his wine glass downing the last of its contents. "You have an exclusive contract with Veray to sell your work. You can't sell it anywhere else."

I feel defeated and weak. I collapse back onto the couch taking a deep breath to try and fuel myself. "I'll figure it out somehow."

"This is how." He reaches for the check again, holding it in front of me.

"No." I shake my head from side-to-side. "I can't."

"Why not?" he asks sharply.

"I can't be indebted to a man again." I steel myself as I continue, "don't you see? I'd be going from being under Mark's thumb and control to being under yours."

"And that's a bad thing because?" his tone suggests he's trying to make light of the situation.

"I don't even know you." I hold my head in my hands feeling a rush of pain at my temple. I'm no stranger to stress headaches and I can feel an intense one barreling down on me. "How can I just take your money?"

"I'm offering it to you." He kneels in front of me. I feel his finger trace a line across my forehead. "You're not taking it. It's a chance for you to start over. You can get your own place."

"I can't." I pull back harshly from his touch. "Besides, you must want something in return."

"I don't."

"That can't possibly be true." I stand readying myself to make my exit. I need to get home to my own bed so I can nurse my headache and sort through this evening.

"Where are you going?" He stands too so his body is blocking my path to the door.

"Home." I push past him. "Or technically, Mark's apartment."

"Not yet." His hand clenches my elbow forcing me to stop.

"We're done here." I turn abruptly and wrench my arm free. "I'm not for sale."

"Fine." His jaw tightens. "There must be something you own that has some value that you can sell to me then."

"Hmm...let me think." I place my finger on my chin clasping my teeth together as if in deep thought. I know I'm being childish but at this point I don't care. "There's nothing. I'm a pathetic loser who has to rely on her cheating ex to provide for her. My mother would be proud of me if she was alive today."

The look of horror on his face mirrors what I feel inside. I can't believe I'm discussing my precarious financial situation with him. How did we go from talking about intimacy at dinner to this? I feel suffocated and the door out of his apartment is my only escape hatch. "I just want to leave and you have a plane to catch."

"I do." His eyes tear into me but the kindness and tenderness that was there this afternoon in my bedroom is now replaced with something darker. It's clear he's not happy with my resistance and I fear that I haven't seen the last of that blank check that now rests squarely on the table.

"Thanks for dinner and...everything," I manage to awkwardly say.

"Leonard will drive you home and he'll be available all weekend if you need a driver. He'll give you his number."

"That's generous but I can make it where I need to be on my own," I mutter. "I don't have any plans anyways." I know he can hear the disappointment in my voice. I was looking forward to spending time with him over the weekend and more than that, looking forward to our promised intimacy. That has not only collapsed beneath his need to rush out of town but it's been shattered into fragmented pieces by his desire to hand me a blank check so I can shift from being Mark's kept woman to being his.

"I'm sorry I offended you. That's not what I wanted." He clutches my hand leading me to the door of his apartment.

"I don't like the situation I'm in, but I'm not for sale." I open the door and glance back at him.

He reaches above my head to close the door. "One more thing." I feel his finger slide over my jawline before he tilts my chin up so my eyes meet his. "Don't talk to Mark or Liz this weekend."

I don't respond. Instead, I stare into his eyes for a moment, before I shake my head, open the door and walk out without looking back.

CHAPTER SIXTEEN

THE PERSISTENT BUZZING OF THE INTERCOM JARS ME AWAKE. I LOOK at the clock by the bed and realize it's already after ten. I'm not a late sleeper but I spent much of the weekend pacing and thinking about Jax's offer to give me a clear path out of Mark's life. I finally fell into bed at three this Monday morning, emotionally exhausted but also timidly excited of the prospect of a new space to live and work in.

"Hello." I clear my throat once I realize I sound sleepy and uninterested. I pray it's just one of the doormen and not an actual living, breathing visitor.

"Ms. Marlow, is that you?" An unfamiliar male voice shoots back at me.

"Yes. Who is this?" I instinctively tie my robe tighter around my nude body feeling slightly exposed even though the man attached to the strange voice is three floors below me.

"It's Leonard. Mr. Walker's driver." He sounds much too chipper for an early Monday.

"Leonard?" I reach for my phone on the foyer table wondering if Jax called or texted me. All that greets me is a few missed call notifications from Liz and a text from my sister asking when I'll visit.

"Yes, Ms. I'm here to pick you up. Mr. Walker has a surprise for you." The exuberance in his voice is grating.

"I'm sorry, Leonard, but I'm not aware of any surprise," I shoot back quickly into the intercom.

"That's why they call it a surprise." I swear I hear him giggle between words.

"I'm not ready to go out." I glance down at my robe. "I'll need some time."

"Will an hour do? I can steal a coffee break while you get prepared."

"Okay," I agree even though I'm about to call Jax to demand to know what the surprise is.

"I'll be here promptly at eleven. See you then, Ms."

"Sure. See you," I call back to him before dialing Jax's number. The call shifts to his voicemail almost immediately. I tap out a quick text asking him to call me before I race down the hallway to shower.

"LEONARD, let's say you knew what the surprise was. Would you tell me?" I ask playfully from the back seat of the sedan as Leonard steers the car through the busy late morning traffic.

"Absolutely not." He laughs as he glances back at me.

"How long have you worked for Jax?" I quiz as I watch the many people briskly walking down the sidewalks all with some place to be.

"Since he returned from California so a few months now I suppose."

"Is he a good boss?" I throw the question out mainly to keep the conversation going.

"Of course." Leonard clicks on the signal light as we head into the bustling neighborhood of Chelsea. "We're getting very close now."

I glance down at my phone and realize there's still no response from Jax. My heart races slightly at the thought of seeing him again combined with a surprise. I know it's going to be related to his blank check but at least now I'm prepared to offer him something in return.

"Here we are." Leonard pulls the car to the curb in front of an impressive pre-war building on West 27th Street. I survey the exterior relishing in all the intricate details that speak of the architecture in this part of Manhattan. This is a neighborhood I haven't spent much time in but its beauty and charm have always been alluring.

"Thank you." I smile at Leonard as he helps me from the car. He leads the way into the building, stopping briefly to shake the doorman's hand. I silently follow him to the elevator and he motions for me to enter before him. I watch as he reaches inside to insert a key and press the button for Penthouse Two and then he pulls back.

"You're on your own now." He waves as the doors close and I take a deep breath realizing that once the doors open again Jax will undoubtedly be waiting for me. I look myself over in the mirror that adorns the entire left wall of the elevator. I pinned my damp hair messily up before putting on a peach backless sundress with white heels. Even though I'm secretly still seething at Jax's unconventional proposition, I haven't been able to stop thinking about his raw power and pull in bed. I want him to be impressed when he first sees me again.

I can tell instantly from his expression when the elevator jerks to a stop and springs open that he is. His hand flies to his chest in response to my withered, "Hi."

"Beautiful, you're here." He pulls me into his chest and I melt when I feel his arms encircle me. "I thought about you all weekend. I'm sorry we left things the way we did."

I step back to look up into his face. "I'm sorry too. I wasn't sure I'd hear from you again."

"I can't stop you, Ivy." His expression softens as he stares into my eyes. "I'm beginning to wonder if I'll ever be able to."

The tenderness of his words catches me off guard and I look down from his glance. I had thought about this moment all weekend and had rehearsed over and over again what I'd say. But now I'm frozen, my eyes locked on the walnut planks of the floor, wishing I could just stay in this room with him forever.

"Let's talk about why we're here." He lets go of me and walks across the expansive room to a row of windows. I look past him and out the windows. I'm captivated by the sight of the elaborate architecture of the neighboring buildings. It all speaks of the rich and stunning history of the city.

"This view is breathtaking," I whisper as I follow him across the room.

"It is." His eyes jump with happiness. "But you haven't seen the other views."

"The others?"

He reaches for my hand and guides me across the barren space to another bank of tall windows. The view from these is even more spectacular as my eyes settle on the Empire State Building. "It's so close. It must be beautiful at night when it's lit up," I say in wonder.

"Soon you'll know." His hand brushes against my back as he moves closer to me.

"Soon I'll know?" I repeat back while my mind works to connect the dots. "You're moving here?"

"No." His breath caresses my neck. "You're moving here, beautiful."

My eyes quickly scan the space and I finally drink it all in. It's immense, open and stunning. The walnut floors are warm and rich in tone. The walls are a stark white just waiting for inspiration and the ceilings must be at least ten feet tall. "It's perfect," I say under my breath. "But..."

"No, Ivy. No buts. We're going to figure out a way for you to live here. It's ideal. Come, let me show you."

We move through the space, Jax leading me smoothly by one hand while the other rests on my back. He steers me past the quaint kitchen and through a long hallway. We stop to glance at a bathroom finished in light marble tones. As we pass one bedroom his hand slides lower until it's touching the bare skin at the bottom of my back. "This will be your room."

I turn towards the last doorway and I'm instantly immersed in a lovely inviting space. This is the only furnished room in the apartment.

There's an elaborate king sized bed, a gorgeous antique dresser and a large walk-in closet. "It's amazing. It's so big."

"It's perfect." He moves to sit on the edge of the bed, guiding me so I'm standing directly in front of him. "It's your new beginning."

I sigh as I look down into his eyes in the dim light of the room. The blinds are drawn and just one small sliver of light bounces through the corner of the adjacent bathroom window. He's incredibly handsome and I shiver at the thought of being alone and this close to him again. I place my hands on either side of his face, relishing in the soft touch of his skin. His hands move farther down my back and he gently pulls me towards him. I sigh the moment my lips touch his and I'm greeted by the hunger of his kiss.

I fall onto the bed, one of my shoes sliding to the floor with a vacant thud. The noise breaks my focus and I sit up abruptly breaking free of his kiss. "Should we be doing this?" I run my hands over the skirt of my dress desperately trying to compose myself. "I don't think the broker would appreciate us having sex on the bed if they're trying to sell this place." I stand and I'm instantly unsteady. I bend down scrambling to find my shoe which I seem to have inadvertently kicked under the bed. Shit. Now I have to crawl around on all fours to find my shoe? Jax will surely find that sexy.

"Ivy, stop." I feel his hand on mine. "I bought the bed. I had it delivered yesterday."

I sit next to him again, pushing the wayward hairs that have fallen into my eyes back into place. "Why?"

"Beautiful." He sighs deeply as he wraps his finger around a few strands of my hair, playfully pushing them back behind my ear. "You told me that Mark and Liz were together in your bed. I know that has to hurt. I wanted you to have a new, fresh start in every way."

I'm struck by how compassionate and thoughtful the gesture is. I feel tears rising to the surface but I push them back. I don't want him to see me as overly emotional especially, not now. "That's incredibly thoughtful of you." I manage a weak smile. "But, Jax, we need to discuss this. How we can make this work. I won't be a bought woman."

He lets out a hearty laugh as he pulls me down on my back into the softness of the duvet cover. "We'll work out an agreement."

"An agreement?" I tense at the sensation of his finger on my jaw. I know that he's about to kiss me and when that happens I'll be lost to him again.

"Stop talking." He leans closer until his lips brush against mine. I taste his breath and I'm instantly lost in the rush of desire for this man.

I reach for his suit jacket, pushing it boldly off his body. He complies and shifts slightly so I can access the buttons on the light blue shirt covering his chest. I stop once I realize that he's wearing cuff links and he breaks our kiss to skillfully remove them, tossing them on the bed behind us. I run my hands down the length of his chest. My fingers lightly graze the toned skin. I feel him fidget under my touch and I glance down to see his erection straining against his tailored slacks.

"Take your dress off," he orders before biting my lip causing me to moan loudly.

I obey. Pulling myself from the bed, I dutifully push the dress from my shoulders, revealing my breasts and the peach panties I'm wearing. I kick my other shoe off and stand before him on display.

He rises off the bed and stares at me as he unbuckles his belt and drops his slacks. His cock jumps as it's freed and I can't help but drink in his entire body. He's beautiful and I want every inch of him. It's never been like this for me. I've never felt this utterly consumed with desire for any man before.

"Your body is beautiful," I whisper, well aware that it's not typically what a woman would say to a man but acutely sensitive to the fact that he's likely heard it from countless women.

"I've never seen anyone as beautiful as you." He leans over and claims my mouth again. His tongue is hot, hard and unyielding. I feel all of my resistance fall to the floor along with my panties. He pushes them from me before pulling me onto the bed on top of him.

I whimper when I feel his lips leave mine. His breath is hot on my neck as he whispers in my ear, "Ivy, have you been checked?"

I pull back and sit astride his stomach. I can feel his cock resting against my ass cheek. "Checked?"

"Tested, checked." He holds my hands in his. "Have you been to the doctor to be tested since you and Mark ended things?"

"Oh, yes." I blush, realizing my innocence when it comes to intimacy is on full display yet again. "I did. I had to. You know." I close my eyes, pushing any thought of Mark and Liz away. I can't think of them right now or ever again.

"And you're on the pill?"

"Yes, for years now. What about you?" I want to appear just as invested in this conversation as he is.

"No, I passed on the pill." He smirks before he pulls my hands down until they are resting on either side of his head. "I love that you're the way you are."

"What way is that?" I blush, knowing that he's referring to my lack of experience.

"Sweet. Perfect. Ivy." He stares into my eyes before he continues, "how many men have there been?"

"In my bed?" I can't break his gaze. It's as if he's drawing the answers from the depths of my soul. I'm embarrassed to respond but I feel compelled. He wants to know and I want to please him so desperately.

"One." I say it with assurance. It's the truth. It's who I am.

"One," he repeats back, his eyes scanning my face and settling on my lips.

"I won't ask." I murmur, knowing that I don't want to know the answer.

"I couldn't answer." He settles his gaze on my shoulder. "I don't count anymore."

"I understand," I say it with a small smile even though the pain that is coursing through my heart speaks of my disappointment. He can't remember them all. How many does there have to be before you forget them all?

"Kiss me, beautiful. I have something I want to ask." I push my naked chest into his as I run my tongue along his bottom lip before covering his mouth with mine. I pull his breath into me, languishing in the feel of his soft experienced lips against my timid ones.

"I want you to be my first." I feel the whisper of the words against my lips. I don't move. I'm certain that I've misunderstood what he's said. "My first," he repeats it again, this time louder and more pronounced.

I sit back up and my hand instinctively reaches to cover my breast as a burst of the cool air in the apartment rushes over my skin. "I'm sorry. What did you say?" I ask, fearing that he's going to ask me to do something with him I'm not ready for yet.

"Christ. Look at you. Your skin, the shape of your breasts, your lips. You're more than I ever imagined a woman could be."

My hips instinctively start to move. I reach for my nipple and trace my finger around it. His words have fueled my desire. I've never felt more alive than I do in this moment.

"I've never been with a woman without protection." His eyes are glued to my breast. "I've never felt a woman's desire directly. I want to feel your wetness, your warmth, all of you without any barriers."

I stop as I absorb what he's saying. "No condom?" I ask timidly afraid that I'm misunderstanding him.

"No condom." He pulls me close to his body again. "I've never been inside a woman without one. I can't stand the thought of anything being between us. I need this. I need you."

"Please, yes," I manage to say as I shift my hips so his cock is close to my entrance. "I need that. Please, now."

"Not now. Not yet." He moans as his cock pushing against my clit. "Savor that feeling, beautiful. Use my body to give yourself pleasure."

I reach down and wrap my hand around him, pulling his hardness towards my aching clitoris. I tremble the moment the tip of it touches me. My body impulsively reacts and I circle my clit with its head, pulling on it, straining to curve my body so I can enjoy every sensation.

"Use me. Take from me. It's all yours." He's breathless now and I look down to see how engorged he is. I'm close to the edge but I can't breathe if he's not inside of me. I swiftly shift my hips and in one quick movement I take him completely within my body.

He almost screams as his back arches and his hands grasp the side of my hips. "Fuck, Ivy. Fuck."

I lean back and rest my right hand on his leg. I reach for my clit with my other hand and slowly rock back and forth, feeling the length of him inside of me. "This is so good. How can it feel this good?" I ask without thinking. I can't think. All I can do is feel and breathe and listen and want.

"You're going to come for me, beautiful." He pushes his body harder into mine.

I'm falling into something. I feel my body losing control. I'm rushing towards the edge. "I never knew it was like this," I cry out. "Please, don't stop."

"Never." His voice is hoarse. "You're so wet. You're mine."

"I'm going…" my voice trails as I feel my pulse racing.

"Now. Come for me now." He barks as he pushes his hips up from the bed, burying his cock deep within me.

I reach back as I come. I feel the rush take over my body. I gasp as I feel him fill me when he reaches his climax. I collapse onto his chest. My breathing labored. The room is silent save for the pounding of his heart beneath my ear.

"You're quickly becoming my everything," he whispers between heavy breaths.

I can't speak. I don't respond. I just silently nod as one single tear falls from my cheek onto his chest.

———

"WE'RE GOING TO VERAY, LEONARD." Jax holds tight to my hand as he closes the car door.

"Certainly, Sir."

"Did you like the apartment?" He throws the question at me.

"What's not to like?" I playfully respond. "It's exquisite. It's so open and large."

"You could create a perfect studio there."

I sigh. "It would be amazing. All that natural light and the space. I could hire someone to help me with production if I worked from there. But, Jax, we need to discuss this."

"We are," he says quietly.

"No, I mean really discuss the terms." I pull my hand from his grasp. I want him to take this discussion seriously. He's helped me see that a new beginning, free of Mark's financial grasp would be the best step I could take right now.

The sound of a phone ringing startles us both. He reaches into his suit pocket and shrugs his shoulders. "It's not me."

I clumsily fish inside my purse before I feel my fingers land on my phone. I pull it from the depths and scan the screen. It's a missed call from Mark.

"Who was it?" he asks.

"No one." I push my phone back into my bag, not wanting to discuss Mark at this moment.

"So, it was Mark?"

"Does it matter?" I ask expectantly. I don't want Mark to tarnish this for me. I finally feel as though I can see a future and I desperately want to leave the past where it belongs.

"It will always matter until you're free of him." Jax shifts his body away from me so he's staring out the car window now. "Are you going to call him back?"

My stomach tightens at the question. "No."

"Is the apartment the only thing tying you to him?" His voice is anxious.

"There's more." I grit my teeth together as I say it anticipating his reaction.

"More?" he repeats as he circles back around so he's completely facing me. "Like what?"

"I actually wanted to talk to you about it." I run my hand through my hair. It's fallen everywhere now and I expected to have this conversation looking more like a business woman than someone Jax just fucked.

He sits in silence, an expectant look on his face.

"Mark, well... when we split...you know after he cheated..." my voice trails as the car comes to a stop.

"Sorry for the interruption, Mr. Walker, but we're here." Leonard jumps from his seat to exit the car.

"We'll continue this in my office," Jax says as he takes a step out of the car. He walks ahead of me as I struggle to tactfully exit the car having left my panties back at the Chelsea apartment.

The elevator is at full capacity as we ride in silence to the seventh floor. I follow him to his office, only stopping to wave briefly at Teresa. I make a mental note to send her those earrings I promised as Jax closes his office door behind me.

"Sit, Ivy." He motions towards a leather couch. He takes a seat behind his desk.

"Are you angry with me?" I stand in front of the desk, my hands nervously fidgeting with the leather strap of my purse.

"Angry?" He finally makes eye contact with me. "Why would you ask that?"

"You changed in the car." I search for the right words before continuing, "I know you don't like Mark and what he did to me."

"You're right." He flips through the messages on his desk before opening his drawer to remove a pad of paper and a pen. "He's an asshole who hurt you. I can't stand him."

I move to sit on the couch and take a deep breath. "I don't really like talking about him."

"We need to." He pushes his suit jacket off before moving to sit next to me. He brings the pen and pad of paper with him.

"Are you taking notes?" I try to lighten the mood but his expression doesn't change.

"Perhaps." He studies my face before he speaks again. "Tell me about your ties with Mark."

"Okay." I place my purse on my lap and adjust my necklace. I take a deep breath and look directly at him. He's looking past me to a bookcase in the corner. I've come to recognize his aloofness as a tactic he uses when coping with uncomfortable situations.

"Mark and you?" he prompts me again.

"When Mark cheated and we separated we didn't involve any lawyers." I spit it out.

"That was unwise." The pen in his hand gets to work jotting something down on the paper.

"I'm sure it was." I try not to feel offended by how impersonal he's acting. "Mark offered to give me something to help I guess or maybe to quiet me, I'm not sure."

"Quiet you?" His eyes jump from the paper to my face. "In what way?"

"We were always on the society page for being at this party or that party. The Post ran a story on our impending wedding. When news broke that we weren't together, the media was asking a lot of questions."

"So he bought your silence?" He shifts his body away from me.

I shake my head from side-to-side. "I didn't want to speak to anyone about what happened. I was so humiliated by it." I glance past him to the window and the bright sunshine showering his desk. "I just wanted to crawl into a hole."

"What did he offer you?" His brow shoots up in anticipation.

"Shares. I own part of his company," I say regretfully. "He insisted I take them. I don't have any part of the day-to-day operations. Mark has my proxy."

He only nods his head up slowly up and down. "You mean shares in his real estate company. What's the name of that again?"

"Intersect Investments."

He writes more before he looks at me. "How much do you own?"

"Ten percent." I feel like I'm being interviewed for a loan. The impersonal nature of our conversation is wearing.

"Mark owns the rest or are there other partners?" His business tone continues as he furiously takes notes.

"There was another partner. He was an older man. I only met him once. His name was Tom." I pause, searching my memory for his last name. "Tom something. He died though and I'm not sure what happened with his shares. Mark talked about buying his estate out but then things between us fell apart and I have no idea where that went."

He nods in silence before standing to toss the notepad onto his desk. "You're a very wealthy woman, Ivy." Finally a smile brightens his face again. "Or you're going to be."

I arch my eyebrow in question. "How so?"

"If you sell those shares to me, you'll be able to buy the apartment in Chelsea and live comfortably on the rest of the proceeds for a very long time."

"I don't know how much they're worth." I stand to pace the floor. "Mark never told me and I never asked. I've forgotten about them for the most part."

"I'll have my business advisors research it but I'd say off the cuff, your ten percent is worth more than ten million." The way the number rolls off his lips so nonchalantly is unsettling.

"Ten million? As in dollars?" I know my mouth is half agape and I don't care. I shake my head certain that I misheard that number.

"At least." He reaches to punch a number into his desk phone. "Probably more. I promise I'll offer you a more than fair price."

I stand in silence as I listen to him order someone named Gilbert to his office for a meeting immediately. I reach for my bag and fumble through it again searching for my phone.

"I have to go, Gilbert. Get here as soon as possible." The phone clicks back into its base as I thumb through my phone's address book.

"Ivy, what are you doing?" He's behind me now, peering over my shoulder.

"I need to tell Mark if I'm selling my shares, no?" I ask excitedly.

"Not yet, beautiful." He pushes my phone back into my purse. "Let me talk to Gilbert first and get a sense of what we're working with and we'll draw up some contracts. Then we can discuss telling Mark." He kisses me lightly on the forehead.

"You're giving me the chance at a new life," I whimper through building tears. "How can I thank you for this?"

"I'll come up with a way or two." He smiles right before his lips slide over mine.

CHAPTER SEVENTEEN

"THANKS FOR THE RIDE, LEONARD." I CALL TO HIM AS HE STEPS BACK
into the car after dropping me in front of my apartment. I turn to look
at it, joy running through me as I realize that soon I won't have to be
here anymore. I'll be free of all the difficult memories of this place and
of my former life with Mark.

"Ms. Marlow, there you are." Oliver rushes to greet me as I step
into the lobby. "This arrived for you a short time ago." He hands me a
rectangular box. There's no return address but the word FRAGILE is
stamped in bold red letters across the front of it.

"Thanks, Oliver." I reach to rub his shoulder gently. "How's your
wife today?"

"She's as wonderful as ever." His face beams.

"Perfect." I walk to the bank of elevators and press the call button. I
push my purse back onto my shoulder as I fumble with the package.
I'm curious about its contents hoping that it's a surprise from Jax. I hear
the signal that the elevator has arrived and the door opens. I step
forward without taking my eyes from the package and walk straight
into someone.

"Sugar."

I freeze and my body tenses immediately. Anger rises quickly to the surface before I even look at her.

"Ivy, I've been waiting here for hours. We have to talk." Her voice is cracking.

I finally lock eyes with her and she's a mess. Her hair is unkempt, her clothing hanging from her frame. She's not wearing any make-up and the redness around her eyes is a clear sign that she's been crying. I realize in that moment how vulnerable she looks. "I don't want to talk, Liz."

"This is important." She grabs my arm forcing me to take a step back.

"Don't touch me," I seethe.

"Ms. Marlow." Oliver is standing beside me now. "Can I help?"

"I'm fine." I try to sound reassuring." We're going to talk here, in the lobby, for a moment."

"I'll be right over there." He points to the reception desk which is only a few feet from where we're standing.

"Thank you." I move towards a bench that sits adjacent to the elevators. "Why are you here?"

"You never answer my calls or texts." She takes a seat on the bench.

I sigh heavily and tap my foot against the floor. "We have nothing to talk about. Nothing."

"Jax," she blurts out. "We have to talk about him and you."

I'm instantly agitated when I hear her mention his name. "No. You don't get to say his name. We will never discuss him or anything else for that matter." I walk to the elevators and press the call button again.

"He has secrets. He's using you," she hisses loudly.

I feel assaulted again, this time by her words. I'm fuming as I turn one last time to look at her. "Go to hell, Liz." With that I step into the elevator. As the doors close I cling to the package, my body shaking from the sobs.

———

I STEP into my apartment and place my keys and purse on the foyer table with trembling hands. I hadn't expected to see Liz and her continued anger unnerves me. It was obvious that she wasn't going to allow me to be happy regardless of where things stood with her and Mark. For the first time since discovering they were lovers, I feel a sense of calm about their betrayal. I'm moving forward with my life and I have to stay focused on that.

I slide onto the couch with the package in my lap. I reach for the corner, ripping the tape away. The lid pops open and the contents are nestled within several layers of gold tissue paper. I carefully peel away each layer until I get a glimpse of the edge of a frame. The frame. I rip the rest of the paper away as my eyes flood with tears. It's the picture of my mother and me. The frame masterfully restored. I turn it over, surveying each corner, studying where the splintered wood had been only a few days ago. It's perfect. The glass is new and the image itself is exactly as it was. I recall Jax's words about trusting him with it. He was right. I could trust him with it, and with my future.

I reach for my phone to call him to thank him for the gift and realize I've missed a call. I excitedly check who it's from. Disappointment ripples through me at the sight of Mark's name. I need to deal with him and since I've already given Liz a small piece of my mind today, seeing Mark seems logical too.

When I emerge from my apartment an hour later, I feel refreshed. A quick shower and a change of clothes have given me time to weigh my decision to confront Mark this afternoon. I know he'll still be at his office and if I broke the news to him about selling my shares before it was leaked through the grapevine it would make the transition easier for us both. I know I shouldn't give a second thought to his feelings regarding the transfer of my part of his business to Jax, but I don't want any lingering hostility. I need this to be over. I need Mark out of my life.

I slip into the back of the taxi Oliver has hailed for me and I once again try and call Jax. There's no answer so I leave a brief voicemail asking him to call me back. I glance out of the window of the taxi knowing that soon I won't be in this neighborhood. I need to speak to Mrs. Adams about my decision tonight.

I pay the driver before stepping out onto the curb. I adjust the hemline of the navy blue shift dress I'm wearing and glance down at the nude heels. I'm coming to see Mark as his business partner, not his former lover and I want to keep my composure intact. I anticipate he'll be rife with questions about who I'm selling to but he'll ultimately have to accept my decision.

"Hi Janice." I greet the young woman sitting behind the reception desk in the lobby of the building. "Is Mark still here?"

She grins before she picks up her phone. "Is he still in?" She's curt with the person on the other end. She covers the receiver with her hand and holds the phone a few inches away. "Do you want me to announce that you're here?"

"No. I'll just go up." I decide that it will be easier to share my news with Mark if he doesn't have any warning about my arrival.

She hangs up and turns to me again. "Carrie picked up Phyllis' phone." I see a not-so-subtle eye roll. "Apparently she left early today so you can just go in when you get up there."

I nod. The fact that Mark's personal assistant isn't hovering over his office is a welcome surprise. Phyllis never liked me and if I don't have to deal with her antagonistic attitude today that removes one hurdle from my path.

I board the elevator for the swift trip up to the twenty-third floor. I can't recall the last time I stepped foot in the building but after today I won't have to be here again. That knowledge alone gives me the courage I need as the doors fly open and I step out into the lavish space that houses Mark's personal offices. Carrie, one of the human resources manager's pops her head out from around the corner. "Ivy, how lovely to see you." She gives me a comfortable hug.

"It's so good to see you too, Carrie. How are you? Your husband? The kids?" I smile as I remember fondly all the dinners Mark and I shared with her family.

"Good, good and good," she exclaims.

"You're here to see him?" She crooks her finger towards Mark's office.

"Guilty as charged," I joke.

She hooks her arm in mine. "Allow me to lead the way."

"It's odd to be back here," I confide in a low voice. "It's been so long since I've been to see Mark."

"I'm a little shocked to see you now." She knocks tentatively on his slightly ajar office door. When there's no response, she pulls it open farther, peering inside. "Ah, the dictator isn't here."

I laugh at her description of Mark. "I can wait for him, yes?"

"Sure." She motions for me to enter the office." Let me see if I can find him." She scurries out of the door and down the hall.

I pull my phone from my purse again hoping to see a message from Jax. There's nothing. I place my purse down on one of the leather chairs facing Mark's desk. I hear voices near the door. I turn to look but I don't see anyone so I walk to the bank of windows overlooking Central Park. I soak in the view, relishing in how beautiful the city is at this time of year. My gaze follows the window's shape and my eyes come to rest on the shelf I'm standing in front of. I suddenly realize there are numerous framed pictures, some of me. I reach back for Mark's desk chair and lower myself as I scan the pictures. I settle on one of Mark and me at a gala fundraiser last year. Something in the background of the picture catches my eye. My breath stalls.

"I can't find him anywhere." Carrie's voice startles me and I drop the framed image in my lap. "Ivy?" I hear her voice in the distance coming closer. "Ivy? Are you okay?"

I feel as if I'm floating in mid-air. I can't speak. I manage to pick up the picture with my right hand. I shove it at her.

"Oh shit," she whispers. "I can't believe he still has pictures of the two of you."

I shake my head from side-to-side and manage to pull a deep breath from my lungs. "Carrie, I..I..." I stammer.

"Ivy, should I get someone? Are you not feeling well?"

"No. It's just that." I turn the framed picture so it's facing her now.

"Who is that? That man in the background. The man looking at Mark and me. Do you know that man?"

She pulls on the reading glasses that have been dangling from a delicate chain around her neck. She peers at me and then at the picture. "I know him," she says matter-of-factly. "He's gorgeous, don't you think?"

I manage a very weak smile. "Who is he?"

"Jax Walker," she purrs his name.

"How do you know him?" I ask tentatively, not wanting her to realize that her answer may change the entire course of my life.

"He's Tom Walker's son." A soft smile envelopes her lips. "Tom was Mark's partner. Jax inherited his share when Tom died. That was such a hard time for all of us. He was such a good man and..." her voice trails off into the ether as the sudden pounding in my ears drowns out everything.

I can't hear.

I can't think.

I can't feel.

I can't...

PART TWO

OBSESSED

Part Two of
The Obsessed Series

Deborah Bladon

CHAPTER ONE

"YOU'RE AN ASSHOLE." THE WORDS SOUND HEAVY AS THEY LEAVE MY lips. They should. They carry with them all the vile distaste I feel for him in this moment.

"Excuse me?" Jax glances up from where he's seated behind his desk. His tone is strong and unyielding. If he's surprised by my words, he's masking it brilliantly. "What are you doing here?"

My head shoots to the right where an older man is sitting. His gaze is downcast but it's clear from the way he's clenching the laptop resting on his knees that he's uncomfortable.

"Are you Gilbert?" I throw the question at him knowing that he must be the man Jax barked at on the phone earlier. He was summoned to help Jax manipulate the shares I hold in Mark's company from my grasp.

He nods, his eyes glued to his lap.

"Leave," I spit out.

"Ivy, what the hell has gotten into you?" Jax stands, dropping the pen he was holding with a dull thud onto a stack of papers on his desk. "You can't order him to leave."

"Leave now, Gilbert," I seethe, my eyes never leaving Jax's face.

"Go." Jax flicks his wrist in the direction of the door. The older man scurries out of the room. His haste makes it clear that he recognizes that I'm about to explode.

I turn to slam the office door behind him. I reach inside my bag searching for the cold metal of the framed picture. As my fingers find it, I feel pressure on my shoulder.

"Ivy, what's wrong with you?" His breath is a whisper against my neck.

I shiver and pull free from his grasp. "This." My voice lacks emotion as I pull the frame from my purse and shove it into his hands in one swift gesture.

I study his expression as his eyes quickly skirt over the picture. "What? It's a picture of you and Mark."

"In the background. Look." I push the edge of the frame coaxing him to hold it higher. I want him to focus on the picture. I want him to see what I see. I want his eyes to lock on his own face, in all its smug, egotistical glory waiting in the shadows studying his prey.

"Fuck." He drops the frame on the floor. It bounces before the glass crashes into splinters.

I don't flinch. "You're worse than him," I scowl. "You used me."

His eyes lock on mine. His tongue traces a path around his lips. He swallows hard before he opens his mouth. "No. Don't say that."

"It's true. You're both lying bastards."

"I'm nothing like Mark. Nothing." He leans in closer to me as he stretches the word across his lips.

"You're worse." I turn away reaching for the doorknob.

"You're not leaving until I explain." He grips my elbow, pulling my hand back towards him.

I flip around to face him pulling my arm free. "I'm leaving. Don't try and stop me."

He throws both hands in the air as he takes a firm step back from me. "Fine. You're too emotional right now to hear me anyways."

"I never want to hear what you have to say. Never." I stomp my foot as I pull the door open.

"You'll hear me. I'll stop by your place later tonight," he says, the words casually rolling from his tongue.

I shake my head at his overt arrogance. "Why? Why would you come by my place?"

He looks past me to the hallway before he speaks in a whisper, "we're not done until I say we're done, beautiful."

I let the doorknob slip from my grasp and walk with weighted steps towards him. I stop inches from him, leaning in close until my lips almost touch his. "We're done . Whatever this was..." I lazily run my right hand down the front of his shirt before waving it in the air between us. "It's over."

He catches my wrist in his hand, pulling it to his lips. "You know that's not true."

"No." I sigh as I jerk my arm free once again. "The only truth I know is that you fucked me so you could steal Mark's shares away from me. That's the truth. Anything else leaving your lips is a lie."

"That's what you think?" He throws his head back with a hearty laugh. "You actually think I slept with you as part of a business deal."

"You did," I blurt out. "Your father was Mark's partner."

"So?" He raises his brow in quiet confidence, irking me even further. "One has nothing to do with the other."

"You're delusional." I stare at him with the realization that he's being dead serious. He truly believes that our personal relationship is separate from his business relationship with Mark. "You stalked me and seduced me so I'd give you Mark's shares."

"You're giving me nothing," he hisses through tight lips. "I'm buying those shares from you for much more than they're worth."

"Bullshit." There's anger coursing through me and I know that it's always quickly followed with tears. I won't cry in front of him. I won't.

"Ivy. You know nothing about my business dealings with Mark." He sits on the corner of his desk. He fingers one of the exquisite cuff links on his shirt before looking back at me. "For that matter, you know nothing about Mark's business at all."

His words cut into me. He's right, of course but the veiled suggestion that I'm naïve doesn't sit well with me. It pushes me closer to the verge of tears. I bite my lip to halt them. "Why do you do that? Why?"

"Do what?" He shrugs his shoulders. "What am I doing?"

"You're making me feel like an idiot. You did it when I told you about Mark and the women he slept with. You're doing it again now." Despite my best efforts to ward off the tears, they spill out. I sob wishing I could redo the past few weeks of my life.

He stands and reaches for me. I stumble back until I can feel the doorknob in my hand once again. I turn it and pull the door wide open.

"Stop," he pleads. "You're upset. I need to explain."

"You need to go to hell," I mumble as I step out into the hallway.

"WHAT WAS YOUR HUSBAND LIKE?" I take a small sip of the Earl Grey tea.

Mrs. Adams stares out at the window of her apartment, the pelting rain creating a mosaic of water spots on the glass. "He was strong, very kind. Did you know he asked me to marry him on our second date?"

"I didn't know that," I fib. She has told me this story more than a dozen times but her gentle company this dismal afternoon is helping me forget what happened with Jax two days ago.

"He said he knew he loved me right then and there." She looks down at the gold band still nestled snugly on her ring finger. "I was sixteen."

"You loved him very much too." I feel the sting of tears bite at the corners of my eyes.

"I did." Her soft smile comforts me. "He was the love of my life."

"Do you think we all have that?" I reach for a tissue to wipe the tears. "A love that is once in a lifetime?"

"It's different now." She stands and slowly walks towards the window, her gaze lifted into the clouds. "Back then men respected women."

Her remark bites although I know that wasn't her intention. "You're right," I mutter.

"Mark wasn't good for you." She points her finger at me. "That young man you were with the other day seems very nice."

"I won't be seeing him again." I feel the ache in my heart as the words leave my lips. "He was using me."

"What do you mean?" She moves back to the chair next to me. "Using you in what way?"

"I'm not sure." I'm embarrassed that I can't offer her any more details. "I just know that he wasn't honest about who he is."

"Perhaps he has his reasons." She pats my hand with hers. "The right man is waiting for you, Ivy. He may be closer than you think."

"I'm happy on my own." I look down at my finger aimlessly tracing a pattern on the leg of my jeans. "I'm going to take a few days at my sister's place to recharge."

"Boston is beautiful this time of year." She hesitates before continuing, "Will your father be there too?"

I flash to an image of the last time I saw my father. It was more than a year ago when I had told him I was marrying Mark. The disappointment that had washed over his face had been unmistakable. He never approved of our relationship. He had expressed, with pointed clarity that I was making a mistake I'd soon regret. That day, in all my infinite and lovesick wisdom I had told him that if he didn't accept Mark, he didn't accept me. Now, all I wanted was his help to sort through the maze of betrayals that compromised my so-called-grown-up life. I just couldn't find the internal strength to swallow my pride to tell him that he's been right all along.

"I don't think so." I glance at the clock shaped like a cherub sitting atop her television. "I should probably get going. I have a meeting in a few minutes. It's a business thing."

"Of course, dear." She grabs zealously to the armrest of her chair to pull herself from the soft cushion yet again.

"No, please, don't get up." I motion for her to settle back down. "I'll tidy these dishes before I leave."

"You might want to give him another chance." Her soft voice carries through the silence of the apartment into the kitchen. I stop washing the tea cups for a brief moment waiting for her to explain the comment. Silence follows.

"Give who another chance?" I peek my head around the doorway to see her grinning back at me.

"That handsome fellow. You know, Max was it? Or was it Rex? There was an x I'm certain." She peers off into the distance as if she's going to pull his name from the ether.

"It's Jax." I take a deep breath. "And no," I whisper as I place the dishes back in the cupboard. "No second chances."

CHAPTER TWO

MADELINE TOLD ME TO MEET HER AT THE RESTAURANT FOR A LATE lunch at three. It's three-thirty. With any hope she's been biding her time with vodka sodas while flirting shamelessly with any waiter within twenty feet of her. I brusquely shake my drenched umbrella a few times before I pull it together and walk through the door. Despite my best efforts and a killer light blue dress, I'm not feeling very powerful or authoritative today. I'm the one who called this meeting so I better find my backbone before I reach her table. The maître-d watches me intently as I try to smooth my hair back into place. The rush of humidity outside has awoken the dreaded natural curl.

"Ms. Veray's table is right this way." He extends his hand in an eloquent loop and I wonder if that's something they teach you in maître d school or if it's a personal trait. Perhaps he embellishes every movement so it appears as though he's ready to launch into a spectacular circus act without warning.

I follow him through the crowded restaurant, my eyes cast down. I run through my mind exactly what I had rehearsed saying to Madeline today. This meeting is a first step in a new direction for me and it absolutely has to go as planned. I need Madeline to agree to my proposal so

I can start building a new life away from Mark, Jax and their bitter feud.

"Ivy, don't you look lovely?" Madeline's voice startles me and I almost run right into the back of the maître d. I stop dead mere inches from his shoulder and that's when my breath catches. Madeline's not alone.

"She looks beautiful. I love your hair like that." Jax smiles as he holds up a glass of wine in my direction. "Come. Sit. Have a drink. Let's talk business."

It wasn't supposed to be like this. I thought I'd never seen him again and here he is oozing smugness, confidence and holding court with Madeline awaiting my arrival. Damn her for telling him about this. Damn him for intruding when he knows I want nothing to do with him.

"I'm sorry I'm late." I ignore Jax and focus solely on Madeline.

"Not a problem." He chuckles. "We've been catching up. Did you know Madeline took you up on your suggestion to call Mark?"

The flippant way he throws Mark's name into the air enflames me. I look above me, draw in a deep breath and roll my eyes. What I imagined to be a power lunch in which I'd chart a new course for my business has now turned into a recounting of Madeline's interactions with my bastard of an ex-fiancé.

"I did." She pauses to take a leisurely drink from the glass in front of her. "But he's not interested. Are any men in New York interested in sex at this point?"

The silence that answers her question is enough to make me cringe. My gaze moves beyond both of them to a table where two women are having lunch. The slim contour of their chins and the similar shape of their noses speak of their biological connection. The maturity of one suggests that's she's the mother. I watch them laugh, speak and smile at one another and it instantly reminds me of why I'm here.

"Madeline, I wanted to talk to you about my collections," I say it calmly.

"Yes, of course." She straightens herself in her chair. "That's why we're here, isn't it?"

"It is." I turn my body towards her. "As you know I started my business to honor my mother's dream."

She nods her head as she sips from the glass in her hand.

"I didn't know that," Jax says with surprise. "Your mother wanted you to be a jewelry designer?"

I sit silently in place, my eyes honed in on Madeline. I don't want to look at Jax. I don't want to talk to him or explain something this personal to him.

"Her mother wanted to be the jewelry designer," Madeline corrects him. "But she died right after Ivy was born so Ivy carries the torch for her. It's a beautiful story."

I search her expression trying to determine if she's being sarcastic or not. She's impossible to read so I wait for Jax's inevitable response. There's nothing.

"I know that I signed an exclusive contract with you but I'd like to rework the terms of that if possible." As I speak I notice Madeline's head subtly nodding up and down. My heart takes that as a positive sign. I may just get out of this meeting with the promise of a brighter future for my business without being tied exclusively to Veray.

"Absolutely not." His words are unconditional.

"Jax." Madeline gestures across the table in his direction. "Quiet down. I want to hear what she's thinking."

"It's not open for discussion." I can feel his eyes on me as he pushes his opinion on Madeline.

"It's still my company. It's wide open for discussion," she snaps back.

I can't resist the urge to turn and look at him. His eyes lock with mine and he raises an eyebrow. I don't flinch. I may have won this small victory but I don't assume I'll defeat him. His influence over Madeline is unmistakable but I came here with a mission and I won't stop until she at least hears me out.

"Tell me more about what you're thinking." She lightly taps my hand as it rests on the table.

I turn my attention back to her and clear my throat before I begin my plea. "I'm very grateful for all the exposure you've given me over the years, Madeline. You took a chance on me when no one else would."

She smiles. "You have real talent, Ivy. It was an easy chance to take."

"That's kind of you." I can sense Jax staring at me but I continue, undeterred from my need to get out of my contract with Madeline so I can get away from Jax in every way possible. "I feel that my business will benefit if I make my pieces available to more people. You know, a broader audience. I want to establish an online presence. Maybe set up my own website to sell some things I haven't consigned to you."

"No." His voice is stern and the tone is unrelenting.

"Shush." She waves her index finger at Jax before motioning for the waiter. "I was once a young woman struggling to make a name for myself too. I wouldn't be where I am now if someone hadn't given me a chance back then."

I instantly feel a weight being lifted off my shoulders. I sit silently waiting for her to continue after she orders another drink. I'm startled when I feel a hand on my knee. My body impulsively darts from my chair and as my legs hit the table the glass of wine in front of me tumbles into my lap. "Shit," I whisper. "No. No. No."

"Ma'am. Let me help you." The waiter bolts to my side of the table, napkin in hand. He starts blotting my dress trying to absorb the quickly spreading red stain.

"Please don't." I wave his hands from me. I look down at my ruined dress. It was so expensive. This meeting was crucial and now it's all for naught. "Excuse me." I push past the growing crowd of wait staff gathered at our table to help. "The washroom?" I question a young woman racing in my direction with a bottle of soda water in hand. She points to the left as she shoves the bottle into my open hand.

"I can't believe him," I mumble under my breath as I walk into the elaborately decorated powder room. I reach for a scented towel from the pile next to the sink. I drench it in soda water and begin the laborious task of trying to clean the bright red stain from my dress.

"You can't believe who? Jax?" I jump at the sound of Madeline's voice behind me. "What's going on with you two?"

"Nothing," I lie as I stare at my dress wondering how I'm going to find the courage to walk past him and out of the door of the restaurant. I'm tempted to climb out the small square window that is beckoning to me above the radiator. If I had even an ounce less pride I'd already have at least one foot firmly planted on it trying to hoist myself up.

"You slept with him, didn't you?" Madeline takes a healthy swallow from the glass she carried in with her.

"I don't want to talk about this." I glance up at her desperately wanting her to see within my expression that I'm on the precipice of falling apart.

She leans against the counter so she's facing me directly. I hear the faint echo of her empty glass against the marble countertop as she places it down. "I can tell. He's territorial with you."

"That's not all he is."

She laughs. "True. Obviously it didn't end well."

"It didn't really even begin." I become more animated with my unsuccessful attempt to clean the stain out of my dress. Maybe if she thinks I'm focused on that she'll go in search of another drink or a man to buy her one.

She reaches for my hands to stop me. "Ivy, look at me," she says tenderly.

I pull in a deep breath and raise my eyes so I meet her gaze. "What is it?"

"Don't let him intimidate you."

"He doesn't," I snap back at her.

"He does," she says. "I saw him doing it just now back at the table."

"I wouldn't call it intimidation." I rub the now pink cloth roughly across the fabric of my dress. I want her to take her observations and walk out the door before she hits the nail on the head and I break apart.

She douses another cloth in soda water before handing it to me. "Men like him have secrets."

"What kind of secrets?" I nod as I take the fresh cloth and throw the other into the sink next to her.

"Secrets that drive them." She turns to look at herself in the mirror. "Secrets that make them crave control."

I move so I'm standing next to her. "Do you know his secrets?" I stare at her reflection in the mirror.

She slowly moves her head from side-to-side as she traces a bright red, perfectly manicured fingernail around her top lip. "I'm not close enough to see it. You are."

"He's done nothing but lie to me." I fumble with the cloth in my hand again. Admitting that is hard. I'm ashamed that I let him seduce him. I'm embarrassed that I slept with him and I'm sick to my stomach over the fact that I was falling for him.

"Did you ask him why?" She turns so she's facing me directly. "Why did he lie?"

"To get back something that belonged to his father."

"Some people would do anything for their family."

I don't respond. I rub the cloth against the now faded stain on my dress.

"Look at you," she says. "You're a prime example of that."

"How so?" The understated suggestion that I'm like Jax stings but I don't show it. I know that she already sees me as an emotionally bruised little dove who has stepped into the vulture's trap.

"You came here to fight for your mother's dream today." She softens. "I admire that. He does too. Don't let that dream die, Ivy."

"I won't." I smile weakly. "I can't."

"I'll have Teresa call you to set up a time for you to come to my office so we can talk more." She picks up the empty glass and takes a step towards the door. "It'll be just the two of us but I can't do anything without his approval. Keep that in mind."

I smile softly and nod.

CHAPTER THREE

THE WEAK KNOCK AT THE DOOR RUSTLES ME FROM MY DREAM. I SIT UP straight and realize I'd fallen asleep on the couch after getting back from the restaurant. I'm still wearing the stained dress and now that it's wrinkled I couldn't look worse for the wear. I'm a sight but seeing Mrs. Adams will give me a boost.

I flinch as my bare feet hit the chilled hardwood. I forgot to close the windows when the sun started to set. The rain today had caused the temperature to dip and now I'm feeling the remnants of that in the air.

The knock is repeated just as I pull open the door. "I fell asleep, Mrs. Adams..." My voice fades as I realize it's Jax standing in the entranceway. Time freezes. I stare at him.

"I didn't mean to wake you." His voice is smooth. The tone is warm. "I wanted to drop this off." A gray garment bag floats into view. I feel as though I'm still caught in the dream. I was dreaming of him, wasn't I? Of his arms around me.

"What are you doing here?" My eyes scan the hallway behind him. "How did you get up here?"

He takes a step towards me and I retreat. He uses the opportunity to slide past me into the room. "The doorman remembered that we worked together. I told him I was your assistant and I had a delivery."

"You can't be here." I don't want this. I don't need this right now. "I want you to go."

"Give me two minutes." He motions towards the living room. "I have something for you."

I shake my head in earnest. "Why?"

"Two minutes." He holds two fingers in the air and throws a grin in my direction.

I hesitate before I allow the doorknob to slip through my fingers. I know this is a mistake but I don't have the emotional tenacity right now to argue with him. "What is it, Jax?"

"It's taken the last few hours but I found one." He flips around so his back is facing me. I hear the sharp pull of the zipper of the bag.

"Found one of what?" I take a step in his direction wondering what he's going to pull out of that bag. My sleepiness mixed with anger is making me anxious. I feel like someone who has been reluctantly pulled onstage to become the unwilling assistant of an overly zealous, inexperienced magician.

"This." There's a wave of fabric in the air but in the dim light of my apartment I can't make out what it is. I take a step closer.

"I found it in Philadelphia. They rushed it to me." He's exuberant.

I stare at the fabric. It's the same color as the dress I'm wearing. "That's my dress," I whisper.

"No." A wide grin covers his face. "Your dress looks like hell. This dress is perfect." He pushes it toward me.

I reach for it. I run my fingers over the fabric. It's the very same dress I'm wearing. I found it in a small boutique years ago. How could he have found a replacement in mere hours? How? "How did you find this?" I whisper under my breath.

"It's not important." He shoves his hands into the pockets of his slacks. "I ruined the one you're wearing. It looked so beautiful on you."

I look up at his face. In this moment, in this light he looks vulnerable and kind. The gesture was overwhelming and sweet. How can one man have so many complicated parts to him? "Thank you but I can't accept it."

The pained expression that washes over his face is palpable. "Why not?"

"I don't want anything from you." I place the dress down on the couch next to the garment bag. I smooth my hands over the dress I'm wearing wishing I had changed when I got home. I feel exposed in this dress. Back at the restaurant he knew the profound effect that his touch had on me. He still knows. He'll always know.

He steps towards me and I instinctively retreat. My hand jumps up in reflex. I don't want him to touch him. I can't promise myself I'll resist him despite everything I've learned about him the past few days.

"Are you scared of me?" I see the confusion on his face.

"Not scared." I tremble from the chill in the room. "Confused."

"It's freezing in here." He slides his suit jacket off. Before I can protest he's moved closer and is wrapping it around my shoulders. His hands tenderly rub my arms through the dense fabric.

I stare at his face. "Why?"

"You left the windows open." He looks past me down the hallway. "I should close them for you."

As he starts to pull away, I greedily grab his shirt to hold him in place. "No. Why did you lie?" I know I'm about to cry and I don't care. I need to know. My body is craving the truth.

"It's so complicated, beautiful."

"I need to know. Please." I know I'm pleading and I'm shameless. I haven't slept in days. I have to understand what happened. Why he went to such great lengths to manipulate me.

"When you walked into the restaurant today I melted inside." He pulls his finger across my jaw and I flinch. His touch is magnetic, even now.

"You used me." I toss the words at him. "You used me to get those shares away from Mark."

He studies my face before he responds, "I admit I wanted Mark to pay for what he did."

"For taking the business away from your father?" I ask.

His brow furrows momentarily and he hesitates. He pulls in a deep breath and looks down at the floor. "Yes," he says, his voice is barely more than a whisper.

"So I was just a pawn? A means to an end?" I pull back harshly from his grasp. I shrug the jacket off my body and it tumbles to the floor.

"No. Absolutely not." He stares directly into me. "I've wanted you since the night that picture was taken."

"What picture?" My emotions are quickly racing to the surface.

"The one you brought to my office."

"The one where you were creeping in the background?" The question flies from my lips like a skewer pointed right at him.

"I remember everything about that night. I remember the first moment I saw you." He reaches behind him as if to steady his balance. His hand fumbles for assurance as it finds the edge of the couch and he lowers himself onto it.

I follow his lead and sit in the chair across from him. I don't speak.

"You were wearing a black gown and your hair was falling down your back. I walked up behind you as soon as I saw you. The fragrance of your skin was intoxicating. I was reaching for your shoulder. I wanted so badly to talk to you. I couldn't breathe being that close to you and then…" his voice trails as he looks down and fumbles with his fingers.

"I don't remember seeing you," I say it softly not wanting to interrupt his thoughts.

"You were so focused on him. He walked in and you went to him." He shakes his head as if to erase the image.

"Yes," I manage to say. I remember that night vividly. Mark and I had spent the afternoon looking at venues for our wedding reception. I had been floating on cloud nine that entire day and the gala was the icing on the proverbial happiness cake.

"That's when I saw it." His tone shifts. There's a sliver of anger edging it now.

"Saw what?"

"You kissed him. You put your hand to his face and there it was.

That ring. The ring and I knew." His voice cracks. "I knew you belonged to him."

"We were engaged then." I offer although it's a fact that I'd rather forget.

He stands and walks towards the window. I watch as he silently closes it, latching the lock into place. "I went back to Los Angeles. I couldn't understand how someone like him could get a woman like you."

"Someone like him?" I prompt.

"Mark does unspeakable things." He clenches his fist and raises it slightly as if he's ready to punch the window. "He's evil. You're an angel. You never belonged with him."

"Brighton told me about your father. I didn't make the connection until I was in Mark's office." I offer. "You should have told me you were Tom Walker's son."

"I was testing you." He turns so he's facing me again.

"Testing me?" I chuckle as I say the words. "Testing me how?"

"Mark has done things. Things that he'd tell you are in the name of business. Things that damaged people I cared for." His eyes darken as he continues, "I had to know whether you knew who I really was or not."

"You don't think I would have told you right away if I had any clue you were Mark's business partner?" I sneer.

"Mark knew I wanted you, Ivy." He walks towards me stopping just short of where I'm standing. "He used your shares to manipulate me."

"So that gave you permission to manipulate me?" I poke my index finger into his chest.

He captures my hand in his, holding it firmly. "No, there's no excuse for that."

"How did he manipulate you?" I ask losing confidence in my ability to be objective. I try to pull my hand from his but he only squeezes it together.

He looks down briefly before answering. "He used the guilt I felt over my father to give him free rein with the business. He drove it into the ground before I even realized what was happening."

"What guilt?" Again I jerk my hand but his thumb begins to softly caress my palm. "What happened with your father?"

"I was a horrible son." His bottom lip trembles and for a fleeting moment I think I see tears well in his eyes. "I was everything he didn't want me to be."

I nod in silence knowing that exact feeling. My father's disappointment in me is echoed in the pain I see in Jax's eyes.

"When he died I vowed to change that." He pulls my hand to his face and lightly runs his lips across it. "I'm sorry I didn't tell you who I was. I was worried you were still tied to Mark and he was using you to entice me."

I jerk my hand away in one quick movement. "You knew I wasn't part of Mark's world anymore. You knew when I told you about the others he had slept with."

"Everyone knew he was cheating on you, Ivy." He runs his hand through his hair, pushing it back from his forehead. "Some women are okay with that."

"Okay with being cheated on?" I raise my eyebrow. "Who in their right mind would be okay with that?"

"Women who don't want to give up what they have for their pride."

"I'm not like that," I say the words with determination. "I just want to be free of Mark."

"I'm giving you the chance to have that." His voice is low and determined. "Just take my offer and you can have your freedom."

"I don't think so." I shake my head slightly. "Then I'm tied to you."

"In what sense?" He stills and stares directly at me. "How would we be tied together?"

I feel flush at the sudden realization that I've once again blurred the lines between business and pleasure. "I just thought...or assumed... that we'd still..." I sigh giving up any attempt to explain the ridiculous thought that we'd still be lovers after everything that happened. What's wrong with me? Why do I still want someone who used me to get back at Mark?

"That we'd still what?" He runs his hand down my shoulder now until it's resting on my wrist. "That you'd still be my lover?" He leans closer as his tongue runs lazily over his lips. He's going to kiss me now. I know it. I want it but I can't let it happen.

"No, of course not," I scoff. "That we'd still be tied together because of Veray." I pull that from mid-air and I high five myself internally for coming up with it.

"Oh, that." He pulls his eyes across my lips before he takes a step back. "I forgot about that."

I shake my head in mock amusement. "Of course you did. It's nothing to you, but it's everything to me."

"How could Veray be everything?" He smirks and I'm certain he's about to burst out laughing.

"It's all I have." I purse my lips together holding in all of the conflicting emotions that are bearing down on me. "That's it."

"No, beautiful." He reaches for my hand again. "You have much more."

"That's right." I let my hand fall into his. "I have all that money you're going to give me when I hand over control of Mark's company to you."

"I'm offering you much more than your ten percent is worth." He traces a finger over my knuckles and I shiver at the touch. "Ask around. Do some digging. You'll see that your shares aren't worth a fraction of what I'm giving you."

"So you're doing me a favor?" I tilt my head to the left anxiously anticipating his predictable egotistical response.

He stares at me. His gaze narrows as he leans in closer. I close my eyes wanting the world to melt away. I want to fall back into that bed in the apartment in Chelsea when he told me he wanted me to be his first. When he said I was his everything.

"Ivy." I feel the whisper of his words on my lips mere seconds before his breath connects with mine. He pulls me into his kiss. His tongue tenderly running over mine, coaxing me. I lose all sense of space, or time or reason. I reach for the back of his head, pushing his mouth into mine. Moaning into him.

His hands encircle my waist. I feel his arousal as my body melts into his. I'm spun around quickly, I can't open my eyes. I don't want to. I feel the couch on my back. I feel him on top of me. Tell him to stop I plead with my heart. Tell him.

"Jax," I say softly against his lips. "Please."

"I need to taste you now, beautiful." His hands race up my thighs reaching my center. He rips my panties off and instantly enters me with two fingers. My back arches at the sensation. "You want me," he growls.

I push my back into the cushions. My body can't stop. I'm rushing towards my release when I feel his breath on my clit. I whimper knowing that when his tongue touches me my hunger for an orgasm under his touch will finally be satiated again. I bite my lip as he tastes me. He delicately pulls my clit between his lips. I can't stop myself. I don't want to stop. I wrap my hand into his hair and push him into me. "Please, Jax, please."

"This is where I belong." He breathes against me before encircling my swollen clit again and again with his tongue. I let my body take control and take me over the edge. I moan loudly, clutching his hair with both hands. The desire races through my veins. He slows the pace. It feels like he's slowly and deeply fucking me with his tongue. I push my hips into him, wanting him to taste more, wanting to give him more. I'm near my edge when he moans deeply into me. I fall over the cliff and the pleasure tears through me. I feel it in every inch of my body. I'm so spent. I can't move.

"Beautiful." He barely touches my lips with his own and I taste both of us. "I'm leaving."

I open my eyes and he's there. So close. So tender. "But we didn't." I motion down with my eyes. I thought he'd want to be inside of me. I thought he'd want to feel me, all of me.

"Not yet," he whispers against my mouth. "I want you to take my offer. I want you to understand that I want a new life for you."

I scan his face. I want so much to kiss him and to tell him to stay with me. I want to fall asleep wrapped within the warmth of him. I just stare.

"Call a securities attorney tomorrow. Get him to contact me." He brushes his lips across my forehead before he stands up. "I want this done as soon as possible. I don't want it hanging between us."

I nod my head. He's slipped again. I can see it in his eyes. Tender, loving Jax has become ruthless, obsessed Jax in an instant again. He scoops up his suit jacket and I watch him leave through the corner of my eye.

CHAPTER FOUR

"Thank you for coming." I awkwardly reach to hug him across the table. "Did you find the place okay?"

His eyes skirt around the room before he responds, "It's not really my kind of place, princess."

I smile at the familiar endearment. "I know, dad. But the steak here is great and I know how much you love steak."

His face lights up at the suggestion of a slab of beef cooked to perfection. "I don't even need to look at the menu now, do I?"

"I'll order for both of us. The train, it was good?" I feel my resolve loosening a bit. Summoning my father to Manhattan may not have been such a bad idea after all.

"It was great. I read the whole trip." He glances at my left hand as he stills. "Is Mark coming?"

The waiter approaches and I order our dinner before turning back to face my father and the conversation I've been dreading for the past six months. "He's not, dad. It's over."

"I told you so." The hairs on my neck prickle at the declaration.

"I know." I respond calmly. "You were right."

"What happened?"

"He cheated on me." I hate those words. I hate the taste of them in my mouth. I hope this will be the last time I ever have to repeat them.

"Mark?" he snaps back. "Our Mark cheated on you? I don't believe it?" The sarcasm in his voice is obvious.

I run my index finger around the handle of the fork sitting in front of me. "He did with many women."

"What women?" he asks with contempt. I can tell that he's angry. I don't blame him. He warned me. He told me that Mark was no good for me and now I have to concede before I can ask for his help.

"One was Liz," I mumble under my breath hoping he won't remember the name of my best friend.

"You're joking?" The words fly out accompanied by small traces of the bourbon he's drinking. I'm surprised he didn't spit the entire mouthful in my direction.

I breathe a heavy sigh. "I'm serious."

"What kind of people are you associating yourself with, Ivy?" his voice cracks.

"I had no idea, dad. I should have listened to you." I tremble knowing that I was too stubborn back when it mattered. My father was wise, he was strong and he was genuine. If his inner instinct had told him that Mark wasn't good for me that should have raised a red flag in my head. I wish I could undo the past few years. I wish I had taken my father's advice to heart.

He stands and I panic. He's leaving. He's so embarrassed by what I've done with my life that he's going to walk right out of this restaurant, get back on a train headed to Boston and I'll lose him again for the next few years. My eyes well with tears as I bury my head in my hands.

"Princess." His voice is right next to me. "You should have called me. I would have come and given Mark a piece of my mind."

I throw my arms around his neck and pull him to me. The overwhelming scent of his cologne takes me back to when I was a little girl and I would sit on his lap for hours while he read to me each night. This is my home. This is where I belong.

"You would have hit him, daddy." I giggle as I pull back to look at his weathered face.

"I could take him. I'd sucker punch him when he was texting on that fancy phone of his." He winks at me.

I laugh out loud. I feel a sense of calm and contentment. I haven't laughed like this with my father in so long. I finally feel anchored again. "Thank you for coming." I cup his cheek in my hand. "It means everything to me."

"You mean everything to me." He kisses my palm. "Now where's my steak?"

———

"NO ONE CAN GRILL a steak like your mama could but that wasn't half bad." My father wipes the last remnants of mashed potatoes from the corner of his lips. "Now let's get to the nitty gritty of why I'm here."

I look across the table at him and I feel a nervous knot form in the pit of my stomach. "It's about Mark and some shares I have in his company."

"That real estate company he owns?" He takes a long sip of the water as he gazes over the glass at me.

"Yes." I nod. "He gave me ten percent when we split."

"It must be worth something?" He's scanning the dessert menu and running his finger across the page as if to check the prices.

"Someone told me it was worth ten million." I cringe as I say the number. My father comes from humble beginnings and although he worked hard to make a very comfortable life for me and my sister after our mother died, we didn't have anything in excess ever.

The menu falls from his hands onto the table as his jaw drops. Then, as if in slow motion, he shakes his head from side-to-side a few times. "I heard you wrong, princess. My hearing isn't what it used to be."

"No, you heard me right." I swallow the last few drops of red wine that have been taunting me from the bottom of my glass since before dinner arrived. "I was told the shares are worth ten million dollars."

"You're rich." A wide grin takes over his face. "You're rich, Ivy. Sell them back to him."

"No." I know this is the point where I should start explaining about Jax. I should launch into a detailed description about how we met and what he might or might not mean to me, but telling my father I'm involved with Mark's business partner can't go over well. I'd just mended one broken fence tonight. I didn't want to break another.

"Mark doesn't want the shares?"

"I don't know. We haven't discussed it." I shrug my shoulders and steady my breath before I continue. "Actually, Mark's partner wants to buy the shares."

"Sell them." He says it matter-of-factly as if there's no room for consideration of any other idea.

"Do you think I should?" I quiz wanting him to tell me it's the absolute best idea I've ever had.

He motions for the waiter before he turns back to me. "Will it mess things up for Mark if you do?" He throws me a playful grin.

I can't help but smile back before I nod.

"There's your answer." He winks before ordering something decadent off the menu for dessert. "You only live once, Ivy. Make him pay."

CHAPTER FIVE

"YOU'RE EXACTLY AS I REMEMBER YOU, IVY." HIS VOICE IS DEEP AND melodic and I'm surprised by how much he's changed since I was younger. He's even more attractive. His jaw has filled out and his black hair is a perfect contrast to his deep blue eyes.

"I'll take that as a compliment." I try to smooth out a crease in the skirt of the red dress I'm wearing. "I'm thankful that you could see me at such short notice, Mr. Moore."

"It's Nathan." He motions to a leather chair situated directly in front of his desk. "I chased you with frogs when we were kids. I don't think Mr. Moore is appropriate."

I laugh at the memory of our shared childhood. "How is Sandra? I haven't spoken to her since graduation."

"She's still back in Boston. Well, actually she's living in Medford now. She got married. You knew that, right?" He leans back in his chair.

"No." I do little to veil the surprise in my voice. "To who?"

"Travis Mitchell."

"Shut up." I blurt out before pulling my hand to cover my mouth. "I'm sorry." I giggle at the wide grin on his face.

"I know, right?" He runs his hand over his chin. "He knocked her up right after graduation."

"She has a child?" I'm shocked hearing the sordid tale of my best friend from high school's adventures in marriage and motherhood. I can't believe she married the boy who had been shamelessly declaring his love for her since middle school.

"Two kids." He reaches across his desk to retrieve a framed photograph and hands it to me.

I bite my lip at my first look at the two angelic faces smiling at me. "They're so beautiful."

"Madison and Mackenzie," he says it with pride. "They're great. I go back at least once a month to get my quality uncle time in."

I smile as I try to absorb the information he's throwing at me. I miss Sandra. I need to call her and congratulate her on her life. "I envy her in some ways," I say quietly.

"Me too," he confesses. "But all of that and more can be yours as soon as you become Mrs. Mark Carleton."

"You heard about that?" I wrinkle my nose.

"Everyone back home heard about it. It was in all the papers." He cocks an eyebrow.

I sigh. I'm going to have to explain to my childhood crush that I'm no longer marrying the man everyone still seems to think I'm devoted to. "We're not getting married. That's part of the reason why I'm here."

"I'm sorry to hear that." There's no indication of emotion in his tone. "I wondered why you needed a securities attorney."

"My dad mentioned your name when he was here for dinner the other night." I look past Nathan to the stunning view of midtown Manhattan that sits outside his windows. "He thought you were still in Boston. I was surprised when I realized you were here in New York."

"I moved out here a few months ago when I turned thirty." He chuckles before he continues, "I guess I needed a change of scenery."

"I love it here." I lock eyes with him. "It's been good to me."

"Apparently it has if you need my services." He grins as he opens a tablet. "What can I do for you, Ivy Marlow?"

"I own shares in Mark's real estate investment firm. I want to sell them." My stomach tightens as I say the words. I'm actually moving forward with this and as soon as Nathan gets involved, there's no turning back.

"Then I'll make sure you sell them." He pushes his chair back and effortlessly stands. He seems so much taller than I remember.

I follow his lead. "Is that it?"

"For today." He walks to where I'm standing. "I'll have my assistant draw up a contract and he'll send that over to you this afternoon. Once you sign that I can access everything I need to and we'll come up with a fair asking price and start looking for an interested party."

"Someone is already interested." I blush when I say it.

The corner of his mouth turns up slightly. "I'm not surprised."

I stare into his eyes as my heart plunges back to my early teenage years. I'd swoon over pictures of him in Sandra's house and melt whenever he walked into the room. I briefly have a flash of what my life might have been like if he had actually taken notice of me when I was seventeen and desperately infatuated with him.

I shake my head to clear my thoughts. "I'll wait to hear from you."

He places his hand on my back before opening his office door. "I'll be in touch very soon."

———

"THERE YOU ARE, DEAR." Mrs. Adams greets me as I exit the taxi.

"What are you doing out here?" I reach for her arm, helping to steady her as she limps towards me through all the pedestrian traffic. "You should be inside."

"Nonsense," she scoffs as she allows me to lead her toward the shade of the building. "It's a beautiful day and I was just taking a small walk."

I tilt my head towards her knowing that she's way too independent for her own good. "I just wish you'd ask Oliver to walk with you." I try not to let my concern overtake my tone.

"That young man was here looking for you again." She stops mid step to point her finger at me. "You know the one."

"Jax," I say.

"Yes. I don't understand that at all. Who names their child Jax? Is that short for something?"

I smile. "I don't think so. It's one of those hippie names."

She nods her head in agreement as I lead her into the elevator and press the button for our floor.

"Did you talk to him?" I ask hoping that my curiosity isn't carrying through to my tone.

"I didn't." She steps out into the hallway and starts in the direction of her apartment as I follow. "I saw him knocking at your door so I peeked out to see what was going on."

I try to stifle in a laugh. Mrs. Adams was definitely better than any security system I could have installed. Somehow she still was able to hear every small noise and knew everyone's business often before they even did.

"I was tempted to tell him to go away or I'd call the police." She fumbles with the assortment of keys trying to find the ones that unlock her door. "But I thought better." The door finally flies open and I guide her inside.

"I'll deal with him." I lead her to her favorite chair before I walk towards the kitchen. "Do you want your tea iced?" I call over my shoulder.

"Yes, dear, with lemon."

"Jax is actually going to buy the shares I have in Mark's company." I hand her the tall glass of tea before sitting across from her. "It's going to help me a lot."

"Whatever makes you happy, dear." She pats her small hand over mine. "Just be careful with your heart."

"I am." I stand to leave. "I have to be."

CHAPTER SIX

"THIS IS JUST A PRELIMINARY DISCUSSION SO KEEP THAT IN MIND." Nathan pulls out one of the padded office chairs at the long rectangular conference table.

"Okay, I understand." I swallow hard before sitting down. "Do you think I look okay for this?" I scan my plain white dress before I soak in the sight of him in his expensive dark suit and stunning blue shirt and tie. "I feel underdressed."

"You look amazing," he says after taking the seat next to mine. "I have to dress beyond my means. It's part of my job. It makes me look intimidating, don't you think?"

I giggle at the expression on his face which is a mixture of a grin and a scowl. "Your tie intimidates me or maybe the pattern hypnotizes me. That has to count for something."

He throws his head back with a hearty laugh and I can't help but giggle at the sight of it. It reminds me so much of when we were children and he'd pull a prank on Sandra and me.

"I've always loved your laugh." I reach for his hand to squeeze it. "It reminds me of home."

He holds my hand in his and I jump at a sound near the doorway. It's the unmistakable grumble of a man clearing his throat for effect, not for purpose. I don't have to glance in that direction to know that it's Jax and he's not pleased by what he just saw.

"Who are you?" He wastes no time in marching up to the table.

"Nathan Moore." Nathan shoots to his feet and offers his hand. "I'm representing Ms. Marlow."

Jax blatantly ignores Nathan's hand. His eyes are locked on me and I can tell from the scowl overtaking his brow that he's not happy with my choice in attorney.

"This is Jax Walker," I interject.

"Nice to meet you, Mr. Walker and…" his voice trails as Jax's attorney enters the room.

"I'm Gilbert Douglas." His thick English accent surprises me.

Nathan takes his hand before everyone settles back into their chairs.

"Ms. Marlow is prepared to sell." Nathan opens a non-descript manila folder that he placed in front of him on the table when we sat down. "These are her terms." He slides a single piece of paper across the table in Gilbert's direction.

Jax snatches it up and studies the numbers against the subtle protest of his attorney. "This wasn't what we agreed to."

"She feels this is more than fair," Nathan explains.

"I wasn't talking to you," Jax barks. "I was talking to her."

Nathan shifts his body in his chair so he's sitting completely upright. "You'll address me, Mr. Walker. As I explained when you came in the room, I represent Ms. Marlow in this matter."

Jax clenches the edge of the table in his right hand. I can see the vein in his neck pulsing and I know he's about to explode. It's obvious to everyone in the room that Jax isn't going to be complacent.

"Mr. Moore." Gilbert's voice breaks the tense silence. "This offer is appreciated but we're going to need time to discuss it. You understand, of course."

Nathan nods. "It's what she wants and if Mr. Walker wants these shares, it's not negotiable."

"I see." Gilbert nods his head. "We weren't aware that she was interested in my client's holdings in Veray Jewelers."

"As you can see, she's willing to agree to less in terms of a monetary offering in exchange for his shares in Veray." Nathan slams the folder shut. "Give me a call when you've made a decision."

Jax stares at him as he prepares to stand. "We're not done, Moore."

Nathan pulls my chair gently away from the table and reaches for my hand to help me stand. "We're done until you agree to these terms. Now, if you'll excuse us both."

I reach for my purse and follow Nathan's blatant lead. I don't want to turn around to see Jax's expression. I know he's pissed. Not just at my attempt to wrestle Veray away from him but by the fact that Nathan's hand is slowly moving down my back as he guides me out of the room.

"That went well, don't you think?" I smile at Nathan as we reach the bank of elevators. "Do you think he'll give it to me?"

He reaches down and taps me on the tip of my nose with his index finger. It makes me giggle. It's the very same gesture we shared when we were growing up. "You did great, Ivy. You definitely have the advantage. I'm proud of you for taking this on."

I smile at the comment. All I wanted growing up was his attention and approval. Now that I have both, I'm feeling like that awkward seventeen-year-old girl again except the man I'm crushing on is back in the boardroom with steam coming out of his ears.

"Here's our ride." The chime of the elevator reaching our floor rings through the air.

I take a step forward when I feel a hand stroke my elbow and take hold. My breath catches. I don't even need to turn around to know that Jax is right behind me.

"After you." Nathan sweeps his arm in the air in the direction of the now open elevator. He jumps when he notices Jax standing in silence right behind me.

"She'll take the next one." Jax pulls me towards him.

"Mr. Walker, you shouldn't be talking to me client alone." Nathan steps into the elevator and holds his hand over the door.

"I'm not talking to her as your client." Jax takes a step back and I'm forced to follow.

"What are you talking about?" Nathan searches my face for some understanding.

"It's okay." My eyes dart to Jax's face. "We have something else to discuss. I promise I won't talk about the sale without you."

"I'll call you tonight." He moves his hand so the door silently glides to a close.

"This way." Jax's hand moves to mine and he pulls me abruptly into a corridor next to the bank of elevators.

"What are you doing?" I hiss. "I don't want to talk about the contract with you. I can't."

He pushes me against the wall before separating my legs with his knee. I'm pinned against the wall in this seemingly abandoned corridor. "Are you fucking him?"

I scan his face looking for any evidence of a smirk or a grin but there's nothing but cold seriousness. "You didn't just ask me that."

"Are you fucking Moore?" He repeats this time with measured force in his voice. "Answer the question."

"Am I fucking Nathan?" I repeat it back.

"Christ, just answer it." He pushes his body harder into mine. I'm certain that I can feel him becoming aroused.

I roll my eyes and try to break free of his grasp. "I'm not answering that. It's insulting."

"He wants to fuck you." His breath traces a path down my neck. "He couldn't keep his hands off you."

"You're crazy." I push harder now, knowing that if I truly wanted to break free I could do it, but part of me is relishing in his jealous rage and how hard he's become.

"He was practically drooling over you." He touches the tip of his tongue to my neck and I whimper. "You had to notice. You're not that naïve, beautiful."

I realize that two can play his twisted game. "I wanted him too," I whisper into his ear.

He retreats. His body pulls back from mine and his hands leap to my face. "Say it again."

I scan his eyes looking for anything that would indicate that my words stung him. I see a faint trace of disappointment. "I wanted him too when...." I let the words trail as I move my face until my lips are hovering next to his.

"When what?" He leans forward and pulls my bottom lip between his teeth.

I flinch at the pain and pull back. I run my tongue over the bruised spot. "When I was seventeen."

"When you were seventeen?" The confusion in his voice is mixed with something else more telling. Happiness? Relief? It's too vague to place.

"He was my best friend's older brother. I wanted him so much," I say the words not caring what he thinks.

"But he didn't fuck you. There was only one," he whispers it with reassurance.

"I wanted him. I thought about it when I touched..." I blush at the mere mention of the fact that the thought of kissing, making love with and coming with Nathan was the only fodder for my desires back then.

"When you touched yourself?" His lips claim mine as the words leave his mouth. I drop my purse to the floor as I grab hold of his shoulders. I can't get close enough to him. I'm addicted to him and he knows it.

I pull back from the kiss when I feel his hands tugging at the bottom of my dress. "No, not here," I say in barely more than a whisper. "I've never. People will see us." I fumble for the right words to tell him that I won't have sex in the middle of the day in an office building.

"No one will see us." His hands don't hesitate as he reaches the edge of my silk panties. I feel him dip a finger inside and pull it across my wetness. "You're ready. I want to be inside you, right here, right now."

"Jax, no, please. No." I whimper without any conviction as I hear the sound of him undoing his belt. The soft pull of his zipper follows and he flips me around until I'm pressed against the wall.

"Tell me to stop now, beautiful." His words are drowned out by the sensation of his cock pressed against me. He pulls my panties aside and expertly slides himself into me in one fluid motion.

I muffle my gasp with my own hand and brace myself against the wall with the other. He pulls my hair into his fist and gently jerks my body closer to his. A guttural moan rises from deep within me and I press my wetness into him.

"You're never going to want another man again," he purrs into my ear as he finds his rhythm. His free hand grabs hold of my hip and he violently pushes himself into me. I brace myself harder against the wall not wanting to hit it with each of his powerful thrusts.

"Fuck, yes." I whimper. I can't hold in the pleasure. I want to scream but I know I can't. "Harder."

"You're mine. Say it, beautiful."

I can't speak. I can only feel. This isn't me. I don't have sex with men like him in public places. I don't. I can't stop myself. I can't stop wanting him.

"I'm so close," I manage to softly say.

"Come with me," he growls into my ear. I feel my knees buckle as I find my release. He pulls me closer with both hands now, holding me steady as he moans deeply in my ear. "My Ivy."

CHAPTER SEVEN

I PLACE ALL THE EXTRA PIECES I'VE CREATED OVER THE YEARS ON THE
floor in my foyer. There's dozens and I smile at the array of designs
and the unique nuances in each one. None of these made the cut in
Madeline's eyes but they're breathtaking to me and I know others will
envision wearing them as soon as they see them. I reach toward the
table and grab my camera. I want to catalogue each piece with a photograph so by the time the deal with Jax is completed and I have his
shares in Veray in my pocket I can set up my own website to sell these
one of a kind creations online.

There's a knock at the door as soon as I take the first image. I know
it can't be Mrs. Adams since I helped her get into a taxi hours earlier as
I arrived home after my encounter with Jax. "Why does this building
even have a doorman?" I ask under my breath.

I throw the door open and I'm greeted by the sight of Nathan in
the hallway. I blush when I realize all I'm wearing is a short
sundress. My air conditioner is acting up again and my apartment
feels like a moderate oven awaiting a batch of chocolate chip
cookies.

"Nathan." I smile at him. "Come in please."

He takes a large step over the threshold then freezes in place when he notices all of the earrings, necklaces, rings, bracelets and brooches scattered all over the floor. "Is this a bad time?"

I silently close the door behind him. "No. Not at all." I push the wayward tendrils of my ponytail back into place. "I'm just sorting through some of my extra stuff."

"This is your stuff?" He falls to his knees right where he is and gently picks up a pair of light green glass earrings. "You made these?"

"I did." I lower myself to the floor too being extra careful to tuck the edge of my dress under my knees. "I made all of these."

"Ivy." His face brightens with a wide grin. "You're so gifted. Why haven't I heard about you? Where have you been hiding this talent?"

"In one small showcase at Veray Jewelers." I reach for a necklace that is embellished with a delicate silver sparrow. "This is one of my favorite pieces."

He takes it tenderly in his hand. "It's a sparrow." His eyes connect instantly with mine. "Sandra's favorite bird."

"I was thinking of her when I made it years ago." I continue," remember when she picked up that injured sparrow and she nursed it back to health? We couldn't have been more than ten-years-old then."

"I do remember." He studies the intricate details I worked into the tiny bird. "Sandra would be amazed by this."

"Will you give that to her when you see her?"

"She'll love it." His eyes scan the entire expanse of the pieces. "Ivy, seriously, you made all of this?"

"Yes." I grin widely. I don't often get complimented on my work and hearing him tell me what he thinks of it gives me the confidence I need to keep moving forward with my plan to start a website and get my own customers instead of being under Veray's control forever.

He moves to stand and I do the same. I realize then that I haven't asked him what he's doing at my place.

"I'm sorry." I motion towards the living room. "Please come in. Can I get you anything? Ice tea, a soda, maybe some wine?"

"Just water if you don't mind." He takes a seat on the couch as he pulls the collar of his dress shirt away from his neck. "Is it hot in here or is that just me?"

I stand silent for a minute before I realize I've misinterpreted what he said. He's hot. I almost told him that. Shit. My seventeen-year-old brain needs to grow up. "My air conditioner is on the fritz. The super promised he'd be up sometime this year."

He laughs as I head to the kitchen to retrieve a water bottle from the fridge. I hold it against my chest briefly before walking back into the room and handing it to him.

"It's a nice apartment." His eyes scan the length of the room. "Did you and Mark live here together?"

"It's his apartment." I don't see any reason to sugar coat the truth. "I'm hoping I can get a place that is just mine once the deal goes through."

"I actually stopped by to talk to you about that." He pulls the cap from the bottle and swallows a large gulp. "I'm sorry I didn't call but I had dinner in the neighborhood and thought I'd take a chance that you'd be here."

I nod. "I'm almost always here," I say quietly. Since my friendship with Liz was shattered I haven't gone out much. I miss it.

"Maybe we can have dinner sometime." The casual way he throws it into the air surprises me. I purse my lips together thinking about how to answer when he elaborates. "Just as friends, of course. Old friends who've recently reconnected."

"I'd like that." I breathe a sigh of relief. If it was a date, Jax wouldn't approve but he's not in control of me, is he? At this point we don't seem to be more than random fuck buddies so is a date out of the question? I glance at Nathan and realize he's staring at me. Christ, he must think I'm still as immature as that girl who used to follow him around hoping to get him to look at me.

"You and Jax. What's up with that?" He nonchalantly asks as if he's inquiring about something as mundane as the weather or the last movie I saw.

"What do you mean?" I'm going to employ the dumb blonde act and pray that he falls for it. Who am I kidding? He's an attorney.

He smiles coyly. "He's either in love with you or he needs anger management classes."

I laugh out loud at how preposterous the idea of Jax being in love with me is and that anger management classes seem like something Jax could excel at.

"He's not in love with me." I trace my index finger along the arm of the chair. "He'd probably fail anger management classes."

"I'd agree with that," he mutters under his breath.

"He can come across as rude, or arrogant or something." I find myself trying to explain Jax's less than welcoming attitude earlier. "But I think he's a good person deep down."

"Are you two involved?" He keeps pushing the subject. "I need to know, Ivy. I don't want to try and negotiate a deal with him blindly. If there's some sort of personal relationship I'd like to know."

I feel flush. I have to admit to this man that I haven't seen in years that I'm sleeping with the person who insulted him earlier today. I nod my head slowly up and down.

"I knew it," he replies. I can't gauge his reaction but I do sense disappointment or anxiety in his voice. "This complicates things for me."

"I'm sorry," I offer. "We're not exactly involved. We're not together like couples are together."

He looks as confused as I feel. I know I should explain more so I sigh while I search for the words.

"You two are just sleeping together?" He throws me a lifeline as if he wants to save me the embarrassment of having to explain that Jax and I just have sex at this point.

I nod. "It was moving in another direction but then I found out about his father and the company." I grimace at the words. The bitterness still sits within me. I hate that Jax hadn't divulged that he was Tom's son when we first met.

"His father used to be Mark's partner, right?" He pulls the lid from the water bottle again and swallows what's left. He places the empty container on the table.

"That's right. I didn't find that out until he offered to buy my shares." I hang my head towards the floor. This is humiliating. In the short span of five minutes I've confessed to Nathan that I'm still sleeping with a man who manipulated me and lied to me.

"That's low." He points out.

"I know." I catch his glance and see pity there. I don't want him to pity me. I want him to help me get away from Mark. Maybe I want him to help me get away from Jax. I don't know. I can't stop and think about all of this. All I can focus on is what Jax and I did in that corridor earlier.

"Is he hiding anything else?" he asks softly.

I look towards the windows as I measure my answer. Why haven't I asked Jax that question? Did I not want to know? "I don't think so."

"I hope not." He stands and I follow his lead. "Find out if he is, Ivy. That's leverage we can use. He may not budge on Veray and anything he doesn't want to come out may be your guarantee to get exactly what you want."

I nod realizing that I have no way of doing that. I'm not certain that Jax will actually be honest with me if I ask him such a pointed question. My heart drops as I absorb that thought.

CHAPTER EIGHT

"IVY, I HEARD YOU WERE HERE." I FEEL HIS HAND ON MY SHOULDER and I spin around to face him.

"I was just picking up my consignment check." I smile at him. He looks gorgeous. He hasn't shaved in a couple of days and the slight growth of beard makes him appear less perfect. Imperfect Jax is someone I could definitely get used to.

"You should have told me you were coming." He places his hand on my back to guide me in the direction of his office. "I would have saved you the trip. I could have brought the check to your apartment."

I step through the doorway of his office pulling in a breath to try to calm my nerves. So far my plan is going flawlessly. He has no idea why I'm really there. "No, that would be silly. I like to come by so I can catch up with Graham."

"Who?" He raises an eyebrow. "Who is Graham?"

"One of your assistants." I heave a sigh. "Hopefully my assistant when I take over."

He moves to shut the door. I can't help but notice that he subtly turns the lock. He thinks we're going to sleep together right here in his office. I've become nothing but a fuck buddy to him. I push my anger down and focus on the task at hand.

"You know we can't discuss that, beautiful." He pulls on the end of my hair. "This dress is stunning on you."

"Thank you," I whisper as I try to temper my discomfort. "I can't stay long. I have an appointment to get to."

"With that attorney of yours?" The animosity in his voice isn't disguised at all.

"You have a problem with him." I bite my bottom lip so I won't launch into a full blown smile. "You have a temper tantrum whenever we talk about him."

"Hardly." His jaw tightens.

"Liar," I playfully spit back at him.

"I'm not a liar." He catches my waist between his hands. "Never call me that again."

"You lied to me once." I nuzzle my face against his neck. "How do I know you aren't holding more secrets inside?"

"We all have secrets." He traces a line along my cheek before tilting my chin up so my gaze meets his. "Some secrets aren't meant to be shared."

I study his eyes trying to find some semblance of emotion in them. I can't tell if he's being facetious or telling me discreetly to back off.

"You made me share my secret about Nathan. You made me tell you all about what I wanted him to do to my body," I tease knowing that it will elicit a reaction that I can use in my favor.

"You wanted him to but he's never made you feel what I make you feel." His lips brush against my neck and I instantly feel my resolve weakening.

"He still wants me. You were right." I push the issue, knowing that Jax's jealousy is a tool that I can easily use to my advantage.

"How do you know?" He pulls back from me and greedily grabs my upper arms. "He told you that?"

"He didn't have to," I say quietly. "I could see it in his eyes when he came over the other night."

"Why the fuck was your attorney at your apartment?"

I continue the façade knowing that it's bringing all of his emotions to the surface. "He stopped by and my air conditioner was broken. I was wearing a short sheer dress and the way he looked at me."

His eyes gloss over and there's a mixture of pure indignation and disappointment. "You shouldn't have let him in."

"Why not? He's my attorney."

"What happened? What did you do?" Irritation envelops the question.

"Nothing." I step back from his grasp. "I'm not a whore. I didn't sleep with him."

Relief washes over his face and he reaches for me. "I can't stand the thought of another man touching you. Please don't give yourself to anyone else, Ivy. Please."

I hear the pleading in his voice and it stirs a familiar place within me. I don't have to question Jax about his secrets. I already know what he's hiding. Why had I been so blind to this? I can't believe I didn't see it before today.

"What was her name?" I whisper against his chest.

"Who?" He exhales loudly as if he's losing his patience with me.

"The woman who cheated on you."

He turns away and walks toward his desk. I can see his shoulders trembling. "No woman has ever cheated on me, Ivy."

"You are a liar," I say it, not caring that it sounds harsh. "Maybe that's how you deal with it. You lie to yourself and everyone else about it."

He looks straight ahead, avoiding my glare. "Not everyone is cheated on. I'm sorry that you were but you're projecting your pain and disappointment."

I smirk, shaking my head from side-to-side. "Maybe you can fool the world into believing that you're cold and heartless. Maybe you move from one woman's bed to another to help you feel more like a man because she stripped that away from you when she slept with someone else. "

"Maybe I'm just fickle." He doesn't flinch.

"Somebody broke your heart. She tore it into so many pieces that when you think about it, you can't fathom how you can put it back together again. So instead of trying you built a barrier around it to keep everyone out. You use women to get back at the one who rejected you. "

"Are you done analyzing me? I have a meeting to get to. "He moves back towards the doorway.

"I'm done." I sigh, frustrated again by his refusal to open up to me.

"Leonard will pick you up for dinner at eight tonight." The way he casually throws the comment out in midst of our current discussion, irks me.

"Not tonight." I reach for my phone, scanning through the numbers. "I have plans."

"Plans?" He finally looks in my direction. "What plans?"

"Dinner with a friend." I don't elaborate.

"What friend?"

"No one you know." I walk past him, opening the office door. "Wait. You don't know any of my friends because you and I are just fuck buddies."

"Don't be so juvenile." He grabs my forearm, forcing me to stop my retreat out the door. "Who are you having dinner with?"

"It's not your concern." I pull my arm from his grasp.

"It is. I made plans for us to have dinner."

I look into his eyes. "I need a break from this." I sweep my hand over the air between us. "Whatever this is. I just need some time off."

"What does that mean?"

"It means I'm tired of trying to understand you. Maybe I should just embrace this for what it is. Two consenting adults who like having sex."

"We're more than that. You know that we are."

"No." I turn to leave not able to look him in the face. "We're two virtual strangers who like having sex. End of story."

"Do you really believe that?" His voice is soft, there's a vulnerable edge to it.

"I believe that I've shared too much about my life with you. I regret that. This is so unbalanced it's laughable."

"It's not."

"It is so." I stop before I walk through the doorway. "You're never going to chase the pain away by controlling me. It doesn't work that way, Jax. Get over her. Call me when you do."

CHAPTER NINE

"I WAS SHOCKED THAT YOU CALLED, SUGAR." LIZ HESITATES BRIEFLY AS if she's contemplating embracing me before she takes a seat across from me in the crowded midtown Starbucks. "I couldn't believe it."

I nod and stare at her face. She looks tired and weak. I know that the past few weeks had to have taken their toll on her too. I saw the obvious anguish in her eyes when she realized that Mark had been unfaithful with others. Maybe she did really love him. "I thought it was time for us to talk."

"I'm so grateful. I knew you'd forgive me."

I pause and run my finger along the rim of the lid of my coffee. "This meeting isn't about forgiveness. I can't get there yet. Honestly, I'm not sure I ever will."

She sobs loudly before pulling her hand to her mouth. "Okay. That's fair. Mark…"

"I'm not here to talk about him," I interrupt her. "Please don't bring him up. If you do I'll leave."

She nods in silence. I can tell that she's in a wretched emotional state but I can't find any compassion within me for her. She pretended to be my best friend for years all the while she was rolling around in my bed with my fiancé. I'd even asked her to be the maid of honor at my wedding. She's stolen things from me that I may never get back and I can't deal with that right now on top of everything else.

"The other day when you came by you said something about Jax." I hate that I've had to resort to looking to someone who betrayed me for information on him. I sense that she knows something though and I'm aching to find out what it is.

She nods her head quickly up and down. "Brighton told me something."

At the mention of his name I make a mental note to call him. He seemed willing to share more information about Jax the night we went to Madeline's party. Maybe if I pushed him a bit he'd open up and give me some insight into what or who caused Jax to build such an impenetrable barrier around his heart.

"What did he tell you?" I wince as I ask. Why am I here and how can I trust anything she says to me?

"He said that Jax only wanted some shares. I guess in Mark's business? And that they would do anything to get them away from you." She enunciates each word slowly as if she's recalling exactly what Brighton said, syllable-by-syllable.

"He said, 'they', you're certain of that?" I take a sip of the coffee in a mistaken effort to slow my pounding heart. Caffeine is only going to add to the adrenaline I'm feeling.

"Absolutely," she says it with conviction. "I asked him directly if he said, 'they' and not 'him'. I knew you'd want to know."

I feel a slight pull at my heart at her desperate attempt to get back in my good graces. I miss her so much but I can't tell her that. I can't trust her. I'm even wary to believe this. "Thanks, Liz." I feign a small smile. I know it took courage for her to agree to meet me.

"I don't want you to be hurt again, Ivy." A single tear leaves her eye before she scoops it up with her index finger. "What I did to you was horrible. What I did to our friendship."

"It's too hard to talk about." I feel my own tears coming on strongly. I take a deep breath holding them in. "I should get going. Thanks again for coming down here to see me."

"I'd do anything for you." She manages a small smile. "One other thing I wanted you to know."

I steady myself for what she's about to share. I hope it's something related to Jax. I can't shake the idea that he collaborated with someone else to manipulate me into selling my part of Mark's company.

"I told Mark I can't ever see him again." Her voice is steady and strong. "It's over forever."

I feel let down by her proclamation. I don't care what she does or doesn't do with Mark at this point. I just nod in silence as I rise from my chair and walk straight towards the door and out of her life for good.

———

"IT'S NOT AS THOUGH I have anything of substance to report." I lazily kick the heel of my stiletto under Nathan's desk as I sit in the chair facing him. "Has there been any movement at all on the contract?"

"He doesn't want to give up Veray to you." The exasperation in his voice is evident. "I don't know why he's holding onto that so tightly. He bought into it less than a year ago and it's not pulling in a huge return for him at this point."

I shrug my shoulders. "Your guess is as good as mine as to why he won't let go of that."

"I do have a guess." He bows his head before he continues, "I think he's holding on to it because it's his last link to you. Well, you know, other than the sex."

I shudder at the mention of sex with Jax. "Actually, I ended that," I say it like I mean it but my body betrays the words. I've spent the last four days replaying each of my intimate encounters with Jax in my mind. I can't even imagine wanting anyone else.

"You ended it?" He sounds as puzzled as I feel inside about it.

"I went to see him as we discussed. You know to try and trick him into telling me something about what he might be hiding."

He nods. "Obviously it didn't go very well."

"It started off great but then I had an epiphany." I suck in my breath when I think about how Jax looked when I confronted him about being cheated on.

"An epiphany? What happened?"

"Mark cheated on me. It was devastating. It's why I ended things." I stop to gather my thoughts before continuing," I realized the other day that Jax was cheated on too."

"He told you that?" He presses for more information.

"He didn't have to. I saw it in his face. I could hear it in his words. He's scared of being cheated on again."

"Well, shit," Nathan exhales sharply. "That doesn't help at all."

"Sorry to disappoint, counselor," I tease as I rise from the chair. "Oh, wait, there was one other small thing but I don't think it's important."

"The devil's in the details, Marlow. What is it?" He laughs. "Everything matters when you're working on a deal this large."

"A mutual..."I pause when I realize that I can't refer to Liz as a friend. That's not who she is anymore. Can I say enemy? Or maybe betrayer? How about relationship wrecker?

"A mutual friend?" he offers.

"This woman who knows Jax's brother pretty well she told me that they had a discussion about him." I feel comfortable with that description of Liz.

"Ivy, don't leave me hanging here." He taps my fingers with his to bring my focus back to him. "What did this woman tell you?"

"She said that Jax's brother specifically said that they would do anything to get my portion of Mark's business away from me."

"So Jax and his brother did this together?"

"No." I sit again wanting to explain but not knowing how without revealing my relationship with Liz and Brighton. "They as in Jax and someone else. The brother said..." I raise my hands to empathize that I'm quoting Brighton. "They would do anything to get Mark's shares away from me."

"Ah, I get it now." He nods his head up and down.

"It's not an exact quote mind you. Don't get me to swear that's it in a court of law."

He laughs heartily. "Do you think it's significant? Or do you think it's more a lost in translation thing?"

I purse my lips together. "I have no idea. I'd ask Brighton, Jax's brother, but I found out he's in Europe right now."

"That's okay Detective Marlow." Nathan stands and reaches for me with his hand. "I'll take it from here."

CHAPTER TEN

"I DIDN'T EXPECT YOU TO CALL SO SOON." I BRUSH PAST HIM AS I WALK through the door of his apartment.

"I can't stand this." He shuts the door behind me. "I thought a lot about what you said to me."

I nod before I turn to walk into his apartment. I try to contain my excitement but I've been floating since he called a few hours ago to say he needed to see me. This is what I wanted. It's what I've been waiting for.

"Sit down, Ivy." He motions towards the couch before disappearing into the kitchen. I place my purse down softly on the coffee table and cross my legs. The black dress I chose is comfortable and crafted to hug each one of my curves. I want this night to end all of the scattered nonsense that has been clouding the space between us. I need it to.

He returns with two half-filled wine glasses in hand. He settles in close to me and hands one to me. I take a small sip before placing it down next to my purse. Getting tipsy makes my emotions tumble to the surface and that's the last thing I need tonight. I want him. I know he wants me. I just need him to open up and tell me what's really going on.

"You were right, beautiful." He lazily rests his right hand on my knee. "Someone did cheat on me."

I feel a surge of energy rush through me at the moment his hand makes contact with my skin. Stay focused Ivy. You can't get to the bottom of this if you're constantly thinking about what he can do to your body. "I thought so."

"It's still hard to talk about." He gulps most of the contents of his glass in one movement before placing it down next to mine. "I want to share."

"It will help." I rest my hand on his, stroking his index finger with mine. "It helped me to talk about what happened with Mark."

He nods and smiles softly. "I met her a few years ago. We worked together."

I feel a twinge of jealousy run through me. I wanted this. I wanted to know the truth but am I really prepared to hear him talk about how much he cared for another woman? How much she hurt him?

"She was different. Unlike anyone I'd met. Brash and direct. She made it clear right after we met that she wanted me. Most women aren't like that." He stops to lift the glass to his mouth again.

"Most women aren't like that," I repeat. I'm not like that. Was that why he was so indecisive with me?

"That's actually a good thing." He pulls my hand under his now and squeezes it. "She was nothing like you."

I nod, deciding right in that moment that I'd absorb that as a compliment. I needed to. They weren't together anymore so that meant something. It had to.

"I fell for her fast and hard." He breathes in a deep sigh before he continues, "it was bound to crash and burn at some point. I just didn't see it coming."

"What happened?" I ask tenderly. I know what it feels like to share details of a betrayal of that magnitude. I know how exposed and open I felt and I want Jax to know that I understand the depth of that pain.

"Things were going great," he admits. "I was crazy about her. It was one of the only times I've dated someone exclusively."

Again I feel the dark edge of jealousy rise within me. It's over.

That's what matters. I can't think about whether she meant more to him than I do. I can't cloud my judgement with petty thoughts like that. "She sounds very special," I say weakly.

"At the time I thought she was." He looks at me before raising his hand to brush away a wayward piece of hair that has fallen onto my cheek. "I didn't understand how special a woman could really be back then."

I blush knowing that he's now talking about his feelings for me. Despite everything that has happened between us I want him to want me. I want him to need me and maybe even love me.

"There was another guy we worked with." There's a slight edge to his voice now. "He was her boss. She did assistant work for him."

I nod not wanting to interrupt. I squeeze his hand coaxing him to continue.

"He was an arrogant bastard," he seethes. "He took whatever he wanted and he wanted her."

"I'm sorry." I stare at his face. His jaw is tightening, His eyes have clouded over. "How did you find out?"

"I didn't walk in on them or anything." He pulls back a touch and picks up the glass. He finishes what's left before he speaks again. "She actually just came right out and told me one day."

I pause before I respond. He wants me to respond I can sense it by his silence. "That takes courage," I offer.

He places the glass down before he turns so he's directly facing me. "She wasn't courageous. That wasn't it." He shakes his head and stares down at our entwined hands.

"Mark didn't tell me about any of them until I stumbled on an email," I say through gritted teeth. I'll never get used to saying that. It still stings each and every time I repeat it.

"I didn't realize that. Who was the email to?" he questions before standing to walk back into the kitchen to refill his wine glass.

"It's strange." I adjust my dress slightly as he sits back down next to me. "I can't remember her name now. Back then it felt so important and life changing. I guess I just blocked it out because I wanted to forget the entire thing."

"What did it say?"

"The email?" I take a small sip of wine to settle my anxiety over talking about Mark again.

He nods. "Do you remember what it said?"

"Not word-for-word anymore." I stare at the shape of his hand. It's so strong and unyielding. I love his hands. I love feeling his hands on me. "The point of it was that he was waiting for her in his hotel room. He sent it to me by mistake."

Something shifts slightly in his stance. His hand becomes more rigid. The tempered tone of his breathing changes. "Where was he when he sent that to you? Do you recall?"

"Yes," I whisper. "He was away on business. Chicago."

His breathing stalls briefly and he jerks his hand from mine. I sit silently while he finishes his second glass of wine in one large swallow. "How do you do it?" His voice is barely audible.

"Do what?" I lean in closer.

"Talk about it?" He turns to face me again.

I search his eyes for some semblance of understanding. "It helps me make sense of it all I guess."

"I hate her." I instantly see the tears welling in his eyes. "I hate what she did to me."

I just want to wrap him in my arms and cradle him next to me. "I know." I sense the tears rising to the surface now and I don't hold them back. "It's a horrible pain. That level of betrayal. I know."

He embraces me tightly, pulling my head into his chest. I hold him closely as sobs course through his body and mine.

"I would never hurt you like that." There's panic in his voice as he pulls away from me and grabs my shoulders with his hands. "Never. You know that. Tell me you know that, Ivy. Tell me."

I look deeply into his eyes. Everything has changed. The veil of darkness is gone. He's pleading. He's wanting. "I know," I say it with strength of belief in his words.

"I don't know how I deserve you." His lips claim mine and I hungrily pull him towards me. He scoops me up and carries me. I don't care where we're going. I don't care where we end up. This is where my heart needs to be.

He lays me gently on his bed before he pulls back and starts unbuttoning his shirt. I sit up. I reach for his belt. I need to taste him. I've wanted to for so long. I pull the belt from his slacks and deftly undo the zipper and clasp. I push them quickly to the floor and pull his magnificent cock into my hand. I stare at it. I love every part of him. I love all the pleasure he's given me.

"Oh, Jesus," he moans as my tongue circles the wide tip. I pull it into my mouth. As I gently run my tongue along the base of its crown, I feel it swell between my lips even more. I pull more of him into me. My hand gently stroking its entire length. He's so large. It's so much. I want to please him.

"That feels so good," he growls. He buries his hands in my hair, pushing me to take more. I slide him deeper within my mouth. Then pull him out. I lick the entire length. Soft gentle strokes, then harder. His hands pull lightly on my hair.

I take the length of him into my mouth now. I hollow my cheeks and I find my rhythm. I pleasure him. I'm stroking, licking, biting, tempting. I want to taste him. I need that so much.

"Stop." He pulls back abruptly. "I want to come inside of you." He's breathless as he claws at my clothes, his cock bobbing up and down in the air. I try to reach for it but he pushes me back. I'm undressed and so wet. So wanting. He pulls my body into his. I finally feel him in my hand again and I try to guide him inside of me. He flips me over in one fell swoop until I'm on top.

"Ride me." He pushes my body down until my wetness is pressed against him. "Use it. Use me."

I take him inside. I almost scream from the sensation. He holds tight to my hips. He pushes himself up from the bed. I press down. He's so deep within me. So deep.

"Jax, please." I move back and forth, pulling him deeper and deeper. "I need to come."

"Not now. Not yet," he commands.

I try to hold in my release. I lean down and run my tongue over his neck, down his chest. I take one of his nipples between my teeth. I feel his body tense. "I'm there," he screams. "Now, Ivy, now."

My body shakes as I feel him fill me with his desire. I collapse onto his chest. He wraps his strong arms around me and tenderly kisses the top of my head.

"I'm never letting you go."

"Never," I whisper.

CHAPTER ELEVEN

"WILL YOU GIVE IN ON THE VERAY ISSUE NOW?" I PLAYFULLY RUN MY finger around his nipple.

"After that, I'll give you anything you want, beautiful." He brushes his lips against mine again and I inhale his scent. I could spend all day every day with this man in this bed.

"I want the contract to be done." I perch myself up on one elbow so I'm looking directly at him. "I want us to get that out of the way."

"Me too." He tenderly runs his hand down my cheek. "I want that attorney of yours out of your life as soon as possible."

I laugh gleefully. "What is it about him?"

"Nothing." Jax winks at me. "I just don't want you hanging out with the guy."

"Let's see." I tap my index finger on his chest. "Could it be his broad shoulders and perfectly sculpted ass?"

He raises an eyebrow as he listens intently to me.

"No, maybe it's his gorgeous blue eyes. Or could it be his jet black hair?" I tease.

"He's a lawyer." Jax reaches for my hand and pulls it to his lips. "I don't trust them. You shouldn't either."

"He's a good guy." I frown. "I've known him since I was a kid."

"That doesn't make him trustworthy, beautiful." I feel his tongue trace a pattern across my palm. "It makes him an old friend, that's all."

"Speaking of old friends." I yank my hand from Jax's grasp. "I wanted to talk to you about something."

"Something more important than me ravishing your body one more time before I let you sleep?" He rolls over so he's facing me and I feel his semi-hard cock rub against my stomach. My arousal is instant.

"Yes." I moan as he pulls me to him. "Please, wait. I have to ask this."

"Ask what?" He glides his hardness over my mound. I feel it briefly brush my still swollen clitoris.

"What?" I ask as I greedily move my hips to try and pull him inside of me.

"Nothing," he says as his lips crush mine again. He growls as he enters me hard and fast.

I almost come the instant his fullness reaches its tip. I'm already aching from earlier. I can't take much more. He can push me to the edge of utter fulfillment so quickly. I start to move my hips to try to take even more of him in.

"That's it, Ivy." He responds in kind. He pulls me closer so every possible part of me that can be touching his naked body is. "Drink me in. Swallow me. Use me."

I speed up the pace of my hips. I fuck him harder. I pull him deeper. I can't get enough of him. I'll never get enough of him.

"Fuck, you're so tight." He pulls my bottom lip between his teeth as he lets out a deep guttural growl. "You're so wet. You're mine."

I come from the sound of his voice, from the feeling of him buried so deep within my body. I scream out his name as he pushes himself into me before his body shudders.

———

"YOU WERE GOING to ask me something earlier, weren't you?" He places the steaming mug of coffee down on the nightstand next to where I'm sitting on the bed. I'm wrapped in the sheet we just made love on.

"Do you always serve coffee in the nude?" I giggle as I pick up the mug.

"Be careful." He reaches to pull it away from me. "It's hot. Let it cool for a minute."

I pretend to pout as he sits next to me. I drink in the sight of his naked body. He's so comfortable sharing himself with me now. He's opened up. I can see it and I felt it when he took me into his bed.

"I need to go to Boston to see my dad." I purse my lips, knowing that it may be too early to bring this up but it's something I desperately want.

"You've never mentioned him before." He reaches for the mug now and takes a sip himself before placing it back down. "Is he alright?"

I take a deep breath. "He's fine. We were actually estranged for a few years."

He raises an eyebrow and I know instinctively that he wants more details about that.

"My Mark years." I wrinkle my nose hoping that will explain enough that I won't have to go into specifics.

"I like your father already." He reaches for the mug again and hands it to me after taking a sip of the steaming, fragrant coffee.

"I asked him to take the train here so we could talk about things and it went really well." I smile as I remember the huge bear hug my father had given me on the platform at Grand Central Station before boarding his train home.

"I'm glad." He rests his chin on my knees and stares into my eyes. "Family is really important."

"I agree." I reach for his hair and pull it through my fingers. He closes his eyes in response and lets out a faint moan. "That's why I wanted you to come with me to celebrate his birthday this weekend."

He snaps his head up so quickly that I have little time to react. I pull his hair by mistake and he yelps.

"I'm sorry." I giggle. "There should be a warning when you move like that."

He pulls his hand into a fist and playfully shakes it at me. "I should punish you for pulling my hair out." He reaches to rub his scalp.

"I'll kiss it and make it better." I pull my bottom lip out and whimper.

He launches his body towards me and I melt into his arms once again.

CHAPTER TWELVE

"WILL YOU COME WITH ME TO BOSTON THIS WEEKEND?" I PLACE MY left foot into the stiletto I dropped in the living room last night. I scan the floor looking for its partner.

"Is it really that important to you?" He comes around the corner dangling my wayward shoe from his finger. He kneels down and helps me slide my foot into it. Before he stands, he sensually runs his hand along my calf.

I look down at him before answering. "I want you to meet my father. I just want him to see that I've made a good choice in selling my shares to you."

He embraces my legs briefly before he pulls himself to a standing position again. "If you want me to be there, I'll be there."

"You don't know how much I appreciate that." I feel my heart leap. I know that we've made tremendous strides forward since last night but asking him to come home with me to meet my dad is something I didn't expect he'd agree to.

"I told you I'd do anything for you, beautiful." He leans forward and lightly brushes the tip of my nose with his lips. "I meant it."

"Well..." I fling my arms around his neck and nuzzle my face into his shoulder. "There is one more thing."

"Again, Ivy?" He starts to unbutton the perfectly pressed light blue dress shirt he put on not more than fifteen minutes ago. "You're insatiable but I'm not complaining."

I giggle as I impishly tap his hands away from his collar. "No, not that. I'd prefer to be able to move for the rest of the week so I'll take a rain check."

"What is it then?" He motions for me to sit on the couch. "And for the record, the rain check expires this evening so you'll need to cash it in before midnight."

"'Like a pumpkin?" I tilt my head to the left in mock confusion.

"Sure, Cinderella." He reaches for my hand and cradles it in his. "What is the one more thing?"

"This feels like a new beginning to me," I say it sheepishly. I don't want to assume that he's feeling the same hope in our future that I am.

"It's a new beginning for us." He tips my chin up so I'm looking directly at him. "Today is our new beginning."

"Thank you," I whisper. I shift slightly on the couch not because I'm uncomfortable physically but emotionally I feel uneasy about what I'm about to say next. "I saw Liz recently and we talked about you."

"Liz? Your friend who slept with Mark?"

The moment he says it I appreciate how ironic the words are. She was my friend and she did sleep with Mark. I just never imagined those two phrases would be joined together. "Yes. She came by my building a few weeks ago and said something about knowing secrets about you."

His gaze darkens. "What secrets could she possibly know about me?"

"I wondered about that too." I feel embarrassed by my confession. "So I asked her to meet me for coffee."

"Why would you put any faith in anything she said?" His voice is crisp and harsh.

"People lie sometimes. That doesn't make them horrible."

"Are we talking about her or me?" he demands.

"Her." I hesitate before continuing, "It wasn't as though she had something to tell me that was life altering."

"Of course she didn't." His body relaxes and he pulls my hand to his lips to give my palm a tender kiss. "She knows nothing about me."

"There was one small thing she said that I didn't understand." I want to clear the air completely. I want all of my doubts to evaporate and the only way I can do that is to ask him about it.

"What's that?" He peers past my hand to my face.

"She said that Brighton told her that you...well...that you and someone else...I think he meant someone else, were working together to get my shares." I stumble through the words knowing they make little sense to me and to him.

He drops my hand and I have little time to respond. It falls with a thud into my lap. A flash of panic washes over his eyes.

"What?" he whispers.

I feel the pit of my stomach drop. "Brighton told Liz that they were working to get my shares, not you, they."

"That's ridiculous," he scoffs. "Brighton is always putting his nose in where it doesn't belong."

"You reacted." I press the subject. I know I wasn't imagining the brief moment of alarm that washed over him. "When I said it, you were panicked."

"I was angry," he snaps. "Brighton has always stuck his nose into my business. His imagination runs wild and it's caused me nothing but problems in the past."

"I didn't know."

"Our relationship is strained, at best. A lot of that has to do with our mother. I don't want to get into that now but one day I'll explain why Brighton resents me." He stands now and straightens his tie.

I take that as my cue and I stand too. "One more thing, Jax."

"What is it, beautiful?" He reaches to adjust the collar of my dress.

"You're not hiding anything from me, are you?" I tilt my head to the side wanting to draw out anything that is left lingering within him that relates to me or Mark. "You've told me everything about the Mark stuff, right?"

His brow arches and he brushes his lips quickly and softly against mine. "I'm not holding anything back. I handled the Mark stuff like a royal asshole. I regret that. "

"Please don't hide things from me." I know I sound like I'm pleading. I know I likely sound pathetic but I don't care at this point. I can't move forward if this beautiful man in front of me is hiding anything else.

"I won't. I won't risk it." He pulls me into a tight embrace. "I can't lose you. I can't breathe without you."

CHAPTER THIRTEEN

I INSIST WE TAKE THE TRAIN TO BOSTON AND JAX USES THAT TIME TO temptingly tease me each moment he possibly can. By the time we arrive at my father's front door I'm feeling desirous, giddy and excited about how my father will react when he meets the man I'm crazy about.

"Promise me you'll behave," I say as I hold my finger over the doorbell of the humble home I grew up in.

"I promise," he says the words with a grin at the very same moment I feel his large hand grab my ass through my jeans.

"Princess, you're here." My father pulls me into a warm embrace when he opens the door. I hold tight to him. It's been years since I've been back and it's been longer since I felt so welcome.

"Dad, this is Jax Walker." I move aside so my father can get his first look at Jax.

"It's good to meet you, sir." Jax extends his hand and my father tentatively grabs it. He shakes it all the while giving Jax a thorough once over.

"Nice to meet you, Jax." My father motions for us both to come in.

"I'm going to show Jax where we'll stay and then we'll come down to visit. Is that okay?" I need to get Jax's first impression of my dad and I can't exactly do that with him standing directly in front of me.

"Sure." My father nods. "I'll brew up a pot of coffee for us."

"Follow me." I loop my arm through Jax's after he picks up both of our overnight bags. He follows me up the long staircase to the second floor of the brick townhouse I grew up in. "We're in here." I open the door and step through first.

"This is quaint, princess," he teases.

I throw my hands onto my hips and pretend to be disgruntled. "Cute, Mr. Walker."

"I love that your father calls you that." He scoops me into his arms and brushes his soft lips against mine. "I can't believe I'm standing in the house you grew up in."

"I can't believe it either." I move away from him and walk to the window. I glance down at the small backyard I used to play with my sister in. I run my hand along the faded fabric of the curtains. "My mother sewed them herself before I was born," I whisper.

"I want to know more about her." He comes up behind me, pulling my body into his. "I want to know all about young Ivy Marlow and how she became the amazing woman she is now."

I turn and bat my hand playfully against his broad chest. "There's not much to tell."

"I doubt that." He pulls on my earring. "You're the most fascinating person I've ever met. I want to know everything there is to know about you."

"Like what?" I look up into his eyes.

"Like what's your favorite flower?"

"Daisies," I answer immediately.

"What's your favorite color, what's your favorite book, what movies make you cry, what movies make you laugh..." he stops to catch his breath.

"Is that it?" I pull away and sit on the edge of the bed. It's covered with the same pattered bedspread that I used to dream on when I was a little girl.

"That's only the start." He sits down next to me.

"The inquisition will have to wait. We have a coffee date waiting for us."

"THERE'S one thing I'm foggy on, Jax." My dad stirs another teaspoon of sugar into his second cup of coffee. So far the conversation has been going well but that could change at the drop of a hat depending on which direction my father decides to steer things.

"What's that, sir?" Jax sips on his coffee. I can tell it's not up to his standards because he's barely touched it.

"Ivy tells me that you own part of Mark's business." He pushes the statement with an even tone.

"That's right." Jax nods and offers nothing beyond that.

"But she also said that you own part of that jewelry store that sells her trinkets." He leans slightly forward in his chair and I know that the horizon is about to change. Things are headed into darker territory.

"That's also correct." Again Jax is being vague. He's not going to elaborate on anything without some coaxing.

"How does that work?"

"What exactly do you mean?" Jax glances at his watch and I curse under my breath. He's becoming increasingly uncomfortable and we haven't even gotten into the hard questions yet.

"He owns a lot of different businesses, dad." I decide to move things along. I hope my answer will be enough to appease my father's curiosity.

"He can speak for himself." My dad isn't going to back down from this. "I want him to explain why he needs to take Mark's business away from him."

Jax clears his throat and shifts in his chair so he's facing my father directly. "I'm not taking it away from Mark, sir. I'm taking it back from him."

"What's the difference?" He isn't buying Jax's charm like most people do.

I feel Jax rest his hand on my thigh and give it a slight squeeze. "Mark and my father were partners for years." Jax takes a deep breath before he continues, "my dad died last year and when he did he asked me to take back control of the company because he felt Mark was neglecting it."

"Go on." My dad gestures with his hand for Jax to continue talking.

"I tried to talk reason with Mark but he wasn't receptive to that. I wanted us to work together to rebuild the company." Jax runs his finger along the chipped rim of his mug. "So I had to do what was necessary to get it back into my hands and Ivy is helping me with that."

"Do you think your dad would be proud of you?" There's a definite softness in my father's tone.

"I hope so." Jax peers beyond my father's gaze to the wall behind him. "That's what I hope for. That I can make him proud and save the company he worked so hard to create."

"I wish you luck with that." My dad rises from the table. "I'm going to rest for a bit now. I'll see you at the restaurant later for the party?"

"We'll be there." I stand to embrace him. "Thank you, dad," I whisper in his ear.

He only nods as he walks out of the room.

———

"YOU'RE WEARING that to my father's birthday party?" I clasp my hand over my mouth as I stare at Jax.

"Um, yeah. Why?" he says smugly with a hint of humor running beneath it.

"You look like a clown." I throw it out there. He does. He's wearing a bright red shirt, jeans and a somewhat tattered and torn paper hat with the words Happy Birthday emblazoned across the front of it.

"So, you don't like red?" He pulls on the hem of the shirt.

I don't respond. I only tilt my chin up slightly in the direction of the hat on his head.

"Oh," he says it with mock surprise. "The hat? You don't think it matches the outfit?"

"Where did you get it?" I turn back around towards the mirror on the wall to finish applying my mascara.

"In your closet." He gestures towards the tiny closet in the corner of the room. "It's full of treasures."

I stare at his reflection in the mirror. "What treasures? What's in there?"

"You don't want to know." He pulls on the elastic strap that runs beneath his chin to hold the hat in place. As he releases it, it snaps back and he jumps.

I can't help but laugh at his pained expression.

"Maybe I need to lose the hat?" He gingerly pulls it off his head and studies it. "Where did it come from?"

"The paper hat factory?" I beam.

"Funny girl." He moves to kneel in front of me now. "Did you wear it when it was your birthday when you were a child?"

"Every year." I smile gently at him.

"Every year? Why?" He looks puzzled.

"We didn't have much money. I got the hat at a friend's party so I brought it out each year on my birthday and on my sister's birthday and we wore it." I exhale sharply. It's both a difficult and joyous memory. "I just wish my mother had been there to see me wear it."

He kisses the tip of my nose before he carefully places the hat on my head. "It's perfect." He grins.

I reach to remove it. "It's not my birthday, I can't wear it today."

"Don't." He stops my hand in mid-air. "Today is your birthday to me."

"What does that mean? You're not going to take a picture of me in this funny hat, are you?" I tilt my head to the side and purse my lips together.

"No." He rolls back on his heels. "I'm going to give you something. Don't move."

My heart starts racing as I watch him walk towards his bag. He fumbles through the clothing and pulls out a long, rectangular box. It's wrapped in gold paper and tied with a delicate lace ribbon.

"Happy Birthday, beautiful." He kneels before me again and places it in my lap.

I stare at the box, transfixed by its beauty. The paper glimmers in the soft afternoon light coming through the window. I gently pull on the edge of the ribbon and it falls off. I look up at him and he's sporting a wide grin. "What is it?" I whisper under my breath.

"Open it and find out." He kisses my cheek and then rests his head against mine so we can watch the unveiling together.

I remove the paper and open the deep blue velvet box. The contents steal my breath away. It's one of my necklaces but it's different. I pull it from the box and study it closer. It's a round gold pendant that I had emblazoned with several small crystals. There had been six but now there are many more and they're not crystals, they're a brilliant blue. They dance in the light.

"Do you recognize it?" Jax's breath washes against my cheek.

"Yes. I think I do." I cradle it in my palm. "It's different than I remember."

"There are twenty-six stones now. Twenty-six sapphires." He points to one of them.

"They're beautiful." I'm struggling to understand the significance of them.

He leans back now and cradles my face in his hands. "I was born in September. Those sapphires represent the twenty-six years I had to live without you."

My body trembles and I can't see. I sob audibly.

'No, no." He presses his lips to the tears. "No tears."

I nod although I can't stop the overwhelming emotions I'm feeling.

"It's something that we made together. Something you can keep close to you." He pulls it from my hand and clasps it around my neck. "Do you like it?"

"I love it." I smile through my tears, "I love..." I stop myself I can't say that yet.

"I love you too, Ivy."

CHAPTER FOURTEEN

"HOLY HELL, IT'S HOT IN HERE." JAX INSTANTLY BREAKS A SWEAT when he walks into my apartment after our train ride back to the city. "Why didn't you turn on your air conditioner before we left?"

"It's broken." I pull an elastic band from the drawer of the foyer table so I can put my hair into a ponytail. "I'll open some windows."

"How long has it been like this?" He fans himself with one of the newspapers he picked up with my mail.

"I'm not sure. At least a week." I pull open the weathered latch on the window and push it upwards to open it. The warm midday air comes rushing in. "Great, it's hotter outside than it is in here. This isn't going to help."

"You can't stay here." He marches into the kitchen.

"It's fine." I flip through my mail as he walks back in with two chilled water bottles in hand.

"I almost climbed into the refrigerator." He laughs. "It's not fine. You can't live here."

"I can and I do." I trace my finger along the edge of an envelope that is emblazoned with stickers claiming I'm a guaranteed prize winner.

"Gather some things. You're coming to my place." It's a demand that he's trying to veil as a request.

"I'm really okay here." I toss the letter into the trash. "All of my work is here and I'm falling behind."

"Beautiful, you should come live with me." He grabs both my hands in his. "Just move in with me."

I'm stunned into silence. He is actually asking me to leave this apartment and move into his? This is moving too quickly. Just days ago I was certain he was nothing but a lying, conniving, cutthroat, power hungry bastard. Now I'm going to move in with him?

"It makes perfect sense." He leans over to pick up my mail and shove it into my overnight bag. "Grab whatever else you need for tonight and I'll send someone over tomorrow to finish packing your things."

"No." I shake my head weakly. "No. I can't."

"You will." He pulls out his phone and points his finger to silence me. "Leonard, come get us at Ivy's. Come up to her apartment. We're bringing some of her things home."

"So that's that?" I stomp my foot. "I don't get to decide?"

"What is there to decide?" He walks down the hallway towards my bedroom.

"What if I want to stay here?" I have to almost run to keep up with his large steps.

He pulls one of my large suitcases from the closet. "Fill this up."

"Jax. Stop." I pull his hands so he'll sit next to me on the bed. "This is overwhelming. I can't think."

"Beautiful, I love you. I don't want to waste any more time away from you. You can't stay here. The air is so thick and hot. It's not good for you. Come and be with me." He scoops up a bead of sweat that is running down my forehead.

"It's really too soon," I say it without any conviction.

"According to who?" He gently pulls at the necklace reminding me of how tender and loving he is.

"I need some time here to gather my stuff together." I search his face for some understanding. "I want to talk to Mrs. Adams too."

"I understand." He stands. "I got a little ahead of myself. It's hard not to." He leans down and brushes his lips against my forehead.

"I want to live with you," I whisper the words under my breath.

"Why don't you take whatever time you need to get organized and I'll come get you when you're ready? Does that work for you?" He kneels in front of me now.

"Yes, thank you." I kiss him softly before I wipe the sweat from his brow.

"I'll get Leonard to bring over some floor fans." He winks. "I don't want to come back and find you melting."

I laugh as I wrap my arms around his neck.

———

"I'M GOING to move in with a friend." I hand Mrs. Adams a tall glass of water.

"That makes me smile, dear." She reaches for the glass and I notice her hand trembling.

"I'm going to really miss you." I know that I'm going to cry. "But I'll come back every Saturday to get your groceries and help you run errands."

"I'd love that." Her eyes well with tears. "You've been like a daughter to me, Ivy."

"You've helped me so much." I sob now, knowing that I'll miss her terribly. I'll miss the way she woke me too early in the morning to share mundane gossip with me and I'll miss the biting comments she throws at me when she thinks I'm being too flirty or risqué.

"I worry about you." She pats me hand with her own. "I worry that you're going to have your heart broken again."

"Not this time." I pull on the necklace so it's closer for her to see. "He gave me this."

"Who did?" She's genuine with the question.

"The hippie." I laugh.

She bursts out laughing. "Rex did? He turned out to be a good boy after all."

I smile at the fact that she can't remember Jax's name. "We worked through everything."

"I hope he'll be your Mr. Adams." She reaches to touch my cheek. "You need that, dear."

I press my palm over her hand. "I want that."

CHAPTER FIFTEEN

"I'M NOT SURE WHAT YOU SAID TO HIM, BUT JAX'S ATTORNEY CALLED me this morning and said we're good to go with the contract exactly as you want it." Nathan motions for the waiter.

"That's such great news." I smile at him before directing my attention to the young man who rushed over. "Just an iced tea would be great."

"So, that's it. You're going to be part owner of Veray Jewelers. How does that feel?" He claps his hands together as a wide grin runs over his lips.

"Promising and exciting," I say as I soak in the ambiance of the restaurant he chose for our celebratory lunch.

"Have you been here before?" He leans his elbow on the table and scans his smartphone quickly.

"No. This place is new for me, but I really like it." I'm being genuine. It's earthy and casual. I like the atmosphere and I can tell from the content looks on the other diners' faces that the food is delicious too.

"I did some digging." Nathan leans back again in his seat and crosses his legs.

"What kind of digging?" I nod to the waiter as he places the large glass of iced tea with lemon down in front of me.

"We'll need a few more minutes with the menu," he coolly says. "I'll let you know when we're ready."

"Digging?" I repeat. My curiosity is definitely peaked at this point.

"Remember that confusing comment you got wind of? Something about the fact that more than one person was trying to take over Mark's business?"

"I already asked Jax about that. He said it was nothing." I take a long sip of the tea. It's welcome given that I walked here from my apartment and I'm feeling extra parched.

"He said it was nothing?" he asks. His expression speaks of some confusion. "And you believe him?"

"Things have changed between us" I absentmindedly run my fingers over the necklace Jax gave me. "We went to see my dad this past weekend for his birthday."

"You were in Boston?" He smiles broadly. "I was there too. I wish I'd have known that. I could have taken you to see Sandra."

I sigh. "I hadn't even thought of that. Dammit. Does she ever come to visit you here?"

He shakes his head. "Nope. It's too hard for her with the kids."

"I'll give her a call then." I reach for my phone. "Can you give me her number?"

He rattles off her phone number by heart and I make a mental note to text her after lunch. I'm definitely going to stop by to see her next time I visit my dad, hopefully with Jax in tow.

"Back to that comment, Ivy." He's being cautious. I can tell. "I don't want to overstep any boundaries."

"Did you find out anything concrete about it?" I ask even though I don't want to know. I can't imagine he's learned anything that will surprise me. I asked Jax point blank about it and he assured me that there was no one else involved in his quest to get my shares.

"Nothing with actual evidence." He finishes his martini. "I did ask around."

"Are you ready to order?" I feel slightly panicked inside. Everything is so perfect at this point. I don't want him to throw something at me that will make me question Jax's honesty. I've pushed and pushed Jax on that and I'd know if he was being dishonest.

"Sure." He motions again for the waiter and we both relay our orders. His phone rings and he excuses himself to take the call. I glance down at my phone and scan through the numbers. I stop at Jax's. Part of me wants to call him just so I can hear his voice and he can reassure me that the necklace holds as much meaning as I believe it does. He wouldn't have given it to me if he was still being deceitful. I would have seen that within his eyes when he looked at me last night when we were making love.

"Sorry about that, Ivy." Nathan sits down again. He obviously stopped at the bar given the fact that he's got another martini in his hand. "As I said I was asking around about Jax."

"It's really okay, Nathan." I hold up my hand to stop him. "I've asked Jax about it and I do trust him."

"You should hear this. You need to know it especially if you're involved personally with him again." His words have a biting tone to them and I feel an undercurrent of something else.

"You don't approve of him, do you?" I push the question at him.

"No. He's a smug, arrogant ass." He takes a large drink from his glass. "You shouldn't trust him either."

"I'm not hungry anymore." I stand to leave. "We weren't supposed to get personal with this, remember? Strictly client and attorney."

"Don't let your feelings blind you." He doesn't move a muscle. "You did that with Mark. Don't make that mistake again."

"You have no right to say that." I pick up my purse and turn to leave.

"You're still that little girl I chased when I was a kid," he calls after me. "Don't let him steal that part of you away."

———

"I CAN'T IMAGINE what you think we have to talk about, Mark." I push past him towards the bank of elevators as I nod in Oliver's direction.

"Jax Walker." The way he says his name cuts into my bones. I can't stand Mark and I don't want to hear him even utter the name of the man I'm in love with.

"What about him?" I ask impatiently as I press the call button.

"We're not doing this here." He reaches for my elbow to push me into the elevator car that's just arrived.

"Don't you dare touch me," I sneer. "Ever." I'm already irritated from my meeting with Nathan and now I have to deal with Mark and all his incessant ramblings.

"Get in, Ivy." He walks past me into the car and I have no choice but to follow. "You need to hear this whether you want to or not."

"I'm so sick of this bullshit." I push past him when we reach the third floor and I fumble with my keys. My hands are trembling. This push and pull between Jax and Mark is wearing and I just want the feud to be over. I'm tired of being caught in the middle of it.

"What the hell is going on?" he demands after stepping into the apartment. "What are all these boxes for?"

"I'm moving," I announce nonchalantly. "I'm leaving this afternoon."

"You're not moving in with him? Ivy, tell me that's not it." He's pleading with me now.

I turn to face him. He's still looking as tired as ever. The peach colored polo he's wearing doesn't help his pale complexion. His jeans hang on his hips loosely. His world is crumbling and his outward appearance isn't masking that at all. "My air conditioning broke. I need a place to stay so for the time being I'm moving in with Jax."

"Don't do that." His voice is impassioned. "I know I'm not someone who can tell you what to do but this is a huge mistake."

"Why? Why Mark?" I spit the words with disdain at him. "You don't get to have an opinion on this. You made that choice when you decided to fuck my best friend."

"Grow up." His eyes glaze over with anger. "Wake up. Can't you see what's going on?"

"You're talking about the company, aren't you?" I push the words towards him with a hint of entitlement. "You hate that I'm handing control of your precious company to Jax."

"I could care less about that at this point." He runs his hand through his greying hair. "Do what you want with those shares. I don't give a fuck."

I twirl around to face him directly now. "You're kidding, right?" I chuckle. "That company is what you live for. Well that and bedding as many women as possible."

"Shut up," he snaps. "Just shut the hell up and listen to me."

"No." I march towards the door and fling it wide open. "Get out. You shouldn't have come here."

"I'm not leaving until you hear me out." He stomps his foot as though that will intimidate me enough that I'll slam the door and sit down to listen to him.

"Ivy, what's going on?" Mrs. Adams weak voice calls to me from her doorway.

"It's nothing. Go back inside," I call back to her. The last thing I need right now is Mark getting into a shouting match with her.

"I'm going to call the police," she yells back towards me. "They'll come take him away."

"Don't you dare do that." Mark lunges past me and down the hallway.

She quickly slams her door and he turns again to look at me before pressing the elevator call button.

"Don't bother me again." I start to close the door.

"Ask him about Brooke."

"Who?" I feel my pulse quicken at the mention of a woman's name in relation to Jax.

"Brooke." His mouth curves into a tainted smile. "Ask him."

"Wait." I march forward to press the call button holding the car on my floor. "Just tell me, Mark. Who is Brooke?"

"I'm not hanging around here." He reaches outside the car to push my hand from its place. "Apparently the police are on their way and you're not worth the trouble."

"Whatever," I spit back as I take a step away from the closing doors.

His hand bolts to hold the doors open. "Oh, and sweetheart, keep those keys. You'll be back here soon enough."

————

"I EMPTIED the top two drawers in my dresser so you can put your unmentionables in there," he teases.

"Unmentionables? Like my dildos?" I twist my lips together and roll my eyes.

Jax blushes. I've never seen that happen and I'm smitten with how genuinely embarrassed he looks. "I meant your lingerie, but I guess if you brought..." his voice trails as I reach up to kiss him softly.

"I didn't bring anything unmentionable with me." I walk over to where he's placed my suitcase on the bed. "Just these panties and things." I hold them up and he takes them, tucking them neatly away in the top drawer.

My confrontation with Mark keeps ringing through my ears but after he left I spent time saying goodbye to Mrs. Adams. She had convinced me that Mark was just being petty and throwing random names at me to try to jar me into distrusting Jax. She pointed out that Mark had lost and had always been a sore loser. Besides, I didn't want to begin my new life with Jax with a barrage of questions about some woman I wasn't even sure existed. If Mark ever gave me any real, concrete proof of this Brooke person and her involvement with Jax, I'd bring it up.

"Ivy, are you listening?" He's bent his knees so his gaze directly aligns with mine.

"Yes. Well, actually no." I giggle. "I was daydreaming."

"About all the fun we're going to have in this bed when I get back from my meeting?" He adjusts the necklace so the pendant is dangling loosely between my breasts.

"Can't we have fun before your meeting?" I suggestively pull on the sash of my dress causing it to fall open. "I bought these new unmentionables just for you."

His gaze slowly runs the length of my body, stopping to drink in the sight of the new black bra and panties I ordered a few weeks ago. He pulls me to him and I shrug the dress from my shoulders. His lips claim mine and I feel his tongue expertly caress mine just as his hand reaches my breast. "I can't," he whimpers into my mouth.

I pull back and unhook the clasp at the front of my bra causing my full breasts to rub against his shirt. "My nipples are so hard. Just look." I lean back slightly so he can get a full view of me running my hands over my breasts. I stop to pull on both nipples.

"Fuck." He falls to his knees and takes both breasts into his hands. His mouth clamps down on the left and I flinch when I feel his teeth pull at my nipple. "I have to go. I can't miss this."

I lean back until the back of my knees hit the bed. I let myself fall backwards while he's still settled on the floor. "I'll have to take care of this myself then." I push my hand into my panties and across my very wet cleft. "I'll think of you." I close my eyes as I hear him rustling.

"Hell," he growls as I feel the panties being ripped from me. His mouth finds my clit immediately and he hungrily licks and bites it. He pushes his hands under my ass, pulling my center into him. He knows how close I am. He knows I need this.

"Come for me," he whispers and his breath pushes me over the edge. I reach my climax instantly and intensely. My entire body shudders and he holds me as I slowly push myself back into the bedding.

"I'll never get enough of you." He kisses me tenderly on the forehead as he pulls a light blanket from the foot of the bed to cover me. "Sleep now. I'll be back as soon as I can. I love you, Ivy."

"I love you, Jax," I tell him softly as I drift off, his footsteps lulling me to sleep.

CHAPTER SIXTEEN

I AWAKEN TO THE SOUND OF MY PHONE RINGING. THE MOMENT I OPEN my eyes I realize I'm in unchartered territory. I'm in Jax's bed, naked. I scramble from the bed to search for my smartphone. I find it resting on top of my clothing in my still unpacked suitcase.

"Hello," I mutter into it.

"Ivy?" Jax sounds concerned. "Are you all right?"

I hold the phone away from me so I can clear my throat. "I'm okay. I just woke up."

"Just now?" he chuckles.

I scan the room looking for a clock but I don't find one. I realize that the sun is setting so I must have been asleep for much of the afternoon. "I've been asleep for hours, haven't I?"

"You have." He sighs. "I like that. It means you're comfortable in our place."

I smile when he says 'our.' My mind may still be questioning whether this is moving too fast after everything we've been through but my heart is winning that battle. This bed, this man's heart and this life is where I belong now.

"I'm going to be another hour or so," he says it with resignation. "I'm doing my best to get out of here as quickly as possible."

"That's okay." I try to veil my disappointment. "I'll take a shower and wait for you."

"No," he says it boldly. "You'll wait for me to shower. I want to shower with you every day."

"I'd love that. I'll make myself something to eat."

He laughs. "That's impossible. There's no food in the house."

"Nothing?"

"Stale cheese and bread would be all that's on the menu." There's definite amusement in his voice.

"I'm not that adventurous. I'll get dressed and go grab something." I stand and search in the darkness for my panties.

"There's a desk in the office. All the takeout menus are there. Choose something and put it on my account."

"Which place?" I turn on the bedroom light and I'm instantly blinded by the bright light.

"Any of them." He hesitates before continuing, "I eat out a lot."

"Should I wait for you?" I finally find my hidden panties.

"No. Order two of what you want and I'll eat when I get home."

I smile when I hear those words. I'm in his home. Our home. This is the first night of our new life. "I miss you."

"I miss you, beautiful. I'll be there as soon as I can."

———

I DRESS AGAIN EVEN though my body is craving the warmth of a shower. I want to wait for Jax for that. I promised I would and the notion of the two of us showering together every day is heavenly to me.

I wander down the hallway in search of his office. I haven't ventured this far into his apartment before and I'm awestruck by the art work that lines the walls. It's obvious that some of it is Brighton's but others are more vibrant and have so much more life to them.

I flick on the light switch in the office and I'm greeted by a large oak desk and a library of books covering two walls. I stand still and just drink it all in. This is his life. These are his books and the place where he comes to work. He's let me in and I'm never going to leave.

I sit behind the desk and giggle once I realize my feet don't touch the floor. The chair is luxurious tanned leather. I take in a deep breath and the scent of his skin wafts through the air. I pull open the top drawer of the desk. It's filled with assorted pens, business cards and a few coins.

I move to the left and pull open the top drawer on that side. I laugh out loud when I see just how many takeout menus there are. I gather them into my hand and pick them up. I'll look through them and choose something I know Jax will enjoy.

The silence is shattered by a sharp bump. Something must have fallen from between all the menus. I look down and don't notice anything. I push the chair back and fall to my knees to retrieve whatever it is. I don't want to lose anything that is important to him.

The natural light in the room is fading and the light fixture on the ceiling isn't throwing enough light in my direction for me to see under the desk. I wave my hand blindly beneath it and come up empty handed. I'm impressed by the lack of dust although I can't imagine Jax on his hands and knees doing any housecleaning. I smile at the thought of that.

I reach back onto the desk to retrieve my smartphone. I'll use the light from that to continue my search. I'm beginning to doubt that I dropped anything but I have to be certain. I shine the light in my line of sight and I'm instantly rewarded. It bounces off something shiny that's a few inches farther than my reach. I lie on my belly and stretch for it. I finally have it within reach. I grab it with just the tips of my fingers and finally scoop it into my palm.

I sit back down. I place the flash drive next to the pile of takeout menus. I fan them out so I can look them over. My eyes run across them all waiting for something to jump out at me. It does. It's not the Chinese food restaurant that proclaims to have the best egg rolls in all of Manhattan and it's not the Italian bistro that uses only homemade meat sauce like your mama used to make. My appetite is lost in an instant. The moment my gaze settles on the flash drive and what's written on it, I can't even fathom the thought of eating anything.

Brooke. That's all that's written across it in dark lettering. Brooke.

I close my eyes. Mark couldn't have been right. He was so smug and boastful. He knew about her. He knew about the woman this flash drive contains information on. I pick it up and hold it gingerly in my palm. Brooke. It can't be her, can it? How would Mark know about the woman who broke Jax's heart? Was her name Brooke? Why hadn't he offered her name? Why the hell didn't I ask her name?

I push the takeout menus to the floor so that I can open Jax's laptop. I flip the cover open and the screen pops to life. I stare at the flash drive. My gaze shifts back to the computer. I shouldn't. I should put it back and ask about her.

I slowly pull the cover back from the drive and hold it next to the USB port on the side of the laptop. He said he didn't have any secrets. There can't be anything on here that will shock me. He would have told me. He promised.

I push the drive in and the computer begins to whir and whine. The light on the flash drive flickers and my heart stalls. I wait with baited breath. A box pops up prompting me to open a folder. I hover my finger over the enter key. I know when I press it I can't turn back. I lower my finger and close my eyes.

A video screen appears and I'm instantly struck with the image of Jax in a bed. He's naked save for a white sheet covering his groin. He's talking to someone off camera. I turn up the volume and crane my neck towards the speaker hoping to hear what's being said.

"Do you think this is good, handsome?" The unmistakable sound of a woman's voice bursts through the speaker.

I pull back and clench my hands against the edge of the desk.

"It's perfect, angel. Now get in bed." Jax motions for her to come in his direction.

She pops onto the screen. She's wearing lingerie. She's tall, brunette, and strikingly beautiful. She's Brooke. I know it without him saying her name.

"You're so naughty, Jax." She snuggles in next to him pulling the sheet over her body. "I can't believe you want to tape us making love."

Tears instantly flow from my eyes. I know that I should turn it off now. I don't want to watch him making love to anyone else. I don't want to know if he did the same things to her that he's done to me.

"You're so gorgeous," he says it while staring directly at her. "How could I not want to watch you coming over and over again?"

"You're amazing." She kisses him then and I turn away. He's going to make love to her. He recorded it and kept it.

"No, you're the amazing one. I'm still in awe of how far you've gotten with Mark."

I twist the chair back around. I strain to hear the recording. Did Jax just say Mark's name to her?

"You've made no progress with Ivy yet, have you?" She traces a path down his chest with her finger. "Remember, you're not allowed to fuck her."

I feel faint. This isn't happening. She didn't just say that to him.

"Why would I do that? I have you, Brooke." He grabs her hand in his and brings it to his mouth.

"Do you think I'm blind?" She throws her head back with a hearty laugh. "I saw the way you were staring at her at the gala last night. You want her."

"I want her shares." He grabs both of her arms and holds them over her head. "Just her shares. Don't forget that's what this is about, angel."

"How could I possibly forget?" Her voice has taken on an overly sweet tone. "I seduce Mark. Then I blackmail him into giving me some of his shares. You seduce Ivy into selling her shares to you and we take over. I get half and you get half and they get nothing. Your father would be so proud of you, Jax."

He pushes her harder onto the bed. "Of us, angel."

"And what's our number one rule?" He brushes his lips against her forehead as she moves beneath him.

"No sex with Mark. No sex with Ivy."

"You belong to me," he purrs. "Only me."

A loud crash breaks my concentration and I almost fall from the chair. I turn to the side and through my veil of tears I see Jax. A broken vase is at his feet. Daisies scatter the floor.

PART THREE

OBSESSED

Part Three of
The Obsessed Series

Deborah Bladon

CHAPTER ONE

THE DAISIES. THEY'RE STREWN EVERYWHERE. THEY LOOK LIKE A SCENE from a highway crash when vehicles are thrown about from the sheer force of the impact. Some are bent, others are broken. I have to pick up the daisies.

I slam the laptop shut and drop to my knees in silence. I don't flinch when a piece of the broken vase wedges into my knee. The crimson line that mars the water on the floor breaks its flawlessness. There's no pain. I can't feel anything. My chest is tight. It's as if my heart has wrapped itself up inside a cocoon.

"Ivy, stop." Jax's voice is faint. It sounds muffled. I can't hear.

I pick up one of the daisies and hold it between my fingers. It falls over. The life has suddenly been heaved from it. It can't be saved.

"You're bleeding. Get up." He's closer now. He's standing over me. I can't look. "Say something." He's reaching for my hand. My voice isn't there. I can't pull it from me.

"I'm going to get a towel for your leg." There's a crunch of glass as he pads over the vase crushing the fragments of it, mutilating the remaining daisies.

I push myself up off the floor, the daisy still dangling from my fingers. I reach for my phone on the desk. My eyes fasten on the flash drive. I pull it from the side of the laptop and clench it firmly in my fist.

"Let me see your leg." He's there at the door again, a white towel hanging from his hand.

I walk past him. My leg is wet. I look down and there's blood. I have bandages at my apartment. I need to go home.

"You're cut. I have to fix it." He's pulling on my shoulder. I don't turn. I keep walking.

"I can explain what you saw." There's desperation in his tone. Not like the tenderness that was there when he was talking to Brooke. Mark was right. There was a Brooke. Liz was right. They did work together to take the company. Nathan knew. They all knew.

"I'm going home," I whisper. I think I whisper. My voice is barely audible. It's echoing in my ears.

"You can't. You're not going anywhere," he says.

"Home," I repeat. I move through the door of the bedroom. I pull my suitcase open and throw the flash drive in. I flinch when I realize he's on his knees, dabbing the towel against my leg. I drop the daisy to the floor when I pull my leg back harshly.

The suitcase slams shut. His hand rests on top of it. "You need to sit down. You're bleeding. You're upset," he says hoarsely. "It's not how it looks."

I pull my chin up. My eyelids are heavy. I look past him to the bedroom wall. "Home, now." I tug the words from somewhere deep within me. I slip my feet into my shoes that had fallen next to the bed when he gave me so much pleasure earlier. So much pleasure then and so much pain now.

"Please stay," he pleads. "You don't understand."

I pull the handle of the suitcase. His hand falls away. "I understand," I mutter as I jerk the zipper shut.

His hand glides through the air. He's going to touch me. I pull back and the suitcase falls to the floor with a dense thud. He stops.

His shoulders slump forward. "No, you can't understand. I have to explain."

"I understand," I mumble as I turn to walk out of the room, the suitcase's wheels haphazardly skidding along the hardwood floor. "Brooke and you. I understand. You..."

"Brooke means nothing to me," he cries. "Just stop and listen. There's more on that flash drive. Come back to my office." He's begging now.

"No." I feel defeated. I don't have the energy to care. "She belongs to you. Only you," I murmur.

"You belong to me." He exhales loudly.

I shake my head violently from side-to-side. "You make me sick."

"She means nothing to me." He blocks my path. "You don't understand what you saw."

I close my eyes. I can't comprehend what he's saying. He thinks I'm that naïve. He thinks I'll believe him over what I saw with my own two eyes. "I know what I saw." I push on his chest with one hand.

"No, you don't," he hisses. "You didn't see it all."

"I saw more than enough." The shock that overtook me after hearing the conversation between Jax and Brooke is now rapidly being replaced by anger. "Get the hell out of my way. I'm done."

"Come with me now, Ivy." His hand is pulling on my forearm. "You're going to watch it. All of it."

I pull my hand back so violently that it slams against his chest. "Fuck you, Jax." I swing open his apartment door and pull my heavy suitcase through. "You're disgusting."

He falls to his knees in the doorway. "Don't do this." His voice is breaking. "You can't leave me."

"Watch me." I turn to step into the hallway.

"I love you," he whispers through sobs.

"How dare you?" I turn back around to glare at him. I follow the path of his eyes to my chest and my fingers settle on the necklace he gave me. The beautiful necklace I stare at in the mirror each morning as I brush my teeth and put on my makeup.

"I do." He reaches to wrap his arms around my legs.

I take a step into the hallway. "You're such a fucking liar," I scream the words at him. I twist my fingers around the pendant. I feel the cut of the delicate chain into the back of my neck as the metal breaks free.

"It's all been a lie." I launch the pendant and chain into the air before turning toward the stairs.

––––––––

"I'M LEAVING NEW YORK." I trace my index finger along the inner seam of the jeans I'm wearing.

"You're going to have to explain that decision." Nathan motions towards me with a bottle of water. "Thirsty?"

I nod and sigh. "It's complicated."

"Does it have to do with your boyfriend?" His eyes dart up from his computer.

I pause before I answer. "I don't have a boyfriend."

"What are you calling him now? Your lover?" If he's attempting to hide the amusement in his voice it's not working.

I clench my teeth together and let out a puff of air. "A self-absorbed, malicious, son of a bitch?"

"Ouch." He feigns grabbing his chest in mock distress. "That's harsh, especially for you, Ivy."

"He's an asshole." I unscrew the top of the bottle and take a heavy swallow. I know that if I'm going to get what I want I have to confide at least a little in Nathan. I'm hoping that I won't have to share all of the sordid and ugly details of Jax's underhanded plan to take over Mark's company.

He peers at me for a few moments before he speaks. "You didn't call this emergency meeting to tell me Jax is a prick, did you?"

I shake my head slowly from side-to-side. "The deal hasn't been finalized, has it?"

"All that's left is your signature on a few stacks of papers and you're home free." He picks up a manila folder that is stretched well beyond its limits with assorted documents.

"I want to see what Mark will offer for my shares," I say it calmly even though I can hear the constant pounding of my heart echoing in my ears.

His eyes jump from the papers he's hunting through to my face.

"What do you mean you want to see what Mark will give you? Jax gave you everything asked for."

"It's not enough." I pull a deep breath from my lungs. It's only been two days since I saw the video of Jax and Brooke. I've been teetering on the edge of an emotional abyss since that moment and I'm going to do everything in my power to pull myself back from that ledge. The dozens of calls and texts from Jax that I've ignored haven't helped. "I want Mark to make me an offer."

"The deal's been finalized." He leans back in his office chair, gripping his hands on the armrests. "Why would we bring Mark in now?"

"He should have a chance to buy my shares." I uncross my legs and stand. "I don't care who owns the company. I just want to get as much out of this as I can."

He turns in his chair to follow me to the bank of windows. "You're saying you're willing to sell your shares to Mark if he offers you more than Jax?"

"Yes." I lean against the windowsill. "I just want the best possible deal so I can start a new life in Boston."

"Ivy. What the hell is going on?" He stands now wrenching his hands together. "You're not telling me everything."

"I'm the pawn in an ugly and bitter war between Jax and Mark." I bite my lip trying to pluck the last bit of remaining strength I have from within me. "Neither of them cared about me. Why should I care who wins their battle?"

He studies my expression. His eyes scan mine looking for a clue. I know he's searching for any hint that may explain my hasty decision to involve Mark.

"You can contact Mark's attorney, can't you and find out if he's interested?" My gaze falls to the floor. I want to get through this meeting without the humiliation of having to admit I have a flash drive in my purse that contains a near naked confession from Jax admitting he and his lover tried to manipulate Mark's company away from him.

"Of course." He tilts his head to the side. "What about Veray? You were dead set on getting that away from Jax. Mark can't offer you that."

"I don't care about that anymore." I try to ground the words in sincerity but his expression speaks of his doubt. "You can tell Jax and his attorney I don't want it."

"Now, that I know is a bold faced lie." He taps the tip of his finger to my nose. "You're a lousy liar, Ivy. Why give up on Veray at this point?"

I pull back so I'm out of his reach. As charming as he is, I don't want the constant reminders that he views me as a child who can't make her own decisions. "I'm going to talk to Madeline today. With any luck I can reason with her and she'll release me from that exclusive contract she's been hanging over my head for years."

"And if that doesn't work?" He cocks an eyebrow. "Then what?"

"Then you'll sleep with her." I smirk as the words leave my lips.

He chokes on the swig of water he's just taken. "I'll what?" He coughs.

"All the woman ever talks about is how she can't get laid." I laugh as I reach for my purse. "She'd definitely release me from my contract if you made her happy in that way." I wink and pull up my shoulder.

"I've met the woman." He chuckles as he lowers his body back into his chair. "You can't pay me enough to touch that."

CHAPTER TWO

"IVY, HOW DID YOU KNOW I LOVE THIS RESTAURANT?" MADELINE'S voice carries over the buzz of the jam packed, Upper East Side bistro I've chosen for my mission to get released from my contract with her.

"*Because they serve alcohol.*" Those are the words perched at the edge of my lips. "It just screamed your name to me," I say as she takes a seat across from me.

"I've never been. It's quaint." Her eyes subtly survey the room. I've known Madeline long enough to realize that if an attractive man is in the vicinity her focus won't be settled on me.

"I came once with Mark." I toss his name at her hoping she'll take the lure and shift her attention back to me.

"I called him, you know." She motions for one of the waiters who dashes over to the table. "Vodka soda. Ivy?"

"I'm fine." I nod towards the glass of lemon water I ordered when I arrived thirty minutes ago. Punctuality has never been Madeline's strength. "How did that go?" I press on, "was he interested?" I feign a smile while inside I'm seething. Talking about Mark ranks at the top of my list of things I like to do right next to thinking about Jax.

"I might have mentioned it to you when we lunched with Jax." She runs her eyes over the screen of her smartphone before placing it down on the table. "I don't know what Mark's problem is. Is he involved with someone?"

"I have no idea." I take a sip of the now tepid water. "We don't talk much."

"What exactly happened with you two?" She doesn't acknowledge the waiter at all as he places her drink down. "Rumor has it that he was sleeping with half of Manhattan."

I feel my face flush crimson. "There were other women involved, yes," I murmur.

"A man like that can't be tamed." She peers over the thick glass while she downs a generous mouthful.

"I suppose not." I bite my lip to stifle a laugh. "He's not my problem anymore."

She glances at her phone again. "Lucky you. Now you've got Jax to keep your bed warm."

I shake my head evenly from side-to-side. "Anything that was going on between us is officially over."

"What did he do?" She reaches across the table to cover my hand with hers. "He fucked around on you too, didn't he?"

Her assumption jars me and I breathe in a heavy sigh. "Maybe, I don't know." I realize that I'm answering honestly. Is he still sleeping with Brooke? Considering his drive to get my shares into his hands I'd venture a guess that he's lounging in bed with the tall brunette as Madeline and I speak.

"You pick the wrong men, Ivy." She pulls back into her chair again, any compassion that might have been there evaporating into the air as swiftly as her drink is disappearing.

"I know," I say.

"Men in Manhattan are a different breed. They're flakes. Most of them can't keep their dicks in their pants through dessert." She empties the glass before waving her hand in mid-air at the back of our waiter who is obviously busy taking another table's lunch order.

I laugh out loud at her brutal description of the male population of New York City. "Are men in Boston any better?" I ask as I watch her hand movement increase in voracity even though the waiter hasn't once turned in our direction.

"Boston?" She freezes as she spits out the word. "Why would you ask about Boston?"

"I'm moving back." I stare at her motionless hand drifting in the air. It's as though she's an enthusiastic third grader aching to answer the detailed math equation the teacher has posed to the class. In Madeline's case the equation in question is another vodka soda. I silently wonder if her hand is actually going to continue to defy gravity until the long winded waiter finally remembers he has other patrons to tend to.

"You're leaving New York? When?" Her hand falls with a thud to the table which instantly causes the waiter to rush over. "Another." She doesn't glance at him as she points at her empty glass.

"Soon. I'm just tying up some loose ends," I say snappily. I don't want to dive into the reasoning behind my running for the hills, or in this case, Boston. "That's actually why I asked you to join me for lunch."

As if on cue, the waiter is back with Madeline's drink in hand. "Are you ready to order?" he asks.

She shoos him away with a flick of her wrist. "What is this about, Ivy?"

"We talked about it briefly when we had lunch with Jax." I feel an ache when I say his name. "It's about my exclusive contract with you."

"Oh that." She picks up her phone and lazily runs her thumb across the screen.

"Do you need to make a call?" I'm slightly annoyed that her focus so far has been on virtually everything in the room but me.

She doesn't tear her eyes away from the screen as she answers. "No. I'm waiting to hear back from Jax. I've tried calling him all morning about our meeting and he's ignoring me."

"About our meeting?" I wave my hand over the table. I can't believe she's actually trying to get Jax involved in this again. I know, full well, that she still owns the majority in her company and doesn't need his final approval for anything.

She casually puts the phone down before taking a small sip from her glass. "No. He asked me to meet him later today at a building I'm not familiar with. I need him to pick me up or I'll have to hire an escort. One can't trust strange neighborhoods in this city."

I muffle a giggle at her cautiousness. "Maybe you should consider a full-time bodyguard," I teasingly say.

She holds the glass in her hand in the air. "Now that's a great idea. As long as he'd be up for a few extra responsibilities." Her emphasis on the word up is quickly followed up with a not-so-subtle wink.

I laugh out loud at this point. I'm not sure I've ever met a woman who was so blatantly obvious about her lacking sex life. No wonder Nathan rebutted my playful request that he sleep with her. She'd likely tear him to shreds.

"Back to business, Madeline." I push through the giggles and bring my voice back to an even grade.

"You want out of your contract, yes?" She finishes her second drink and I wonder how she manages to stand up straight most afternoons.

"That's right." I realize that the window of opportunity for me to talk to sensible Madeline may be rapidly closing if she gets another drink in her hand before any food lands in her stomach. "I'd still design exclusive collections for Veray but I want to branch out on my own."

"So, we're not talking about you pulling everything out of the store?" There's a slight slur to her voice already.

"Absolutely not," I say convincingly. "I'll do a special collection just for you each season and those won't be sold anywhere but at Veray."

"Why wasn't Jax on board with this?" The waiter rushes over with another vodka soda in hand. He obviously knows where his tip is coming from since I've ordered nothing but the water which is still barely touched.

"He's a man." I throw the comment out knowing that it will bring a smile to her lips.

I'm right when I'm greeted with a roar of laughter. "He's a dude." She pulls the words across her lips as she swallows half of the clear liquid in the glass.

I can't help but laugh almost as loudly as her. "So we have a deal?"

I press knowing that this is the moment when I have to reel Madeline in.

"Deal." She offers her hand across the table. "I'll have my attorney send the papers to you. Tomorrow is good for that?"

"Tomorrow is absolutely perfect." I raise my glass and feel some of the weight melt off my shoulders.

CHAPTER THREE

"Déjà vu." Nathan pulls the chair away from the stark wooden table while I settle in next to it. "Doesn't it feel like we were just here?"

I smile faintly at the mention of our last meeting in this building with Jax and his attorney. It was only a few weeks ago but in the scope of my life it could have been years ago. Everything has changed so dramatically since that day. That day when Jax had taken me so brazenly in the hallway outside this room. "It does, yes," I manage to say weakly.

"Remember to let me do the talking." He pats the top of my hand before pulling a folder out of his briefcase. "Now that we know what Mark is willing to give us, we have a lot more leverage with Jax."

Leverage with Jax. His words echo in my ears. I have all the leverage I could ever need in my purse. The flash drive I had taken from Jax's apartment the night that our relationship imploded had been weighing heavily on my mind and my heart the past few days. If I gave that to Mark and he heard Jax and Brooke plotting to take over the company it would change everything.

"Put on your game face." Nathan's words pull me from my thoughts and I glance across the sparsely decorated room to see Jax and Gilbert walking through the door.

Jax looks nothing like he did the night I left him on his knees at his apartment door. The growth of beard on his face suggests he hasn't shaved since then and his chosen attire of blue jeans and a black sweater seem out of place in this corporate environment. His hair is disheveled and his eyes are locked on my face. I glance at him briefly before I drop my gaze to my lap. I hear his heavy footsteps as he rushes towards the table.

"Did you watch it?" His voice is frantic. He slams his fist against the table.

"Watch what?" Nathan interjects. He stands in response to Jax's obvious anger.

"Ivy, look at me," he demands.

"Sit down or we're leaving." Nathan's tone is measured and calm. "If you don't control your temper, we're walking out of here now and we'll finalize a deal with Mark this afternoon."

I don't look up. I can't. I feel all the emotions of that night rippling back to the surface of my heart. I'll cry if I look at his face. I'll break into a million pieces in this cold, barren boardroom if I think about him and Brooke in bed together.

"Bringing Mark into this negotiation is underhanded." Gilbert takes a seat directly across from Nathan which means if I look up I'll be staring straight at Jax.

"I sent over our new terms yesterday. Have you both had a chance to look it over?" Nathan ignores Gilbert's accusation. "It's more than fair in light of the circumstances."

I dart my eyes towards Nathan. What does he mean? He throws me a sly grin and I realize he's bluffing.

"What circumstances?" Gilbert poses the question to the room.

"Ivy, you need to watch the whole thing." There's a tremor in Jax's voice as he quietly says the words. "I know you have it. You took it when you left. Just watch it. Please."

"What the hell is he talking about?" Nathan reaches for my arm.

"Don't." Jax pushes against the table as he stands. "Don't touch her."

I shake my head slowly before I raise my eyes to finally look directly at him. "I can't watch it," I murmur. "Why would you ask me to?"

"You have to, beautiful." His eyes lock with mine and I see all the pain that has washed over me reflected back in his face. "Trust me." He pulls his hand to his chest and that's when I notice it. Dangling from the corner of Jax's balled fist is a gold chain. The broken clasp is slowly waving back and forth in the air as he moves his hand. It's the necklace. It's my necklace.

"Someone needs to explain what's going on." Nathan's voice interrupts my concentration.

"I can't trust you." I won't back down regardless of how lost and broken Jax looks. "You are nothing but a liar. I know what I saw. I know what I heard."

"No, you don't." He's on his feet again. "You don't understand what you saw."

I bolt out of my chair. "I know exactly what I saw. I saw you fucking another woman. A woman who you were working with to blackmail..."

"Enough!" The strength of the word rebounds across the barren room. "Give her whatever the hell she wants."

I stand in stunned silence as he calmly tosses the necklace on the table, turns and walks out the door without looking back.

CHAPTER FOUR

"I HEARD IT." NATHAN'S VOICE BREAKS THROUGH THE MUNDANE HUM of the busy restaurant. "Blackmail. It was clear as day."

I stare at him over the rim of my wine glass. I don't respond. I'm not going to. I hadn't meant to toss that word out when we were meeting with Jax and Gilbert earlier and I instantly regretted it once I had.

"I'm not letting this go." He gazes at me for a second before dropping his eyes to the menu.

"There's nothing to let go." I follow his lead and scan the expansive offerings. I have absolutely no appetite and this celebratory lunch that Nathan suggested isn't exactly where I want to be.

"You said something about blackmail." He doesn't pull his eyes away from the menu. "You can't expect me to ignore that."

"Just drop it." I roll my eyes.

"No." He places the menu down before leaning against the table with his elbows. "Spit it out, Ivy. What the hell is going on with you two?"

I take a slow drink of the hearty red wine I'd ordered when we first arrived. "There's a flash drive."

"That's what he was talking about when he said you took it from his apartment?"

I nod." I found it in a drawer. I watched it," I grimace. "Then I left and I took it with me."

"He was with another woman?"

I exhale sharply. "Yes."

"That's rough." He picks up the glass of scotch and brings it to his lips. After taking a leisurely drink he continues, "So he was cheating on you?"

I flinch at the question. "It was recorded over a year ago. Jax and the woman were talking about at a gala that Mark and I attended."

"You're pissed that he fucked someone before he met you?" He flashes me a smile.

I take another drink trying to gather my thoughts. I don't want to give away too many details. "There's a lot more to it than that."

"Like what?" He pushes for more even though I know he's fully aware that I'm incredibly uncomfortable.

"I can't talk to you about this, Nathan," I bristle. "Suffice it to say that I saw who Jax really was when I watched that video."

"If Jax was blackmailing someone you need to tell me, Ivy." His tone shifts and I see a veil of seriousness overtake his expression. "You understand that, don't you?"

I nod my head slowly up and down. He's right, of course but as much as I despise Jax and what he and Brooke were plotting together the last thing I want is to be pulled into any more legal drama with him and Mark. "There's nothing to tell."

"I don't believe you," he grumbles. "But I trust you to know what's best for you."

I tear slightly at the words. Hearing that from Nathan means a lot to me. I've come to see him as a sort of surrogate big brother the last few weeks. His belief in me is comforting. "Thank you for saying that." I smile faintly.

"I mean it. I'm really proud of you." He grins. "I'm starving. Let's eat."

———

I PLACE my fork down after picking at the spring salad the waiter delivered to our table over thirty minutes ago. The idle chatter that Nathan and I have shared over lunch about our childhood has reenergized me. The idea of getting home to finish packing so I can finally leave New York in search of a new life in Boston is my sole light at the end of the tumultuous tunnel that my life has become as of late.

"I've got one last question about Jax?" There's a definite suggestion of trepidation in his voice.

"Must you?" I joke.

"I must." He playfully nods. "In the meeting earlier he kept telling you to watch the entire video. I'm assuming you haven't?"

I raise my eyebrow in response.

"Seriously." He pushes the plate that contains the last remnants of the ribs and fries he devoured to the edge of the table. "You didn't watch the whole thing?"

"Why would I?" I bark back. "Would you want to watch someone you love having sex with another person?"

"So you do love him?" He places the white linen napkin atop the plate.

"No." I violently shake my head from side-to-side. I wonder if I'm trying to convince Nathan or myself more.

"I'm going to play devil's advocate for a minute." He breathes in heavily before he continues, "I haven't exactly been subtle about my dislike for Jax."

I smile faintly at the declaration. "True," I whisper.

"He looked like shit today." He reaches across the table and places his hand over mine. "Ivy, he's torn up inside. I could see it the minute he walked in the room."

I pull my hand back harshly. If this is some kind of bro code thing, I'm not going to listen. If Nathan knew the whole story he wouldn't be taking Jax's side. "I don't care," I blurt out.

"Think about it for a minute." There's a small pause. "Why is he asking you to watch the entire video if he knows it's going to hurt you even more?"

I shrug my shoulders. "He doesn't have a heart."

"You're wrong." He shakes his head slightly. "There's more to that video than what you saw. Whatever that was."

"I turned it off before they made love." My voice trembles as I continue, "I can't watch him with another woman. I can't."

"I get that." His deep voice is barely more than a whisper. "There's something on it he needs you to see. If you can't watch it, I'll do it for you. You owe it to yourself and to him to see the entire thing."

The moment is broken with that one simple word. Owe. "I owe him nothing." I stand and reach for my purse. "Nothing. How dare you suggest otherwise?" I feel a rush of tears. "You have no idea who he really is. What he's capable of."

"Calm down." He's on his feet now too, reaching for my arm. "I didn't mean to upset you."

"I'm not upset." I wave his hand away. "I'm tired of all of this bullshit."

"Let me take you home." He reaches into his suit jacket to pull out his wallet. "I just need to settle our bill."

"I'm fine on my own." I brush past him and I don't turn back as I head straight for the door.

CHAPTER FIVE

"Dear, have you finished packing?" Mrs. Adams asks as I open the door to my apartment.

"Almost." I motion her in. "I need to pick up a few more boxes for my clothes and then I'm all set."

"You young girls have more clothes than you know what to do with." She limps past me towards the living room. "Back in my day a lady had one skirt for Sundays and one for the rest of the week."

I smile at her remembrance of her youth. "Can I make you some tea?"

"Yes. That would be lovely." She settles onto the sofa as I walk towards the kitchen.

I stand in silence as I wait for the kettle to boil. I keep hearing Nathan's words ringing in my ears. Do I owe it to Jax to watch the entire video? I've almost thrown that flash drive into the trash so many times I've lost count. Now I'm beginning to wonder if watching it will actually be the way to get the closure that I need.

"Do you want milk or lemon?" I place a small flowered tea cup and saucer in Mrs. Adams trembling hand.

"Lemon, please." She smiles faintly. "I came over to talk to you about your hippie friend."

I squeeze half a lemon into her tea before taking a seat in the chair across from her. "Jax. What about him?"

She sips carefully at the hot liquid before placing the cup and saucer on the table in front of her. "He was in the lobby when I came home from the doctor yesterday."

My cup instantly begins to shake when she mentions his name. "He what? I'm sorry. He shouldn't have been here." I try to contain my surprise. Why would Jax come here when he knows I want nothing to do with him? "I'm sorry if he bothered you."

"Not at all, dear." She reaches again for the saucer resting it and the tea cup on her lap. "He came to see me actually."

"He came here to see you?" I don't even try and veil the shock in my voice. "Why on earth would he do that?"

She sighs before taking another small sip from the cup. "He's troubled. That boy is very troubled." She stares down at her lap as she shakes her head slightly. "I feel badly for him."

"You feel badly for Jax?" I'm questioning not only her better sense but Jax's motivations. He had no right coming to my building to accost Mrs. Adams and make her feel sorry for him.

"He hurt you," she says softly. "It's upsetting to me that he did that."

I nod. I don't want to interrupt her. My curiosity is peaked now.

"He told me that you saw something that broke your heart." Her weathered brow furrows as she frowns. "I told him that he had to make it up to you."

I smile at her boldness. She was never one to hold back her opinion and now that she's explaining her conversation with Jax, I'm grateful that she's as honest and direct as she is.

"Some things can't be made up," I whisper. "Anything that we had is over now. I'm going to start fresh in Boston."

She studies my expression. I know that she can see right through my words. She knows that I'm only trying to convince myself that I don't care for Jax anymore. "Running away never solved anything, Ivy." Her voice is tender but there's an edge of authority to it. "I know you think you can leave and start over but that's not how life works."

"It can work that way." I take a swallow of the tea and realize it's bitter. I reach for the sugar and stir one scoop into the half empty cup. "I have to get away from here."

"From here or from him?" she questions.

"Both," I confess. "I'm surrounded by lies and betrayal here."

"Do you think I'm a good judge of character?" she asks me expectantly.

I smile before I respond. "Of course, Mrs. Adams."

"That boy has a pure soul." She pats herself on the chest. "I see my late husband in his eyes."

My tea cup stops in mid-air as I try to absorb her words. Is she saying she believes Jax is a good person? Why am I surprised by that? He's debonair, charming and manipulative. How hard would it be for him to convince this woman that he's the second coming of her dearly departed soul mate?

"He told me he loves you." Her tone is direct and matter-of-fact. "And I, for one, believe him."

I draw in a deep breath. "I for two, don't." I pull a thin smile across my lips.

She places the now empty tea cup back down onto the table. "He was in pain. I could see it. He just wants you to watch something. A show on your computer. It's called…"

I'm appalled that Jax is so conniving that he's even trying to use my elderly neighbor to further his cause. "He told you…"

"The show is called Flesh Drive," she interrupts. "It sounds promiscuous but he assured me it's not." She snaps her chin down and her expression narrows. "Watch it, dear. He says you'll understand when you do."

Before I have time to protest she's pushing herself up from the sofa. I rush over to help and hand her the cane she rested beside the coffee table earlier. We walk in silence to the door of my apartment.

"Don't you dare leave for Boston before coming over to see me." She pulls me into a weak but tender hug.

"I promise I won't." I hold the door open as she steps through.

"Watch the program." She calls over her shoulder as she slowly walks towards her apartment. "Do it now."

CHAPTER SIX

"WHO THE HELL DO YOU THINK YOU ARE?" I SMASH THE FLASH DRIVE
onto his desk causing him to turn from where he was gazing out the
window, the phone still pressed against his ear.

"I'm going to have to call you back." He's curt with the person on
the other end. "What are you doing here?" His eyes run seamlessly
from my face to his desk where the flash drive with Brooke's name
emblazoned across the side now rests.

I turn to slam the door of his office shut. "You had no right coming
to my building to sweet talk Mrs. Adams into being part of your fan
club."

"What?" A weak smirk flashes across his lips. "I have a fan club?"

"Everyone is suddenly on your side." I know I sound delusional.
I've just realized that I'm standing alone in a room with Jax. This is the
first time we've been in this situation since that night at his apartment
when I finally understood his true intentions.

"Who pray tell is everyone?" His tone is playful and misplaced.

I stare at him. He looks like a completely different person than the
disheveled and scattered mess that he was yesterday. He's dressed in a
navy suit complete with a blue and white pin stripe shirt. He's pushed
his hair back from his forehead and his face is now smooth. Any

remnant of his outer pain has been cleaned up by a shower and a shave. I feel completely out of place in my worn out jeans, white t-shirt and pink cardigan.

"Mrs. Adams and Nathan," I murmur. Why am I telling him this? "They said I should give you a chance."

"Moore is on my side?" He leisurely undoes a button on his suit jacket as he sits. "So you haven't watched it yet?" He nods his chin in the direction of the flash drive.

"I'm not watching it, Jax." I follow his lead and sit in one of the two leather chairs facing his expansive desk.

"Do you remember when we went to visit your father?" He reaches for the flash drive and rubs it between the index finger and the thumb of his right hand.

"Of course I do." My throat is burning. I'm anxious and frustrated. His calm demeanor is doing very little to help ease any of that.

A small smile spreads across his face. "It was perfect."

I sit in silence. I can't allow myself to relive those memories. He's right. It was perfect. The entire trip was everything I wanted and needed. I left Boston feeling intensely that Jax adored me and would do anything for me.

"Your father asked me about my father." He stares at the flash drive flipping it effortlessly between his fingers. "My father was always very disappointed in me when he was alive."

I feel my anger retreating and I'm frustrated by my own emotions. I don't want to listen to his excuses. I know what I saw and I know what I heard. "I'm sorry for that but..."

"Your father's approval is important to you too," he interrupts. "I saw it that day."

I nod silently. I've always wanted my father to love me more. I've always known that he secretly blames my birth for my mother's death. I understand that voracious need to win the approval of a parent but rehashing my second-rate childhood and how it relates to Jax's isn't what I came here for.

"Yes, that's true but I didn't come here to talk about that." I state boldly. I can't back down from this. I want Jax to understand that manipulating Mrs. Adams into doing his bidding for him just isn't acceptable.

"Before the gala…" He leans forward in his chair before he continues, "doing whatever was necessary to win back my father's company was all I thought about."

"That's obvious on the video." I motion towards the flash drive he's still lazily running along his fingertips.

"Everything changed at the gala. Everything changed when I saw you." His voice breaks and he looks down into his lap. I can hear him drawing in a heavy breath in an effort to temper his emotions.

"No, that's not true." I push back. I don't want him to think that he can pull on my heart strings again and I'll forgive him. This time is different. I understand his need to honor his late father's memory but I won't let my guard down. "On the video you say it's the day after the gala. You were plotting to blackmail Mark after the gala so you're lying again."

He slowly raises his head until his eyes are in line with mine. I lock onto them searching for any hint of honesty within him. "Did you believe me when I told you I loved you, beautiful?"

The question jars me. How dare he ask me something so personal when we're in the middle of a discussion about his underhanded corporate conspiracy? "Don't talk about that." I spit the words out with distaste. "How can you use someone so easily like that? How can you pretend to be something you're not?"

"I've never pretended with you." He studies my face with his eyes. "I told you I loved you because I do. I've never loved a woman before."

I laugh out loud. "That's such bullshit. You admitted you were cheated on. It was Brooke who cheated on you, wasn't it? She cheated on you with Mark. How sick and twisted is that? The woman you loved cheated with the man I loved?"

He's silent in response. I sit waiting for the expected explosion of anger but he stares directly into me, his eyes not faltering.

"You and Brooke plotted against Mark and me." I point my index finger at him. "The two of you deserve one another. I just have one question."

He tilts his chin up. "What's that?" he asks in a whispered tone.

"Why did you break the rule? Why did you fuck me?" I seethe.

"You said you loved me, Ivy." He picks up the flash drive and balances it on his palm. "I know that you meant it."

"So what if I did?" I snap back. "I was in love with who I thought you were not the real you."

"You're mistaken, beautiful." He pulls himself to his feet in one fluid motion. I push my body back into the chair. I want to keep as much physical distance as I can between Jax and me.

"I'm not." I fumble for my purse. I know I placed it next to the chair when I sat down and now I can't find it. I just want to get out of here.

"I haven't made love to anyone since I saw you at the gala that night." His voice whispers across the back of my neck and I jolt myself back into an upright position. He's there, hovering over me. I can smell his skin. He's so close.

"Why are you lying?" I try to retreat into the chair but the soft leather resists. "I saw you in bed with Brooke. I saw it."

He leans back against the desk giving me a slight reprieve from his imposing presence. "I was in bed with Brooke. Nothing happened."

"No. You're lying. You think I'm an idiot. You've always thought I was naïve." I scowl.

"You're, by far, the most amazing woman I've ever met." His voice lowers. "I knew it the instant I saw you at the gala. I would do anything for you."

I stand. "You're so delusional."

"How so?" He mirrors my stance and towers above me.

"You and Brooke worked together to manipulate Mark and me. It's all there on the flash drive, yet you continue to deny it," I chuckle." The proof is right there, Jax."

"Indeed it is, Ivy." He opens his hand and holds the flash drive at my eye level. "If you would watch the entire thing, you'd understand."

"I understand everything I need to understand." I grab the flash drive and toss it back on his desk. I try to push past him so I can leave but his body is blocking my pathway to the door.

"That's obviously not true." He lowers his head until his lips are hovering mere inches from mine.

"It's true." I pull back. I can't think straight when he's this close to me. I'm beginning to doubt my own resolve.

His index finger traces a faint line across my chin. "I fell in love with you at the gala. My life changed that night."

I shake my head partly to disengage from his heated touch and partly to clear my thoughts. "You've been manipulating me since we met at Brighton's gallery opening. It's all been so you could take control of Mark's company."

"That's your perception, beautiful." He takes one step closer. "I'm only guilty of wanting you and my father's company."

"Do you really think this will work?" I throw my hands in the air in sheer frustration. He honestly believes that he can seduce me into forgetting what I saw on the video.

He grabs my wrist in one fell swoop. "What do you mean?"

I try to pull it free from his grasp but he's not relenting at all. "Let go of me." I glare at him.

"Not yet," he whispers as he pulls my arm to his lips. I flinch as I feel him run his lips across my skin.

I shiver from the touch. "Stop it." I jerk my arm again and this time he effortlessly lets it drop from his clutch. "You can't seduce me. You can't convince me that you're not the manipulative jack ass that I know you are."

He arches his brow and his expression darkens. "Oh, I'll convince you, beautiful."

"Give up, Jax," I scowl. "You won. You get your father's company and you got to fuck Mark's ex. Way to go." My words are dripping sarcasm and I don't care.

He swallows hard before he speaks in a pained whisper, "You think I'm a monster, don't you?"

I'm taken back by his response. "I think you'll do whatever is necessary to get what you want."

He lowers his head into his hands. "That's not who I am."

I stare at him. His shoulders have softened. His posture has shifted.

If I didn't know better I'd swear my words bit into him. "You've manipulated me since we met. You've withheld the truth."

He pulls his head up so he's looking directly into my eyes. "I should have been honest about my father."

"You used me. You used me to get what you wanted. You let me believe in you." I feel all of my emotions rushing past the barrier I've tried to create within my heart. "I fell in love with you. I thought you were him. I thought that was you."

"You thought I was who?" He jolts to his feet again.

"Him." I sob as I turn towards the door. "Mine." I can't form the words to tell him that I envisioned our future. That the innocent part of my heart wanted to build a life with him.

He reaches for me and pulls my body into his chest. I struggle to break free.

"I am him. I've always been him." His voice cracks. "Believe in me. Trust me."

I twist around swiftly breaking free from his arms. "You don't see it." I struggle to form the words through my sobs. "You can't do that..." my voice trails as I point behind him to the flash drive. "You can't do that and then expect me to just pretend I didn't see it."

"You don't know what you saw." He raises his voice, frustration laced within it. "Until you watch the entire thing, you're never going to know the truth."

"I can't." I stumble back towards the door. "Why the hell do you want me to watch you fucking her? Why?" I scream the words at him.

"I didn't fuck her. I couldn't. I wouldn't have." He picks up the flash drive and lays it in his palm. "Take this. Watch it."

I stare at it. Brooke's name is taunting me. I scoop it up and throw it in my purse again. "You're not worried that I'm going to hand this over to Mark and ruin your chances of taking over the business?"

He pauses as if he's contemplating the question. "The business doesn't matter to me anymore."

"Yeah, right." I snap. "That's all that matters."

He brushes past me. "I have a meeting to get to." His hand curls around the handle of the door. "I can have Leonard drop you off at home and I'll take a cab."

"I'll take the cab." I move quickly towards the open door. "For someone who doesn't care about the business you're certainly in a hurry to go to this meeting." I know I'm being childish but the way he's dismissing me stings.

"It's not a meeting for that." He motions towards the bank of elevators. "Everything I do is for you. Everything." With that he steps into the open elevator.

I stand in silence as I watch the doors close.

CHAPTER SEVEN

"I'M NOT SURE WHAT DAY I'LL BE THERE, DAD," I CALL TOWARDS MY phone where it's perched precariously on my pillow. "I haven't finished packing yet."

"I can barely hear you, princess." His voice bounces off the now empty walls of my bedroom.

I scurry over to the bed and pick up the phone. I hold it to my lips. "You're on speaker phone, dad. Is this better?"

"Much better." I hear relief wash through his voice. "You're on rotary dial by the way."

I giggle at my father's reluctance to embrace technology. "Really dad? Is that why you sound like you're sitting at the bottom of a tin can?"

He laughs and the sound lifts my spirits.

"I'll let you know when I'm ready to come down and then we can go apartment hunting together." I work to fold one of my dresses with my free hand but it's more of a mess than when I found it bunched up on the floor of my closet.

"Nonsense. You're going to live here with me." I can hear how adamant he is by his tone.

"Maybe temporarily, dad," I offer in response. I do want to rebuild my connection with my father but living together may not be the best approach to take.

"It's settled then. I need to run over to your sister's now. I'll give her your love." He's not leaving me any room for a rebuttal.

"Sounds good. Love you, dad." I stare at the phone waiting to hear his response.

"I love you too, princess," he says quietly before ending the call. It's a small offering but it brings tears to my eyes. I know that once I reach Boston, I'll feel safe enough to find my footing again.

I glimpse at the time on my phone and realize that it's after seven. I need to eat something. I silently wonder if Mrs. Adams might be up for a quick stroll to the diner down the street. I drop the dress I've been unsuccessfully trying to fold into the large cardboard box near my closet. I'll worry about sorting through everything once I'm settled in my new place.

I grab my purse from the bed and rummage through it for my keys. I curse when I realize I can't find them. "What the hell," I whisper under my breath before dumping the contents onto the blanket. I pull my hand through the assorted pens, notepads, candy bar wrappers and receipts before my fingers settle on something metal. "Eureka!" I joke to myself when I throw my hand up in the air. I stare at it when I realize it's not my keys. I'm holding the flash drive above my head.

I feel my knees going weak so I sit back on the bed. My laptop is within arm's reach on the nightstand. I pull it into my lap and flip it open. I push back the cover of the flash drive and hold it next to the USB port. I feel a sense of nausea wash over me. Why am I doing this? Why subject myself to this?

My mind darts back to Jax's office when he assuredly told me to watch it. Since that conversation I've been certain that he was calling my bluff. He handed the flash drive back to me because he was convinced I wouldn't watch it. I need to prove I'm stronger than he thinks I am. I push the drive in and hold my breath.

A folder pops onto the screen and I click the now familiar file to start the video. I close my eyes when I hear Brooke's voice. I want to mute the sound but I'm going to get past their conversation. I'm going to see what Jax wants so desperately for me to see.

It seems like an eternity until I hear Jax say, "You belong to me. Only me."

I cringe and close my eyes as I await the sounds of their lovemaking. I fumble for the flash drive. My heart is screaming at me to pull it out. My body won't let me.

"I've waited forever for this." Her voice is breathy. I recoil at the sound of the desire in it. I peek at the screen through the corner of my eye.

"Do you know what would make me hard?" He leans back pulling his body away from her.

She breathes an exaggerated sigh. "Tell me."

"Hearing how much power you have over him." He rests his head on his elbow. "Play it for me again."

"Now?" She eases closer to him.

"Get it for me." He points toward the nightstand. "Play it. Let me hear how in control you really are."

She runs her eyes over his face and chest before she leans back and picks up a phone. I watch as she rolls her thumb across the screen. She carefully holds the edges of the phone between her fingers pointing it in Jax's direction.

"Baby, it's me. It's Mark. I've been thinking about you all day. Fuck I wish it was you I was marrying. I wish we could get Ivy out of the picture. If we could, everything would be yours. All the shares, the money, that apartment you want. I'd give you anything if you were my wife. Call me as soon as you get this. I miss you."

I wince at the sounds of Mark's voice on what seems to be a voice-mail message as I watch her place the phone back onto the nightstand. "I have him right here, in the palm of my hand." She holds out her hand in front of Jax's face.

"Tell me you don't want him," he says.

"Are you crazy?" she snickers. "He's too old for me. Just the thought of him naked disgusts me. I wouldn't touch that with a ten foot pole."

"You're such a stupid bitch." His voice is barely audible. Did he just call her a stupid bitch?

"What did you say?" The confusion in her tone is blatantly obvious.

"Get the fuck out of my bed." Jax's voice booms through the speakers.

My hand jumps to my mouth and I stare at the screen. He's pulled the sheet back from his body and is sitting straight up glaring at Brooke. He's wearing nothing but boxers.

"What?" Her stunned expression mirrors my own. "What's wrong with you?" She's pulling at his arm coaxing him to lie down next to her again.

"You seriously thought I was going to sleep with you?" He laughs before pulling himself up. "Get dressed. Get out."

She doesn't move. She's frozen in place. I can feel her shock resonating through me. "What..." her voice trails as she helplessly stares at him.

He's standing next to the computer now and all that is visible is his right arm. "You ruined my parents' marriage. Did you really think I'd want my father's leftovers?"

Her stunned silence is now giving way to something else. Rage. "You're crazy," she screams it at him. "I never slept with your father."

"Shut up," he barks back at her. "He told me everything before he died." He leans far enough forward that there's a flash of his back on the screen. "Everything," he pulls the word along his lips, enunciating every syllable. "You were blackmailing him, you bitch. You haven't changed your playbook at all. You're doing the exact same thing with Mark."

She's up on her knees now. She reaches for a glass from the night-stand. She levels it in Jax's direction and he moves his body completely in front of the computer. I can't see what's happening, but the dull thud suggests that the glass hit him square in the chest.

"Why are you doing this?" Her voice is louder now. I can tell she's closer to where Jax is standing.

"I wanted to see how far you'd take things with Mark." He doesn't move. "I know you already slept with him. He was bragging about how he tapped his hot assistant last week."

"So what? "she scoffs. I curse inwardly wishing Jax would shift his body enough that I could get a glimpse of the rage on Brooke's face.

"I don't give a shit what you do with him." He moves slightly left now and I can make out Brooke reaching down next to the bed gathering up clothing.

"You're just jealous." She throws the words in his direction with a smirk. "That's why you turned on me."

"Turned on you?" he asks mockingly. "You're the one who came to me with the idea to steal their shares away. That's all on you."

"Your father should have left his part of the company to me." She points a bright red fingernail at Jax. "He told me he would. It made me sick every time he fucked me. He was a stupid, horny old man."

He leans forward before he says anything. "You're the company whore. You disgust me. You'll do anything for a dollar."

"And you won't?" She throws her head back in careless laughter. "You're ready to destroy Mark's relationship just to get what you want."

"You're wrong." I can sense the movement of his head in the way his shoulders teeter back and forth. "Ivy is off limits. I'd rather give up the company than sink to your level."

"You're going to have to." She stands now and steps into her skirt. "You're not even half the man Mark is. You'll never get those shares away from Ivy. You might as well give up now."

"Don't say her name again," he snaps at her.

"She's nothing," she spits the words out. "He loves me."

He can't contain his amusement and he roars with laughter. "He loves Ivy. You're his whore."

"I'm not his whore." She reaches down to pick up one shoe, her eyes still scanning the area next to the bed.

"You're right." Jax shifts his body in front of the screen yet again. "You're one of his whores."

"If you care so much about Ivy, why don't you run and tell her what Mark is doing?" Her question rattles me.

"I will tell her." He walks forward now. I get my first glimpse of her fully dressed standing in the doorway of the room.

"When?"

"You don't get it, do you?" I watch as he pulls on a pair of faded jeans and a black t-shirt. "I watched my mother suffer when she found out my father was cheating on her. You think I'm just going to march up to Ivy and announce it?"

"Why should you care what she feels?" There's definite contempt in her tone.

"She's not like you." His expression is hard and unyielding. "She's not like anyone."

"So you're just going to let her marry him, is that it?" She adjusts her watch. "You're going to let her believe in him forever?"

"She'll know before the wedding." He stands and motions for her to leave the room. "I won't let her marry him."

I sit in stunned silence as I hear the muffled sound of their footsteps and a door closing. I watch the screen for what feels like hours until Jax reappears alone. He walks over to the computer, punches a few keys and the screen goes black.

CHAPTER EIGHT

I STARE AT THE DOOR TRYING TO CONTROL THE POUNDING IN MY CHEST. I just need to press the buzzer and Jax will let me up. I have no idea what I'll say to him. I glance at my hand. The broken necklace is dangling between my fingers with the flash drive pressing into my palm. I have to tell him I watched it. I have to tell him I understand now.

I push my purse further onto my shoulder as I reach towards the panel that houses all the buzzers. "Excuse me," a woman's voice startles me. The street is dimly lit and in my overwhelmed state I hadn't noticed anyone walking up the steps.

"I'm sorry." I step back and watch as she unlocks the heavy door to the building with her keys.

"Are you coming in?" she asks as she holds open the door with her foot.

I nod and follow closely behind her marvelling at how she can balance two bags filled with groceries, a briefcase and a container of take-out all while using two different keys to unlock the door.

"Where are you headed?" She smiles as we reach the base of the stairs.

"I'm here to see Jax Walker," I say softly now wishing that I had stayed behind and buzzed him. I'm not certain of how warm a reception I'm going to receive when I start pounding on his apartment door.

"He's that way." She nods towards the wooden stairs. "I'm this way." She points with one free finger to a hallway to the left.

"Do you need some help?" I step closer reaching for a grocery bag.

"I'm good." She turns and disappears down the corridor while I pull in a deep breath and begin my ascent of the staircase.

I reach the top and I'm overcome with dread. I glance at my phone and realize it's almost ten o'clock. Maybe he's not here. Could he be on a date? Did he give up on me because I gave up on him? I shake the thought from my head. I came here with purpose and resolve. I can't turn back now. I'm so close to understanding the truth. All I need is for Jax to fill in the missing pieces.

I knock softly on the door before pressing my ear against the heavy wood. I hear nothing. There's no movement inside. I knock again, louder this time. Still there's nothing but complete silence. I don't want to wake Jax's neighbors but I'm not leaving without talking to him. I thump my fist against the door three times and call out his name. The distant sound of swift footsteps is my reward.

I hold my breath as I hear the click of the lock. I stare at the door handle, watching it turn. It's as if everything is in slow motion. I feel a wave of emotion washing through me. Suddenly the door swings open.

"Ivy," he says in a breathless whisper. He's not wearing anything but a pair of blue pajama pants that are sitting low on his hips.

"I just wanted..." I hold up the necklace and open my hand to show him the flash drive. "I watched this."

I'm vaguely aware of his hands grasping my shoulders as he pulls me into the room. I hear the distinctive sound of the door closing before his arms engulf me. I melt into his bare chest, clawing at his skin. I want and need to pull him into me. I inhale the scent of him and rest my forehead against his chin.

"Beautiful," he breathes the word into my mouth before his lips claim mine.

I wrap my hand through his hair as I pull his body into me. I need to tell him I'm still confused. I should explain that I want answers. I want to understand everything. Thoughts are bouncing off every recess of my mind. I should tell him to stop.

"Jax," I say his name as he moves his lips to my neck. "Please."

"Please what?" His hand is moving up my thigh. I can feel it getting closer. He's going to touch me. He's going to feel how aroused I am already.

"Please," I repeat unsure of anything in the moment.

"Please let me love you," he growls as he dips his index finger into my panties. I shudder as he pulls the length of it against my slick cleft. "Let me show you how much."

I don't resist. There isn't an inch of my body that doesn't want this right now. I need to feel him inside of me. I need to know we're connected. "Yes, Jax. Yes."

He drops to his knees. I whimper at the thought of his tongue touching my core. I don't think I can hold back. I'm so close to the brink now. I feel the brush of his hand against my hip as he rips the panties from my body. I'm so open, so exposed and so ready.

"Christ, Ivy. Look how wet you are." His breath whispers across my skin as I feel the first hint of his tongue brushing against my already swollen clit.

I moan in response, arching my back to meet his hungry mouth.

"That's it, beautiful," he growls into my flesh. "Take your pleasure. Use my tongue."

I grab hold of his hair with both my hands and push myself into his mouth. I'm lost in the moment. In the indescribable feeling of perfect pleasure. I buck my hips against him, using him to bring myself closer to the edge.

He moans loudly, lapping at my clit. He pulls it into his mouth, his tongue tempting it. "Come for me," he coaxes. "Do it, Ivy. Come."

I don't want it to end. There is nothing that feels as good as this. Nothing but having him within me. I cry out as I fall over the edge and the orgasm claims my entire body. He holds my legs as I shudder and pull on his hair. He's reaching for me with his tongue and I'm too tender to respond.

"No." I shake my head. "No more." I almost grunt the words. The primal sounds leaving my lips are a mirrored reflection of what I'm feeling.

"More." He pushes up against me and runs his lips across mine. I taste my own arousal. I need to feel him inside of me. I tear at his pajama bottoms, pushing them down as his cock springs free.

He scoops me up in his arms, kicking free of the pants as he heads towards the sofa. He unties my dress, pushing it off my shoulders before he unhooks my bra. His lips cover mine again and I close my eyes, relishing in the touch of his hands on my breasts. He pinches my nipples, gently pulling them between his fingers. I reach for his cock but before I can touch it, he's pushing me onto my back.

"I need to feel you." The words spill out of him recklessly. "I have to…" his voice trails as he pushes the tip of his cock against my clit.

I moan from the sensation and adjust my hips so he's at my entrance. I'm aching and he knows it. He thrusts himself into me in one sold, fluid motion. I gasp at the deep mixture of pleasure and pain.

"Fuck, you're so tight." He pounds himself into me. He pushes harder and deeper and with each thrust my body responds in kind. I grip the edge of the sofa for leverage and drive back against him. I can't get him deep enough inside of me. I can't let him go.

"Harder, Jax," I beg. "Harder."

He grips my hips with both hands and plunges further into me. The sofa moves in time to our rhythm. I can feel it jumping forward each time he pounds himself into me.

"I'm so close," I scream the words.

I feel him pull me closer, his body begins to tremble and in that moment I find my release. He fills me at the exact second the orgasm races through me. "Oh, God, Ivy. Oh God."

We lay in silence, the only sound in the room is our measured breaths.

CHAPTER NINE

"I HAVE QUESTIONS." I ADJUST THE HEM OF THE PAJAMA TOP THAT JAX gave me to wear.

"Drink your tea." He motions to the cup of herbal tea he brewed for me that is now sitting atop the nightstand.

"It's too hot." I wave my hand in front of my lips as if to warn of the impending heat.

"That's adorable." He settles in across from where I'm sitting.

I smile before I continue, "I'm serious, Jax. I came here looking for some answers."

"I want to answer those questions." He sits up straighter. "You watched the rest of the video on the flash drive?"

I nod my head. "I did."

"You understand then." He reaches for the cup of tea. He blows on the liquid before he hands it to me.

I manage a small sip and then realize my hands are trembling. I nervously place the cup back down. "I don't understand everything."

"About Brooke?" He reaches for my hand to quiet it within his own.

"About Brooke, Mark, your parents, the woman who hurt you,

the…"my voice trails as he brings my hand to his mouth and gently brushes his lips across the palm.

He looks up and into my eyes. "Let's start with Brooke."

I nod and feel my breath quickening. Even though I watched the full video I still feel a sense of uneasiness about watching Jax in bed with another woman. I'm not naïve enough to think there was no one before me. He's told me there were many but still the burned images in my mind of him pulling her body into his are hard to carry within me.

"Brooke worked for my dad," he says quietly as he squeezes my hand. I run my index finger back and forth against his palm to reassure him that it's okay to continue. "She was in college at the time. She was one of the interns they hired over a summer."

"Did you work with her too?" I press.

"No." He shakes his head slowly. "I was traveling back then, ignoring my responsibilities. I was running from things."

"What things?" I ask, wondering if this is another road into Jax's life that will unveil secrets I'm not ready for.

He raises his eyes from my hand to my face. "Life things. I wasn't ready to grow up. I wanted the wealth my dad could give me without the responsibility."

I can see the pain in his eyes when he talks about his father. It's the same pain I've long felt knowing I haven't lived up to my dad's expectations.

"I didn't know who Brooke was until my father was dying." His body trembles slightly when he says the words. "My parents had separated months before that and my mother was a mess. She was destroyed by his affair but they wouldn't talk about it."

"The affair was with Brooke?" I ask the question even though I'm already certain of the answer.

He nods. "She was decades younger than my dad. She told him she loved him and he left my mother for her. He hid it…her from me."

"But you found out about her before he passed?" I try to ask it diplomatically. I've seen the wrenching pain that Jax is in because of his father's death and I don't want to exacerbate that.

He pulls in a heavy breath. "The hospital called one morning and said he was asking for me. I didn't know he was there."

I'm taken back by the admission. It offers me clarity. I now understand how estranged Jax and his father really were. I squeeze his hand again reassuring him so he'll continue, offering him understanding.

"He was so weak. He was frail," he whispers, his voice cracking. "We talked for hours. He told me all about Brooke. She had used him."

"That's horrible."

He pauses as if he's gathering up the will to continue. I can tell he hasn't talked of this before but it's been weighing heavily on him. "He asked me to make things right. He knew she was sleeping with Mark too." He casts his eyes downward. "I knew he was cheating on you then."

I wince, not wanting the confirmation that he held that knowledge for so long. "You didn't know me then," I offer in response.

"I knew Mark had a girlfriend." He smiles slightly. "You two were just dating back then."

I flash back to the night that Mark proposed. Part of me hadn't wanted to admit that his philandering had been a part of our relationship before that day. I know now that when he dropped to his knee and pledged his undying devotion to me that he was already being unfaithful. I briefly stare at my now vacant ring finger.

"When did you know we had become engaged?" I know it's a selfish question given Jax's emotional confessions about his father but my curiosity is peaked.

"I didn't know who you were." He pulls himself across the bed so his knees are now touching mine. "When I arrived at the gala that night I heard someone say that Mark and Ivy were engaged. Any woman in that room could have been Ivy." He traces his finger along my ankle. "It didn't matter at that moment to me who she was." He puts extra measure on the word she.

I furrow my brow not quite understanding what he's saying. "You didn't know I was me?" I giggle and shake my head once the words leave my lips. "I mean you didn't realize that I was Mark's fiancée?"

"Once I knew that he had gotten engaged to his girlfriend I was determined to tell her... to tell you about his relationship with Brooke." He taps his index finger against my leg. "Then I walked into the room and standing in the center of all the madness was the most beautiful woman I'd ever seen."

My heart stops for what feels like an eternity. I lock eyes with him and wait breathlessly for him to continue.

"You were searching the room for something. I watched you for so long. You were wearing a beautiful long black gown that showed the gentle curve of your back. Your skin looked so soft." He studies my face as he continues, "your hair was pulled up onto your head." He lifts his finger to trace a line along the side of my chin. "It was falling down in places though so you kept pushing it back with your hand."

I remembered the night but not the details the way that he did. Everyone in the room had melted away because I was so caught up in Mark and in planning my happily-ever-after with him.

"I walked up behind you," he says, his eyes widen as if he's seeing that moment right in front of him. "I breathed in the scent of your skin and I heard your voice for the first time as you said hello to a woman passing by."

I'm awestruck by his recounting of that night. I'm hit by how different things might have been if we'd met then. If he'd pulled his arm around my waist and slid his body next to mine.

"I was reaching out to touch your shoulder and then..." his voice trails as he casts his eyes downward.

"Mark," I murmur.

"He walked into the room and you waved at him." He raises his hand in the air as if to mimic my movements. "There was a flash and something bounced off the light."

"My engagement ring," I say weakly.

He nods in response. "You walked away then. You moved across the floor and into his arms. I knew then that you were Ivy." His hand clenches into a tight fist on the bed between us.

I place my hand over it willing him to let go of the anger. "I still believed in him then."

"I know." His hand softens and he cups it over mine again. "I knew that night that I couldn't let you marry him. I didn't want you to be hurt the way my mother was."

"Would you have told me if I hadn't found out myself?" I ask meekly.

He hangs his head low, his eyes focused on the bed. "Yes," he offers in a shallow voice.

"When?" I press.

"I went back to California after that night at the gala to take care of my mother. Well, actually after that night with Brooke," he corrects himself. "I made it my mission to find out everything I could about you."

"That's how you knew about the article. The Dialogue article that you brought up at Brighton's opening?" I ask excitedly. The pieces are starting to fall into place.

"Yes." He nods.

"What about the woman you said you dated who was wearing one of my bracelets?" I ask.

"There was a woman months ago. It was the only date I went on after seeing you at the gala," he says gently. "She was wearing one of your bracelets."

"How is that possible?" I'm confused. "What are the chances that a woman you'd go on a date with would be wearing one of my designs?"

He pulls back and swings his legs over the bed. "I met her the day I bought into Veray. I was in the showroom with Madeline. There was a blonde woman looking at your pieces."

I move next to him, my feet dangling inches from the floor.

"I thought it was you." He squeezes his eyes shut. "I wanted it to be you. I stood right behind her. She wasn't wearing a ring."

I reach to wrap my arm around his neck and I pull him into me. "I'm sorry it wasn't me. I wish it had been."

He gently rubs his hand over my leg. "Me too, beautiful."

I pull back as a heavy yawn takes over my body.

"Get under the covers." He stands and moves back the blanket exposing the sheet. "It's very late."

"We're not done," I protest, kicking my legs against the side of the bed.

"We're never going to be done. You'll always be mine." He scoops me up and lays my head on the pillow.

I smile at him in the dim light. He looks different tonight. He's happier, lighter maybe. "That's not what I meant."

"We'll talk more tomorrow." His lips graze my forehead. "Sleep now, beautiful."

I sigh as I close my eyes and drift off into a heavy sleep.

CHAPTER TEN

I FEEL HIS BREATH ON MY THIGH BEFORE I OPEN MY EYES. I STRUGGLE to process where I am. It's Jax's bed. The room is dimly lit. It's just the breaking of the new day. I can make out a small silver of light bursting into the room.

"Jax," I murmur as I fumble for him. I reach down and my hand wraps itself into his hair. He's there. He's so close. He's going to make me come again.

"Relax, beautiful." His lips tickle my hip. "This is how you're going to wake up every morning."

"No," I protest lightly. I don't mean it. I want this. I want him. I want to wake up in this bed every single day.

"No?" His body shifts and his lips are touching my chin. I feel his fingers trace a lazy path along my clit. "What do you mean? You don't want this?" He pushes a finger into my wetness. "Your body is screaming for me."

"We just made love last night," I say breathlessly, my voice rising when he slides another finger into me causing me to involuntarily move my hips.

"So?" He traces his tongue over my lips pulling back when I reach to kiss him.

"It's so much." I lick my lips wanting him to taste them.

He catches the tip of my tongue with his, pulling it lazily across. "It's never going to be enough." He presses his lips against mine as he speaks, "I could make love to you all day, every day until I take my last breath and it won't be enough."

I wrap my hand around his head and pull him hard into a kiss. He responds in kind, pushing himself up from the bed, plunging his fingers deeper within me.

"Oh, please." I moan at the sensation.

He pulls back from the kiss and drops his mouth to my breast. I feel his tongue trace a circle around my erect nipple before he yanks it between his teeth and bites it softly. "Your breasts are amazing." He grazes his teeth along the skin of my chest before claiming my other nipple.

"Fuck me, please," I say it without candor. I don't care how it sounds. It's all that I want.

"Not now. Not yet," he says softly. "You're going to come like this. Open, exposed and wanting me."

I gasp as I feel the pad of his thumb push on my clit. I stare into his eyes as the pleasure ripples through my body.

"Take it all. Own it beautiful. "He edges me on, circling my clitoris with just the right amount of pressure as his fingers hone in on my most sensitive spot.

I relish in the feeling of being so exposed, so open to this man. I move my hips below him, moaning with each touch of his fingers and thumb. I push his lips into mine, pulling his tongue between my teeth. "Fuck, it feels so good," I purr. "So good. Never stop."

"Never," he growls before kissing me deeply. "You're going to crave my touch."

"I do," I whimper. How can I lie? He knows it already. My body can't shield the desire I feel for him. It's there, always on display. I can't get enough of him. I ache for him.

He takes my breast in his mouth again, circling the now aching nipple with his tongue. I buck against his hand harder, reaching down to push it into me.

He moans. "You're so wet." He weaves my fingers between his so they're gliding over my wetness just as his are. "Touch your clit. Show me how you do it when you're thinking about me."

His brazen words spur on my desire and I greedily stroke my clit, pushing my finger around it, racing to the edge of my desire. "Jax, yes," I whimper through clenched teeth.

"Come for me, now." He pushes his fingers deeper still as I plunge off the edge and feel intensity unlike any other charge through my body. My body moves uncontrollably, my hips pushing off the bed, my legs thrashing.

I gasp for air. "That was…" I can't speak. I can't breathe.

"That was just the beginning." His lips brush lightly against mine. "Go back to sleep. I want you rested for round two."

———

"YOU DIDN'T COME BACK to bed after…well, you know." I blush as I open the shower door to see Jax soaping his body.

"You're finally awake." He pushes his lathered hair away from his face. "Get in here."

I acquiesce quickly, shedding the pajama top before stepping into the warm water and wrapping myself in his arms. "How long have you been awake?"

"I didn't sleep much at all." He motions for me to push my chin back. I do and I feel his hands pull my hair through the water.

"Why not?" I close my eyes as he pours shampoo onto my head and starts massaging it into my scalp.

There's silence as he pushes me back slightly so he can rinse my hair. I bite my lip wondering why he's not responding. I don't know that my heart can take any more Jax surprises at this point. He gently pushes the water from my forehead before he kisses my nose.

I open my eyes. "Why didn't you sleep?"

He casts his eyes downward, kicking the water that's gathered near the drain with his foot. "You deserve to know everything."

I freeze. He's going to confess something to me. Last night was still part of the lie. He's going to tell me he's really the cold, heartless man I thought he was.

"I did sort of arrange for Liz to be at Brighton's opening."

"Why?"

He studies my face before he responds," I was scared."

"Scared of what?" I push.

His hand reaches behind me to retrieve a bottle of scented body wash. I watch him pour some into his palm before he brings it to my arm. "I couldn't just walk up to you on the street and say, 'hey, I'm Jax Walker and I'm your ex fiancé's business partner and oh, by the way, I'm in love with you.' I didn't know how else to approach you."

I step back so I'm just out of his reach. "So instead you went to all the trouble of getting Brighton to accept Liz as a prospect in his program so by some off chance I'd come to his opening with her?"

"You make it sound far-fetched." He laughs as he steps closer to me again. He picks up soaping my shoulder where he left off before I pulled away.

"It's convoluted. Why would Brighton agree to it?" I cock my head to the side.

He massages my shoulder, driving his finger into the stressed muscles. "You've met my brother, Ivy. If he thinks any woman sees him as the second coming of Picasso, she's in his inner circle at the drop of a hat."

"How did you know Liz loved his work?" I ask pensively. I'm scared that he's about to tell me that he had someone following Liz.

"I didn't." His hand moves down to my right breast. I don't react as he pulls his fingers across it, covering it with the sweet scented soap. "I actually had little to do with her getting onto that prospect list."

"Don't say it was all by chance." I stare into his face.

"Hardly." He shakes his head as his hand runs to my other breast. "Mark actually set the wheels in motion."

"Mark?" I take a step back. I can't focus on what he's saying when his hand is touching my breasts. "Why would Mark set that up?"

"He didn't, at least not knowingly."

"What do you mean?" I fold my arm across my chest. I feel

exposed even just talking about Mark when I'm standing here naked with Jax.

He motions for me to come closer so he can continue to wash me. I wave my finger in the air playfully. "Answer the question, Jax."

"One of the sticking points between my dad and Mark was the art in the corporate offices." He steps back into the water holding out his hand for me to join him.

I ignore the gesture and wait for him to continue.

"Mark was in charge of design and he commissioned a bunch of Liz's work. Those paintings were everywhere. In the personal offices, the boardroom, waiting areas, even in the washrooms. You couldn't escape them and all their glory." The sarcastic tone in his voice makes it evident he's not a fan of Liz's work.

"And your dad didn't want that?"

"It should have been Brighton's work hanging on those walls," he snaps. "Instead there's some nobody getting the recognition that my brother deserved."

I flinch when he calls her a nobody. That's exactly who she is to me now too.

He steps out of the water and moves his body closer to mine now. I try to step back but the cold shower wall is waiting for me. I pull back suddenly as a chill runs through me.

"Come here." He wraps his arms around me coaxing me back into the heat of the water.

"I remember how excited she was when Mark ordered all those paintings. I thought he was doing my friend a favor," I say, my lips breezing across his chest.

"I didn't give it much thought until a few months ago when I saw her in Mark's office. It dawned on me then that she was your friend. I saw you two together a couple of times."

"Where?" I push for more anticipating he'll be hesitant to offer any more details.

"I asked Brighton to come see my office before lunch one day." He proves me right and skips over my question as expected. "I played up

Liz's work and threw in a few comments about how attractive she was and he took the bait."

"You did that so she'd be at the opening and you assumed I'd be there too?" I pull my lips into a tight pucker. "That's so much trouble just to bump into me."

"Actually." He strokes the small of my back with his palm. "I did that because I wanted to do something nice for your best friend. I knew that she was important to you."

"Oh," I murmur trying to absorb the kindness of the gesture.

"When Brighton added her to the list I do admit I suggested strongly that he invite her to his gallery opening and I pressed him to tell her to bring you," he says sheepishly.

"That's why Liz was so adamant about me attending with her." I pull up memories of Liz insisting I go with her even though I had whined about how boring it would be for me.

"I took Brighton to Veray to see some of your collection a few weeks before the opening and then mentioned you were a friend of Liz's and I'd like to meet you." The words come out slowly and purposefully. It's almost as if he's choosing each one very carefully.

"So, you did manipulate him into inviting me?" I stare at his face hoping to catch his gaze.

"I wanted you to be there. I just wanted to be close to you." He locks his eyes with mine. "I can't tell you what it felt like when I saw you standing there alone."

I pull my arms around his waist and rest my head against his chest again. "Jax?"

"What is it, beautiful?" He softly caresses my shoulder.

"Thank you for making sure I'd be there."

CHAPTER ELEVEN

"Why are you getting dressed?" he asks. He shakes his head as he playfully grabs at the hem of my dress.

"I need to take care of a few things today." I pull back and slip on my heels. "I'm meeting Nathan shortly."

"Let me get ready." He pushes past me to his closet and rips a shirt from one of the padded hangers. "It won't take me long."

I tap him on his shoulder trying to divert his attention away from the wardrobe. "You aren't coming with me," I giggle.

"Yes, I am," he says boldly before stepping into a pair of slacks. "I'm not letting you out of my sight. Besides, I don't like the way he looks at you."

"Jax." I reach to button the white dress shirt he's pulled on. "I'm meeting my attorney to talk about my business deal with you. Do you see how that might be just a bit of a conflict?" I tilt my head to the side.

"Ah..." He masterfully ties a blue bold-patterned tie around his neck. "You two are going to scheme to get more from me, aren't you?" he asks teasingly while pulling out the empty pockets of his slacks. "I'm all tapped out, Ivy. You ran me dry with your list of demands."

I laugh loudly as I swat him on the forearm. "It's just to finalize some things with Madeline."

"I heard about that." He kisses the top of my head before he continues, "I'm proud of you, beautiful. You told Madeline who was boss."

"Hardly," I scoff. "I just don't want to suffocate my business anymore. I need it to grow and getting out from under her wing is a good start."

"I'm glad you see that." He walks over to his dresser and loops one exquisite cufflink through the arm of his shirt. "I knew buying into Veray would pay off. It bought you some time."

The comment jars me. Why would he say that? "What?" I blurt out. "What do you mean it bought me some time?"

He turns as he fastens the other cufflink into place. "Veray is on the verge of bankruptcy."

Startled, I don't say a word in response.

"I've known Madeline for years." He's standing in front of me now, adjusting his suit jacket. "She's a horrible businesswoman."

"When did you know it was in trouble?" I inhale sharply. Why hadn't he mentioned this to me before? Is this why he was so reluctant to sell his shares in Veray to me?

"The day after I read in the Dialogue piece that you had an exclusive contract with her," he says it so easily. It's as though the details of that knowledge are lost on him. Does he not understand that I've placed the success of my entire business into Madeline's hands for the past few years?

"I had no idea." My skin is burning in frustration. I feel as though he's been orchestrating my life behind my back for the past year.

"Why did you think I bought into it?" The smile on his face has faded into a frown. "I did that so you wouldn't get stuck in limbo when the creditors came looking for their money."

I'm losing my footing. The room is spinning. I reach behind me to find the edge of the bed. "When were you going to tell me this?"

He stares at my face. "Sit down, beautiful." I feel him push me down until I'm sitting on the edge of the bed. He sits next to me, holding my hand in his lap. "You were so intent on wrestling those shares away from me." A light smile crosses his lips. "I was thankful when Gilbert told me you'd given up on that."

He's throwing so much information at me that I'm having difficulty absorbing it all. "But before I saw the video, but that night..." I pause before I continue, "you agreed to sell those shares to me."

"You fought so hard for that." A ghost of a smile waves across his lips. "If the deal would have gone through that way I would have just bought Madeline out and closed the business."

I feel overwhelmed. He's controlling everything. He's been hiding so much from me. It's as though I'm the puppet and he's pulling all of the strings. I pull myself back onto my feet. "I need to go. Nathan is waiting for me."

He nods in agreement. "Signing those release documents today is a fantastic start. Then we'll work on getting you a studio and maybe a shop of your own. Do you think Tribeca is good or something closer to Chelsea?"

"I put an offer on a space in Boston," I whisper while holding my breath.

"You didn't say Boston, did you?" His question makes me tremble inside. I knew we'd need to have this conversation but I wasn't expecting it to be this morning.

I face him directly. I don't want to appear meek to him. "Yes. I've made plans to move there."

"You made those plans before last night?" He motions towards the bed. The sheets are still rumpled, casting a hint of what took place there.

I stare at the bed for a moment before I respond. "Yes, I did, but I'm determined to make it on my own and Boston is home to me."

The veins in his neck tighten and I can tell that the territorial part of him is quickly sprinting to the surface. "You can't just pick up and move there."

"Don't tell me what to do." My response is quick and intuitive. The words shoot out.

"Why would you leave me?" There's pain in his voice.

I sigh heavily. "My decision isn't about you, it's about me." I cast my eyes down to the bed. "We had a beautiful night. I understand more but I still have a million questions."

"Like what?" he snaps. "What do you want to know?"

I shake my head. "Much more than you can explain in the next five minutes. I need to get to my meeting."

His face hardens before he speaks. "Fine. We'll have lunch after-wards and you can ask me anything you want."

"I hope you realize what that means." I pick up my phone from the bed, turn towards the door and march out of the apartment.

———

"MY MOM WAS TALKING about your sister yesterday when I called her." Nathan reaches over his desk to point to yet another dotted line that I need to sign on.

"How's your mom?" I smile brightly when I ask about Gloria. She was the mom that everyone could depend on to have an open door. Her refrigerator was always full of lemonade and brownies and her heart filled with love when I was a kid.

He turns the page scanning the document. "She's really good. I told her you're moving back and she's excited to see you."

I hesitate before I respond searching for the right words. "I'm reconsidering that move."

"Because of Jax?" The question is loaded and comes with just the right amount of spite in his tone.

"I thought you were on his side."

He puffs out a breath. "He was pretty torn up at our meeting. I take it you watched that video that he was talking about?"

I nod. "I did after coaxing by you and my neighbor."

He cocks an eyebrow. "Your neighbor?"

"Not important," I say quietly.

"What was on it?"

I stare out the window behind him. "Jax and a woman." I finally answer. "She was plotting to take over the company with him."

"Mark's company?" He pushes back into his chair.

"Yes or Jax's father's company I guess depending on who you ask." I shrug my shoulders.

"So blackmail was mentioned?" he asks tentatively.

"Off the record?" I joke.

"I hereby evoke client, attorney privilege." He laughs as he waves the pen in his hand in the air mimicking a magic wand. "We're good to go."

I smile weakly. "The video started with the two of them in bed. I thought he was going to make love to her." I shudder as I think about what I felt the moment I first saw them in together.

"That's all you initially saw?"

"Yes. I stopped it at that point when Jax walked in." I stand and walk to the windows. "I finished watching it yesterday."

"And they didn't?" His words are clipped.

"No." I stare out at the expansive view. All the people milling about the city's streets look so small and insignificant. There's so many of them. Hundreds upon hundreds at any given moment. "Do you think it's odd?"

"That he didn't fuck her?" His voice is on my neck now. I shiver at the sensation.

"No." I turn and look up into his vibrant blue eyes. "Do you think it's odd that the only two men I've ever loved own a company together?"

His eyes scan my face. I know that he still sees that shy and vulnerable seventeen-year-old girl that stared at him across the baseball field. "You're doubting him still, aren't you?"

I shrug my shoulders. "Maybe or maybe I'm just doubting myself."

"I think that you're a beautiful woman who needs to listen to this..." he gently grazes his finger across my forehead before he continues, "instead of this." His finger hovers above the space between my breasts. "Get all your questions answered, take some time and then everything will make sense."

"How did you get so smart, Nate?" I ask tapping my finger to the tip of his nose.

He blushes. "Law school, Ms. Marlow."

"Are we done here?" I move past him back to where my purse is resting in a chair. "I have a lunch date."

"You've signed everything I needed you to sign." He gathers together the papers that now cover his desk.

"Did you know Veray was in financial trouble?" I throw the question at him as I reach for the door handle.

"Jax's lawyer was pretty insistent that I talk you out of taking over his interest in the company," he says. "So I had a pretty good idea there were some issues with the company's structure."

"I found out today he bought into it to save it from bankruptcy because I sell my stuff there," I admit.

He lowers himself into his chair. "How do you feel about that?"

I slowly open the office door. The sound of people milling about is mixed with a cell phone ringing in the distance. "Numb."

He nods as I turn to walk out the door.

CHAPTER TWELVE

"How's Moore?" The loaded undercurrent that is swirling beneath the question doesn't slip past me.

"Dreamy," I say with little emotion as I sit down across from Jax.

"Dreamy?" he repeats. "Who even uses that word anymore, Ivy?"

I pull my eyes into a squint. "Obviously, I do."

"You just say those things to get under my skin." He raises his wineglass to his lips.

I take a small sip of the ice water in front of me. "I say it because it's true. Nathan is hot."

"You're goading me now." He pushes his body into a more upright stance. "Why?"

I motion for the waiter and order myself a martini. "This territorial, I caveman, you woman thing is wearing on me."

"Excuse me?" He tries to stifle the laugh that accompanies the question but it's useless.

"I'm being serious." I don't break a smile. I don't even really know who this man is. Our entire relationship has been nothing but a series of lies, betrayals and corporate maneuverings. Last night was a start towards the truth but I'm craving more and I'm not afraid to ask for it.

He studies my face as if he's gauging whether or not I'm sincere. "It's just who I am," he says dryly.

"Were you always that way? With the women you bedded?" I nod as the waiter places the martini on the table. I drink from it, savoring the taste, anticipating the slight buzz it will give me. My courage always seems to make an appearance when alcohol is involved.

"The women I bedded?" He looks past me pretending to do a search of the room with his eyes. "Where's the Ivy that left my apartment this morning? You're an imposter, aren't you?" The laugh that follows the questions irks me.

"None of this is funny to me." I take another swallow of the drink. "I told you this morning that I have a lot more questions."

"Ready. Set. Go." He points his hand at me as if he's shooting a revolver. "Ask away, beautiful."

"Who was the woman you said cheated on you? When did that happen?" I lob both questions effortlessly at him. He doesn't bat an eyelash.

"Maria. I can't recall her last name right now." He pauses to sip from his wineglass. "It was right after college. She was blowing our boss for cheap favors and a dollar more an hour than what I was getting."

"You're joking," I say sarcastically. "That's who broke your heart?"

"I was crazy for her," he admits. "The day after she told me about their affair, I quit and took off."

"Took off? As in left the job?"

"As in left the city. Hell, I left the continent." He shrugs. "I guess I was running from the pain. It was the first time I was rejected."

"You're over her now." It's more a statement than a question. "Do you think the possessiveness stems from that?"

He stares intently at my face. "I've never been possessive. I'm only that way with you."

I chuckle before I respond. "I clearly recall you saying something to Brooke in that video about her belonging to you."

His face rushes crimson and he scowls at the words. "I said that to her to make her feel safe enough to confess what she was doing. The words slipped out."

"It's strange." I shift my gaze past him to a couple seated behind him. I envy the simple way they are holding hands, the way he leans in to listen to her speak. "The words hold less meaning to me now. Now that I heard you say them to her."

"They meant nothing before you." He reaches casually across the table to place his hand over mine but I retreat.

"What about my shares in the company?" I slip into a new topic, not wanting to dwell on the loss of our connection's innocence.

He stares at my hand as if it's left a trail behind it on the table when it dodged his grasp. "What about them?" he asks nonchalantly.

"Is there a reason you just didn't tell me who you were and then ask to buy them?" I ask before raising the glass to my lips again to finish the drink.

"Mark cheated on you."

His statement is unexpected and I grip the stem of the glass, wishing the waiter would stop by with another. "That's common knowledge, yes."

"Do you honestly think that you would want anything to do with his business partner?" he asks without emotion.

I don't know how to answer that. Until a few weeks ago I assumed that Tom Walker's widow was Mark's irrelevant and silent partner. I had no idea that his son, my new lover, was the man who held Mark's company's future within his hands. "I don't think that that's relevant." I pause before I continue, taking the time to carefully craft my response. "I think what matters is that you didn't give me a choice. You just swooped in, pretended to be something you weren't and almost snatched Mark's company away from him."

"Why do you insist on calling it Mark's company?" His words are biting. "It belongs to my father. It's mine now. Why can't you see that?"

I don't react. I don't want him to see how weary this is making me.

"Mark has driven the company into the ground. He's taken every-thing my father built and tossed it aside because he couldn't focus enough on the business at hand. He was too busy fucking anything that passed by him in a skirt," he fumes.

I sit rigidly letting the words soak into my skin, my heart and my soul. Mark. It's all about Mark. It's always been about Mark.

"Christ, Ivy." He pushes his chair and stands. "I didn't mean that."

I silently watch him walk around the table. He crouches before me. I close my eyes. "Please, just go," I whisper as I wave my hand thoughtlessly in the air.

CHAPTER THIRTEEN

"YOUR WISH IS MY COMMAND." MARK'S OVERLY ZEALOUS GRIN GREETS me as I swing open the door of my apartment.

I move to allow him to walk in. "Cut out the theatrics, Mark and get in here. The NYPD will be breaking down my door with a battering ram in about two minutes if Mrs. Adams sees you're here."

"Good point, sweetheart." He uses the word naturally and I suddenly wonder if he does it as way to unnerve me. I decide that this time I'm going to completely ignore it.

"Moving back in?" He nods towards the stack of boxes littering the foyer.

"Nope," I say curtly. "I'm moving to Boston."

"Boston?" He twists the word around his tongue as if it's repulsive.

"Boston," I parrot back to him.

"Why the hell would you go there?" He walks into the living room and settles himself onto the couch. I follow behind and take a seat in the chair opposite him.

"My life isn't your business anymore," I growl. "I didn't ask you over to talk about that."

"Fine." He stares at his fingernails. It's a tactic he's long used when he wants me to believe he's not interested in what I have to say. It's childish, humiliating and pure Mark through and through.

"Let's talk about Brooke." I lean back into the chair, relaxing my shoulders.

"So I did peak your curiosity when I mentioned her." He sits upright. "Is that why you left him?"

"Who said I left him?" I purse my lips together.

He studies my face trying hard to mask the look of surprise that is running along his brow. "You're moving away so it's obviously over."

"Jumping to conclusions isn't smart, Mark," I chuckle. "Sleeping with Brooke probably wasn't one of your brightest moves either."

"I didn't sleep with her." The words fall off his tongue so quickly they almost bounce into one another.

"What's that?" I crane my neck forward as if I didn't hear him. "You didn't sleep with her?"

"Jax did," he spits back at me.

"Yeah, no." I shake my head lightly back and forth. "That's a lie."

He runs his hand over his brow pushing away a few small beads of sweat that are forming. "So now you believe him over me?"

I breathe in heavily before I pull a wide grin across my lips. "Actually I believe that if she would have slept with Jax she wouldn't have gone near your bed."

"What the fuck does that mean?" He jerks forward, his knees banging into the coffee table.

"You kind of suck in bed." I shrug my shoulders. "Jax, on the other hand..." I let my voice trail as I watch him squirm.

"Shut up." A vein on his forehead bulges as he tosses the words at me. "What the hell would you know?"

"I finally know what an orgasm is," I say in a breathy tone.

"You're vile." He lunges to his feet. "You called me all the way over here for that? To tell me Jax is better in bed than me?"

"Better is an understatement, sweetheart." I stand now too.

"What do you want, Ivy?" He moves swiftly towards the door of the apartment.

"I want to know why I keep hearing that there were company

shares in my name before we even separated." I place my hands on my hips in defiance. I won't back down from this.

He scoffs. "Who told you that? It's not true."

"Brooke did." It's a lie but it's only skirting the truth. I did hear her say it with my own two ears when I was watching the video.

"She's a lying bitch." His hands are trembling.

I know I'm circling something big. I just don't have any idea what it is. "No, she's a whore and a lying bitch but that's just semantics."

"When did you talk to her?" He pushes the question at me as he takes a step towards me.

I don't retreat. I'm not going to allow him to intimidate me a moment longer. "That's not relevant. What is relevant is that you gave me a ten percent share in Intersect Investments when we separated and apparently I owned at least that for some time before that day."

"You did not," he screams at me.

"I've always wondered why you didn't involve any lawyers in that transaction." I tap my index finger to my chin. "Brooke helped me understand why that is."

All of the color drains from his face. "I paid her to keep her mouth shut."

"Obviously not enough." I temper the tone of my voice. I have to keep baiting him. "She told me everything."

His foot begins drumming extraordinarily fast against the hard-wood floor. It's a sign that he's panicked. I remember it clearly from the day I confronted him about his affairs. "Fuck her. She told you about the forgery, didn't she?" he asks, his voice cracking.

I nod my head. Forgery? Did Mark forge my name? Was he using my proxy before I signed the documents giving it to him?

"When Tom died I had to do something." He starts pacing back and forth in the foyer. "Jax could have taken over. Putting those shares in your name was the only thing I could think of."

I stare at his face. How could I have not realized how destructive he was? How did I not see through the thin veil of goodness that he wore for me?

"You're not going to the FTC with this, are you?" He lunges at me and grabs my arms. "Is she going to testify that I made her impersonate you? Or that I paid her off to keep quiet?"

I almost feel my knees buckle. I can't speak. I can't believe that all of this has poured out of him. All I wanted when I called him over here was some closure. I just wanted to know why Brooke had mentioned those shares right after the gala when Mark and I were still together. I wanted this to be the last time I'd ever see him.

"What do you want?" He takes a step back from me. "I'll give you the apartment. You can sell it and buy one in Boston. Do you want money? What? Tell me what?"

"Nothing," I whisper. "I want nothing."

He glares at me as he marches towards the door. "I'll be back. Think about what you want and I'll be back."

I slide to the floor as the door slams behind him.

CHAPTER FOURTEEN

"If you knew something about someone that you didn't care about but that information could damage someone you love, what would you do?" I ask while I stare at my hands in my lap.

"That depends, dear." Mrs. Adams takes a heavy breath. "Is this about your fellow?"

"It is." I smile lightly. "Someone has done something that is illegal and if I report it, the consequences of that could hurt Jax and me."

She squints her eyes as she looks toward the midday sun pouring into her apartment. "I think you need to ask him about it."

"I'm not sure I can do that." I rush back in my mind to that moment at the restaurant when Jax was seething with anger about Mark and his father. If I give him this ammunition there's no telling what he will do with it. At the very least the three of us will be pulled into a very complicated investigation with the FTC. All I want at this point is to leave Mark behind me. I just want him to stop being such a force in my relationship with Jax.

"Ivy, come sit here." She pats her wrinkled hand on the couch next to where she's sitting.

I move from my position in a chair next to the window, to sit with her. She reaches for my hands. "Dear, lies break people apart. You know that."

I nod. I know she's talking about Mark and it's ironic that she has no clue that my problems have come full circle right back to him.

"Don't be like Mark. You're better than him." She lightly squeezes my hand. I can tell it takes a lot of effort for her to do it. "Do the right thing. Your fellow will understand."

I sigh. I know that she's right.

"Never tarnish your heart." She taps my chest with her finger. "You have to tell him. If you don't, you're a liar too."

Her words bite not because they are cruel or malicious but because they are grounded in fact. She's completely right. I have to tell Jax and I have to report Mark.

———

"YOU'RE SUCH A GOOD COOK," I say as I place the fork down on the plate. "Where did you learn how to cook pizza that's this good?"

"My mother was an amazing cook." He reaches for my plate and places it in the sink along with his own. "It was one of the things we always did together when I was child."

I smile. I love when Jax talks about his childhood. Each time he has it's always brightened his face and brought a lilt to his voice. "That's such a beautiful memory to have."

He reaches for my hand to pull me from the chair. "It's one of my favorites."

I watch his back as he leads me down the hallway to the bedroom. "Isn't there a rule about waiting at least a half hour after you eat before having sex?"

He stops, turn and lets out a ferocious laugh. "Do you know how charming you are?" He brushes his lips across my forehead. "I just wanted to show you something?"

"I've seen it and it's impressive." I giggle. The one glass of white wine I had with my dinner is already having the desired effect on me. I need to bring up my conversation with Mark but first I have a few questions for Jax.

He shakes his head as he chuckles. "There's something in your drawer for you." He motions towards the dresser. I flash back to the day I was moving in and he had shown me the emptied drawers that were reserved for my unmentionables as he called them.

I glance up at his face and his gaze is clear and steady. There's no apprehension there. Tonight he's just my Jax. He's not the ruthless businessman determined to ruin Mark. I don't want to tell him what I've learned about Mark but I know I have no choice.

"Open the drawer, beautiful." He reaches for my hand and holds it to the metal pull.

I yank it open and I'm greeted with the sight of my lingerie I left behind when I raced out after seeing the video. Beside it is a plain white envelope with my name on it. On top of that is the necklace. The beautiful necklace that Jax had designed for me was now fixed.

He reaches past me to pick up the delicate chain. "Turn around," he whispers into my ear."' I'll put it on you."

I do as I'm told and I feel a shiver course through me as he grazes my neck with his fingers after securing the clasp. "Thank you," I say breathlessly. I feel complete again. I cradle the necklace in my hand, wishing that I could make the world swallow everything up and chase it away so that all that existed was Jax and me in this moment, in this room, forever.

"It belongs on you." He kisses my neck. "Now open the envelope." There's a giddy edge to his voice and I whip around to look at the expression on his face. It's exuberant. He's excited and I feel my stomach flip flop as he hands it to me.

I raise an eyebrow expectantly as I watch a wide grin take over his face. "I can't wait." He's almost bouncing up and down. "Rip it open."

I do it knowing that if I hadn't at that exact moment he was liable to take it from me and do it himself. I stare down at a beautiful invitation. I run my finger over the raised lettering before I pull it closer so I can read it. The information is sparse. It only lists a date and time and an address in SoHo.

"Is this another of Brighton's shows? If it is I'm going to have a headache next Friday." I scrunch my nose up.

He chuckles. "I won't subject you to another of those. No." He takes my hand and sits me down on the edge of the bed. "Next Friday at eight o'clock you need to be at that address." I'm so focused on his words that I don't protest when he starts to undo my dress.

"Why?" I moan as I feel his hand brush against the thin lace of my bra. "Is it another apartment?"

His finger plunges beneath the lace pulling on my erect nipple. He buries his face into my neck. "No, you don't need that. You're going to move back in here."

"I am?" I ask faintly. Of course I am. I want to.

"When you're ready this is your home. This is your bed." He pushes me gently onto my back and the invitation flutters out of my hand and onto the floor.

I catch his lips with mine and pull him into a deep kiss. I need this. I want him like this. I have to have him one last time before I arm him with what he needs to ruin Mark. "Please, Jax," I purr into his mouth.

He tears at my dress, pulling my body from it. I'm tangled within the sheets, trying to undress him. He stands and quickly unburdens himself of his clothing. I stare at his body. His beautiful, magnificent body. It's the body that taught me what pleasure really is. It's the only body that I can imagine having within mine.

He reaches behind me to unhook my bra. I watch as he carefully traces my right nipple with his tongue. Pulling it into his mouth for light kisses followed by bursts of pain when he clamps his teeth around it. His hand moves between my thighs, dipping below the lace. He traces his finger along the wetness, tempting me, taunting me.

"I want you," I beg. My body is trembling. The ache to be one with him is almost immeasurable.

"Not now. Not yet," he murmurs against the tender flesh of my nipple before pulling his finger from my folds.

I hold my breath as he reaches behind me to unhook my bra allowing both my breasts to spill out. He traces his tongue from one nipple to the other. Biting, licking, kissing. I reach down to touch myself. I want to come. I need to.

He shakes his head to warn me off. His hand clasps mine pulling it to his cock. I eagerly take it. I love how it feels. I can't close my hand around it but I stroke it. I want him to feel as much pleasure as he gives me. He lets out a guttural moan.

I feel as though I'm floating as he pulls the panties from me just as his lips find mine. He tugs my bottom lip between his teeth. He nips it, sucks it. He's tempting me, pushing me closer and closer to the edge.

"Please," I almost sob.

He inhales sharply the moment he slides himself into me. "Fuck." The word rolls slowly off his tongue and onto his lips, spilling into my mouth with his breath.

I grab his hips, pulling desperately. I need him. I can't let him go. "So good," I whisper into him.

He moves faster, thrusting harder, pushing with everything he has. My head thuds into the mattress, my whole body moving with each measured plunge he makes. He speeds the rhythm and I reflect it in my own movements. I push harder, pull more.

"Look at me," I scream.

His eyes pop open and he stares into mine as he fucks me. "Ivy." The word leaves his body as a moan.

"Now," I command. I can't hold it any longer. I have to come. I stare into his eyes. I see deep into his soul.

"Christ," he grunts as he falls over the edge with me. His body trembles. I hold fast, wanting him to pump everything he is into my body.

"I love you." His breath caresses my cheek. "I love you, Ivy."

CHAPTER FIFTEEN

"I MEANT IT WHEN I SAID YOU SHOULD LIVE HERE." HE'S CLAD ONLY IN boxers now as he sits on the bed. He lays a plate of fruit and cheese on the sheet and hands me a bottle of sparkling water.

"I'd like to," I reply. It's one of the things I think endlessly about I want to say but I temper my reaction. I still need to confess to Jax that Mark has committed fraud.

"Drink." He tilts the bottle towards my lips. "I want you to finish that and all this."

I laugh at the prospect. "We just had pizza, Jax." I take a small sip of the cold water. "I'm not hungry."

He cocks a brow as if he's questioning my response. "I am." He pops a red grape into his mouth followed by a slice of white cheese.

"Can we talk about something?" I reach to place the bottle of water on the nightstand. I'm feeling so anxious. I don't want him to notice that my hands are now trembling. I'm grateful that he gave me a t-shirt to wear. I know that the conversation we're about to have is going to make me feel emotionally exposed. The shirt helps me to feel some comfort and protection in a sense.

"Anything." He munches on a crisp piece of apple.

I cast my eyes downward as I take a breath to quiet my nerves. "It's about Brooke."

He stops chewing and stares at me. "What about her?" he asks out of the corner of his mouth.

I watch him pick the plate up and reach past me to place it next to the water. He scoots closer to me.

"Why did you make that recording?" It's a neutral place for me to start. I want to understand his true motivations for filming Brooke and for coercing her into playing that voicemail that Mark left her.

"She was out of control." His eyes idly scan the room. "She came to me weeks before that and tried to seduce me."

"Really?" I ask although I'm not surprised. It was the first assumption I'd made after viewing the entire file on the flash drive.

He nods. "She played that voicemail for me to prove that I could trust her," he says as he locks his eyes on my face. "I'm sorry you had to hear that."

"It wasn't shocking." I mean the words. "Mark was very good at hiding his true self."

He reaches for my hand and strokes it with his. "I wanted her to back off. Not from Mark. I didn't care about him at that point. I just wanted her away from the company."

"Because of what she did to your dad?"

His expression shifts slightly to one of concern. "She really fucked up his life. My mother's too. I couldn't watch her ruin the company and it felt like she was going to do that."

"Was she delusional?" I ask because I want to understand what she was really after.

"My father promised her the moon and the stars and half of the company." He waves his hand in the air as if motioning to the sky beyond the ceiling.

"During their affair," I mumble.

"She gave him something. Attention maybe, a sense of love. I don't know what but he needed it and he was willing to give her anything in return."

I lean forward. "Do you think that was just pillow talk?"

He looks into my eyes. I see sadness there now. I know it's difficult for him to talk about his father's weaknesses. "He was never going to give her anything once he found out she was sleeping with Mark too. He told me that when he was dying."

"What did she want from you? Did she really believe you'd be on board to blackmail Mark?"

"Maybe," he says it without conviction. "Before my dad died she bought an apartment she couldn't afford. He paid her mortgage and when he was gone, that evaporated so she panicked."

"And the recording?" I leave the question open ended on purpose.

"The recording was meant to push her into just disappearing. I thought if I threatened her with it, she'd bolt before Mark saw it. It wasn't the best laid plan but I wanted to corner her. Make her feel the same pressure she made my dad feel."

"Did you ever play it for Mark?"

"I didn't have to." He reaches past me to grab the bottle of water. "My mom took a turn for the worse so I left for California. Once she died I came back and Brooke was gone."

"Did you wonder what happened to her?" I push the subject wanting to know if he has any inkling that Mark paid her off.

"I've always secretly hoped she fell into the Hudson River on one of her morning jogs." He laughs the comment away.

I smile meekly. The idea of that woman falling into the river conjures up images of men with cement shoes in hand and thick Jersey accents who are getting paid in unmarked bills.

"My guess is that she nailed some executive to the wall and he married her."

"Is that an uneducated guess?" I'm wondering exactly what had happened to her now.

"Not entirely," he says. "I heard a woman from payroll talk about Brooke's husband in the lunchroom one day when I stopped to get a coffee."

I breathe a sigh of relief which I try to conceal with a cough. I know that once I explain to Jax about Mark's corporate maneuverings that Brooke will likely be dragged back into the mess that Intersect Investments is going to become when an investigation is opened.

CHAPTER SIXTEEN

I WALK BACK INTO THE BEDROOM AFTER SPENDING AT LEAST TEN minutes in the washroom splashing cold water on my face. It's time for me to tell Jax about Mark. I'm terrified. Not by the idea of him knowing what Mark was doing behind closed doors but by the fact that it may set in motion a series of events that will impact our relationship for good.

"So there's something I have to tell you." I sit back down on the edge of the bed. I'm wishing I had fully dressed. The things I am about to tell Jax feel too weighty for just a t-shirt and panties.

He pulls me closer to him so my hand is resting on his leg. I love his legs. They're so strong, so imposing. He's everything I ever wanted and needed and now I'm going to change the course of this forever.

"It sounds serious." He tilts his chin down so his eyes align with mine.

I nod and breathe a heavy sigh. "So serious."

"You can tell me anything, beautiful." He brushes his fingers along my chin and I reach for them with my hand. I cradle his hand in mind pushing it into my skin.

"It's about Mark. He came to my apartment."

"When? Why?" His fingers go rigid and the tenderness that is there is erased with irritation.

I relax and his hand falls from my face into his lap. I stare at it before I answer. "I asked him to come see me."

He bolts to his knees. "Why would you do that? What were you thinking?"

His coarse tone rasps against me. His constant hatred of Mark is crushing at times. I feel like I'm tied to the middle of a thick rope in a tug-o-war game. I didn't ask for it. It's not what I wanted.

"Something wasn't making sense to me. I needed Mark to clarify it." I speak calmly. It's the truth. I wanted Mark to explain about the shares and about the timing.

He settles back onto his heels now as if he's a rabid dog who has been pulled back to the prone position by its owner. "What didn't make sense?"

I look down at the bed. I want to choose these next words carefully. "When I watched that recording of you and Brooke for the second time something hit me square in the face."

He scans my face looking for anything that will clarify my words. "What?"

"Y-you…two talked about my shares in Mark's company," I stutter. "About taking them away from me."

He rubs his hand across his brow. "We did."

"I didn't have any shares back then," I say slowly.

His eyes dart up and down my face. I know that look. He's going to question whether I'm being naïve again. "Are you sure? Mark had your proxy then."

"I'm positive," I snap back. "I didn't sign my proxy over to him until after we separated."

He jumps to his feet and steps off the bed. "I think you're mistaken on the timing." He doesn't look at me. His eyes are focused on the floor as he rubs the back of his neck with his left hand.

I stand and walk past him towards the living room. I hear his footsteps following me. I need to find my purse. I reach inside it grabbing onto the folded documents I slipped into it earlier. "I'm not mistaken." I turn and face him.

"What is that?" He nods towards the papers in my hand.

I unfold them and study them briefly. "When Mark made me sign my proxy to him we went to a notary public. He didn't want a lawyer involved. I asked for a copy." I shove the papers into his hands.

He greedily runs his eyes over them, soaking in the signatures, taking in the dates. "These state that Mark gifted those shares to you a little over six months ago." There's a difference in his tone now.

"Yes." I know this is the point in the conversation when I have to tell him about Mark's confession. "He forged my signature on other documents. Documents that gave him my proxy a year or more ago."

His eyes leap to my face. "How do you know this?"

I stare into him. He's shifting. I can see it before me. His ruthlessness is rushing to the surface again. "He told me."

"What? He told you?" He almost laughs in merriment. "Tell me exactly what he said."

I try to pull the conversation with Mark back to the forefront of my mind. I don't know his exact wording. I can't recall every pinpointed detail of what he said. "I'm not sure exactly what he said."

He grabs my arm forcefully and I flinch. "Remember, Ivy. You have to remember."

I try to tear myself from his grasp but his hand is unyielding. "You're hurting me, Jax. Let me go."

"Think about this carefully." He ignores my request. The papers swing past my face. "What did he say to you?" He spits out each word separately the way a person would do if they're talking to someone who doesn't comprehend the language.

I wrench my arm free. Pain bites through it. "He said that he was worried that I was going to go to the FTC. He forged my name on documents and Brooke helped him."

"Holy fucking shit." He jumps up and down. "You've got to be fucking kidding me."

I stand in silence staring at him in all his wanton joy. He's giddy. His eyes scan the documents for a second time.

"What else?" He doesn't raise his eyes from the paper he's focused on. "What else did he say?"

I wince at his words. I don't want to talk about this anymore. I want to go back to the bedroom. I want all of this to be a bad dream.

"Ivy." My name snaps across his lips. "What else?"

I stare at him. He's not the same. The man from the bedroom is gone now. "He said that he paid Brooke off."

He doesn't reply. He's racing down the hallway. I stand in silence hearing only the distant sound of his voice. He's telling someone that he has the golden ticket. I don't know how much time passes. It must be only moments, although it feels like endless hours. I'm still standing exactly where he left me. My hair rumpled, his t-shirt covering my body as he sprints past me, fully clothed and charges out the door.

CHAPTER SEVENTEEN

"WHERE DID YOU DISAPPEAR TO LAST NIGHT, BEAUTIFUL?" JAX IS standing in the doorway of my apartment. It's now approximately sixteen hours since he left me alone in his living room.

I move to the side so he can walk in. "You were the one who disappeared on me." My words are spiked with resentment. "You just ran away with your golden ticket."

He smoothly slips his suit jacket from his shoulders and thoughtfully folds it before placing it over the back of the chair in my living room. "You heard that," he grimaces.

"I did." I motion for him to sit.

He takes a spot on the couch and I can tell from his posture that he's expecting me to sit next to him. I move towards the chair and perch myself on the arm.

I wait for him to check his phone before I speak again. "So what happens now?"

"You could sit on my lap," he growls patting his slacks.

"With Mark? What happens?" I ignore his innuendo. I don't want to slip into anything intimate with Jax until we discuss what I'm feeling.

He rolls his eyes and the gesture bites into me. This cocky version of Jax isn't nearly as appealing as the man who gave me the necklace or the one who took care of me in the shower. "Why does it matter, Ivy? Don't you dare say you care about what happens to that asshole."

I stare sullenly at him. "I care what happens to me."

"You're fine." There's a definite edge to his voice. "I'll take care of you."

"What about our deal?"

"What deal?" He's focused on his phone again.

"The shares..." My voice falls off as he pulls the phone to his ear.

He raises his index finger as if to stop me from speaking. "Gilbert. Tell me what you know. When will the FTC meet with me?"

I stand and walk towards the bank of windows overlooking the street. I stare down. There are a few people scattered along the sidewalk. I spot a couple holding hands. There's a woman pushing a stroller while a very happy toddler laughs and tries to bat the low hanging leaves off the tress they pass. It's all so simple and so uncomplicated.

"Those papers changed my life, beautiful."

I turn to see him still seated on the couch, his eyes cast down toward his phone.

"Is our deal on hold now?"

He bursts out laughing. "Of course it is. As soon as the dust settles and Mark is locked up, the company is completely mine."

I don't move from my spot by the windows. I need physical distance from him in this moment. "How long before the dust settles?"

"A year. Maybe more?" He throws it out as more a question than an answer.

"You're really happy, aren't you?" I'm not sure why I want to know that. Or why I need confirmation of it. The wide grin that has been on his face since he waltzed through the door is answer enough.

"Ecstatic." He leaps from his spot on the couch and moves quickly towards me. "Almost as happy as when I'm inside you."

I feel him slip his hand into my dress. "You're going to fuck me now?"

"I don't have a lot of time." He's pulling at the buttons, exposing my bra. His hands dive to unfasten his belt.

"How thoughtful of you to pencil me in." I push the dress from my shoulders. "Do you want to just fuck me here bent over the windowsill so we don't waste any time walking to the bed?"

He freezes. His hands stop in mid-air. His shirt unbuttoned, his slacks hanging open. "Ivy," he whispers my name.

"You better get started." I bite my lip to hold back a sob. "You need to leave soon."

"What's wrong, beautiful?" His hand grazes my cheek and I pull back.

"I can't do this anymore." I reach to pull my dress back on. "I can't."

"Do what?" he asks, his voice slightly raised.

"I'm so tired." I move away from him now, seeking out the comfort of the chair. I sink into its cushion. I fumble with the buttons on the front of my dress before I give up in frustration.

His legs come into view and I watch as he silently sits on the coffee table. "What's going on?"

I close my eyes. I pull in a deep breath to cage my emotions. "Our relationship is all about Mark."

He shakes his head. "No, that's not true. There's much more to it than that."

"We always come back to him. To how much you hate him."

"He ruined my father's life." He barks the words at me.

"Your father is dead. He wasn't perfect." I try to find compassion within the words. "No one is perfect."

He slides his hand along his thigh, balling it into a fist when it reaches his knee. "You're going to defend that bastard, aren't you?"

"Who?"

"Mark?" he seethes. "That's what all this is about, isn't it? That's why you wouldn't fuck me just now?"

The irony of his words isn't lost on me and I can't control the laugh that falls out. "Wow."

"Wow?" He stands and rapidly does up the buttons on his shirt, before tucking it in and fastening his belt.

"You always go back to Mark. Always." I pull in a deep breath and exhale slowly.

"No, you do that." He throws my words back in my face.

"It will always be like this." I hang my head.

"Like what?" he asks absentmindedly, his focus pulled back once again to his smartphone.

I don't reply. I sit in silence waiting to see when he'll notice. Several moments pass as he taps out what seems to be an email on his phone.

"Where were we?" He reaches behind me for his jacket and pulls it back on.

"You were leaving." I stand and motion towards the door. "Goodbye, Jax. Let me know when the dust settles."

He stops and stares into my face. I can see countless questions bouncing in his eyes but he doesn't open his mouth to speak. He just follows my suggestion to the door, opens it and slips through.

CHAPTER EIGHTEEN

"I KNOW THAT LOOK." MRS. ADAMS PULLS MY CHIN UP WITH HER finger. "You're upset about a man."

I giggle as I squeeze her hand in mine. "You should have been a psychic."

"I could have been one." She winks. "That or a chorus girl on Broadway."

"You would have driven the men wild," I say jokingly.

She bursts into laughter almost spilling the glass of lemonade she's holding into her lap. She places it down on the table before she turns to look at me. "I'm glad you're staying here for now, dear."

I gaze past her to the foyer of my apartment. "Me too." I haven't told her about Mark's legal issues or that I may have to move out of the building at a moment's notice if his assets are seized. It's all too worrisome and complicated for her to manage.

"Have you spoken to your fellow today?"

"Not today," I reply softly. Not since he walked out a week ago after our confrontation regarding Mark. I haven't tried to text or call him and I've heard nothing from him at all. I assume he's been too wrapped up in making Mark pay for his misdeeds. That along with the restructuring of his father's company would soak up all of his time. At least that's what my heart is telling me.

"It's getting late." She glances at the vintage silver watch on her right wrist. "I need to get home."

It can't be later than four I imagine. After our lunch we had stopped here for a glass of lemonade. Spending time with Mrs. Adams on this Friday afternoon was just what I needed to boost my spirits. "I'll help you to your door."

She gossips about one of the women who lives on the floor below us as we walk the few feet to her apartment door. I assure her that I'll stay away from the widow Pennington now that I know that she's a hussy.

As she opens the last of the locks she turns back to me. "I'll see you tonight, dear."

"Tonight?" I ask softly.

Her eyes dart from my face to the wall behind me. "Tomorrow." She pats herself on the forehead. "Old brain," she chuckles.

I giggle as I help her through the door.

I STARE at the luxurious embossed card that Jax had given me last week. It's almost seven and I'm still undecided on whether to be at the noted address in an hour. I wish I knew what he had planned when he prepared this. My eyes settle on the date. I catch my breath. Today would have been my mother's birthday. This was the day she was born.

I bolt from the bed and start searching through my still unpacked boxes of clothes. I have no idea what awaits me at this building in SoHo but I know now that I need to be there. I smile as I pull a simple black cocktail dress from the second box I rummage through. I move on to one of the boxes of shoes and find a red set of heels.

I hurriedly shower, bunching my hair into a passable upswept mess and put on minimal make up. I stare at my bare neck in the mirror after applying my mascara. I rush into my bedroom opening a small wooden box on the nightstand. I carefully pull the necklace from it and sit down as I fasten it around my neck. It's back where it belongs.

I grab a clutch and toss my phone, wallet and keys into it. I stand and take one last look at myself in the full length mirror in the hall. I look tired. My hair is an absolute disaster but I'm presentable. I look hopeful and that's more than I have looked or felt in a week.

I hold tightly to the card as I take the elevator to the lobby. After stopping to greet Oliver and kiss him on the cheek I gaze past him to see a car parked at the curb. It's Leonard, Jax's driver.

"Ms. Marlow," he says as he opens the back door of the sedan for me.

I slide in silently waiting for him to take his seat behind the wheel. "Will Jax be joining us here?" I hold out the card knowing full well that Leonard already knows my destination.

"No Miss," he says curtly. "Mr. Walker is out of town I believe."

"Wait," I snap as he starts to pull the car away from the curb. My heart has dropped to my feet. Why am I going to this address if Jax isn't even in the city?

He doesn't respond as he drives the car through the maze of traffic in Manhattan.

I slink back into the seat and stare at the card in my hand again. Why would he send his driver to get me to go to a place alone? Maybe he arranged it all before last week and Leonard was just following directions. As soon as we arrive, I'll ask him to take me back home.

"We'll be there soon," he calls to me.

I stare silently at the window watching the city rush by me. If there was any question about my relationship with Jax it's been answered now. He's so busy with bringing Mark to task that he forgot to cancel these plans. I feel foolish.

The car pulls to a stop in front of a storefront. I can't make out the sign in the dim light. It's not illuminated and the banks of windows are all covered with brown craft paper. I wait patiently while Leonard walks around the car to open the door for me. I reach for his hand as I step out. My eyes search the sidewalk. It's barren save for the expected foot traffic of a Friday evening.

"Stand here." Leonard directs me by elbow to a spot not more than a few feet from the deserted store.

I search his face looking for any explanation. He's expressionless as he points towards the storefront and takes a step back.

I pull my eyes to the building, wishing I could just slip back into the car, go home and crawl into my bed.

My breath catches as the sign springs to life. Lights pop into the darkness and my heart stops when I read the script writing. Whispers of Grace. Grace. My mother's name.

The door bursts open and I'm overtaken with images of my father's face, my sister and her husband, Mrs. Adams. I see Madeline beyond them, and Nathan. I think I catch a glimpse of Sandra, his sister waving to me from behind the doorway.

I reach to hug my father, burying my face in his chest. "Dad," I whisper. "What...what is this?"

"Come." He pulls me close and guides me through the doorway into a beautiful space filled with jewelry cases. He leads me to one and I peer inside. Nestled beneath the sparkling lights are my pieces. My bracelets, my necklaces, rings that I designed and earrings too. I stare in astonishment. These are the pieces I've had at my apartment. I had packed them to take them to Boston.

'How?" I ask not really absorbing the scope of the space I've just entered.

"Wait until you see your studio." His words are so carefree and happy.

"My studio?" I can't comprehend what he means.

"Your studio, your store." He waves his free hand around the room. "This is all yours, princess."

I stare at the space, drinking in every nuance and detail. My eyes stall on the crystal vases filled with daisies, the business cards stacked neatly at the door and the exquisite glass table I assume is for consultations for commissioned pieces.

"You did this?" I search my father's face for answers.

"I helped with the design." He pulls his shoulders back with pride. "Jax did this."

"Jax?" His name falls from my lips with a quiet sob just as my eyes settle on Brighton's expansive painting from the gallery. The painting I was standing in front of when Jax first spoke to me so long ago.

"Come this way." He pulls me toward the back of the space and opens a door that leads to a staircase. I follow him as he takes each step slowly, the arthritis in his knee making him a slower version of the vibrant man who chased me around the playground in my youth.

Just as he reaches the top step he flips on a light switch and the room is filled with warm, white light.

"This is your studio." He moves aside as I leave the last step and walk into the room. It's breathtaking. A large table is the focal point along with carts filled with supplies. I walk the perimeter of the room slowly pulling it all inside of my mind.

"I can't believe this." I hold my hand over my mouth in astonishment. I've had tears streaming down my face since I saw my father bolt out of the door onto the street. I'm finally overcome with emotion and I reach for the side of the table to balance myself.

"There's something for you." He points to an envelope in the center of the table. "I'm going back down to have some of that fancy champagne."

"Yes," I whisper.

"Take your time, princess. This night is yours."

I listen as he descends the stairs one at a time. When I hear the door close behind him I reach for the envelope. There's nothing on the front of it and its flap is hanging open. I reach inside pulling a handwritten note from it.

MY BEAUTIFUL IVY,

YOU ARE the shining light of my life. I love you more than I ever thought it was possible to love someone. You hold my heart in your hands. It is yours. That is forever.

. . .

I HAVE MADE MISTAKES. Too many mistakes. I've been thoughtless, selfish and calculating. Those are my faults. I tried so hard to guide you into my world when all along you were guiding me into your world. A world that is pure, simple and based in love.

I CREATED this space for you. To honor your mother and to showcase your talent. It is yours. There are no strings attached. I just want you to have it. To use it to create a life for yourself. To show everyone how incredibly unique you really are.

I'VE GIVEN up much of what I own. I've sold my interest in Mark's company (yes, Mark's company not my father's) pending the outcome of the investigation and I'm negotiating the sale of all my other business interests.

IN OTHER WORDS, I need a job. I've never made jewelry but I did work at a video game store for a hot minute in high school. I think that qualifies me to be, at the very least, a part time sales clerk at Whispers of Grace. I haven't included my resume because it's not relevant. If I can have the job just turn around and say, "yes."

YOUR FANBOY

THE LETTER FLUTTERS to the tiled floor as I pull my breath from deep within me where it's been stalled since he walked out of my apartment last week. I stand slowly.

"Will you get me water and food when I'm working so hard I forget to eat?"

"Yes." His voice says softly from behind me.

"Will you bring me fresh daisies every week?"

"Absolutely." His voice is closer now.

"Will you get rid of that painting you hung in the showroom? It's no Da Vinci."

"I will." His voice is so close. His breath is teasing my neck.

"Yes," I whisper as I turn around just in time to feel his lips brush against mine.

PART FOUR

STILL OBSESSED

The Conclusion to
The Obsessed Series

Deborah Bladon

CHAPTER ONE

"You're not serious, beautiful?" He's leaning against the door to my studio, his hands tucked neatly into the pocket of his jeans. The growth of hair on his face makes him look even more stunning than he usually does. I'll never get over how absolutely handsome he is.

"I'm dead serious, Jax." I just need him to accept the inevitable. If he can do that, my life is going to be so much easier.

He taps his shoe against the floor as he studies his fingernails. "You think you have that much authority over me?" He's trying hard to cover the amusement in his voice but it's not working.

I try to suppress a wide grin. I've got him in a place he never saw coming. Now all I have to do is go in for the kill and this nightmare will finally be over and done with. "I know that I do. You're wasting my time."

"I'm wasting your time?" The question accompanies a deep chuckle. God, how I love his laugh. It's so smooth and natural. It means he's comfortable and happy. This is how I want him to always be. This is what fills me with a feeling of being utterly content.

"Yes." I nod and look down at the silver earring I'm working on. "I have a lot to do today. You can pack up your things and leave." I can't meet his gaze again. I just need him to go before I change my mind.

"Just like that? You're going to throw me out on the street?"

"I called Leonard. He's waiting downstairs to drive you home." I know the reference to his driver will hit a nerve within him. Arranging to have Leonard waiting with the car downstairs means that as soon as Jax leaves the shop he'll be on his way home, not on his way back up here to persuade me to reconsider.

"You have this all worked out." His voice deepens. "You were planning on firing me even when I was inside of you this morning and you were screaming my name."

I feel an ache rush through me at the reminder of Jax making love to me just as I was waking up. Being pulled from a dream by the feeling of his lips coursing hot over my right nipple was the perfect way to begin any day. Living with Jax was heaven, but working with him was quickly becoming my own personal hell.

"You can't take it personally," I say curtly. "You're the one who taught me that business is business. That's all this is."

"You don't think I've done a good job?" His voice is clipped. "You're firing me because I fucked up?"

"I'm letting you go because you stalk the customers when they're just browsing the showcases." I suck in a measured breath before I continue, "I see you harassing them when they're walking out of the store without buying anything. It's bad for business."

"It doesn't make sense to me."

"What doesn't make sense to you?"

"None of this makes sense." That's all he offers. He's going to make me put two and two together and decipher what he means on my own.

"Jax, I love you." I pat the empty spot on the edge of the table I'm working on.

He leans against the table. "I love you endlessly, Ivy. Endlessly." His hand reaches to cradle my chin. "I would do anything for you."

"Then leave." I plead with my eyes. "Let me do this alone, please."

"You don't think I'm helping?" A slight frown skirts over the corners of his lips.

I stand and wrap my arms around his neck. "This is my store. I want to make it a success."

"We've been doing that together." I shiver at the touch of his hands on my waist. Even through the heavy material of the knit dress I'm wearing, Jax's touch still makes me weak and desirous.

"Let me do this alone. You need to do something more." This was the part of the conversation I'd been dreading for weeks. Ever since Jax sold off most of his business interests six months ago, he'd been unsettled, unhappy and there was an emptiness within him that was unmistakable.

"I gave up everything for you, beautiful." He bounces the earring in my ear against the tip of his finger. "So you could have your dream."

"It wasn't just about that." I cup my hands around his cheeks. "You know that."

"I was scared." His voice is so low I have to lean in to hear each word. "I was becoming too much like my father. I was being driven by money. I almost lost you because of it."

"You were chasing your dad's dream." I lightly brush my lips across his forehead. "You need to start thinking about what your dreams are."

"I have been thinking about it," he offers. I'm taken back by the words. Every time I've tried to bring up the subject of Jax finding a new business focus he's quieted me by professing his undying need to be by my side twenty-four hours of each and every day.

"You already have something in mind?" The question pains me. I've sensed for weeks that he was lost in thought and not sharing. Even though I know Jax Walker isn't one to share everything openly, it still stings knowing that he's been contemplating something as important as his next step in business without throwing any thought to my opinion.

"We'll talk about it soon." He lifts his head and stares into my eyes. "Right now I have to get off the premises before my former boss calls the authorities to remove me."

"She wouldn't go that far." I grin.

"I'm not taking my chances." His lips brush against mine in a tender kiss before he turns to leave the studio. "What about my severance package?"

"There isn't one." I bite my bottom lip to hold in a broad smile. "You were working for free, remember?"

"Goddammit," he teases as he breezes out the door. "Fired and kicked to the curb with nothing in return, all in one day."

CHAPTER TWO

"WHEN ARE YOU GOING TO TELL ME MORE?" I PICK AT THE LAMB CHOP on my plate. I know Jax spent hours preparing our dinner after I unceremoniously threw him out of the jewelry shop, but I just don't have an appetite.

"About what?" He picks up the goblet of red wine in front of him and takes a hearty swallow before he speaks again," You're sure you don't want wine?"

I shake my head slightly. "About how you plan on spending your time now that you're unemployed." I want to make light of it. I want him to feel comfortable enough that he can open up and share.

"It's not a big deal, beautiful." He nods towards my lamb chop and I shake my head as he pulls it from my plate onto his. "You've barely eaten all day."

"It is a big deal to me." I don't want to sound bitter but since we started living together I've been the one always trying to bridge the emotional gap that is still there. Unless he lets down the barrier that he's built around himself, our relationship is always going to feel as though something fundamental is missing. My life with Jax is beautiful, enriching and more than I could have ever wished for. Even with that knowledge, I still want more. I want all of him, especially the darkest parts of his heart. His secrets had torn us apart too many times. I can't allow that to happen again.

"I was talking to my friend Hunter about investing in some the restaurants his family owns," he says through the corner of his mouth as he quickly devours the lamb chop I barely touched.

"You have the eating part of that down." I manage a smile even though I'm feeling anxious inside.

"You should ask the question, Ivy." His mouth thins. "I know you want to, so do it."

The challenge is meant to push me. He wants me to be the one to acknowledge the elephant in the room. That same elephant that has been stalking us ever since Mark had been arrested for fraud.

If I broach the subject again, the conversation we're having will grind to a halt and Jax will spend the next several hours in his home office with the door closed.

"I'm really tired." I place the linen napkin next to my untouched plate of food. "I think I'm just going to go to bed, Jax."

"Don't." He bites the word out. "Don't run away from this."

"If I don't, you will," I shoot back. "I'll bring up Intersect Investments and you'll slam your fist on the table and run into your office."

"You bring it up at the worst times."

"It hasn't been the right time in six months." I push myself up from the chair. "The deal to buy your shares fell through and you haven't had another offer. You still own half that company and I know part of you wants to go back to it. There. I'm done."

"It's not that easy." His tone is harsh and clipped. "He's not going to pay the way I want him to."

"You can't control everything, Jax." I exhale in a rush trying to temper my rising emotions. "Mark cut a plea deal. That's done. You can't change it."

His shoulders tense as he rises from the chair. "I hate that you can't see how wrong that is."

"I hate that you can't get past this." I straighten and turn to leave the kitchen. "You have to accept that Mark isn't going to prison. You have to accept that he was fined and that he's on probation. That's life."

I close my eyes at the sound of his fist connecting with the table. The unmistakable ring of the silverware hitting the floor and a glass shattering cuts through the dead silence between us. I stand still as Jax breezes past me, the only other sound in the apartment, his office door as it slams shut.

CHAPTER THREE

"DID YOUR HUSBAND HAVE A TEMPER?" I POUR A SMALL AMOUNT OF cream into the china tea cup before handing it to Mrs. Adams.

"He did, dear." She brings the cup to her mouth with trembling hands before she takes a small sip.

"Jax has this sore spot when it comes to Mark." I take a small drink from my own cup of tea and recoil at the taste. It's too bitter. I should have added more sugar.

"Do you think it's because you two almost married?" I wince at her words. I've tried desperately hard to block out all the lingering memories I've had of my long forgotten engagement to Mark Carleton.

"I think he's gotten over that." I reach to offer her one of the sugar cookies I found in the cupboard in her kitchen. "This has more to do with his father's company."

"Your friend is a proud man." She delicately takes a small bite of the cookie. "He's a good judge of character, Ivy. Mark is a loser."

I laugh, shocked by her complete honesty. "He is a loser."

"You need to tell your fellow that you believe in him." She pats my hand lightly. "If he thinks you're ever taking Mark's side it's going to sting more than if you hit him over the head with a frying pan."

It's an interesting analogy and as much as I want to know why she picked that particular implement of havoc, I skip over it. "Mark's been trying to contact me. I haven't told Jax."

"What do you mean?" She motions for me to take the tea cup from her. "How so? Has he been calling?"

"Calling, texting, emailing." I rub the back of my neck. "I haven't responded to anything. I've been deleting all the voicemails and messages without listening to them or reading anything."

"It may be important, dear. I remember you telling me his mother was ill." Her voice is soft and comforting. "Tell your fellow first and then find out what Mark wants."

I nod before I hand her back the cup of tea. She makes it sound so easy. Little does she realize that Mark's name is a literal four-letter word to Jax.

———

"MOORE WAS HERE LOOKING FOR YOU." Jax's gaze fixes on the door behind me. "I didn't realize he knows where we live."

"I mentioned it when I was having lunch with him a couple of weeks ago." I try to play it down. Jax's jealousy over my friendship with my attorney is just another sticking spot between us. If I'm going to bring up Mark's insistent need to talk to me in the next few days, I'm going to have to first put out the fire that is my connection to Nathan Moore.

His eyes shift to my face and I turn away, hanging my sweater up before placing my purse on the chair next the door. "It was nothing."

"You have lunch with the man you crushed all over when you were a teenager, and it's nothing?" He cocks a brow and I swear I see a quick grin flash across his handsome face. He looks relaxed, standing next to the couch, pajama bottoms hanging low on his hips and a stark white t-shirt covering his chest.

"You know it's nothing," I say wryly. "Did he say what it's about?"

"Check your messages." He nods towards my smartphone. "He must have called."

I glance down at the screen and scroll quickly through the recent missed calls. Nothing from Nathan and surprisingly nothing from Mark either. Maybe he has given up. Maybe I won't have to explain his desire to talk to me to Jax after all. I breathe in a heavy sigh of relief at the promise of that.

"Are you hungry, beautiful?" His hands are on my arms now. "Or did you eat with Mrs. Adams?"

"No." I shake my head, grateful for his tender touch. "Just tea and cookies."

"So lady like." His hands glide effortlessly to my hips. "My Ivy. So demure."

I smile at the veiled invitation to prove otherwise. "I'm not demure, am I?"

I rock myself against his body, feeling his cock through the thin material of the pajama bottoms. He wants me. He's already straining, hard and yearning for my body.

"You blush when I tell you I want to fuck you. You close your eyes when you're about to come." His hands move behind me, slowly pulling the zipper of my dress down. "I'm going to take your clothes off right here and you'll tell me you want to go into the bedroom but I'm going to take you right here, against the door."

I feel a surge of crimson rush through my face. I'm blushing, he's right. He's so direct. He's always been with me. I don't protest when he handily unclips the front of my bra pushing it from my body.

"All that's left in my way are these pretty lace panties." His hand traces a path over the front of my cleft. "I knew you'd be wet."

"Always for you, Jax." I bend to push the panties down, stepping out of my heels as I do. "I'm always ready for you."

His clothes are off and he's on his knees in an instant, pulling my left leg over his shoulder as his mouth claims me. I grab for his hair to steady myself while his tongue licks and parts me, pulling the desire to the surface. My body aches for release, it aches to feel him inside of me. I can't ever get enough of him.

"Jax, please," I moan through gritted teeth. It feels so good. It's too good.

"Take it, beautiful." He breathes heavily into my folds as his finger finds my opening.

I shudder at the raw intimacy of the touch. My body bucks helplessly against the door, trying to claim more from him. I push myself into his face, clawing at his hair, needing to come.

"God, yes," I whisper through a veiled moan as I race to the edge. I can't temper what I feel with him. I've never been able to. I want him too much. I crave his touch endlessly.

"Come, Ivy." The command is lost in the moment. I'm enjoying it too much. I don't want it to end.

I lazily roll my hips towards him, pulling his hair, pulling him into me. I crave this. I want this. I try to hold on. I want to savor it. "Jax." My voice is a breathless whisper as I feel the pleasure rushing through my body. I buck my hips against the door, unable to contain the pure rawness of the desire.

"Beautiful, please." He pulls my clit into his mouth, sucking on it while his finger hones in on my most sensitive spot.

I feel the orgasm building. I'm so close to the edge. I want to scream his name but my body won't let me. I can't speak. It's too much. It's too good. I bite my lip as I feel the warmth course through me slowly and evenly. It's too good. It's so good.

"My turn." He's on his feet now, his lips pressed into mine. "I have to fuck you. I've been waiting all day."

I'm still lost in the feeling of coming so hard when he lifts my legs around his waist and carries me to our bed. His lips flutter over mine, kissing me, sharing my most intimate taste.

I cry out as he enters me in one swift movement after tossing me on the bed. His large, muscular frame hovers above me as I feel the entire length of him within me. I grab his ass, pushing him harder, needing to feel completely and utterly connected to him. A small moan escapes my lips as he finds his rhythm.

"You're so beautiful." He groans through gritted teeth as he surges his body forward.

I gasp at the depth of him and grip harder to his body. He's fucking me so hard, driving his body relentlessly into mine. It feels so good. Too good. I'm close to coming again.

"Jax," I whisper into his shoulder. "I'm so close."

He levels back on his feet and pulls my hips closer into him. "I have to watch you come. I want to see it on your beautiful face."

I stare into his eyes as the pleasure falls through me. I call out his name as I feel him buck even harder.

"Christ, Ivy. Yes." He moans loudly as he pumps himself into me.

He pushes me back and pulls his body over mine. I feel his hand cupping my ass as he pushes deeper into me. I accommodate and push back up, pulling my sex around his cock.

I'm gifted with a low, guttural moan as he feels me gripping him tightly. "It's so good," he growls. He fucks me harder, pushing my ass up to meet each of his thrusts. I can't control my need to come again.

"Ivy, come." Two words, the rawness in them unmistakable. The need within his voice is palpable.

I scream his name as I feel him pump himself inside of me. The deep thrusts filling me with his desire. My nails clawing into his skin as I hold on tightly, knowing that I can never get enough of this man.

CHAPTER FOUR

"DID YOU FIND OUT WHAT MOORE WANTED?" JAX PLACES A GLASS OF freshly squeezed orange juice down on the bathroom counter as he stares at my reflection in the mirror.

"I was too busy last night to call him and ask." I wink and see a sly smile glide over his perfect lips.

"Too busy making me come," he says in a breathless whisper. His hands pull the towel away from my body.

"It's cold in here," I shriek as I reach to pick it up from where it fell on the floor.

He takes off out the door in a flash and I hear him call back down the hallway, "I'm getting your robe, then you're going to eat the breakfast I made you."

My stomach turns at the mere mention of food. Today is the day I'm going to deal with Mark and that has to begin with me telling Jax that my former fiancé is essentially harassing me. I haven't spoken to Mark in months. After finding out about his affair with Liz, and how he had manipulated control of the company he owned with Jax, I wanted nothing to do with the man anymore.

"Brighton's coming back to town tomorrow." Jax is back, covering my naked body with a plush white robe. "I'm going to have lunch with him later in the week. He'd like to see you too."

I smile at the mention of Jax's older brother. Since Brighton has been away showing his art in Europe the past few months, they've gotten a lot closer. I know my insistence that he work on his relationship with his brother has had some impact but I also know that Jax has come to realize that holding a grudge against Brighton wasn't helping either of them.

"I'd love that." I pull my hand across his cheek. "I've missed seeing him."

"Me too, beautiful." He cups my hand in his as he kisses my palm. "I'll let you know what day it is."

I nod as I turn back around to finish straightening my long, blonde hair. I watch Jax's reflection through the corner of my eye as he scans his smartphone. I want to ask him what he's going to do today but I'm fearful that he'll retreat back into the brooding and quiet part of himself that he is whenever I bring up the possibility of him going back to the helm of Intersect Investments. His father's company meant the world to him until he felt he was losing me. He gave it up and now I feel a slight hint of resentment coursing through the air between us whenever either of us mentions it.

"Ivy." My name escapes his lips in a hushed tone. "Ivy, sit down."

I turn to face him, the hair brush still clutched firmly in my grasp. "Why? You want me to suck you off right now?" I tease. "I have to get to work."

"Ivy, sit." His tone matches the glare in his eyes. "Sit."

I reach to grab hold of the edge of the counter and lower myself onto the closed toilet seat. "Jax?" I mumble his name. "What?"

He runs his hand along the back of his neck before he glances at his phone again. "Ivy, it's…"

The loud hum of my own phone breaks the moment. I stand to retrieve it from the bedroom. He blocks my path. He leans against the doorway, his large frame making it impossible for me to escape.

"I should get that." I press my hand against his solid chest. "It may be about something at the store."

"It's not, beautiful." His hand covers mine pushing it into his skin. "Ivy, I don't know how to tell you this."

"Tell me what?" I feel panic rushing through me. The expression on his face is unlike anything I've seen before. "Jax? What's happened?"

"It's Mark." His tone is even and calm. "Ivy. Mark is dead."

CHAPTER FIVE

"It was a car accident. Liz was in the car too. They said he didn't stand a chance."

The words echo through me and I'm remotely aware that it's Jax's voice reciting them. I can sense him in the distance. I can feel his hands around me but it's as if an abyss has swallowed me whole. Mark is gone. Liz is hurt. Everything in the world is different. It's never going to be the same again.

"He called me," I say the words into Jax's chest, my lips running along his skin. "He kept calling me."

"What?" He leans back slightly. "Ivy, what?"

I shake my head slightly. I can't tell him now. I need to go. I need to go somewhere and do something.

Jax jumps at the sound of my phone ringing again. "We'll stay here today. You can't go to work."

I need to go to work. I have a custom piece that I have to complete before the weekend. "I have to go." I yank back from his embrace and try to push him out of my way. His body is too large. He doesn't move an inch.

"Ivy." I feel his hands cupping my face. "Please. Stay with me."

I pull my gaze to his face and it's covered in concern. He pushes my hair back behind my ear, his finger lingering to trace a path down my cheek.

"Jax," I whimper as I look up at him. "Mark."

"I know." He pulls me back into his chest and I wind my arms around his waist. "He's gone."

He's gone. The words reverberate throughout me. Mark is gone and I may never know what he wanted to talk to me about.

———

"THERE'S some concern about her family." A middle-aged nurse pats me on the shoulder to get my attention. "No one has come to see her."

I keep staring through the cloudy glass at Liz laying still in the ICU. Her body is motionless. Her thin frame attached to countless tubes and wires.

"I called them," I offer. I had called them. I spoke to Liz's father who said he wanted an update whenever I could provide one but his schedule 'didn't allow' him to get away right now. It took all the strength I could muster in that moment not to scream at him.

"She's in bad shape." She points absentmindedly at the glass. "She's got a long road to recovery."

I can only nod in response. Judging by what Liz's doctor shared with me earlier combined with what I'm seeing with my own two eyes, Liz's life may never be the same again. Both her legs had been crushed on impact when Mark's car had slammed into a guardrail on the West Side Highway. She'd suffered a severe concussion and countless cuts and bruises to her face and torso. She was barely recognizable.

I watch the nurse walk silently down the hallway as I gaze through the glass. She promised me she wouldn't see him again. She swore it was over. Now, her relationship with Mark had changed her life in a way she never could have predicted.

"Ivy?" Jax's voice is in my ear the moment I feel his hand pressing on the small of my back. "Are you ready to go?"

I turn and smile at him noticing that his eyes never leave my face. He hasn't asked about Liz's condition and his only interest was in driving me to the hospital today so I wouldn't be alone. He's never forgiven her for cheating with Mark and for hurting me that day she pushed me in my apartment. That was the day I fled into his arms and realized just how much I needed and wanted him.

"I need to go see June." I drop my gaze to the floor. Bringing up Mark's mother isn't easy but I promised her I'd stop by today to help her deal with some of his funeral arrangements.

"I'll take you." He reaches to take my hand in his. "We'll go see her now."

"You don't have to do that." I want my words to sound lighthearted. I don't want to drag Jax down into this pit of depression and confusion that I'm wallowing in. Even though I've been over Mark for a long time, his death is haunting me in a way I never could have predicted. It's also showing me that Mark had very few people in his life that cared enough about him to even mourn his passing.

"It wasn't an offer, beautiful." He brushes his lips across my hand. "We're doing this together."

I reach to grab his arm as I lean in to him. "Thank you, Jax."

CHAPTER SIX

"HOW WAS THE FUNERAL?" IT'S A MISPLACED QUESTION AND I CAN tell from the expression on Nathan's face that it's not one that he wants to be asking.

I plop myself down in a chair in front of his expansive desk. "Horrible. There weren't even ten people there. His mother was distraught. I couldn't wait for it to be over."

He brushes his lips across my forehead and squeezes my shoulder through the plain black dress before he sits next to me. "We need to talk."

"Jax said you came by the night before Mark died." I realize that was more than a week ago and I should have put some effort into getting in touch with Nathan before now.

"I came by to tell you he was dead." The words are direct and without emotion. Even though he's now my attorney, and an old friend, Nathan hasn't ever asked anything about Mark. He's never been overly curious about why I ended my engagement to him. His interest in that relationship has always been limited to my financial interest in Mark's company.

"You didn't tell Jax, did you?" I cringe when the question leaves my lips. I want to believe that Jax didn't find out about Mark's death until the moment he told me, but I've had lingering doubts all week. After we'd made love that night, he'd gotten out of bed and had spent hours on the phone.

He chuckles softly before he answers." He told me to go to hell in no uncertain terms, Ivy. I couldn't get two words in."

"I'm sorry," I whisper. "He has issues with you."

"I've wondered about that. What's that about?"

I close my eyes as he leans closer and his breath caresses my cheek. "Nothing. It's nothing." I can't confess to him that I told my boyfriend that I used to masturbate to thoughts of Nathan's naked body intertwined with mine.

"You're blushing." His finger grazes my cheek and I instinctively pull back. I have to focus.

"I'm not." I smile sheepishly. "Why did you want me to come by?"

He studies my face with his piercing blue eyes before he stands to walk behind his desk. "I can't believe I'm going to say this but it may be best if Jax was here for this."

"Jax?" I can't temper the surprise in my tone. "Why would he need to be here?"

"It may just be easier for him to hear it coming from me than from you."

"What?" I feel my stomach drop with the question. This has to do with Mark. It must. I haven't consulted with Nathan in any official legal sense since Mark was arrested. The deal for Jax to buy my shares of the company had been put on hold while the board wrestled with what to do when wind of the scandal hit the papers. The fact that both Jax and I still retained shares in the company was a subject neither of us ever brought up. We both viewed it as a mute until Mark had sorted through his next step.

"Do you want to call him and ask him to come down?" It's a genuine question but it's laced with a challenging undercurrent. Nathan doesn't believe I can handle whatever he's going to share with me. That's because he still views me as the young girl who chased him when we were children.

"Just tell me already, Nate." I grip the arms of the wooden chair trying desperately to temper both my rising anxiety and my anger. I don't have to involve Jax in everything I do. I can handle whatever this is alone.

"Mark left everything to you," he says each word slowly, carefully and loudly.

"Mark what?" I heard him just fine. I desperately want him to repeat it back so I'm certain that there's been no misunderstanding.

"His attorney called me. They read the will. He left everything to you."

"That can't be right." I stand and immediately feel my knees buckle. I reach for the edge of his desk just as I feel his hands grab my waist. "No. Mark wouldn't do that, Nate. He wouldn't do that."

CHAPTER SEVEN

"Ivy, beautiful." His voice is barely more than a breathless whisper as he leans back on the couch. "This is so good. So good."

I smile up at him as I circle the head of his cock with my tongue. I couldn't wait to take him when I came home from work. I couldn't wait to claim him. I had to taste him. I needed to give him pleasure before...

"Christ. Yes." He bites the words out with a guttural moan. His hands lock in my hair, pulling it free of the ponytail I neatly tucked it into this morning. "You're so good."

I moan in response. My tongue licking the length as I slide both hands up and down his shaft. He's so hard, he's so ready. We both needed this so much.

"I want this to last." He pulls on my hair to try and slow my rhythm but I can't. I want this as much as he does. I want him to see how much he means to me.

I moan around his cock and his body tenses at the sensation. He's getting so close. I can feel it.

He twists my hair within his fingers as he rocks his hips off the couch. "Fuck, Ivy." The words are harsh and come from a place deep within.

I look up and his eyes are closed, his head rolls back onto the couch, his breathing is labored.

I twist my tongue once again around the head and I'm gifted with a drop of cum. I eagerly lap it up. "Come, Jax," I coax softly around his throbbing cock.

He pushes his head back more and his body angles up as the first thick burst hits the back of my throat. I swallow hungrily, squeezing his cock softly to get all that he has to offer me. I lap greedily at the tip, cleaning him with my tongue before I rest my head against his strong thigh.

"Beautiful." He's hands are pulling on me, motioning for me to sit up next to him.

I do and he tugs me into his lap. I can feel that he's still semi-erect as he rests against my thigh.

"I love you so much," I whisper into his neck. "You know that, don't you?"

He nuzzles his face into mine. "I feel it in here." His hand jumps to his chest and I cover it with my own.

"I would do anything for you, Jax." My voice trembles with the words. The raw truth within them is so profound. I would do anything for this man. This is the man that I love more than life itself.

"You can do that again in about an hour." He pinches my side and I feel a sigh of relief at the small reprieve form the intensity that has been swirling around me since I left Nathan's office just an hour ago.

"Maybe you can return the favor in an hour," I tease. My body aches at the mere thought of Jax's head between my legs. His skillful tongue can pull a climax to the surface so quickly. It seems almost effortless but it's his intimate knowledge of my body that makes it so intense.

"I can right now." His hands snake their way up to the hem of the grey wraparound dress I'm wearing.

"Not now." I inch forward so my chest is touching his. "Now I need to talk to you about something."

"Anything." He pulls me closer.

"Not like this," I say the words although I don't mean them. I want to hold onto him like this forever. I want to cling to his body for dear life. I don't want the words that I'm about to say to him to change anything but I know that they will.

"Why?" I feel him retreat and I know he's waiting to meet my gaze. I can't look up at him just yet.

"You need to put your clothes back on." My breath skirts across his bare chest. My eyes clinging to the strong muscles of his well-toned arms.

His hands grasp my face and he pulls my head up so it's level with his. "What's this about? Nathan? You saw him today, didn't you?"

I slide my body off of his to allow him access to the clothes I pulled off him the moment I got through the door.

"I did." I don't want to do this. I can't stand the thought of Jax knowing that Mark left everything he owned to me including controlling interest in the company he shared with Jax.

"Is that why you ravaged me?" There's a playful glint in his eye as he pulls his jeans and blue sweater back on. "You were thinking about Moore?"

I laugh. "No. Of course not. I couldn't wait to get home to you."

He leans down and pulls his lips slowly across mine. I sigh at the intimacy of the gesture. I love kissing him. I could kiss him for hours and never tire of it.

"What's it about then?" He walks past me to the kitchen and I curse inwardly. I just want him to sit back down so I can tell him this without any more thought. I can't keep playing the possible scenarios of how he's going to react over and over again in my mind.

"Can you come sit down?"

There's absolutely no response. Only the sound of dishes moving and drawers being opened and closed greets me. I sit in utter silence, not moving for what feels like an eternity.

"Here's some fruit." Jax reappears with a small plate piled high with sliced apples, strawberries, bananas and oranges. "Eat and drink this." He pushes a bottle of water towards me.

"I'm not hungry." I sigh. "I just want to talk."

"You've lost weight." He pushes a piece of apple between my lips. "That dress has never been that loose on you."

I smile at the concern in his voice. "I'm fine. I just haven't been hungry." How could I have an appetite when I've been dealing with the non-stop stress of Jax working for me and now Mark's death? It's a wonder I can get one meal a day down.

"Eat, beautiful." He tempts me with a piece of strawberry. "I'm worried about you."

I nod and take the fruit between my lips. I eat a quarter of the fruit on the plate and take a long sip of water before I raise a brow. "Is that enough, Mr. Walker?"

"It's a start." He kisses me gently. "I just want to take care of you."

"You do." I stroke his brow with my hand while I stare into his eyes. "You take such good care of me."

He silently reaches for my hands as his eyes scan my face. He's searching for a clue about what I want to talk about. He's anxious. I can see it between his brows. His forehead is furrowed. That's a sure sign that he's feel apprehension. I've seen it too many times not to know the meaning within it.

"Tell me." The words slide off his lips. "Tell me what it is."

"You're not going to like it." I preface my confession with the hope that it will temper his reaction. I know it won't. I know that he's going to be gutted when he realizes that my ex fiancé left his entire estate to me.

"Just tell me." His bottom lip quivers and I instantly realize that he has no idea what I'm about to confess. I can see the uncertainty in his expression.

"It's about Mark." That feels like a good place to start. If I can spit the truth out in small doses maybe Jax and I can get through this evening without the roof blowing off of our apartment.

"What about him?" His body language speaks louder than the words as he pulls back from me. I grimace at the sharp contrast between his stance now and what it was not more than two minutes ago.

"It's about his will."

"What about it?" He shoots the question back at me so quickly that I almost physically recoil from the force of it. This is it. This is the moment when I have to tell him.

I adjust the skirt of my dress before I respond. "I'm in it."

The corner of his mouth twitches. "What did he leave you?"

"Everything," I say the word so quietly I'm not sure it even left my lips.

"What?" He leans in closer, his eyes never meeting mine. "What did you say?"

"Everything," I repeat louder. "Mark left everything he owned to me."

CHAPTER EIGHT

"THAT CAN'T BE RIGHT?" HE SNAPS BEFORE HE BOLTS TO HIS FEET. "That bastard wouldn't leave you anything."

The words bite through me even though I know they shouldn't. Mark and I were over. We had ended our relationship more than a year ago now but knowing that he named me as the sole beneficiary of his will meant something to me. It had nothing to do with the business or the properties. It just meant something.

"That has to be an old copy of his will." His arms cross. "He wouldn't leave you a red cent after what happened between you two."

"He did." I stand and reach to retrieve my heels. "The will is valid. I'm the sole beneficiary. Everything he owned is now mine."

"You're happy about it?" The words sting more than any slap on the face could have. I don't deserve the question. I don't deserve his insistent need to remind me that I almost married a cheating asshole.

I drop my heels to the hardwood floor with a dull thud. "Why would you ask me that?"

"Answer the question, Ivy." The challenge in his voice is clear. He's speaking in a measured tone. He's not showing any emotion whatsoever. This is the Jax Walker who always appears when Mark becomes a part of the conversation. Even in death he was impacting the most substantial relationship I'd ever had.

"No." I push my hands onto my hips. "It's insulting."

"It's insulting that you'd consider taking anything from a man who treated you like shit."

I feel my stomach turn at the words. I pull my hand to my lips, push Jax aside and race to the bathroom. I just make it in time as I feel my body reject the food as my mind tries to reject the harsh words of the man I adore.

———

"DO you think you should see a doctor?" I feel the bed shift as he sits on the edge.

I roll over, not wanting to face him. "I'm fine. It's been a very stressful week." The words are a veiled lie. Most of the stress I'm feeling is being thrown at me by Jax, even if he's not aware of it. Anticipating his reaction to my news about Mark wasn't nearly as bad as the reality.

"We need to talk about Mark." His tone is clipped and determined.

"It's late and I'm not in the mood." I feel numb. I can't even find the strength within me to cry. I didn't ask Mark to leave me anything. The fact that he did has now impacted everything.

I feel his arms encircle me from behind as he presses his body into my back. "I'm sorry." The words are so faint, but the meaning is there. I know he's being genuine. I know he feels badly for what he said.

"I don't know why he didn't change his will." I pull his hand to my lips. "But he didn't."

I only feel a nod against my shoulder in response. The silence is overbearing. He's waiting for me to confess to him that I'm going to refuse all of it.

"Nathan is going to help me sort through it all with a probate attorney." I know his reaction to that news isn't going to be well received either so I continue, "I'd like you to be involved too. I want you to help me with this."

I feel his entire body tense at my request. I almost whimper out loud when his hands pull away from me. "I can't. I just can't."

I listen in silence for what feels like hours until I hear his breathing slow. He's fallen asleep. He's abandoned me with the burden of having to deal with Mark's estate all alone.

CHAPTER NINE

"What about if I just handed everything over to Mark's mother?"

"It's not that easy, Ivy," Garrett Ryan, the probate attorney that Nathan introduced me to, says as he leans back in his office chair. "It's more complicated than that. There are taxes and life insurance policies and Mark had holdings in many businesses overseas."

The words all run together in my mind. I had asked Jax to be here with me. His business mind can comprehend all of this much better than my creatively driven mind can. He'd refused. He claimed he was busy and didn't have the time.

"I'll explain all of this to Nathan." I know Garrett can sense my trepidation in dealing with the details of Mark's will. "I know legally he can't help you with the fine details of this but he can spell it out in layman's terms so it's easier to digest."

I smile at the muted suggestion that I can't absorb what he's telling me. I can't be offended. It's obvious that all of this is over my head.

"I'm going to work my way through all of Mark's assets and then we'll set up a meeting again." He stands and reaches his large hand over the desk towards me. I take it and he squeezes it. "I promise that Nate and I will get you through this."

I look up into his kind green eyes. "Thanks Garrett."

"There is one thing before you go." He shuffles through a few papers before he lowers his tall frame back into his office chair. "This business that Mark owned... Intersect Investments? You have shares in that too?"

I nod my head in silence.

"And Nate said your boyfriend has some also?" The question is laced with uncertainty. Garrett and Nathan had gone to law school together. I sensed that Nate was sharing much more with him about my life than just the required legal history.

"He owns the remaining shares, yes." I can't think past the words. Jax and I haven't discussed the ramifications of us owning the business together. My assumption that he'd want to join forces to bring the business back to life seems to be horribly misplaced right now. He hadn't brought up the possibility at all and that fact had been wearing on me for days.

"Do you two have a plan for how you want to move forward with that?" It's an obvious question. It seems innocent enough but it bites through me with the force of a rabid dog.

I pull in a heavy breath before I begin, "I haven't discussed it with him yet."

"That's interesting." The words linger between us. He doesn't offer anything more and I know that if I want to know what his inference was, I'm going to have to push.

"Why is it interesting?"

"Jax Walker is your boyfriend, right?" I'm surprised by the mention of Jax's name. He knows Jax? He's looked far enough into Mark's will that he knows who his business partner is?

"Yes. Jax and I are together." Why did I answer like that? We are together, aren't we? He's more than my boyfriend.

"His attorney..." the words trail as he glances at a pad of paper next to his phone. "Gilbert Douglas contacted me this morning."

I feel anger burn through me. "Jax's attorney called you?" The question is almost rhetorical. Garrett already spelled it out to me. He knows the name of Jax's lawyer. Why the hell is Jax having his lawyer call mine when he can't even bring himself to say two words to me about any of this?

"He did." He nods his head as his eyes skim over the note pad. "He wants to know about the shares you've inherited. He's putting out feelers for what you might be looking for in exchange."

"Jax wants to buy the shares I inherited from Mark?" I push myself up from the chair as if that's going to give my anger more room to expand.

"He does. You can discuss those terms with Nate once we get through probate."

"That's not going to be necessary." I pull open his office door. "I'm dealing with this on my own."

CHAPTER TEN

"YOU CAN'T RESIST ME, CAN YOU?" HIS LIPS ARE ON MY NECK THE moment I walk through the apartment door. As angry as I am with him, I can't help but melt a little at the feeling of his hands on my waist.

I pull back slightly. "You already know the answer to that question." I pat him on his cheek. The entire way home from Garrett's office I envisioned slapping Jax across his face, but now that he's standing next to me and I'm staring into his beautiful brown eyes, I can't fathom ever intentionally hurting him.

"You didn't come home in the middle of the day so I could ravage your body?" The way he raises his brows playfully suggests that he already knows that I have an ulterior motive for not being at the jewelry store.

I wish it were that simple. I wish that I could fall into his arms and into our bed for the rest of the day. The thought of rolling around help-lessly in Jax's arms for hours is heaven to me. I need that. I need him. I need to get through this conversation with us whole and together.

"I know that you aren't interested in helping me deal with Mark's estate." My tone is so harsh and the way he steps back from me suggests that he notices it too.

"I can't help you." It's an admission he hasn't made before. "I can't."

"I know." I slide the heavy grey sweater from my shoulders. "Because you hated Mark."

He reaches out to adjust the collar on the plaid dress I'm wearing. "It's not that."

My stomach drops at his words. "What do you mean it's not that?"

"I think you know what I mean." The fact that he reaches for my hand to cradle it tenderly in his signals that he's feeling some sense of guilt. It's the same gesture that he does whenever he brings home a huge bouquet of daises after we've argued.

"Why?" My voice cracks as I ask. "Why would you go behind my back like that?"

"Beautiful." His hand sweeps across my cheek. "This is business. That's all it is."

I shake my head slightly as I try to form the right words in my mind. "No. It's not business. It's us."

"I need those shares, Ivy." He pushes a piece of hair from my forehead. "I want my father's company back. Helping you deal with Mark's estate would be a conflict of interest for me."

"So you're going behind my back to get them?" It's more dramatic than I intend. He didn't really go behind my back. He went to my attorney. He took the necessary steps he needed to in order to purchase a company that he wanted. It's the same thing he'd do with any other company. The only difference is that I owned this one.

"You're taking this all wrong." His tone is too calm, too measured for me. I'm fuming inside. "I'm going to offer you fair market value for them and you'll accept and that will be it."

He says it so effortlessly, as if it's fact. "You're assuming too much," I say the words in spite. I'm angry with him for not talking to me before I went to see Garrett.

"What does that mean?" He tips my chin up so I'm looking directly into his eyes.

"I was beyond humiliated today when I sat in that lawyer's office and heard that my boyfriend wanted to buy my dead ex fiancé's shares from me." I feel too numb to let any emotion seep into the statement.

"Imagine the shock on my face since I hadn't heard a word out of your mouth about it." I tap him on the lips with my index finger.

"You're confusing business with pleasure again." He tilts his head to the side. It's too playful of a gesture for me. It only incites me more.

"Maybe I am." I take a heavy step back. "Maybe that's not all I'm confused about."

His chest expands as he takes a deep breath. "What is that supposed to mean?"

My eyes close briefly as I feel the tears approaching. "It means that I thought we were moving towards something. Something...something that would mean that we'd share everything with one another."

"You're not making sense, Ivy," he says flatly. "I don't know what you're talking about."

"I guess that's the problem, Jax." I push past him to head down the hallway. "I'll have Nathan call you with a number."

CHAPTER ELEVEN

"MY BROTHER IS AN IDIOT." BRIGHTON TAKES A SMALL SIP OF THE coffee he ordered when he first arrived at the café in midtown. "He seriously didn't get that you were talking about marriage?"

I shake my head and manage a weak grin. "I went to sleep and when I woke up he wasn't there. I'm not even sure if he slept in our bed last night."

"When I saw him the other day he was all about Mark and his business." He places his hand over mine. "I asked him what you thought of that but he ignored the question. Classic Jax move."

"I just assumed that we'd deal with the business together." I roll my eyes with a slight chuckle. "Not exactly together. I thought Jax would run the business for both of us."

"You were right to make that assumption, Ivy," he sighs. "I've never seen a more perfectly matched couple than the two of you."

"I feel like I made a big mistake." It's a confession that I've been holding in since I learned of Mark's death.

"Dating my brother?" He cocks a brow. He can't be serious. He has to see how endlessly devoted I am to Jax even when he's being an ass.

"In pushing him back into the business world." My jaw tightens as

I think about how I brought up the subject of Intersect Investments repeatedly. I put the idea in Jax's mind and once Mark died, he ran with it full steam ahead. Right now it didn't seem like he cared who he ran over to get what he wanted, even if that person was me.

"How are you going to handle it?" The question is ripe with assumption. I know Brighton well enough to know that he thinks I should sit down and tell Jax exactly what I'm feeling. I'm not sure how I can ever confess to the man that I love that I assumed that our shares in the business would merge since we'd be married one day.

I take a small sip of herbal tea. "I'm going to let it play out. I'll see what Jax offers and what my attorney considers a fair deal."

"You're playing hardball?" A faint chuckle skirts the edges of the question.

"I'm playing in Jax's world." I pull a small smile across my lips. "Let's not talk about this anymore. What's going on with you?"

He darts his eyes over my head before he speaks. "Liz."

It's only a name but it still has a profound impact on me. "You know she was badly hurt in the accident that killed Mark?"

"Jax told me." His brow pulls together. "I'm really worried about her."

"I thought when she withdrew from your program that you two were done." Brighton and I hadn't ever spoken about Liz after he learned that she was one of Mark's lovers. Jax had shared that juicy tidbit of information without realizing that Brighton was developing feelings for my former best friend. When he'd finally offered her placement in his mentoring program for burgeoning artists, she had pulled back and withdrawn.

"We talked a lot when I went to Europe." He stops to take a sip of the coffee. "When I ran away to Europe."

"Have you been to see her?" Guilt overlaps the question. I hadn't been back since I was there with Jax. I didn't know how to push aside all the hurt and anger I still felt for her.

"I go every day." He taps his finger on the edge of the wooden table. "I was hoping you would go with me sometime."

I feel panic race through me. I'm not sure I can face Liz. "I hadn't thought about going back."

"She needs support, Ivy," he says glumly. "I'm all she has."

I tip my head back to stare at the ceiling. Maybe it was time to finally put the past to rest. Maybe forgiving Liz would bring me closure too. "I'll come. Once."

CHAPTER TWELVE

"Jax is here," Libby, the new store clerk, calls up the stairs as I'm just putting the finishing touches on a necklace.

"Send him up," I call back down. Since when did Jax ask to be announced when he arrived at my store? The fact that he had someone call up to warn me coursed through me as an ominous sign. I wasn't expecting to face him until tonight. After my coffee with Brighton, I'd come straight back to the store to get started on the constantly growing list of custom pieces I needed to finish.

"Beautiful." His voice wafts through the air and surrounds me. "I couldn't wait to see you."

I look up from my place at the table and I'm certain my mouth is hanging open. It's the first time in months that I've seen Jax dressed in a suit. His attire, since he walked away from corporate life, has been jeans and sweaters or t-shirts. I'd forgotten how gorgeous and commanding he looked when he was ready to take control in the business world.

"Holy crap." The words slip out before I realize and I pull my hand quickly to my mouth. I feel so underdressed. I was so tired after our argument last night that I only had the energy to pull on jeans, a white blouse and pin my hair messily on top of my head.

"You like?" The gleam in his eye has been missing too. I smile when I see it there dancing around the edges, pulling on his handsome face.

"I love," I say quietly. I do love. I love him. I love who he is and I even love how much of an ass he can be at times.

He moves so he can lean against the side of the table I'm sitting next to. He reaches for my hand and I let him take it. I need to feel that connection. I want to be close to him. I can't let this issue with Mark pull us apart.

"I'm sorry," he says the words quietly. They're not words that he speaks often so I know that when he does, they hold more meaning than with most other people. "I didn't handle things well."

I look down and rub my thumb over his. "This can't come between us." I want to say more. I want to tell him that he doesn't have to buy the shares. I want to tell him that I trust him enough to just give it all to him.

"I don't want it to." He doesn't want it to. That's different than he won't let it. I know Jax and business and I know he won't let much get in the way once he's focused on an end goal.

"You're dressed up today. Are you going to a funeral?" The words leave my mouth before my mind has a chance to catch them. It's a reminder of Mark and the fact that Jax wouldn't go to the funeral with me. I didn't want to drag any memory of Mark into our conversation and I have. I'd done it within the first twenty seconds of us talking.

"A business meeting." He doesn't even flinch at my reference to a funeral. He's going to let it slide past him and I'm grateful that he does.

No details are offered and I don't press. I don't want to. I don't want anything to set him off today. I know he's been on edge since we first spoke about my inheriting all of Mark's estate. I just want this moment in time to be peaceful, drama free and quiet.

"I saw Brighton." I stand. I want to feel his arms around me. I need to. "We had coffee a little while ago."

"He told me." His hands encircle my waist and he pulls me between his legs. "He said you two talked about Liz."

I nod as I stare into the depths of his eyes. Something has shifted since last night. He's less tense. He seems happier. "He wants me to go with him to see her."

"Will you?" I feel his finger touch my chin lightly.

"For him." I tilt my head trying to grab more of his touch. I'm so hungry for it. I feel as though we haven't connected enough the last few days. I miss it. I miss him.

His brows rise. "You're good to him. I'm trying to be better to him too."

My mouth curves. "You're a good brother." I mean the words. Jax has tried desperately to strengthen his connection to Brighton the past few months. Doing that electronically hasn't been easy, but he's been putting in the effort.

"I can't stand when there's tension between us, beautiful." His words whisper over my lips as his mouth claims mine.

"I don't want that either." I pull back from the kiss. "It kills me inside when we're not on the same page, Jax."

"Me too." He breaks my gaze to look down. "It's hard, Ivy."

He doesn't have to say more. I know he's talking about Mark and about my seemingly never ending connection to him.

"I won't let this come between us." I close my eyes as I say the words. I can't let this come between us. I need him too much to let that happen.

"We won't," he corrects me before he glides his lips over mine again.

I can only melt into his arms, letting him pull me away from everything and into the heat of his kiss.

CHAPTER THIRTEEN

"YOUR BODY IS SO BEAUTIFUL." HIS BREATH GRAZES OVER MY MOIST folds. He's helped me climax with his tongue and lips and I'm already feeling so spent. "I need to make you come again."

"No," I pull the word from somewhere deep within me. He was waiting for me at the door when I got home from work. Naked and waiting. He'd licked me until I came right there on the spot after he pulled my jeans and panties off. Now, he's done it again, not twenty minutes later in our bed.

"No?" He traces a pointed path with his tongue over my swollen clit. "You want me to make you come again."

"I can't." I try to sound as though I mean the words, but I don't. I can't ever get enough of Jax pleasing me. He knows my body better than I do. He knows how to bring me to the edge of an intense orgasm with just a few strokes of his skilled tongue. He also knows how to push me past my limits so I feel more pleasure than I ever imagined was possible.

He ignores my protests and pulls my ass off the bed so he can devour me. I almost scream at the sensation of his lips coursing hot over my clit. I pull on his hair, wanting him to take more. I'm already so close again. I don't know how I can come so easily under his touch. "Jax." His name is drawn across my lips like a breathless whisper.

He moans as he sucks on my clit and I pull harder on his hair.

"God, please," I'm almost whimpering from the sensations. It's so much. I can't take it. I feel as though I'm going to plunge off the edge of a cliff into pleasure so deep that I won't be able to breathe. "Please."

He pushes two fingers inside me in one swift movement and I come instantly. I claw at his shoulder, wanting him to stop. Needing him to give me time to feel and breathe.

"I have to fuck you." The words are so direct. It's not a request. It's a command.

I lay still, unable to pull any strength from my limbs. He flips me over quickly, pushing my shoulders down so my back arches. I feel his lips skirt the edge of my ass cheek before his hand glides over my wetness.

"Fuck. You're so ready." He plunges balls deep into me and I scream from the pain. It's so much. He's so wide and long. I'll never adjust to his size. I'll always feel the tender bite of pleasure mixed with the raw pain of being stretched past my limits.

"Jax." I barely spit out the word before I feel another orgasm rolling through me. It's never been like this. I've never felt so many sensations so intensely before.

He quickens his thrusts and pushes on my back, pulling my ass even higher. "This is too good, beautiful" he groans loudly. "I'm going to fuck you forever."

I push back at the sound of the words. I want that. I want to be his forever.

"Ivy," he growls my name through a deep moan and I arch my back more. I want him to take this pleasure from me. I want him to feel it too just like I did. I need that for him. I crave it more than anything.

"Touch your clit." He rubs his hand across my mound. "Touch it."

I pull my hand back to circle my fingers over my swollen clitoris. His hand joins mine and he applies even more pressure. He wants me to come again. He wants me to take more from him.

"Oh, god, yes." My voice is a breathless whisper. I feel as though I'm lost in the pleasure. It's all so much. "I have to come."

"Not yet." He pounds me harder. "Together. Ivy, together."

I nod into the pillow. I push back, matching his rhythm. Our hands are interwoven teasing my clit.

"You're mine." He pulls his hand back and pulls on my thigh. "You'll always be mine."

His words push me to the brink. I can't stop my body's reaction. "Now," I blurt the word out with a loud moan.

"Now," he screams as he races to the edge and fills me with his desire just as I fall into a heap onto the bed.

CHAPTER FOURTEEN

"Ivy." I feel his muscular arms encircle me from behind as he steps into the shower. "Beautiful."

I pull him into me, wanting the closeness to last beyond tonight. I need our connection to be this strong outside the walls of our apartment. "I still can't breathe."

"I'm scared." The words feel foreign and misplaced coming from him.

I turn quickly and reach for his face. It's damp from the water. I push the moisture away and cup his cheek in my hand. "Scared? Of what?"

He doesn't respond. He pulls me into his chest and I wrap my arms tightly around his waist. Even in a semi- hard state I can feel his cock pressing against me. I still want him. If he wanted to claim me again right here and right now, I'd drop to my knees and please him. I'd take him between my lips and pull another orgasm from within him just as he did with me.

"Jax, please," I plead with him.

His body moves slightly and I realize he's sobbing. I try to look up but he's too strong. He's pressing my body into his, molding our two frames together under the heat from the shower.

"Jax." My eyes are filled with tears now too. What's happening? What is he going to tell me? Is that why he took me so ferociously in the bed? Because he's going to do something that will make me not want him anymore? It's not possible. I have to tell him. "Tell me," I whisper into his chest. "What's scaring you?"

"I want us to go away." He moves back slightly so I can tilt my head up to look at him. "I need that."

I nod even though I know I can't leave right now. I have to go through Mark's apartment tomorrow to ready it for sale and I have to finish up the work that I'm desperately falling behind on. None of that matters right now. All that matters is Jax and I.

"You know I've never loved anyone but you." The words cut through me like a razor sharp knife. He wouldn't be saying that unless he believed I doubted that fact.

"I know." I try to temper the fear in my voice but it's almost impossible.

He presses his lips to my temple and I feel a shudder course through him. "I can't survive losing you. I can't."

"I'm not going anywhere." I pull him closer. "I'm not."

"You know I can't live if you're not with me, don't you?" It's a question that he doesn't need to ask.

"I'm not going anywhere." I raise my head and search his face. "What's going on?"

"Ivy." My name escapes his lips in a sob. "I'm so scared."

"Jax." I pull on his arms, wanting to merge our bodies together." Please. You're scaring me."

"Don't die." He pushes his cheek into mine. "Please don't die before me."

"Don't say those things." I sob into his chest. "Don't talk like that."

He doesn't respond. He just pulls me closer, holding my naked body next to his until the shower starts to run cold.

———

"I KNOW this isn't in your job description," I begin before I stop to open a desk drawer. "But I appreciate you coming with me."

"We're friends, Ivy." Nathan turns from where he's standing next to a tall cabinet. "I'll always help in any way I can."

I smile at the reminder of our renewed friendship. Having Nate back in my life has helped so much, especially today when I'm stuck with the task of searching through Mark's belongings trying to decide whether anything is worth keeping.

"I stuck his cell phone and the other stuff from his car there." Nate points to a small, clear plastic bag sitting on the edge of the desk. "I picked it up at the police station yesterday."

I nod and turn my gaze back to the drawer before a sudden realization washes over me. "Do you think there's a charger for the phone here somewhere?"

"I saw one in his bedroom." He tips his head back as he heads out the door into the hallway. "Let me grab it."

I open the bag and carefully retrieve the phone. The screen is scuffed but other than that it's not worse for wear. It's shocking that Mark's smartphone could survive virtually unscathed from such a violent crash that claimed his life and left Liz helpless in a hospital bed.

"Let me plug it in." Nate reaches for the phone before he kneels to plug it into an outlet near the desk. "Give it a few minutes."

I nod and look back at the desk. "Mark called me a bunch of times before he died." It's the first time I've said the words since I told Mrs. Adams weeks ago.

"What did he want?" He doesn't look my way when he throws the question at me.

I glance at the phone and the green bar indicating it's finally charging back up. "I have no idea. I ignored everything and deleted all of it."

"It was likely nothing. I wouldn't worry about it."

"Did the police say anything more about the accident?" I don't know why I've been so curious about what happened on that stretch of road that night. Knowing wasn't going to change the outcome.

"Speed and his blood alcohol level was almost twice the limit." He turns as he sighs. "Liz was apparently hammered too."

I wince at the words. "I should have done something," I mutter under my breath.

"You should have done something?" He turns completely around now. "Like what?"

"Nothing with Mark," I say it so carelessly. Is it horrible that I haven't cried about Mark's death? Is it horrible that I don't feel any sense of loss knowing he's no longer alive? "When Liz and I were still friends I thought she might have a drinking problem."

"You're not responsible for her." He walks over to lean against the desk, his leg almost brushing against my arm. "They both chose to drink and get in that car."

I nod. I know he's right. I know that there was nothing that I could have done to change the outcome of that day.

"The text messages Mark sent me should be on his phone."

"I hadn't thought of that." Nate taps me on the shoulder. "You really missed your calling. You should have been a private investigator."

I laugh before I push myself up to my feet. "I'm going to get everything packed up for charity. Once probate is done we can sell this place."

CHAPTER FIFTEEN

I have a daughter, Ivy. Holy shit, I'm a dad.
   Ivy, call me. I want to tell you about my daughter.
   She's an angel. We need to talk. I'm sorry.

I READ the messages again and again not caring that the rain pelting Central Park at this moment is soaking my clothing from top to bottom. I can't move from my spot on the bench. I can't bring myself to dart my eyes from the screen of Mark's smartphone. Mark has a daughter. Mark was a father. Mark is gone.

The loud ring of my own phone jars me and I fumble in my purse trying to find it. I glance at the incoming number. It's Garrett. He's calling to talk to me about Mark's estate. I know he is. I also know that Jax still wants the company back even though he hasn't brought it up to me directly in days. I know that he's planning his future around it. He has no idea. He has no idea that I can't take anything from Mark anymore. I can't. It all belongs to his little girl.

I pull Nathan's number up on my screen and push the call button.

"I need to see you," I say breathlessly into the phone. "Now."

———

"YOU LIVE HERE?" I try not to sound as shocked as I am. Who knew Nathan lived in such a gorgeous apartment on Central Park West?

"I do." He laughs as I walk into the space. "Do you want a towel?"

"You're hilarious." I throw him a wicked grin. "It's just rain."

"Remind me to get you an umbrella for your birthday." The words are filled with jest and I smile at how comfortable we are with each other. He's becoming more and more like my big brother every day.

"So this is where you entertain the ladies?" I search the room for any sign of a female presence and I find nothing. Nathan's apartment screams very loud and clear that a man lives there.

"One lady." He smiles.

"She's lucky," I murmur. She must be. Being with him surely can't be as complicated as being in love with Jax. Reading the sent messages on Mark's phone has only complicated things more.

"I'm lucky," he replies. "You didn't come over for a tour of my apartment so spit it out. What's up?"

"I finally looked at Mark's phone." It's been two days since Nathan and I sorted through Mark's things and I'd taken his phone and shoved it into my purse. The past two days with Jax had been nothing short of heaven. Long nights making love, cuddling while we watched television and not a mention of Mark at all had made me feel that we were finally getting back on track.

"Was there some deep and dark secret there?" He grins widely as he motions at a bar. "Do you want something to drink?"

"Water." I take a deep breath to steady my emotions. Once I tell Nathan what I saw on the phone everything will change. It will impact my relationship with Jax forever.

He reaches down to a compact fridge and removes a chilled bottle of water that he pours into a tall glass. I take it from him with a trembling hand, downing half the glass in one large gulp. I hadn't realized how parched I was until this moment.

"What was on the phone, Ivy?"

The question lingers there, between us. He's an attorney. He's not a regular friend. He has obligations. He'll do something with the information I give him.

"I should talk to Jax first," I say the words out loud even though I mean to keep them quiet. I've volleyed the idea back and forth about who to tell first.

"You can go in the other room to call him." He motions down the hallway. "It's up to you."

I'm grateful that he's not pushing. That he's not insisting I confess just yet. I need a moment to breathe.

"Ivy." I look up and he's staring directly at me. His brilliant blue eyes are searching my face. "I'm only saying this because I adore you like a little sister. You look like hell. Whatever this is, it's eating you up inside. Tell me. Tell Jax. Hell, tell the doorman. Just get it out."

"Mark has a daughter." The words spill out in a jumble of tears. "There's a little girl. He has a daughter."

Nate reaches to level his balance on the edge of the bar. I see his knuckles turn white. "This changes everything."

CHAPTER SIXTEEN

"IT WOULD HELP HER A LOT IF YOU CAME TO VISIT HER MORE."
Brighton's tone is soft and nurturing but the words strike me as
anything but.

I shoot him a look. "It's taken every ounce of strength I have to
come here today." It had. I had fallen asleep early waiting for Jax to
come home last night. This morning he was gone before I woke, the
only indicator that he had been there at all, a small note on his pillow
saying he loved me.

"She's your best friend." The words aren't meant to slice through
me the way they do. I know he's just trying to help Liz. He's always
had a soft spot in his heart for her.

"Jax is my best friend." I correct him. "She's someone I used to
know."

"Just think about coming here once in a while," he suggests. "Even
if it's just for a few minutes."

"So I can give her false hope that we still have a friendship?" My
tone is harsh. I know it is. I want it to be. "I feel horrible that she was
hurt so badly but it changes nothing between us. She betrayed me.
Why can't you see that?"

"Come and say hello." He pushes the door to her private room open and I'm left with little choice other than to waltz through with a smile on my face.

"Ivy," she says the word and her voice is completely different than I remember it. It's shaky, deeper and the volume so soft.

I pull my eyes across her body. Her legs are both still encased in casts. The bruises that once covered her face are now almost completely faded away. The cut on her forehead is still visible. She looks nothing like the vibrant socialite who tried to convince me that the key to a good life is a strong martini and a rich man.

"Liz." I bite my lip to temper the rising tears. I can't help but feel sympathy for her. I can't imagine how much physical pain she's in.

"Karma is a bitch." She tries to smile and I freeze. How am I supposed to react to that?

"She hasn't lost her sense of humor." I feel Brighton's hand on the small of my back, steering me farther into the room. The only machine Liz is hooked up to now appears to be tracking her vital statistics. The room itself is no less imposing than ICU was. I still feel horribly uncomfortable. I don't want her to bring up Mark. I don't think I can handle it.

"Mark died." She doesn't hesitate. She just barrels into the subject full force.

I nod. "I'm sorry," I say. The words aren't meant to offer comfort. I'm not sure what their intention is. I just know it's the right thing to say in that moment.

"I hadn't seen him in months before that night." Her bottom lip quivers and Brighton runs his hand over her forehead. "He wanted to talk to me about things. He wanted to make amends."

I don't want to hear about that night. I can't allow myself to feel any more sympathy for her. She was sleeping with my fiancé for more than three years. She was making love to him in the very same bed where I wrapped myself around him before I fell asleep each night.

"He still loved you, Ivy." I can't contain the well of emotions that now rushes to the surface. I reach for a plain metal chair that is sitting next to her bed to steady myself.

"Please don't talk about him," I say the words in barely more than a whisper. I don't want to know more about Mark than I already do. I don't want to shed one tear over him.

"He wanted to make it up to you." She taps her hand on the bed. "You never answered his calls."

Her words feel like an accusation and I have to stop myself from pushing back. I didn't come here to argue. I'm not sure why I did.

"I'm sorry that you were hurt." I mean it. I sincerely do. "Mark is gone. Dwelling on the past won't help anyone."

I see tears well at the corner of her eyes before she shifts her gaze to Brighton's face.

"I'm leaving," I say the words knowing that both of them are glad that I'm not staying any longer than I already have. "I hope you continue to get better." It's a small offering but for now, it's all I can muster.

CHAPTER SEVENTEEN

"MARK HAD A DAUGHTER." HEARING THE WORDS OUT LOUD MAKES THE reality of it that more real.

"A daughter?" Mrs. Adams points to a spot on the window. "There's a streak there, dear."

I rub the cloth over the area before I step back to take a look. "That's what I believe, yes."

"You haven't met her?" It's a natural question. Of course she'd want to know that. Up to this point, the only confirmation that I have that Mark has a child are the three text messages I found on his phone. Nathan has been working tirelessly to try and piece together who the mystery child is but so far, nothing has brought any concrete answers.

"I was going through his things." I stop once I realize that I've never confided in Mrs. Adams that Mark left his entire estate to me. "I'm helping with his estate and when I was looking through his phone I saw some messages he sent. There were messages he wrote about his daughter."

"So who is this girl?" She points back at the window and I rub the cloth along the length of it again. Coming back to my old apartment building once a week to help Mrs. Adams with her chores and shopping was a delight until it came time to do windows.

"I don't know. I wish I knew." I shrug my shoulders as I walk past her. I'm determined to put the window spray and cloth away before she notices yet another streak.

"What does Jax think about it?"

I stop in my tracks at the entrance to the kitchen. I haven't told Jax. It's been days and I have yet to tell him that I know that he can't buy the shares I inherited because I won't be keeping them.

"We haven't had a chance to talk about it yet."

"Why, dear?" She's pressing. I know she's doing it to give me an outlet to talk but I'm not sure I can. I don't know why I've avoided bringing it up. I don't know why I've allowed him to make love to me knowing that I'm holding such a big secret within. Part of it has to be that I'm certain that he'll want to talk about the timing and the reminder that Mark cheated on me now likely exists in the form of a child.

"It's very complicated," I offer. It's a weak excuse and we both know it.

"Secrets have no place in love." The words are soft and gentle.

"You're right." I tap her on the shoulder as I walk past her. "I'm going to go talk to Jax now."

She nods her head as she motions towards the door. "Hurry now. You need to tell him before you chicken out."

I laugh loudly as I step through the threshold and close her apartment door behind me.

———

"SHE'S TWO?" I repeat back his words. "She's two-years-old?"

"Two, Ivy." Nathan holds up two fingers as if that's going to help me comprehend the fact that Mark's daughter is just two-years-old.

"I was just on my way to tell Jax about her." I motion towards our building which is less than a half a block away. "I don't know how I'm going to do this."

"He's not there." Nathan steers me out of the heavy pedestrian traffic in the middle of the sidewalk. "I was just there looking for you."

I pull on his wrist to glance at his watch. "It's after seven. He should be at home."

"It just gives you more time to plan out what you're going to say." He taps me on the nose. "You're doing the right thing."

"What's her name?" I've been dying to know the answer. I've been craving information about Mark's daughter since I found out she existed.

"Bailey." A gentle smile pulls at the corner of his mouth.

"Does her mother know about Mark... about his death?" I still struggle to say the words. "Has someone told her?"

"I'm not sure." He glances down at his watch. "I'm running late for something, Ivy."

"Go." I push him into the sidewalk. "I'm good." The truth was that I was happy to have some time to think before I threw all of this information at Jax.

CHAPTER EIGHTEEN

I'M OUT FOR DINNER WITH AN OLD FRIEND. DON'T WAIT UP.

I stare at Jax's text message again. Why would he have to pick tonight of all nights to go out for dinner with a friend? Tonight is the night I want to tell him about Bailey. I want him to see that giving everything to that small girl was not only the right thing to do, it was the legally necessary thing to do.

Please come home soon. I need to talk to you.

I send the message knowing that it sounds pleading. I don't care. I have to get this out of the way now.

I walk into the kitchen to prepare something light to eat. I scan the refrigerator, looking at all the fresh fruit and vegetables Jax always keeps stocked there for me. I feel my stomach churn at the thought of eating anything right now. I'm too nervous. I feel way too much anxiety to even think about food at the moment. All I want is to talk to Jax so we can start putting all of this behind us.

I go back to the bedroom and scan my phone. Nothing from Jax. I lay down while I wait. My mind replaying my relationship with Mark over and over. When we were engaged he slept with someone and created another life. He had the child he always longed for and then he was taken from the world. I feel the sobs rush through me. It's the first time I've let myself feel any sorrow since I learned of his death. I tumble into the darkness of sleep, my body shaking from the sadness.

———

I FEEL his hands on my thighs as I drift back into the reality of the apartment. I glance at the clock near the bed. It's two in the morning.

"Jax?" I reach for him. I need to feel his arms around me.

He lunges towards me and pulls me into a deep embrace. I cling to his body. He smells of perfume and alcohol. He was out with a woman. I can tell. I know. My body is telling me so.

"Where were you?" I whisper the words quietly not wanting to push him into a dark place before we talk about Mark.

"I texted you. I went out for dinner." His words are slurred. His breath tainted with the heavy aroma of whiskey.

"That was hours ago, Jax." I reach to turn on the bedside lamp but his hand stops mine.

"Don't." The word is brittle and hurried. "I just want to fuck."

Normally, my body would ache at the command. I'd be pulling his jeans off and mounting him in one easy stroke. Tonight it was different. Tonight he was different.

"No." I reach to pull myself across the bed. "I don't want that."

"You never want me anymore," he whispers the words into the darkness but they bite through me just as harshly as they would have in the bright light of day.

"I always want you." I know that my attention to Mark's estate has pushed an unspoken wedge between us.

"Prove it." The challenge comes from a dark place. I can hear it in his tone.

"Stop it, Jax." I push the words back at him wishing that I could see more of his face than the shadowy outline that the sliver of light from the hallway is providing.

"Maybe she'd fuck me if I asked."

My stomach recoils at the words. She. There was a she. He was out with another woman. I leap past him and rush down the hallway. I slam the door shut as I heave into the sink. The putrid taste of my own bile not nearly as disgusting as Jax's vile words.

CHAPTER NINETEEN

"I'm leaving for a few days." I pat him on the ass to wake him but he doesn't budge. "Hey jerk, I'm out of here."

He moans quietly before he turns over.

"I'm leaving." The words are more firm now, their intention unmistakable. "Last night was unacceptable. I'm not staying here."

I turn to leave and I feel his hand on my elbow. "Ivy. No."

I ignore him and continue to walk toward the door. He jumps from the bed, teetering unsteadily on his feet as he jumps in my way.

I cringe when I look at him. His brown hair is a disheveled mess. His brown eyes are sunken in and empty.

"Get out of the way." I'm late for work. I need to leave before I say something that we'll both remember for far too long.

"I'm pretty sure I fucked up last night." He runs his hand across his face. "What did I say?"

"I don't have time for this." The truth was I didn't have the time or the patience to deal with him right now.

"What did I say? What did I do?" he asks the questions so fast that they barrel over one another.

"You need a shower." I can't respond to him. I can't tell him that he brought up the suggestion of fucking someone else. If I do it's going to unleash a surge of emotions that I'm not sure I can tame.

"Tell me." He grabs my arm and I pull it back so harshly that I almost lose my footing.

I stare at him, anger coursing through every cell in my body. "You were out until two and when you did finally drag your drunk ass home you were clear that if I didn't fuck you, you had someone ready, willing and able to spread her legs for her so why don't you take her up on that offer today."

His mouth falls open.

"And at least have the decency to change the sheets when you're done." I push past him and stop at the bedroom door. I know I shouldn't do it but I want to sting him as much as he's done to me.

"Jax." I call to him but he doesn't turn around. "Hey, Jax," I raise my voice so it's skirting the edge of a scream.

He turns slowly, his naked body on full display.

"Mark had a daughter so you're shit out of luck with that too." I don't look back as I turn on my heel and walk away.

———

"I DIDN'T THINK you had it in you." Nathan rolls his head back in laughter when I tell him what happened between Jax and me.

"I was just so pissed." I take a small bite of the garden salad I ordered. "I don't know how to talk to him anymore. He's become this different person."

"How old is he?" He bites into his cheeseburger as he cocks a brow waiting for me to answer.

"He's twenty-seven." I shrug my shoulders. I want to say that Jax is twenty-seven going on twelve but I know that's petty and unnecessary.

"He's in a weird place right now."

"No kidding." I take another piece of tomato in my mouth and chew it slowly. "He's in the same place he's always been in."

He looks over the rim of the water glass he's sipping from. "Most of us are pretty settled by the time we're twenty-seven. We have a clear path. We know what we're after. That's not the case with Jax."

I shake my head in disagreement. "He knows exactly what he wants. He's back to wanting that company his father owned and he can't control that. I thought he grew up the last few months. I was wrong. "

"I don't think so." Nathan motions for the waiter. "I think he's chasing after that because he still feels obligated. I don't think it's coming out of a place that's based in need."

I furrow my brow. "I don't get it. You're saying that Jax is only after the company because he feels he should do that but internally he actually wants something else?"

"That's it. You've hit the nail on the head." He orders a glass of bourbon. "Do you want anything, Ivy?"

I shake my head. "I'm still not sure." I need to change the subject. Talking about Jax's immaturity is making me wish I didn't have to talk to him later today. "What else do you know about Bailey's mom?"

"Ah, Bailey." A wide smile covers his full lips. "Her mom is a woman Mark met in Tulsa when he was there on business. It took her months to track him down and when she did, Mark flew out to meet his daughter."

The idea of Mark spending any time with his little girl brings me a small amount of comfort. "How long did he know about her before he…"

"Not more than three months." Nathan rolls his finger along the edge of his glass. "He was set to take off the next day to spend a week with them when the accident happened."

"That's sad." The words sound hollow and empty compared to the tragedy of the situation. Mark didn't really have a chance to be a dad, but maybe his estate could provide a better life for his daughter.

"Garrett needs to see you in the next few days." He reaches into his wallet to pull out a credit card. "We can get things moving right away so a trust can be set up in Bailey's name."

I nod in agreement. That's exactly what I want. I want Mark's estate to go to his daughter and I want him to be a distant memory as soon as possible.

CHAPTER TWENTY

"You need to see a doctor." His breath brushes over my neck. I open my eyes slowly to see him kneeling next to the couch, concerning covering his expression.

"Why?" The word leaves my lips in barely more than a whisper. After spending two nights in Mrs. Adam's guest room I was back home. Being away from Jax was pure torture. I must have drifted into sleep while I was waiting for him.

"You're sick." His voice cracks. "I've been so scared for weeks."

"Scared?" I reach to cradle his cheek in my hand. "Of what?"

"There's barely anything left to you." His hand runs down my side. "You're so pale. You sleep so much."

"It's been so stressful, Jax." It has been. He can't understand how hard it's been trying to manage everything with Mark's estate and his feelings too.

"I wanted to believe it was just stress." He shuts his eyes tightly before he opens them again. I see the moisture gathering at the corners. "I've been so scared that if I took you to the doctor he'd tell me I was going to lose you."

"That's silly." I run my hand along his tie. "I'm fine."

"Ivy." He pulls my hand to his lips, skirting it across them. "Something isn't right."

"You've changed." I blurt the words out without any emotion. "You're not the same anymore and that's so hard. It's too much for me."

"I'm me." He leans forward to graze his lips across my cheek. "I'm still me."

"You were out with a woman." I bite my bottom lip to temper what I want to say. "You said she'd sleep with you if you asked."

"I was drunk," he whispers the words into my hair. "I was out with a woman I went to high school with and her husband."

"You hurt me when you came home."

"What? I hurt you?" He reaches to hug me, pulling me closer into him. "How? Ivy. Tell me."

I know I'm going to cry. Everything that has built up the past few weeks is being pushed down into me. I have to let it out. "Your words. We don't talk about fucking other people. We just don't."

"Tell me you know I wouldn't do that." His tone is pleading. "Tell me you knew I was fucked up and drunk."

"Did you fuck her in high school?" The question feels as though I've pulled it from left field.

He shakes his head as if he's trying to register it. "No. Gosh, no."

"Then why would you say that?" I pull on the lapel of his suit jacket. "Why?"

"To hurt you." The confession is quiet and simple. "You've been so wrapped up in Mark's death. I was being petty and childish."

I stare at his face, wanting to find a concrete answer to all the questions I have. "Something is going on with you. Something isn't right."

"I don't want to run that company." He spits the words into the air as if they're vile and tainted. "I can't go back to that."

"You were making an offer on the shares you thought I inherited." I push for understanding. I need it. I can't deal with this aching gap that has developed between us.

"When you fell in love with me I was Jax Walker, business man." I smile at the words. I did fall in love with him but it had nothing to do with his career choice.

"I don't care what you do." I take a pause before I continue," I just don't want you to work for me."

"I loved being at the shop every day." A small smile pulls on his lips. "Spending that much time with you was the best. I wish I could do that every day for the rest of my life."

"You can," I whisper. "You can do whatever you want. I just want you to be happy. We can spend all the time together you want."

"Making love to you now would make me happy but only if you have the energy."

I push past him and leap to my feet, pulling my dress over my head. "I'll race you to the bed." I scream as he charges behind me pulling me into his arms.

———

"I WOULD HAVE GIVEN you the shares if you would have asked." I run my finger down his chest. It's covered in the light mist of sweat from our love making. "Anything I have is yours. I thought you knew that."

"Everything but that jewelry store I gave you." He pinches my side and I scream out in delight.

"We've been over that. You follow the customers around and then get angry with them when they leave without buying a piece."

"Here's the thing, beautiful." He pulls my leg over his torso so he can rest his hand on my ass. "You're the most amazing jewelry designer in the world. One day people are going to pay thousands of dollars to own one of your designs. The people who walk out of the shop now are missing the big picture. I'm just trying to explain it to them."

I roll my head back in laughter at his words. "Not everyone in the world thinks I'm as great as you do. You know that, don't you?"

"They're idiots." He shakes his head. "How could anyone in their right mind not realize how gifted you are? It makes no sense to me."

"I love that you think I'm special." Even I hear my own words and realize how grossly understated he's going to think they are.

"Special?" He jumps to his knees, pushing me back into the bed sheets. "You're the breath to my life, Ivy. You are the reason I get out of bed every single day. You are my world."

My heart leaps at his words. This is the closest I've felt to Jax in so long.

"You're my world too." I pull my arms over my head and look into his eyes. "I can't be without you. That's not an option for me anymore."

"You'll never have to be." He leans down, his large body hovering over mine. "I'll never let that happen."

CHAPTER TWENTY-ONE

"I'M GOING TO TAKE GOOD CARE OF HER, IVY." BRIGHTON GIVES ME A
brief hug. "I promise you that."

I nod as I watch Liz's bed wheel past me. I know I should stop her
and say something. My mind is telling me it's the right thing to do but
my heart. My heart is telling me to let her go.

"Ivy." Apparently her heart isn't ready for this to be over yet.

"Yes, Liz?" I turn towards where the stewards have stopped her
stretcher near the door to the hospital.

"I'm sorry." Her eyes fill with tears as the words leave her lips.
"You were the best friend I ever had. I'm sorry I messed things up."

I know it's taking most of the strength she has to say the words. I
know it's pulling on a part of her emotions that she usually keeps
buried deep within.

"I know, Liz." I reach to run my hand along hers. "I know."

She only nods in silence as they wheel her through the door to the
waiting ambulance.

"We'll be in Paris in two days. It's the best place for her right now.
The doctors there are doing remarkable things for people like Liz."

I smile at Brighton's cheery disposition. Taking on the task of not
only helping Liz to recover from her injuries but helping her to over-

come her addiction is a huge step for them both. I can tell he truly does love her and I hope, with everything that I am, that she can love him back just as much.

"We're here if you need us." Jax's voice flows over my shoulder as I feel his hand pressing into my back. "I've missed you, Brighton. Come back and visit soon."

His words were almost identical the last time Brighton fled to Europe. The difference today is that there's heavy meaning behind them. They've moved past their differences. Jax no longer sees Brighton as a spoiled artist and Jax is more than an arrogant businessman to him. They are brothers now. I move out of the way to allow them one last embrace before Brighton boards the ambulance.

"I didn't think you'd make it in time to say goodbye." I grab hold of his hand and cradle it in mine. "What kept you?"

"I was talking to Gilbert." He tucks his smartphone into the pocket of his jeans. "He found a buyer for your shares and my shares. They'll run the company with integrity. Bailey's going to have a bright future."

I smile at the mention of her name. I've never met her and I likely never will but that little girl had changed the entire landscape of my relationship with Jax and I was forever grateful for that.

"I promised Mrs. Adams that we would stop by her new place on our way home." I motion towards the parking lot. "She wants to show me the cat that her boyfriend bought her."

"I can't believe she's shacking up with that guy." He pulls me closer into a tighter embrace. "She's a hussy."

I roll my head back in a burst of laughter at the mention of the word. "That's her word for all the single women who used to live in our building."

"So you were one too before you sold your apartment?" He cocks a brow and the serious look on his face only adds to my amusement.

"You saved me from my life as a hussy." I perch on my tiptoes to pull my lips across his. "Jax..." my voice trails as I feel a rush of heat course through me.

CHAPTER TWENTY-TWO

"If you're going to faint, the hospital is the place to do it, beautiful." Jax's gorgeous face is the first thing I see when I pull my heavy eyelids open. I gaze past him a monitor that is beeping out a pulse rate.

"What?" I try to sit up and he gently eases me back onto the stretcher. "What happened?"

"You fell into my arms when I was kissing you." He trails his lips across my forehead. "It was all very romantic."

I smile a weak smile. "I must have been dehydrated. I was so busy at the shop before I rushed here to say goodbye to Brighton."

"That's not what it is." He leans closer, his hand gently rubbing my cheek. "That's not it, beautiful. My beautiful Ivy."

I see the tears in his eyes. He was right. I am sick. I should have listened to him and gone to the doctor when he told me to. I should have taken better care of myself. I should have done so much more when I had the chance.

"Or maybe it's mom now." The words are barely audible.

"What?" He didn't say that. He didn't call me mom.

"I'm going to be a dad and you're going to be a mom." His hand effortlessly glides softly over my stomach. "We're having a baby."

"A baby?" I know what the word means. I don't understand how he can be saying it in relation to me.

"A baby, yes." He nods slowly. His expression is so soft; it's so loving and tender.

"I'm having a baby?" I need to sit up. I need to think about this.

"We're having a baby in six months."

"I'm that pregnant?" I look down to where his hand is resting on my body. "How?"

"You know how." He winks. "It all makes sense now."

I search his eyes for an answer. I need to understand. I pull my hand to his cheek and that's when I see it. Shimmering in the fluorescent light of the sterile hospital room is a ring. A large diamond ring is perched on my left hand.

"Jax." I can't say more than that. I can't think straight.

"I asked you to marry me when you were passed out." He shrugs his shoulders. "I just assumed you were speechless because you were so happy."

"You had this with you?" I motion towards the ring. It's so exquisite. It's one of the designs I've sketched.

"I've been carrying that in my pocket for the past three months." He pats his chest. "And I've been carrying the question in here since I met you."

"We're getting married," I say breathlessly. I feel as though I'm dreaming. Nothing seems real.

"We're having a baby too." He leans down to kiss my stomach. "Our baby, my beautiful Ivy. Our baby."

"A baby." The words come out in a tumble of tears.

"This is exactly what I'm supposed to be doing." He reaches to cover my lips with his. "Taking care of my wife and baby is my life. This is where I belong."

"This is where we all belong. Together. The three of us." I slide my hand around his neck as his lips glide over mine.

EPILOGUE – 1 YEAR LATER

"He's not going to walk for months, Jax." I toss the tiny sneakers onto the floor. "You have to stop buying him things he doesn't need."

"Like that's going to happen." He kisses my cheek as he wraps his arm around my waist. "I can't stop. I want him to have everything."

"He just needs you. Like this." I pat his chest. "Open and loving. You're the most amazing father."

"I am pretty good at this house husband thing, aren't I?"

I pull my eyes around the apartment and wince when I settle on dirty dishes, blankets strewn everywhere, a few baby toys and a laundry basket overflowing with clean clothing. "You're learning."

"I'm happier than I've ever been." The words bounce through me with the excitement that he's attached to them. I've never seen him this content.

"I love knowing that you're exactly where you want to be." I lean in to him, enjoying the quiet solace while our son naps.

"When you leave for work every day and I get to hold that little prince in my arms and tell him stories about how I met his beautiful mommy, I feel like I'm on cloud nine."

"Tell me the story," I tease.

He pulls me towards the couch and motions for me to settle into his lap. "It's like this." He runs his hand along my arm. "I say, Jackson, once upon a time not that long ago, this beautiful woman with pretty blonde hair was staring at a painting at an art show. She thought it was the ugliest thing she'd ever seen and that's when daddy fell in love with her."

I jump to my feet. "Very funny, Jax."

He bolts to his too. "That's a true story."

I race down the hallway trying to suppress the giggles. Everything stops when I feel his hands on my waist pulling me into our bedroom.

"Jax," I whisper into his kiss. "I love you."

"I love you, Mrs. Walker." It's the nickname he's called me since we married right after Jackson was born. Holding my newborn son in my arms while I pledged my undying love to the man I adore had made me finally feel whole, complete and anchored.

I close my eyes as I feel him undo the sash on my dress.

This is my life.

This is my everything.

ALSO BY DEBORAH BLADON
& SUGGESTED READING ORDER

THANK YOU

Thank you for purchasing and downloading my book. I can't even begin to put to words what it means to me. If you enjoyed it, please remember to write a review for it. Let me know your thoughts! I want to keep my readers happy.

It's hard to imagine that Jax & Ivy are over, but like all good things, they need to come to an end. Obsessed was my first serial and will always hold a special place in my heart. I hope it does for you as well.

Stay tuned to my website, www.deborahbladon.com, for more information on upcoming releases and future series.

If you want to chat with me personally, please LIKE my page on Facebook. I love connecting with all of my readers because without you, none of this would be possible. www. facebook.com/authordeborahbladon

Thank you, for everything.

ABOUT THE AUTHOR

Deborah Bladon has never read a romance hero she didn't like. Her love for romance novels began when she was old enough to board the bus, library card in hand to check out the newest Harlequin paperbacks. She's a Canadian by heart, and by passport, but you can often spot her in New York City sipping a latte and looking for inspiration for her next story. Manhattan is definitely her second home.

She cherishes her family and believes that each day is a gift for writing, for reading, and for loving.

Made in United States
North Haven, CT
12 April 2022

18178582R00222